Piqued

AND

Repiqued

Book 5 of the Branwell Chronicles

Judith Hale Everett

Evershire Publishing

Published by Evershire Publishing, Springville, Utah

ISBN 978-1-958720-01-1

Library of Congress Control Number: 2023921133

Books in this series:
A Near Run Thing
Two in the Bush
Romance of the Ruin
Forlorn Hope
A Knowing One
Piqued and Repiqued

To get the ebook of *A Near Run Thing*
for free, and to find out more about the
series, scan the QR code below:

Piqued
AND
Repiqued

Chapter 1

THE ARRIVAL OF Miss Iris Slougham and her mama at Lady Wish-forth's ball would have been unremarkable, had not their little group been honored to include the Lady Athena Dibbington, whose beauty and elegance defied indifference. All heads instantly turned to witness her entrance, and a buzz of admiration rushed through the room. It was enough to mortify any other maiden present, but Iris did not regard it. Indeed, she rather appreciated that all attention was diverted from herself, allowing her to vanish from the minds of the speculative and thus decrease the necessity of opening her mouth. To her mind, it certainly would be better for all involved if that were so.

Following Athena to an advantageous spot at the edge of the room, Iris endeavored to blend into the potted palm beside her mama. Lady Athena was approached by several gentlemen at once, and it fell to Mrs. Slougham, as chaperon, to approve or disapprove her partners. This she did very ably, dismissing three as unworthy out of hand.

But when Mrs. Slougham showed signs of favor to the Viscount Greenbury, Iris whispered desperately to Lady Athena, "Pray, do not abandon me!"

"You know I must, Iris," was the cool answer. "It would be very strange in me to refuse a partner when your mama has pronounced him perfectly eligible."

"But you must be my shield. You know how the gentlemen terrify me—I shall invariably come out with the wrong thing—"

As Lord Greenbury now awaited her, Athena's patience was at an end, and she said rather shortly, "I cannot conceive of what you would have me do for you, Iris, for you will only allow yourself to be intimidated!" But at Iris's injured look she added more gently, "You are perfectly equal to this. You simply must not believe otherwise."

Athena went away with the viscount, leaving Iris to edge behind her mama with a hunted look. But Mrs. Slougham, quick to divine her daughter's intention of making herself invisible, firmly planted her at her own side, in full view of possible suitors. Her efforts were wasted, however, for three sets were played and three partners accepted for Lady Athena, while Iris remained unsought.

Taking matters into her own hands, Mrs. Slougham made a sign to her friend and hostess, and as the fourth set was struck up, Lady Wishforth came up to where they were seated, leading her nephew behind her.

"My dear Mrs. Slougham," she said with a dazzling smile. "You must allow me to present my nephew, Mr. Fazenford. He is just come down from Cambridge and is dying to be known to your daughter."

Mrs. Slougham's keen glance took in Mr. Fazenford's rail-thin figure and blemished countenance through her lorgnette, but she gave a polite smile. "Certainly, Lady Wishforth. Sir, this is my daughter, Miss Slougham. Iris, give your hand to Mr. Fazenford."

Iris, gazing panicked at her supposed admirer, only swallowed and blinked until her mother, with lips tightening, nudged her with an elbow. Iris's hand shot out to grasp Mr. Fazenford's and he bowed stiffly over it. Smiling resolutely, he took a breath.

"You look a mere boy," Iris blurted before he could speak. Her face instantly assumed a beetroot hue as Mrs. Slougham's eyes fluttered closed in horror.

Tittering uncertainly, Lady Wishforth took her nephew's arm and patted it. "Fazenford certainly is blessed with youthful good looks! But he is no mere boy, to be sure. He took honors in his exams, Miss Slougham, and will join Lord Burraston's staff in the autumn. Perhaps more to the purpose, he is an excellent dancer."

She stood there blinking expectantly, but when her nephew did not speak, she gave his arm a little shake. He tugged at his neck cloth, looking everywhere but at the mortified Miss Slougham.

"If you would be so good—that is, if you would honor me—"

But Iris interrupted him. "I did not mean to—oh, pray excuse me!" she cried, standing so abruptly that her reticule fell to the floor. Mr. Fazenford stepped back quickly enough to avoid a collision and watched open-mouthed as she fled the ballroom.

After a moment of shocked silence, Mrs. Slougham bent to retrieve her daughter's reticule and straightened with a pained smile. "A thousand apologies, sir," she said. "I pray you will excuse my daughter, though I do not have any notion of why you should. I regret infinitely to own to you that she is prone to the most ridiculous starts, and I assure you most sincerely it is nothing to do with you or your—" she gestured vaguely at his person— "appearance. It was most kind in you to single her out, however, and I may only wish you will be more fortunate in your next choice of partner. Good night." With a speaking look to Lady Wishforth, she stalked away, following the path that her distraught daughter had taken moments before.

Iris had found a secluded archway in the corridor, and now stood there fanning herself vigorously. All she could think was that Mr. Fazenford had not deserved such rudeness, and that she wished she could go and drown herself. But it was nothing more than what she had prophesied to her parents when they had forced her to come on this ill-judged Season in London. Despite everything, they persisted in the belief that her social ineptitude was born merely of inexperience, and that all she required to blossom into a paragon of pleasantries was to rub elbows with as many members of the *ton* as possible.

As it was, each event boasted so many persons present that Iris's brain was inundated with innumerable observations and suppositions— which did rather the opposite for her success than Mrs. Slougham had expected. For it was not shyness or reticence that was Iris's downfall. On the contrary, she merely suffered from severe frankness.

Miss Iris Slougham was born curious, and from her infancy had watched everybody. So far from quietly considering their vagaries, however, she shared her conclusions with all the guileless honesty of youth—heedless of their propriety, or the station or sensibility of the subject. Her parents had treated these childish revelations with indulgence, trusting that both they and her curiosity would lessen as she grew up, but in this they were disappointed. Though she was subjected to the same rigorous training as every other young lady of her station, Iris simply could not rid herself of the impulse to state her mind and, as she entered her teenage years, could be depended upon to come out with embarrassingly blunt remarks whenever in company.

Looking toward her daughter's imminent come-out and seeing disaster on the horizon, Mrs. Slougham redoubled her efforts to no avail. The more she drilled, the more inept Iris became. At last, her mother resorted to forbidding Iris to speak anything but a polite yea or nay, but this only magnified Iris's terror of misbehaving in company, which in turn increased her gaffes.

With the conviction that she was destined to be a pariah, Iris withdrew from Society, resisting her parents' insistence that she have a London Season on the grounds that it would be a great waste of time and money. She was grudgingly allowed this peculiarity for a few years, but on her twenty-first birthday, Mrs. Slougham put her foot down. She would not brook being thought a skinflint for neglecting to give her only daughter a Season, no more than she would keep a daughter indefinitely in her home who had not at least made a push to secure a husband.

Thus, Iris found herself in London, surrounded by gently-bred persons whose effervescent civility bubbled like champagne from their lips, and whose expectations she knew to be intolerably high. Everywhere she looked was someone whose dress or manner or activities elicited comment in her brain, but none, she was assured, wished to hear her thoughts. Iris dutifully endeavored to keep quiet, but to do so in this company was almost as damning as speaking her mind, for a silent woman was instantly suspected either of thinking herself above her company or of being under-bred, both equally damaging to one's future prospects.

How she was to succeed in securing a husband, therefore, she could not conjecture, for she had yet to inspire anything resembling even vague interest from a gentleman. Even her mother's machinations had failed, as just proved with Mr. Fazenford. The impossibility of it all set her to plying her fan anew, but almost at that moment, Mrs. Slougham appeared, snatching the fan from her and shutting it with a snap.

"What do you mean by acting in so hoydenish a manner? Have you learned nothing these one-and-twenty years?"

"No, Mama—that is, I did not mean to cause a scene—"

Her mother glared. "What am I to do with you? How are you to find a husband if you cannot comport yourself with propriety?"

Iris shook her head, raising her hands. "I told you before we came to London that it was hopeless, Mama."

"No!" huffed her mother, jabbing a finger toward the floor, and continuing to do so with her succeeding words. "I will not believe it! You must only try harder!"

"But I have tried my best, Mama! I swear it!"

"Oh, for heaven's sake!" Mrs. Slougham pressed her eyes shut, pinching the bridge of her nose between thumb and forefinger. "I declare, you could drive a saint mad! With all we have done for you, all we have borne, the least you could do is to sit demurely through one ball, nodding and smiling without opening your lips for more than a 'thank you, sir' or 'if you please, sir.' It is not too much to expect of a daughter so carefully reared! You cannot be forever in our care, I tell you—not when you have every opportunity to find a husband. It will be the most infamous thing if you do not make a match this Season!"

Iris blinked rapidly against tears that pricked her eyes. "I simply cannot tame my tongue, Mama!"

"Do not make excuses, Iris! You are fully capable of making speech with a gentleman, for that is all I have taught you these three years, and it is not as though you are a nitwit! You know precisely what to do, and you will begin this moment! If you do not make yourself agreeable to at least three gentlemen at this ball tonight, I promise by heaven and earth that I will marry you off to Sir Isaac Hornaby!"

Iris's hands flew to her mouth. "No, Mama! You do not mean it!"

"I have never meant anything so truly in my life, my girl! You know he has expressed an interest in you, and will jump at the chance to marry a young lady such as yourself."

"But he is old and horrid, and looks like a toad—"

"Then do not make me do it!" snapped her mother, turning and propelling her daughter down the corridor and into the ballroom.

Iris, gripping her reticule as she stood rigid beside her indomitable mother, looked desperately about for support. Athena was dancing and would be no help, and Diana Marshall, her other lifelong friend, was not even in attendance, having gone to Brighton for her father's health. Iris was entertaining the horrid conviction that she was doomed to marry a toad when she perceived a newer acquaintance, Lenora Breckinridge, moving through the crowd with her mother, Lady Stiles.

When Lenora came up, she was a trifle startled by Iris's instantly dragging her to an alcove and imparting to her the intelligence that she wished to throw herself into the river. Knowing her new friend well enough to recognize this as hyperbole, Lenora made it her business to put herself in possession of the facts and then attempted to soothe the sufferer. But upon being rather hysterically assured of Mrs. Slougham's determination to follow through with her threat, Lenora sent away the gentleman who came to claim her for the next set and led Iris to the refreshment table.

"All will be well, Iris, I assure you," said Lenora, thrusting a glass of champagne into her hand. "There is no occasion for such despair, and so you shall find if only you can calm yourself."

Iris, gulping down her champagne, merely stared wildly, and Lenora perceived that drastic measures were called for.

Glancing about for something to divert her friend, Lenora said, "Goodness, only look at that immense headdress over there! On the lady with the sapphires—do you see? No, I do not believe you can see her, for she is terribly short. Only look for the ostrich plumes waving above everyone's heads—there! I wonder if she wears so tall a head-dress because she is so short? I declare, what an interesting notion! Being tall myself, such an idea had never occurred to me, but as my extreme height is the greatest affliction to me, it stands to reason that excessively short persons must feel afflicted too. However, I cannot agree that so tall a hat is the answer. Upon my word, she really is almost shorter than the ostrich plumes! Thank you, dear."

Lenora paused a moment to take the empty glass which was handed to her, covertly assessing her friend's condition. It had only nominally improved.

Plunging gamely on, therefore, she said, "Not only that, but what would one do if one's plumes were to be bent at a party such as this, I wonder? It could very easily happen, I am persuaded, for it is such a crush that persons are forever bumping into one another and treading on gowns and toes and such. It is not so very unimaginable that an ostrich plume might come between two persons and be bent beyond repair. And then it would dangle down like a fallen bird—how sad! One might be obliged to leave the party and go home, for it would never do to continue so. I vow, it is so dispiriting how fragile things are. Oh, I thought you had finished your champagne—"

She looked from the empty glass in her hand to the empty one in Iris's and blanched. "Oh dear. Did you drink two glasses? That will not do at all."

Lenora quickly took the second glass, placing both on the refresh-ment table. "We are in the suds, for if you do not become bosky, I know nothing of the matter, and then what shocking things will you say? If only one knew what you are like in your cups."

Iris huffed, ending in a hiccough. "We shall soon find out," she said ominously. "Mama will not like it at all."

"Perhaps you should stay by my mama for a while," said Lenora, eying her friend uneasily. "Then Mrs. Slougham need know nothing about it."

They ensconced themselves near Lady Stiles, and Lenora kept a surreptitious eye on her friend, whose anxious expression soon gave way to a dreamy smile. When a gentleman came rather close and Iris did not stiffen in terror, Lenora began to feel optimistic.

"You seem quite calm, Iris. Perhaps you will get on very well after all. My brother Tom is always much braver when he is a bit foxed."

"Perhaps I shall," said Iris, a trifle vaguely. "This is rather a nice ball. That lady ought not to wear pink. That gentleman has hair like a straw field. It seems he wishes to address you, Lenora."

Lenora turned to find the gentleman she had sent off earlier, whose hair was as tidy as it could be, back to claim her hand for the set that was forming. "Miss Breckinridge. Your friend is recovered, I hope," he said.

Grateful that he had not overheard Iris's appraisal of his hair, Lenora placed her hand tentatively in his. "I believe so, Mr. Tenby. Iris, you had better stay here by my mama."

Mr. Tenby's gaze shifted to Iris. "Pardon me, ma'am. I had fancied you to be better. You look very well to me, if I may say so. But I shall not dream of taking your support from you unless you assure me you are quite well."

Lenora watched anxiously as Iris blinked, smiled sweetly and nodded. "You are too kind. But I am very well, sir."

He returned her smile with a little bow. "I am glad of it, ma'am."

Iris turned to watch him lead Lenora away and caught her

mother's eye. Mrs. Slougham nodded in approval and Iris blinked again, swaying a little in her surprise. How odd that a bit of champagne could make so great a difference in the tone of the evening!

The relaxing effects of the champagne continued until Mr. Tenby returned to deliver Lenora to her mama. Iris thought complacently that he seemed a rather nice gentleman, and smiled up at him in the belief that he would take himself off to find another young lady. She was startled, therefore, when he did not go away, but turned and requested her to stand up with him for the next set. Iris gazed at his outstretched hand in bemusement, the oddity of the circumstance making her frown, but Lenora nudged her encouragingly, and a glance to the side confirmed that her mama's gaze was upon her once more. In a flash of spirit, she took Mr. Tenby's hand and stood, and before she could change her mind, he had led her into the set and they were dancing.

Muzzy detachment gave way to euphoria as she progressed through the dance, and she ventured to speak some of the many strange things that came to her mind. In amazement at her own boldness, she observed to Mr. Tenby how a short round man had partnered a tall, thin girl, and that they danced very well together for all they looked so ill-matched. Then she wondered at a young lady who wore so many diamonds that her partner was in a continual squint, and invited Mr. Tenby's opinion on the wisdom in this, for it seemed to Iris that a man cannot admire what he cannot see.

Mr. Tenby seemed in perfect accord with her observations, a circumstance which filled her with a conviction of their joint perspicacity. She was so pleased that after going down the line and taking her place opposite Mr. Tenby at the bottom, she looked into his politely smiling face and said, "Your hair is like a straw field."

His smile faltered, and she experienced the first pang of anxiety that she could remember after drinking the champagne. A vague notion assailed her that it was wrong to say such a thing, and yet she could not recall why it was so. It was an honest observation, but it seemed he had not taken it as such, and she felt it imperative that he understand her.

Drawing upon the last vestiges of her pot-valiance, she said carefully, "It is the color—a lovely gold, like straw in the sun."

He blinked in astonishment, and her heart began to thud, her tongue cleaving to the roof of her mouth in a horridly familiar way as shadows of her forgotten fears began to close in. But then his smile returned and he gave a small bow. "Thank you, Miss Slougham. It is very kind in you to say so."

Iris was so overcome with relief as to be incapable of further speech until he returned her to her seat beside Lady Stiles, at which she thanked him perfectly properly. When he had gone, she happened to glance at her mama, and was pleased to see Mrs. Slougham nod her approval. Iris's courage sealed, she accepted Lady Stiles's invitation to join in a conversation with some military gentlemen, and managed so creditable a performance of amiability that she was certain to be safe—for the time being at least—from Sir Isaac Hornaby's toad-like advances.

Chapter 2

THE HUSH IN the dressing room at number 18 Hanover Square was total as Mr. Jonathan Blysdale, his countenance grim with concentration, completed the intricate tying of his neck cloth and set an emerald pin in the center of its snowy folds. His valet, awaiting at a respectful distance the issue of this, the third, attempt, released a sigh of relief and lay the two unused lengths of starched muslin he had been holding at ready upon the bed. Stepping forward, he assisted his master in easing into the russet brown coat he had chosen to wear for the Countess of Dewsbury's rout party that evening. Smoothing the coat across the fine, broad shoulders, the valet scrutinized his master's person in the large gilt mirror and nodded with satisfaction. Nothing could be more faultless than the form-fitting coat, the green and gold embroidered waistcoat, the cravat tied in a perfect *Trone d'Amour*, and the immaculate brown pantaloons worn over buff stockings with black evening slippers.

Mr. Blysdale, his slate blue eyes surveying his reflection quite as critically as his valet, turned his head to the side and said, "That will do, Hindley. Thank you."

The valet bowed and, in the same movement, picked up the two mangled neck cloths that had been discarded on the floor.

Mr. Blysdale slipped his watch into his waistcoat pocket, took up his hat and gloves from the dressing table and, reaching for his cane, said, "Don't wait up for me. I plan to go to my club afterward."

"Very good, sir," said Hindley, while forming the intention to be hard at work polishing or pressing or what need be in order that he might be still up when his master returned. That a gentleman of Mr. Blysdale's quality should put himself to bed was not to be thought of, no matter his antecedents, but neither should it be thought that Hindley was above his station and wiser than his master.

Unconcerned by the deep doings of his valet, Mr. Blysdale strode from the room and down the curving staircase of his London townhouse, accepting the assistance of the butler in donning his greatcoat against the April evening chill.

"The carriage is waiting, sir," said the butler, returning the cane to his master.

"Thank you, Stomes. I'll be back late. Have the hall boy sleep here on the bench. No need for you to be up half the night just to let me in. Good night."

The butler bowed him out, reflecting—not for the first time—that for a man who came from trade, his master certainly had the way about him of a gentleman born.

Seated in his well-sprung and lavishly upholstered carriage, Mr. Blysdale considered that being a gentleman had its advantages, but there was no denying it was excessively expensive. Little had his father known, in desiring better for his son, just how much of his hard-earned wealth would go toward items that, to a tradesman, were mere luxuries, but that to a gentleman were necessities. The coach, the horses, the driver, the townhouse in Hanover Square, with all its attendant servants and expenses—all were necessary to the success of a young man who wished to make a mark in Society. The fine coat and waistcoat, the tailored breeches and the jewels—all must be used to advantage if Mr. Jonathan Blysdale, son of a Yorkshire textile merchant, and first of his line to achieve both an education and a foot on the social ladder, was to continue on the path his father had set him.

It went without saying that Mr. Blysdale was bound and determined to continue this path. Not for nothing had he endured snubs and slights all through his Harrow days, working tirelessly to erase any hint of Yorkshire from his accent, scoring the highest marks despite the bullying and loneliness, and earning himself a place at Merton College, Oxford. There, he had distinguished himself for his stubbornness in adhering to the rules, insisting on regular study heedless of the prevailing opinion that he was a great gaby—for one need only get hold of a String with which to cheat on the exams, and one's time could then be very much more agreeably spent.

Jonathan had never much cared for the pastimes his more carefree associates thought agreeable, and so he experienced few qualms in disregarding their advice. And it did him no disservice for, in time, his independence and intelligence had won him great respect; indeed, despite a rather solemn manner, he was generally well-liked, held to be a great gun, and to possess excellent bottom. He held a magnetic sort of fascination for young men of aspiration but inadequate spirit to forge their own way in the world and Society. While many sons of nobility and gentry looked at him down their noses—or at the very least, askance—there were those who found themselves in need of his peculiarly unique guidance, and after a year at Oxford, he was the mentor of a handful of high-born young gentlemen whose dependent situations obliged them to value education more than dissipation. His fierce determination to succeed and make them succeed with him, along with a natural aptitude for sport and a willingness to relax once his duties were done, won him their lifelong loyalty and friendship, and enabled him to set his foot securely on the social ladder as his father had hoped he would.

Stepping from his carriage after it had wended its way through the crowds of other vehicles waiting to disgorge their passengers in front of Dewsbury House, Mr. Blysdale entered the stately mansion and surrendered his greatcoat and hat to one of the many footmen inside the door. He ascended the stairs and greeted Lady Dewsbury, who stood at the door of the front saloon, which opened onto a drawing room and another saloon to accommodate her many guests.

"Blysdale!" she cried, offering her hand and her cheek to him. "How delightful to see you, my dear. And looking so fine! I must own I like a little color on a gentleman in the evening, whatever Mr. Brummell may have thought. But I wish you will teach poor Windon to tie his neck cloth, for he never can achieve such a masterpiece as you are forever sporting."

"I am at your service, ma'am," said Blysdale, with the smile he reserved for his old friends. "If you will only tell me where he is, I shall do my possible to correct his appearance."

"What a tease you are! He would never forgive you—or me, for that matter!" her ladyship said, tapping his arm playfully with her fan.

"Then he is here?"

"Oh, certainly, certainly. He is somewhere about the rooms, monopolizing the attentions of some hapless young female, no doubt! You know his way!"

Blysdale did know his friend's way, and smiled his sympathy before bowing to the countess and continuing unhurriedly into the saloon. He scanned the room, taking note of those persons with whom he was acquainted and to whom it behooved him to speak during the course of the evening. There was Sir George Spurdon, Dean of Merton College and Blysdale's mentor; and there was Lady Gwinthwaite, whose son, a true friend in his Harrow days, had been killed at Genappe. One or two others deserved his notice, but the rest would do with a nod and a smile, or a polite how-d'you-do, while Mr. Blysdale seized such opportunities to enlarge his circle through advantageous introduction as he deemed appropriate.

He discovered Lady Dewsbury's son and his old schoolmate, Peter Holydale, Viscount Windon, in a corridor off the drawing room, speaking in dulcet tones to a wide-eyed brunette whose giggles belied her discomfiture, but whose shrinking attitude and darting glances at the doorway to the drawing room did not.

"Playing off your old tricks, eh, Windon?" inquired Blysdale, taking the young lady's hand from his friend's grasp and bowing over it. "Pardon me, ma'am, while I extricate you from his lordship's clutches."

"Blysdale! What the deuce—" demanded his lordship.

Mr. Blysdale ignored him. "The air is rather warm just here, ma'am, and you appear somewhat flushed. May I return you to your party for refreshment?"

Her blushing murmurs were indicative of agreement, and they turned to go.

"See here—Wait! Lady Serena, allow me to take you wherever you wish to go," said her former cavalier, reaching for her hand, but it was moved beyond his reach.

Mr. Blysdale gazed blandly at him over his shoulder. "I believe your offer comes too late, my lord, and so you must take defeat with a good grace."

"No, that's too bad of you!" exclaimed Lord Windon as they walked away. "Do not trust him, Lady Serena! I swear he is up to no good!"

But the lady had gone unhesitatingly with her rescuer, and his lordship was left to curse his friend until, presently, Mr. Blysdale reappeared alone.

"Really, Blysdale, you've no honor at all!" Lord Windon cried.

"And you do, luring innocent maidens into dark corners?"

"I'd no need to lure her! She came willingly enough, for there was no danger!"

"No danger in a secluded corridor, out of sight of her chaperon?" countered Blysdale.

"I had taken her to see Turner's *Tintern Abbey*, just here in the hall." But Blysdale cast him a wry look, and his lordship balled his fists, his brown eyes flashing. "You will paint me a scoundrel, but I am nothing of the sort!"

"Next you will insist it was she who pulled you into the alcove. I trust you meant to communicate to her your intentions."

"My intentions were of the purest—this time," declared his lordship. "Can't go about seducing maidens at my mother's party! Besides, I could no more impose on Lady Serena than I could you, for she is a lady of quality, and the sweetest creature, besides being the granddaughter of the Duke of Norfolk!"

"Then she is not for the likes of you," replied Blysdale, "such a dullard as you are. Did you not sense her distress?"

Lord Windon spluttered at this, but Blysdale went on ruthlessly, "If you cannot perceive that your attentions are unacceptable, you ought not to dispense them so freely. Come, make yourself useful and do the pretty. I wish to be made known to some of your mother's guests."

Ignoring his friend's protests, Blysdale towed him into the next room, snatching a glass of champagne from a passing footman and thrusting it into his irritated friend's hands with a request that he "drink it and stop ragging." Windon did drink, but it was some time before he ceased his bitter animadversions against any and all upstart tradesmen who had the impertinence to think themselves better versed in the rules of propriety than a born and bred nobleman. This censure Blysdale bore with a smile, leading his lordship to a group of young people whose lively conversation had interested him as he had passed through previously.

At length, soothed by the champagne, Lord Windon resigned himself to Blysdale's will and made the introductions with punctilio, while Blysdale exerted himself to please. It was no difficult task for him, blessed as he was with a quick eye and discerning taste, and his excellent education and good breeding furnished him with unlimited resources with which to make himself agreeable. They moved about the room, renewing old acquaintances and making new, until Blysdale's attention was caught by a vision of loveliness just entering the saloon.

She was a tall, elegant young woman, with dark hair and large, grey eyes that took in the room with one measured glance. Her beauty, while uncommon, was undeniable, with her aristocratic nose, alabaster skin, and graceful carriage. As he watched her move about with absolute confidence, Blysdale suspected that she was well aware of her incomparability—but if she was, it did not harm her in his eyes.

"Who is that lady?" he inquired quietly of Lord Windon, who stood sipping champagne at his side.

"Where?" asked his lordship, following his friend's gaze. He started back. "Oh, lord! The Countess of Gidgeborough! You don't want to meet her, I tell you!"

Taking Blysdale's arm, he turned him swiftly round, but Blysdale looked back. "That beautiful creature is Lady Gidgeborough?"

"Beautiful? Are you daft?" Lord Windon peeked over his shoulder and straightened. "Oh, you mean Lady Athena! I thought you referred to her mother, the terrifying dragon beside her."

Blysdale now perceived the small, passably pretty older woman walking with Lady Athena, who resembled her daughter very little except in her weighty presence which instantly dominated the room. She surveyed the company in majestic detachment, quite as Lady Athena had, but her manner was more oppressive. This rendered her terrifying, whereas Lady Athena's grace and beauty softened and justified her, and made her a fascinating subject.

"Is Lady Athena a dragon, as well?" asked Blysdale, watching both mother and daughter closely. "I cannot believe it."

"Oh, not precisely! That is, the old lady's rubbed off on her a bit—stands to reason, you know—but I don't imagine that would trouble you, sauce box that you are. Come to think on it, she may very well level you, which I wouldn't mind being present to witness, after the way you've used me tonight! I'll make the introduction." He ducked back behind his friend as the two ladies advanced. "But not until they've separated, and we can get Lady Athena alone. Regular Tartar, Lady Gidgeborough."

"You know the countess well?" inquired Blysdale, allowing himself to be drawn off into the crowd.

"As well as I wish to. She and my mother are thick as thieves. Can't understand what Mama sees in her, though. Withers one with a glance. Can't do anything to suit her."

Blysdale's brow rose. "You didn't happen to try your tricks on Lady Athena at any time, did you, Windon?"

"Not on your life!" Lord Windon cast him a horrified look. "Wouldn't live to tell the tale! Besides, Lady Athena's above my touch."

"But she is your social equal, is she not?"

Windon gave a choking laugh, "You'd think it, but she wouldn't, nor would anyone believe it. Just look at her!"

Blysdale was looking at her, from his vantage point across the room. She moved gracefully among the guests as if she were a goddess, her very presence demanding their homage. And it was given, though not always freely. He could perceive reticence among many of her admirers, an uncertainty to give what may be rejected. Shaking hands here, bestowing a smile there, entering into conversation with a chosen few, she carried herself with the ease of one who knew her own worth and was assured that none would question nor forget it. Blysdale smiled to himself. Here was a woman who could match him.

The moment the Dragon detached herself from her offspring, Blysdale seized his friend's arm, leading him over to where Lady Athena sat conversing with three other young ladies, whom Windon was reasonably certain were called the Goddesses. Their conversation was short, for one of them jumped up, apparently in high dudgeon, and went to stare, arms crossed over her chest, out a window.

"It's always her way, I warn you," said Windon in an aside, as they came near the group. "She don't have scruples to hold her back from speaking her mind, unlike mere mortals. Too high in her own opinion for that."

Blysdale's smile grew. "The lady is more intriguing by the minute. Come, they've ceased their chatter—introduce me."

A gentle push brought Lord Windon to the ladies' table, and he said, after a nervous cough. "Lady Athena, Miss Marshall, Miss—erm—" He blinked helplessly at the vague-looking lady in question, but she merely stared back, her eyes flicking from his face to Blysdale's and back again while she swallowed convulsively. His lordship cleared his throat. "Yes, well, good evening! May I present my school friend, Mr. Jonathan Blysdale?"

The three ladies regarded them in various states of curiosity, but Blysdale's gaze was focused on Lady Athena. He gained the impression that her imperturbable grey eyes—without leaving his face—had taken in his whole person, but he could not determine if she liked what she saw. Her gaze held his for a long moment, and then she opened her lips.

Before she could speak, however, her inarticulate companion suddenly blurted out, "Slougham!" and then, with a horrified glance at her companions, subsided into blushful mortification.

Lady Athena, with a withering look at her friend, said, "Iris, you refine too much upon your recent accomplishment of speaking two words to a gentleman in company. Pray do not attempt an encore. One word is enough! You have already given Lord Windon a disgust of your manners."

"Athena!" cried Miss Marshall on her other side. "It is no such thing, I am persuaded! His lordship is not so unfeeling, and nor is Mr. Blysdale, to be sure. Pray do not heed Miss Slougham, sir. She is merely unaccustomed to company."

Mr. Blysdale held up a hand, smiling. "No need to apologize for your friend, Miss Marshall. Miss Slougham, I am pleased to make your acquaintance."

As Miss Slougham merely stared like a deer in the cross-hairs, he returned his attention to Lady Athena, whose countenance bore all the hallmarks of pique. He could not be certain, but he fancied she was more affronted by Miss Marshall's easy acceptance of his acquaintance than embarrassed by Miss Slougham's blunder.

Her gaze transferred to Lord Windon, who blanched perceptibly. "Where did you find your friend, Windon? I do not know the name Blysdale, and I confess to great curiosity as to his antecedents."

Windon opened his mouth, shut it again, and then said haltingly, "School, my lady. Oxford. Honors at Merton College. That's where I found him—that is, where we met."

Her eyebrow quirked up infinitesimally as she returned her gaze to Blysdale and appraised him anew. "Oxford? Very proper. But he cannot have been born there."

"Certainly not, my lady," said Blysdale, with a benign smile. "Merely my connection with this tongue-tied fellow. My people are from York-shire. It is a county quite northward, I own, and must account for any unfamiliarity with the family name."

Something flashed in her eyes and she said, pointedly turning away from him to his lordship, "Your friend is impertinent, Windon. You may wish to inform him that to force an introduction is ill-mannered, and will not serve him well in polite circles. My mother is beckoning. You will pardon me."

Rising majestically from her seat, Lady Athena brushed past Mr. Blysdale, leaving a sputtering Lord Windon and an apologetic Miss Marshall in her wake.

"Pray do not heed her, Mr. Blysdale," begged Miss Marshall, looking regretful. "She is merely overwrought."

"If that's so," muttered Windon, seizing another glass of champagne from a passing footman, "she's been overwrought the whole of her life."

Miss Marshall was obliged to stifle a giggle. "Shame on you, Windon. She has her moments, to be sure, and she is never at her best when at a disadvantage. You must comprehend that just now she is laboring under the double irritation of embarrassment at Iris's interruption and a misunderstanding with Miss Breckinridge." With a nod of her head, she indicated the other young lady who was still gazing stormily out the window. "But it will soon blow over, and then Athena will be herself again."

"All the more reason to avoid her, I tell you," said Windon, tugging at Blysdale's arm to drag his attention away from the departing Lady Athena. "She's hot at hand, my boy. Above your touch as well, by Jupiter! You'd have to be a clodpole even to attempt—Leave off and come away!"

Mr. Blysdale's gaze flicked back to where Lady Athena now stood with her mother, his expression far from affronted. In fact, she fascinated him all the more for having snubbed him.

Turning at last from the object of his regard, he smiled kindly upon his friend. "Your solicitude does you credit, Windon. I shall take it under consideration, depend upon it, but now, I must take my leave of you. Miss Marshall, Miss Slougham, it has been my pleasure to make your acquaintance."

Bowing to the ladies, Mr. Blysdale turned and walked placidly to Lady Dewsbury, spoke a few words of thanks and parting, and was gone.

Chapter 3

Two days after Lady Dewsbury's rout, Lady Athena, Diana, and Iris walked together in the Green Park, discussing their engagements for the week as a footman in Gidgeborough livery trailed dutifully behind.

"Mama insists that I attend the Ibbitson's musicale tomorrow," said Iris mournfully, "but I had rather walk naked down St. James' Street than go to another party."

"Iris!" cried Diana, putting a hand up to cover her shocked laugh. "You overstate the case, surely!"

"Can you be in any doubt?" inquired Lady Athena in a tone of long-suffering. "When does Iris ever moderate her speech?"

Iris colored and said defiantly, "I do not think it matters what I say I had rather do, as I should never do it anyway. Mama shall have her way, and I shall be obliged to go to the party."

Diana patted her hand. "There, there, Iris. You are fatigued after the exertions of Lady Wishforth's ball, but that is no occasion for despair. Recollect, your mama has taken back her ultimatum regarding the Toad, so Mrs. Ibbitson's rout cannot be so horrid for you."

"Perhaps," said Iris, without conviction. "However, Mama may change her mind at any moment, for it is just what she would do. She has hinted more than once that Sir Isaac Hornaby is still highly eligible, and so I cannot think myself safe. Indeed, I am persuaded that I will be expected to perform the miracle of making myself amiable again if I attend the musicale, and as there shall be no champagne there, I cannot believe I have it in me."

"As you have already concluded that your mama shall have her way," said Lady Athena reasonably, "it follows that you must find it in you."

"And you shall!" said Diana bracingly. "We will be there to bear you up, after all."

"You ought not to answer for others, Diana," said Lady Athena. "I shall not be there."

Iris turned to her. "But you have been invited, Athena, and I know that the Ibbitsons, of all people, are not beneath you."

"Nevertheless, Iris, Mama and I must decline Mrs. Ibbitson's obliging invitation," said Lady Athena with some asperity. "Lady Sheffield's ball is tomorrow, and it would not do to miss it for an inferior affair."

Diana sighed in comprehension. "To be sure, Athena. One must prioritize, must not one? I, however, will not leave your side for an instant, Iris, and shall make it my business to show you to best advantage."

Iris was still worried, but any further argument she might have made was forestalled by the approach of two gentlemen on the path ahead. She instantly shrank against Diana, staring helplessly at Mr. Blysdale and his companion, Lord Greenbury.

"Good day to you, ladies," said his lordship, punctiliously doffing his hat. "Lady Athena, Miss Slougham, and Miss Marshall, I believe you know Mr. Blysdale."

Diana and Iris dipped curtseys, nodding to Mr. Blysdale, but Lady Athena only bowed her head slightly to his lordship, not deigning to acknowledge his companion.

With a fleeting glance between her ladyship and Blysdale, Lord Greenbury gave a small cough. "It is so lovely a morning for a walk. Will you allow us to join you a while?"

Lady Athena smiled coolly. "Perhaps another time, Greenbury. You perceive we are going in quite the opposite direction."

She inclined her head again, ready to pass them by, but his lordship almost leapt toward her and extended his arm. "It would be an honor to walk any direction with you, Lady Athena."

With a raised eyebrow, she took his outstretched arm. "Certainly, Greenbury—for a short while. We cannot trespass upon your time longer, for I am persuaded you have somewhere to be."

As his lordship disclaimed any obligations upon his time, Mr. Blysdale calmly offered his arm to Iris, who only blinked and colored as she took it, and then looked steadfastly at her feet. She had seen Mr. Blysdale bodily prod his lordship to insist on accompanying them, and she was busily drawing her own conclusions, which were sure to trip off her traitorous tongue as soon as she opened her mouth. She kept her lips pressed tightly together, therefore, while Lady Athena and Lord Greenbury led the way at a dignified pace, conversing on unexceptionable topics. Iris, Mr. Blysdale, and Diana walked three abreast behind and the footman took up a respectful distance at the rear.

Mr. Blysdale spoke first. "It is fortunate that we came across one another. I have been wishing to improve our acquaintance after our brief introduction at Lady Dewsbury's party."

Iris darted a glance at Mr. Blysdale, but only bit her lips.

"Thank you, sir," said Diana. "It was unfortunate that we could not prolong the interview."

"And we are not destined to prolong this one, I apprehend," he said, watching the back of Lady Athena's head. "But perhaps we will meet again soon. Do you attend Lady Sheffield's ball tomorrow night?" he asked.

"Not I," said Diana, sighing. "Nor Iris. We are not acquainted with her ladyship."

"That is a sad misfortune, for myself and for Lady Sheffield. And also, I presume, for Lady Athena, for she will attend, I trust."

"Most assuredly," said Diana. "Athena is acquainted with persons of the highest rank."

Iris, suddenly overcoming her scruples, blurted, "You would do better with an earl or a marquess."

Both her companions regarded her in bewilderment and she blanched, her confidences at an end.

Diana, observing Mr. Blysdale's confusion, gave a laugh and leaned across him, whispering, "Dear me, Iris! Whatever can you mean? You must not leave poor Mr. Blysdale in suspense. Pray, what can he want with an earl or a marquess?"

But Iris would not unclose her lips, and Mr. Blysdale, who was looking between them in the utmost astonishment, received a kindly smile from Diana. "Do not distress yourself, sir," she said in a confiding tone. "I am sure she does not mean *that*, for she is not at all stupid. She may say odd things, but there is almost always sense behind them, I assure you."

He blinked, absorbing her meaning, and looked with interest upon the silent lady beside him, saying gallantly, "Of course, ma'am. It does not admit of a doubt."

This conviction was to remain untested, however, for though Iris looked gratefully at him, she had not been brought to elucidate before Lady Athena's imperative voice arrested further speech between them. "Come Diana, Iris. Thank you, Lord Greenbury, for a delightful walk. We shall not keep you longer. John will see us safely home. Goodbye."

With that, she walked purposefully onward, leaving Diana and Iris no choice but to take a hurried leave of the gentlemen and hasten to catch her up.

"You really ought not to have snubbed Mr. Blysdale, Athena," said Diana once they were out of earshot of the gentlemen. "Not again."

"And why not?" inquired Lady Athena coolly. "He is nothing to me."

Diana persisted. "If he is known to a viscount, he must be something."

"Lord Greenbury may choose his own friends, but not mine."

"Mr. Blysdale surely won't be anything to you if you insist on being so uncivil," observed Iris.

Athena eyed her coldly. "As I cherish no designs upon Mr. Blysdale, it cannot signify. I care nothing for what he thinks."

"He is undoubtedly respectable," offered Diana, "to be so intimate with such members of the *ton* as Lord Windon and Lord Greenbury."

"You are deceived by his airs, Diana," Athena replied, still in that maddeningly superior tone. "Not all members of the *ton* are as discerning as they ought to be. Mama assures me Mr. Blysdale is nobody."

"It cannot be true, I am persuaded, Athena!" cried Diana. "I heard he has a magnificent fortune, and his airs, as you call them, are prodigiously well-bred."

"Depend upon it, his good breeding is only skin deep. Any mongrel can be taught to sit and to heel."

"You are odious, you know, Athena," declared Iris. "Just how much more gentlemanly must he be to win your approval?"

Athena's mouth pinched as she straightened the cashmere shawl about her shoulders. "A great deal, for a true gentleman is born, not self-taught, as anyone with a modicum of breeding would under-stand. I suppose you would think him gentlemanly, Iris, merely because he deigned to take notice of you."

"Yes, and it was well done of him," said Diana, linking arms with Iris. "Society would be vastly improved if more men were like him."

"Then Society would be overrun by commoners and pretenders," snapped Athena.

"It would be vastly preferable to being overrun by snobs and syco-phants," muttered Iris.

Lady Athena stopped and glared at her companions. "What has come over you? How can you even suggest that I accept Mr. Blysdale's acquaintance? His fortune may come from trade, for all we know!"

"My fortune comes from trade," retorted Iris, meeting her gaze. "And yet, you do not snub me."

Athena paused before walking on. "That is nothing to the purpose, for it is many generations ago."

"Yet I am still descended from bakers."

Her ladyship was silent for several paces. "It is neither here nor there, Iris. Your family is unquestionably genteel. I am much mistaken if Mr. Blysdale is not an upstart."

Diana and Iris exchanged looks. Iris made as if to speak, but Diana tugged her arm, giving a slight shake of the head. In annoyance, Iris clamped her mouth shut and walked on, but after they had made their bows to some passing acquaintances, it seemed she could no longer keep silent.

"You'll die an old maid, Athena," she blurted.

"Iris!" cried Diana, wide-eyed. Holding protectively to Iris's arm, she looked with some trepidation to Lady Athena, who gazed frigidly upon her companion.

Iris shrunk a little, yet her impetuous tongue blundered on. "You have a reputation already."

A faint blush rose on Athena's pale cheek. "Certainly I have a reputation, Iris. One that I must uphold by depressing the pretensions of every unworthy man who seeks my acquaintance. Unlike some persons, I owe something to my family name."

"To be sure, Athena," said Diana quickly. "Iris is well aware of the responsibility you bear, are not you Iris? Yes, of course you are. You mistake her meaning entirely, Athena, I am persuaded. Is not that so, Iris?"

Iris seemed caught between mortification and an obstinate determination, but under Diana's pleading gaze, she at last dropped her eyes and nodded. "I only hope that you will not be too careful, Athena. You deserve as much happiness as anyone, no matter your duty to your family."

Athena blinked rapidly and looked away, putting up her chin. "Then you need not be troubled for me, Iris," she said, then continued in a softened tone, "Be assured, I know what I am about. I could never be happy with a man who is beneath me."

"Certainly not!" agreed Diana with relieved accents, and she took Athena's arm, linking them all together as they continued on the path.

"In any event," said Athena, the edge now quite gone from her voice, "I have an excessively eligible match within reach. The Dowager Lady Foxham is to be at Lady Sheffield's ball."

"Good heaven," said Iris, wrinkling her nose. "You'd never accept that stuffy Lord Foxham!"

Lady Athena looked at her askance. "Can you not tame that horrid tongue?"

Iris looked conscious, but before Diana could formulate something to say in her defense, she saw Athena's eyes dance, and she let out a sigh. "Oh, Athena, you must own he is a trifle stiff."

"Stiff I will allow, but not stuffy." Her ladyship's lips turned up in a superior smile. "A marquess must be dignified but never too full of himself."

Iris huffed. "Then Lord Foxham is not for you, for his size indicates he must be stuffed full of himself."

"I have heard he wears a corset," confided Diana.

"And he creaks when he walks!" said Iris. "How mortifying for his future wife."

Athena pursed her lips. "I fancy that once he is married, his wife—if she is of a mind to do so—may alter the situation to her liking."

"To be sure; however, I do not know which would be more tolerable," mused Diana, "a creaky corset or a bulging waistcoat."

Iris agreed wholeheartedly to this conundrum but Athena, her chin raised, remained conspicuously silent until her companions' chatter died away. They looked uneasily at her as she continued on at her decorous pace a few more moments.

She at last spoke. "You mean to steal all the romance from my being wed to a marquess, I perceive, but you must know that romance does not weigh with me in the least. What does weigh with me is compatibility in rank and fortune, which Lord Foxham embodies. He is exceedingly eligible, corset or no corset, and yet you would have me refuse him out of hand, which would be most foolish in me.

There is more to consider here than the likelihood of an offer. Now that I have the Dowager's attention, I intend to take full advantage of her interest. She gives the most excellent parties, you know. Everyone who is anyone goes to them, and if Foxham proves disagreeable to me, perhaps I shall be put in the way of a duke."

Her friends, though chastened, expressed their horror at this latter notion, for all the single dukes were quite elderly and either grossly fat or odiously lewd.

Athena smiled primly, adjusting her shawl. "Lord Foxham is infinitely more eligible when compared with a duke, I see."

Her companions were silenced.

"Even if he does creak." She looked at them askance and then laughed, and Diana and Iris joined her in some relief. They laughed for some minutes, and when at last they had settled into a happy silence, Athena said, "I am grateful for your solicitude, my dears, but there is no occasion for it. Rest assured, I shall be exceedingly careful not to be precipitate in closing with any offer I receive. I know my worth."

"But you must not comprehend it if you can forgo the possibility of happiness in marriage, Athena," pressed Iris. "You do not even seem to desire happiness, and I am persuaded that would be a horrid waste."

Athena glanced at her. "I desire comfort and respectability, and a continuation or improvement of my station. These will make me happier than any lovelorn husband in an inferior situation."

"Love is not so bad a thing," said Diana, "for it can only make the marriage state more comfortable, I am persuaded."

"You have read too many novels, Diana," her ladyship said, tossing her head. "Love does not take nearly so great a hand in a successful marriage as your romances would have you believe. In my sphere of life, marriage is about alliances, and love can have no place in such considerations. It can only confuse the point and hamper the desired outcome."

Iris sighed. "I still would think twice before entertaining the suit of a man who must wear a corset."

Athena huffed a laugh. "I wish you will leave off the corset! You are far more frivolous in your requirements than I, you must admit. At least I have a deeper motive than appearance in all this. You must own that I should be a fool not to enjoy the Dowager Lady Foxham's hospitality wherever it reaches."

"I suppose I must."

"You would do the same, I am persuaded."

"Not if it brought on the attentions of a duke," Iris said bluntly.

Diana giggled at this and Athena shook her head, and they continued on to Grosvenor Square, where Lord Gidgeborough had a house. Athena sent the footman on to see her friends safely home while she went in to prepare for afternoon callers. Her mother was awaiting her in the Crimson Saloon and eyed her pink cheeks with disfavor.

"What have you been doing, Athena, to put so much color into your face? It is undignified. You are heated, I am persuaded."

Athena put the back of her hand to one of her cheeks and said, "Forgive me, Mama, but you are mistaken. I am not heated but chilled. It is a trifle cool outside. The color will fade as I change my gown, if Sarah has not allowed the fire to go out in my room. I will go up directly. I only looked in to tell you I was home and that Lord Greenbury escorted us some way in the park. Pardon me. I will not be above a quarter of an hour."

The color in her cheeks did fade, rather more quickly than it took to change into a morning dress of twilled muslin with an underdress of orange crepe and orange ribbon roses along the flounce and down the long sleeves. She descended to the Crimson Saloon again without haste, entering the room just as a knock was heard on the front door.

"I hope you did not keep Lord Greenbury from his business," remarked Lady Gidgeborough.

"Certainly not, Mama. He assured me he had none but to walk in the park."

Lady Gidgeborough huffed lightly. "He is a good sort of young man, and his father is not likely to last many more years. You are right to entertain his company, for one must not have too few prospects. Not that I count him as a serious prospect, mind you. He is nothing to compare with Lord Foxham, of course."

"Of course not, Mama."

"A marquess! It is what I always wished for you, my dear," her ladyship went on, lowering her voice as the measured steps of their visitors began to be heard on the stairs. "Indeed, I had hopes of a marquess myself, but it did not come off. Your father was in just the position of Lord Greenbury, however, and that is why I counsel you not to discount him completely. One must be prepared for every eventuality."

"One must," murmured Athena as the door opened and the butler ushered in their first visitors.

It was a lady and her daughter, new acquaintances made at Almack's rooms very recently, and Athena listened graciously to the younger girl's chatter about her delight in London and her string of beaux, while her mind ran upon the possibility of Lord Greenbury as a suitor. She thought not. His fortune was respectable and he would be an earl someday, but something was lacking in his air. Even Mr.

Blysdale had more address than Greenbury—but she pushed away the thought. A mere mushroom, no matter how well-educated and instructed in the ways of a gentleman, could never compare to a nobleman born and bred. It simply wasn't the way of things.

Chapter 4

AFTER TWO MORE glimpses of Lady Athena at *ton* parties, but without success at getting even close to her, it became apparent to Mr. Blysdale that his quarry was as elusive—at least to him—as she was desirable. He was not deterred; indeed, if anything, his interest was all the more piqued, for he was no stranger to rebuffs, and he thrived on challenge. He wanted only to find the proper mode of approaching the Unassailable Citadel, and his success, he was certain, would be assured.

As he bent his mind to the problem, he ruminated on what could be learned from his failed attempts. Windon was a flighty creature, though well-bred and highly situated in the *ton*, so it was perhaps not to be wondered at that Lady Athena had snubbed him there. But Windon's introduction had been at least considered before it was discarded—and so magnificently, too! He smiled at the memory of her majestic set-down when the propriety of his antecedents could not be placed with certainty. He could not but feel it was a victory of sorts to have put her out of countenance, even just a little.

He could not doubt he had piqued her curiosity, too, for when next they had met in the park, she had not even deigned to look at him—a sure sign that she had discovered something of his background. His smile grew to a grin and he leaned back in his chair, reveling in the knowledge that he had made her think of him, at least for a time. But Greenbury, with all his stolid propriety, had not fared better than Windon, so character did not seem to weigh with her ladyship. As to rank, they were both viscounts, so—

Here, he sat up, eyes narrowed as he recalled Iris's cryptic utterance at the Green Park. "*You would do better with an earl or a marquess.*" It was made plain now—he had bargained too low in his friends. Mere members of her own station were not enough to excite Lady Athena's respect—he must call in higher authority to represent him. He chuckled, leaning back once more in his chair. Miss Marshall had the right of it—Miss Slougham did have sense, no matter how oddly she phrased it.

Thus it was that Mr. Blysdale, arriving late to Lady Ferndale's soirée and careful to avoid general observation, appeared at the Earl of Hollingsford's shoulder as he was conversing with Lady Athena Dibbington.

"Ah! Blysdale," said Hollingsford, clapping Blysdale on the shoulder and turning back to his cool but somewhat rigid companion. "Lady Athena, allow me to present Mr. Jonathan Blysdale, an excellent man and my son Alverton's very good friend—"

"Forgive me, my lord," said her ladyship with a bow of her elegant head, "but my aunt is just arrived and I must go to her instantly."

Both gentlemen watched in stupefaction her graceful progress through the crowd before Hollingsford turned a knowing gaze upon his companion.

"Dished, sir," he said with a shake of his head. "Told you she was above your touch. Very high in the instep, and no mistake. Her mother was just such a one, and the apple don't fall far from the tree, it appears."

Blysdale nodded. "Thank you for making the attempt, all the same, sir. It seems I mistook my man."

"Your man, or your woman, eh?" Hollingsford squinted at him. "You'd better leave off her, my boy. Why waste your time? You're a handsome man, and your fortune is immense. You could have any one of a number of young ladies, and high-born, too, who don't take exception to your birth. What do you want to go chasing after a lady who don't want you?"

Blysdale smiled, looking after Lady Athena again. "A ridiculous start, I daresay. Mushroom madness."

Lord Hollingsford laughed, clapping him on the shoulder, and went off to refill his wine glass at the refreshment table. Mr. Blysdale made his usual civil rounds and took his leave, reflecting that he had yet to number a marquess among his acquaintance. But this oversight was easily remedied the following evening at Boodle's Club, where he hung casually back from the gaming tables until he had selected both his man and his intermediary. Then, adroitly encouraging the latter to join him at the former's table, he effected the introduction.

"Lord Foxham," said Lord Dewsbury, settling beside his junior at the Macao table, "allow me to make Mr. Blysdale known to you."

So invited among company that respected seniority as much as rank, his lordship allowed the acquaintance, and Mr. Blysdale's native charm and genteel air facilitated its progress. This meeting was singularly felicitous, as Blysdale later discovered during conversation at the quiet points of the game.

"I have had occasion to review your bill before Parliament, my lord," remarked Blysdale to Lord Foxham as the cards were dealt, "and I am moved to congratulate you on your perspicacity. It is most impressive, for you are only recently come into the title, I apprehend."

His lordship preened a bit. "Yes, sir, only a year ago. But it was not unexpected, unfortunately, for my poor father had been ill some time, and he took it upon himself to see that I was more than adequately prepared for my responsibilities."

Mr. Blysdale, a smile of satisfaction curling his lips, looked at his card and laid it back down. "It was well done, and worth the strain it must have been upon him, I am persuaded. My condolences on his death, my lord. He must have been a most excellent parent. It is never easy to lose one's father, whether it is sudden or expected. I should know, for my very excellent father died almost eight years ago."

Foxham murmured what was proper, but Lord Dewsbury put in, "I'll only say that you'd better set up your nursery directly, Foxham, and cut out that miserable worm of a cousin you have as heir."

"It is my intent, sir," said Foxham with all gravity. "It would not do to hand over the noble title of Foxham to so unworthy a line as the Abbershams, for all they are my relations. It would not do at all!"

Dewsbury agreed heartily, shaking his head as much at the result of the round as at the subject of conversation. "Every family has 'em, more's the pity. Poor breeding and bad blood, no matter how careful we are to tease it out."

"Ah, but there I disagree with you, sir," said Foxham, sitting back to allow the purser to rake in their cards. "Bad blood always has a source, and one must only avoid it. It has been my study ever since I succeeded to my esteemed father's honors to discover those families that began pure and have remained so, and I believe I have found out the very best. Indeed, I have a most eligible young lady in my eye—the Lady Athena Dibbington."

Mr. Blysdale, who had every reason to take offense at the discussion, remained as unruffled as he had throughout his long career in penetrating the ranks of gentlemen, merely raising an eyebrow. "I have heard that she is a fine woman, to be sure. But it has not yet been my honor to make her acquaintance. May I know how your suit has prospered?"

"Very well," said Foxham, glancing at his card. "But it is to be expected. Lady Athena has been reared with the same principles and expectations as have I, and we are excessively well-suited. I will continue in the regular course of attentions, but it is little more than a formality."

This statement was met with agreeable murmurs from his lordship's companions, and the game proceeded with every sign of a prosperous friendship developing between Lord Foxham and Mr. Blysdale. As far as his lordship was concerned, this was the case, for Mr. Blysdale had him well in hand, and it was not a week later that the two were found at the same ball, where Lady Athena was also in attendance.

As Lord Foxham had a vested interest in her ladyship, Blysdale could not prime him as he had his previous intermediaries, and thus was obliged to wait upon an opportune moment to present himself. He did, however, propound his great desire to meet the paragon of purity, and Foxham readily agreed to perform the office, but whether from the bustle of the room or the movements of the dance, that moment never came. As the evening wore on, it was borne in upon Blysdale that he had miscalculated his lady's ingenuity, for though he used the same discretion in approaching her as before, she somehow remained elusive. When it became apparent that his object was not to be had without his stooping to underbred tactics, he simply acted as though he had come to dance as usual, and made himself as agreeable as possible to every other young lady in the room.

As the ball wound down in the early morning hours, Mr. Blysdale caught sight of his quarry leaving the house with Lord and Lady Gidgeborough, and knew he had yet again been beaten. But he was not a man to be easily dissuaded from his purpose, nor was he a man above using unorthodox means to get his way. He took graceful leave of his hostess, therefore, and went home to work out another way to win his point.

Of the many servants he employed, Blysdale's secretary was arguably the most useful to him. Thomas Shaw, the fourth son of a barrister, had come to his employer's notice through the services of his elder brother, who was land agent to Lord Alverton. At least, that was how Thomas viewed his extraordinary good luck at having been selected from a pool of no fewer than four-and-twenty hopeful applicants for the post, which had been advertised as being compensated at a gargantuan sum. For a young man who had barely distinguished himself in school, the appointment to such a post was more than a dream come true, and Thomas could not imagine any trait he possessed to have set him apart, but for his brother's connection to Mr. Blysdale.

This, however, was not entirely the case. Blysdale had indeed come to know of Thomas's existence through his friend's land agent, but it was because of an oblique reference he had happened to make in that man's hearing to his desire for a discreet and resourceful servant who could discover useful bits of information. Alverton had laughed at him, saying that what he wanted was a spy, and dashed if he shouldn't put in a request at the Home Office now that Boney had taken up residence on Saint Helena and all the spies must be twiddling their thumbs with nothing to do. But not a week later, Blysdale had received a note from his lordship saying that his land agent had just the man for the job, if he had been serious. Upon inquiry, it was revealed that young Thomas Shaw, tiring of being bullied and set down at school for his lowly station, had discovered in himself a talent for uncovering information that was prodigiously useful in securing his own safety and comfort through the remainder of his school years.

Thus it was that, after a brief but thorough interview regarding his scholastic attainments and secretarial suitability, Thomas found himself the inmate of Blysdale House in London, with a fine mare at his disposal, room and board, and two suits of clothing and two hundred pounds remuneration per annum. It was only after several weeks that the realization dawned that his employer's occasional requests for odd bits of information were not mere curiosity, nor were they aligned with any malicious intent, but were part of a grand plan to smooth his own way into the *ton*. Thomas, having by that time developed a deep respect and liking for Mr. Blysdale, took this in good part and turned himself to developing this newfound scope for his abilities.

When Mr. Blysdale desired Thomas to discover for him all he could of Lady Athena Dibbington's background and connections, therefore, he did not blink.

"Do you wish me to have her followed, sir, or simply to find out about her?"

"Surely it would be excessive to have her followed, Thomas," said Mr. Blysdale with a look of disapprobation. "She is not engaged in nefarious business, after all, nor is she suspected of espionage. However, a glimpse at her social calendar would be helpful."

"Certainly, sir," replied Thomas, blushing for himself, but not the least discouraged—his employer was too good-natured to be taken overly seriously. "How far into the future would you wish to know? These things often change at short notice. However, it will be possible, I expect, to set up a regular inquiry, should it be necessary."

Mr. Blysdale considered the matter, shifting the papers about on his desk without seeing them. "I cannot say whether my business with her may take some time or not, Thomas. Much will depend upon what you find out. Perhaps you had better put a regular inquiry in place, to be safe."

"Yes, sir." With a click of his heels and a bow, Thomas was gone to execute this order, and Mr. Blysdale, with only a few musings on the probable outcome of this request, set to his regular business with every confidence in his secretary's discretion and expertise.

This confidence was not misplaced. Two days later, Thomas presented him with a dossier of Lady Athena's nearest relations, her closest friends, and her expected movements for the coming fortnight. Mr. Blysdale, setting aside the Yorkshire agricultural reports he had been perusing, thanked his secretary and dismissed him, taking up the sheaf of papers. After a thorough reading, he sat back in his chair and thoughtfully considered his findings, among which he was certain was the only irrefutable route to Lady Athena's acquaintance.

There was no question that Lady Athena was well-guarded from the attentions of the unworthy. As the daughter of an earl, she moved among the highest circles in Society, and could pick and choose where and by whom she was received. Her mother, Lady Gidgeborough, accompanied her to every social event, and formed the first line of defense against unwanted introduction. But Lady Athena, as Blysdale well knew, was perfectly capable of depressing pretensions all on her own. She had evaded his every attempt so far, even matching him for slyness, and coming just as close as he had come to impertinence without actually demeaning himself.

It was this that goaded him to persevere. If she had accepted his acquaintance at the outset, he could not tell but that his interest may have waned in time. But she had not—moreover, she had spurned him so thoroughly that a lesser man would have lost all hope and crept away with his tail between his legs. But Jonathan Blysdale was no cur to be scorned. He had not survived the rigors of Harrow and Oxford only to submit meekly to defeat at the hands of the lady deservedly known as the Ice Maiden.

Indeed, it was her very rejection that spurred him on. When he called to mind her magnificent disdain, and her subsequent efforts to thwart him, he experienced no shame or despair. On the contrary, he felt only a thrill—the thrill of certainty that she counted him a worthy opponent.

Now that he had found the sure route to her acknowledgment, he had only to decide whether he was impudent enough to tread it. The thought made him chuckle. Undoubtedly, he was, just as she was majestic enough to punish him for it if he succeeded. But the very thought energized him to his core. It was much like a game of piquet—pique and repique—and he would not hesitate to undertake this course, and thus win himself another round of battle with the incomparable Lady Athena.

Locking the dossier away in his desk, he pulled a clean sheet of hot-pressed paper toward himself and dipped his pen in the standish, scribbling a quick note with his graceful, assured hand. He dusted and folded it, sealing it with a wafer before ringing the bell for Thomas.

The following evening, he met Lord Hollingsford and accompanied him to Brooks's Club, where he was admitted as a guest and shown with his mentor into the dining room. They ordered dinner and discussed various political and social news until a gentleman entering caught Hollingsford's eye. His lordship waved him over. Mr. Blysdale, turning to view the newcomer, saw a solidly-built man running to fat, with a jowled face and black hair that showed grey at the temples. He was elegantly dressed and carried himself well, but the easy smile of recognition he gave Hollingsford confirmed in Blysdale's mind his conviction that he was about to take the upper hand in his unspoken battle with Lady Athena.

Blysdale and Hollingsford both stood to greet their new companion, who took the latter's hand in a hearty handshake.

"How d'ye do, Holly? It's been an age since last I saw you in these hallowed halls. Never say you've defected to Boodle's! Won't have it! Will have to cut you, I warn you!"

As this was said with a jovial grin and a clap on the shoulder, it could not be mistaken as anything but banter, and Hollingsford laughed in return.

"What do you take me for, a revolutionary? I'd sooner swim the channel and join the Frenchies. But you know you're well out, for even if I'd a mind to change, I'm too old for Boodle's! Just ask Blysdale, here. Allow me to introduce you—one of Alverton's cronies from Oxford. Excellent fellow, Mr. Jonathan Blysdale. Blysdale, may I present Edward Dibbington, Earl of Gidgeborough."

Chapter 5

M R. BLYSDALE RETURNED home early the next morning, having spent a convivial evening with Lord Gidgeborough and Lord Hollingsford, both of whom had been glad to accompany him to the gaming tables after dinner, and to allow him to exchange vowels with them. It was not Blysdale's practice to play too deep; however, in this case, he considered the risk outweighed by the reward. He was, as he had anticipated, justified. He ended the night as high in Lord Gidgeborough's esteem as he was in his debt, and with an invitation to join him at dinner the following evening at the club.

Two more such meetings, wherein Blysdale had been honored to both give advice—on the likeliest horse to win at Newmarket the next week—and receive it—on the finest wine merchant and then the most discreet gaming hell in London—and Blysdale had been admitted to the ranks of Gidgeborough's followers. He could not be said to have become his lordship's crony—indeed, he had never aspired to be, for it was both presumptuous and unnecessary. He needed only to be thought of well enough to be granted his introduction to Lady Athena, and then the relationship could develop as it naturally would.

To this end, Blysdale allowed himself to be led to said gaming hell on more occasions than he would ever have thought prudent—indeed, he had never stooped to enter such an establishment before in his life and vowed he would not again after he had attained his ends—and parted willingly with a small fortune on half those occasions. It was money well spent—or lost, as it may be—for within a sennight, he found himself at a card party where Lord and Lady Gidgeborough and their amiable daughter were in attendance.

It was a simple matter to seek out Lord Gidgeborough in the card room, and even simpler to lose ten pounds to him over the course of the evening, thus bringing his lordship into a humor so jovial that he took Blysdale's arm on his way into supper and led him straight up to where his lady and his daughter sat delicately sampling lobster cakes and ham.

"Here you are, my love," boomed his lordship, upon reaching the table. "What an agreeable circumstance!"

Lady Gidgeborough and Lady Athena looked up, quickly perceiving Lord Gidgeborough's companion, and Blysdale suppressed a swell of triumph at the abrupt change that came over their countenances. At one moment they were cool and collected—almost pleasant—at the next they were frigidly civil—caught between indignation and *point non plus*.

Before either of them could make a move to extricate themselves, however, his lordship drew Blysdale toward them. "Here's a fine man I've been meaning to make known to you. Best card player I know below the age of thirty!" He laughed heartily at this and clapped his companion on the back. "Mr. Jonathan Blysdale, my loves. Blysdale, my Lady Gidgeborough and Lady Athena Dibbington."

Blysdale bowed over her ladyship's coldly extended hand, murmuring his obligation to her, and then turned to Lady Athena. While her countenance remained impassively civil, fire snapped in her eyes, but she gave him her hand and allowed him to make his bow over it.

"My lady," he said smoothly. "It is an honor to finally make your acquaintance."

Neither lady spoke, only flashing polite half-smiles and nodding infinitesimally. He returned their smiles with more warmth—and, if he could be so bold, with evidence of better breeding, though he must be forgiven a flash of exultation. He had unequivocally won his repique.

Lord Gidgeborough took a chair beside his lady, motioning Blysdale to take the last one beside Athena. "Nothing like cards to turn a man ravenous," he said, piling his plate with whatever viands were within reach. "Fine pickings here, I must say."

Lady Gidgeborough very nearly rolled her eyes, but restrained herself to merely a look of irritation. "Do refrain from gauche phrases, Gidgeborough, no matter your company. You well know Lady Archibald gives excellent suppers. One need not remark upon it."

She returned her attention to her plate, apparently resigning herself to the inescapability of Mr. Blysdale's society, and unconsciously signaling her daughter to do likewise. Both regained their dignified manner, which allowed them to eat their supper without causing anything near an unpleasant scene, but which did not require either of them to contribute to the conversation that then sprang up. Lord Gidgeborough, who scrupled not to speak across his wife and daughter down the table to Mr. Blysdale, talked of card play and of food, of wine and of parties, and Mr. Blysdale was obliged to respond or risk offending his interlocutor. Unerringly gentlemanly, however, he answered only enough to show respect to his lordship, but not so volubly that he could be accused of rudeness to the ladies caught between them.

In consequence, when they arose from the table, Lady Gidgeborough accorded him a slightly less frigid nod, and Lady Athena, allowing him to pull out her chair, murmured a word of thanks. But the glance she cast him upon this condescension could not, by any stretch of the imagination, be considered conciliating. It was steel and ice and warning—such a look as would send Lord Windon and his like hotfoot out the door. But Mr. Blysdale took it with superb equanimity, for he was of sterner stuff. He chose to take it not as a dismissal, but as a promise. It was only as he could wish, for he had thrown down the gauntlet and, with that look, Lady Athena had taken it up.

She wasted no time in playing her hand. When Blysdale paid a courtesy visit to Lady Gidgeborough and her daughter the following day, he was met with the intelligence that Lady Athena was gone out. He was therefore obliged to spend an uncomfortable quarter-hour's *tête-à-tête* with her ladyship, the Dragon, and to endure an uninterrupted barrage of supercilious slights and insinuations, all uttered with the utmost decorum.

"You are from Yorkshire, I believe," said her ladyship. "A wild country, to be sure, and so far removed from civilized society that one doubts anyone of sensibility or breeding would wish to reside there."

"It is very far from London, to be sure," agreed Blysdale coolly. "However, Edinburgh is not so distant, and its society is lively enough to have drawn the Prince Regent himself to partake in its delights."

"Ah, but His Highness is not known for his discrimination."

Undaunted, Blysdale said, "York offers a charming social scene, and is home, as you must recall, to various notable and learned persons, including His Grace the Archbishop."

She sniffed. "One suspects that His Grace is merely tied by his calling to so distant a place. It speaks much of his integrity and faith that he so nobly and selflessly adheres to his duty."

"He is an example to us all, as I had occasion to mention to him only last Christmas," he said gravely. "Perhaps his example inspires Lord Harewood to continue in residence."

"Oh, Harewood is but a new creation," she said, waving the earl into obscurity. "One need not discuss the wisdom of following such persons in anything."

Mr. Blysdale nodded graciously. "To be sure, my lady. I suspect those such as Lord Mulgrave—whose title your ladyship must admit to have been extant in Yorkshire for centuries—have set the mode for newcomers such as Harewood."

"As he should," she said, eying him with dislike. "Whether they enjoy residing in so desolate a county is another matter—the north is becoming so full of millworks, one does not imagine it will long be a very pleasant sort of place."

"Indeed, there is much industry there, madam, but as the mills are confined to the larger cities, the majority of the county—which your ladyship will acknowledge to be sizable—remains largely untouched."

"A fortunate circumstance, for those who prefer sheep for their company."

"If I may, madam, Yorkshire boasts an array of wonders aside from its healthy and useful livestock, from the coastal cliffs to various ruins to the dales and the moors. It is quite a remarkable county."

"It is only unfortunate that one must endure the inhospitable climate to view these wonders."

"The seasons revolve in the north as well as the south, my lady," he returned, smiling benignly. "The winters are long and dark, and the moors can be bleak at times—Yorkshire is not a residence for the faint of heart, to be sure. But the summers are delightful, and the heather in bloom is a sight to behold. It is then that visitors are best advised to come."

"Or rather begged to come, one should imagine," her ladyship said tartly. "It cannot be pleasant being exiled to one's country seat for the whole of the winter, which I conjecture lasts full twice as long as here in the south. However, if one has chained oneself to the north, one must accept the consequences."

"It is not so harsh to those who are accustomed, depend upon it, madam. Our people are not easily depressed, and must inspire one with their fortitude."

She raised a brow. "The Luddites certainly were not easily depressed, sir; however, I cannot pretend to admire their fortitude. It is just such disregard for peace and order that one cannot approve, but that runs rampant in so uncivilized a quarter as Yorkshire."

"An unfortunate era in our history, to be sure, madam, and one that affected other counties than Yorkshire, you recall. I, myself, have so fastidious a regard for what is right that I must join with your disapprobation of those who are so lost to all sense of Christian duty and respect as to participate in wanton violence. We may be grateful that the perpetrators have been punished and the movement so entirely subdued."

"So we may," she said, her gaze sweeping up and down his person in annoyance.

She continued in this vein until the visit was concluded, but it was no more than Blysdale had been used to endure at school, and he bore it with a sangfroid impressive even to his tormentor, if she had deigned to allow him to know it. It was unnecessary for her to make it known to him, however, for he was experienced enough at the task of bringing a difficult subject around his thumb that he had seen the signs and had taken satisfaction in them. He left Gidgeborough House in the conviction that he would soon have an ally in both Lady Athena's parents.

This was an unfortunate error, however, for Lady Gidgeborough, though recognizing in Mr. Blysdale a man of excellent breeding, education, and even bottom, would not allow these qualities to overshadow the fact of his inferior birth. He simply was not *bon ton*, and thus could never be acceptable to her. She was forced by her husband's regrettable lack of fastidiousness to entertain him as an acquaintance, for as her husband's acknowledged friend, he must be welcome in the house, but she was not required to like him, nor did she mean to. And she certainly would not promote any semblance of tolerance in her daughter toward such a mushroom.

Upon Athena's return from her spurious morning errand, therefore, her mother wasted no time in acquainting her with the particulars of her conversation with Mr. Blysdale.

"He is as ill-bred an upstart as we were led to believe," she concluded, "and it will be well to keep him at a distance."

Nodding coolly, Athena inquired, "Shall you say as much to Papa? For I fear he has taken a liking to Mr. Blysdale."

Lady Gidgeborough pursed her lips. "Unfortunately, any hints in that direction would be in vain. Your papa was ever thick-skinned. It is the greatest affliction to me. No matter—you and I may give Blysdale a wide berth, and if Gidgeborough inflicts him upon us at any time, we need not make him feel welcome. It will only be to encourage social climbing, which must not be done for the world. We are already beset by too many vulgar persons such as Lord Craven must introduce into our ranks. That any self-respecting peer would marry an actress is incomprehensible to me! But it is all of a piece with the male race nowadays."

Athena simply murmured assent to all her mother said and went upstairs to change her gown.

Thus it was that Mr. Blysdale, returning to Gidgeborough House two days later to request Lady Athena accompany him on a drive through Hyde Park, received the tidings that her ladyship was not at home to callers. He left his card, returning the following day, but was again sent away by the superior butler with the intelligence that her ladyship would not be home to callers in the near future.

A visit to Brooks's Club to renew his acquaintance with Lord Gidgeborough bore excellent fruit; his lordship greeted him jovially and entertained him for nearly an hour with various hunting anecdotes, all having taken place in Yorkshire.

"A glorious country, I must say, Blysdale," proclaimed the earl, refilling his companion's glass. "Should like to get up there more often, but it's a devil of a way off, even from Leicestershire. And Lady Gidgeborough don't like it above half. Anything farther north than Warwick is beyond the bounds of reason to her mind. But that's a female all over—can't comprehend the value of good, open country."

Having obtained an invitation by his lordship to accompany him and his family to the theater, Blysdale presented himself betimes at Covent Garden the following evening, only to endure a chilly reception by the two ladies in the box, which mood lasted for the entirety of the play and dampened even Lord Gidgeborough's bluff insensibility.

Electing not to stay for the farce, Blysdale took his leave of the ill-matched party and sent his carriage away, using the walk home to formulate a new plan of attack. In the morning, he called the resourceful Thomas into his study.

"It seems, Thomas, that I have misjudged the Dibbington spirit. We must pursue another course."

"I'm sorry to hear it, sir," replied Thomas. "It seemed as though his lordship had done the thing for you."

"Lord Gidgeborough has done me a great service, and continues to be excessively useful, but his lady is not taking his example. She is proving a most redoubtable opponent."

"Not Lady Athena, sir?"

Blysdale tapped his lips with his steepled fingers. "It is too early to say. We must get around the mother first."

As his employer paused in consideration of his problem, Thomas shuffled a bit on his feet, leading Blysdale to say, "Out with it, Thomas. You have something to say?"

With respectfully lowered eyes, the secretary said, "I cannot help but wonder if the lady is worth all this trouble, sir—meaning no offense, sir."

Blysdale smiled. "None taken, Thomas." He was silent a moment more, gazing into the middle distance before saying, "I have never met a lady so perfectly formed for me, Thomas. Her connections and family are excellent, to be sure, but so are those of any number of ladies in the *ton*. It is not that." His eyes narrowed in the effort of capturing Lady Athena's perfection in words. "Were she a governess or a milk maid, she should have caught my attention and admiration, for she was born to be worshiped—Did you know, Thomas, that she and her friends are called the Goddesses? A singularly apt sobriquet."

He tapped the desk decisively. "I believe it will be wise to discover which of Lady Athena's friends will be most useful to us. See to it, won't you?"

If Thomas thought his employer's interest a trifle imprudent, he did not say so, merely accepting the commission and leaving the study. Two days later, Mr. Blysdale was possessed of another dossier, this time outlining the histories of Miss Diana Marshall, Miss Iris Slougham, and Miss Lenora Breckinridge.

The excellent Thomas had discovered that Miss Breckinridge was a recent addition to Lady Athena's circle—introduced through the kind offices of Miss Marshall, who had a *tendre* for her brother, Mr. Tom Breckinridge—and thus not one of the Goddesses. After a cursory glance through her information, Blysdale set her aside as unhelpful to his cause, for she could not possess sufficient knowledge of Lady Athena's character nor the influence of longtime friendship to be of any use to him.

The Goddesses were another matter. Thomas's inquiry revealed that Lady Athena, Miss Slougham, and Miss Marshall had been fast friends since birth, and could be depended upon to be intimately acquainted with each other's deepest secrets. After nearly two decades of intimacy, there had been nothing strong enough to shake the friendship, though fortune had smiled upon their families in somewhat differing ways. The young ladies were nigh inseparable, and though Lady Athena was exceedingly nice in her social expectations, she never refused an invitation from Diana, and she not only tolerated Iris's oddities amazingly, but had been known to defend her almost to ferocity.

Considering Lady Athena's aloofness to every other person she thought beneath her, this last fact piqued Blysdale's interest more than all the rest. With an effort of memory, he called to mind his first meeting with the Goddesses, at Lady Dewsbury's ball, and recollected Lady Athena's cutting remark to Miss Slougham upon her finding courage enough to tell him her name. Miss Marshall had been of the opinion that Athena had acted from embarrassment. Analyzing the situation with the benefit of his new knowledge, he concluded that her remark, though unsolicitous, had indeed been made without rancor. Blysdale himself had many friends who would so address him, without truly meaning to slight him or even to offend him.

It seemed that, though Miss Slougham embodied much of what Lady Athena did not generally tolerate, her ladyship did not hold her friend in disdain. The Slougham's fortune had come from trade, some generations back, and Miss Slougham, though an heiress with twenty thousand pounds, was otherwise the reverse of the elegant, refined Lady Athena. Everything pointed to her ladyship holding Miss Slougham in aversion, but though she would, on occasion, so far forget herself as to belittle her friend, she certainly showed no inclination to cast her off.

It seemed that Mr. Blysdale's best course—now that he had exhausted Lord Gidgeborough's influence with his daughter—was to make himself agreeable to the backward and strange Miss Slougham. He felt certain he could do this, for he was possessed of unending patience and persistence, and even the most reluctant young lady had not yet been proof against his charms. Besides, it was a challenge, and Jonathan Blysdale was ever up for a challenge. He had been bested by no one as yet, and trusted that he never would be, for he had excellent sense and super-excellent instincts. When he knew himself to be on the right track, he would not back down, and he did not doubt that Miss Iris Slougham was the most qualified of all Lady Athena's friends to give him the key to her acceptance.

Chapter 6

THE VISCOUNTESS OF Brixham's ball was an unusually elegant affair, with plaster columns set beside every doorway to approximate the look of a Grecian temple, and plaster replicas of the more recognizable Elgin marbles scattered about the room. Gauzy fabrics draped tastefully here and there completed the milieu, and one lady was heard to say she felt utterly transported into Ancient Greece. All this was lost on Iris, however, who merely viewed the statues with longing, wishing she could join their ranks and never be expected to say another word in her life.

Though it had been nearly a month since her victory at Lady Wishforth's ball, Iris continued awkward and uncertain in society, unable to trust herself in any but her closest circle. Even there, she said things she ought not, but her friends—even Athena—were more forgiving. If her mother had told her once, she had told her a thousand times that she must tame her rebellious tongue if ever she hoped to receive an offer.

"Gentlemen do not want bluntly-spoken wives," was Mrs. Slougham's unyielding opinion.

Iris did not mistrust her, for every gentleman who had been a recipient of her unvarnished thoughts had recoiled—some civilly and others less-so—most retreating so rapidly from her vicinity as to leave a chill space behind. Only a handful of gentlemen had borne her bluntness with fortitude, Mr. Tenby among them.

As her gaze darted among the dancers from her safe vantage point behind her friend Lenora, Iris spied Mr. Tenby with a golden-haired damsel in a spangled white dress.

"She smiles too much," she murmured, surprising her friend.

Lenora turned to her. "Who does?"

"The young lady dancing with Mr. Tenby. She oughtn't to smile so much. She has a gap tooth."

Lenora craned to see through the shifting movements of the sets. "Oh, dear, so she does. However, it is nothing to the purpose, for her smile lights up her eyes. I have no doubt Mr. Tenby does not notice the gap tooth."

Iris bit her lips, cognizant that she had once more uttered a solecism, but unable at the moment to feel remorse. It had occurred to her that it was excessively unjust that the golden-haired girl could flaunt her gap tooth to everyone without incurring a remonstrance, while Iris must take the greatest pains to hide her particular flaws from the world. But there was very little justice in Society, as she had long ago been made to understand. All her comfort must bow before the great and urgent cause of Matrimony.

The dance ended and she moved more securely behind Lenora, not wishing to be remarked by any of the gentlemen leading their partners off the floor, for she was certain to burst forth with an entirely inappropriate observation on the inequity in social discourse, and she could not look forward to yet another public shaming. But her shield forsook her for the next set that was forming, and Iris, cherishing no desire to deceive an unsuspecting gentleman into believing that she was a proper partner, cast about for a convenient column behind which to place herself.

She was forestalled in this laudable purpose by a gentleman's voice addressing her.

"Miss Slougham, may I have the honor of this dance?"

Panic gripped her throat and she stilled in the hope that she would become invisible and the gentleman would go away, but in this she was disappointed, for he simply repeated his invitation. Civility forced her to face him and endure the consequences, but when she turned, her astonishment chased every other consideration away, for it was Mr. Blysdale.

She blinked, bewildered. "What do you want with me, sir? I am not Athena."

Instantly, she blushed, clamping her lips shut, but the gentleman merely smiled. "I wished to dance with you, ma'am. If I am not mistaken, that is the order of the evening."

Coloring, she swallowed, glancing about for someone to save her from her predicament.

"If you are looking for your friend, I believe she is in the set," Mr. Blysdale observed helpfully, "but Mrs. Slougham is in the card room. If you are in need of her, I will gladly fetch her to you—"

"No!" cried Iris, almost leaping toward him. But then she shrank back, wringing her hands before her. "She will only force me to dance with you—that is—Oh! If only Diana were here!"

His lips twitched as he bent closer to her. "I do not profess to know Miss Marshall well, but I fancy she would be pleased to know she is missed. If you were to furnish me with her direction, I should be gone to retrieve her directly." He bowed. "I am your servant, ma'am."

"Diana is gone to Brighton," Iris said flatly.

Mr. Blysdale's eyes widened. "Ah! I fear my gallantry does not extend that far." He paused and, averting his eyes for a moment, added in a more serious tone, "As I am fully sensible of the discomfort of your situation, ma'am, may I offer myself as a friend? Or do I ask too much?"

Iris regarded him with a slightly furrowed brow. That he was still standing before her, pursuing her acquaintance despite the reticence and rudeness of her manner, was incredible. Very few persons of either sex were willing to overlook her oddities unless obligated by friendship or relationship, and Mr. Blysdale did not fall into either of these categories. As she meditated upon the matter, it occurred to her that this civility may only be of a piece with his good breeding, for he had been kind to her since their first meeting some three weeks ago. But many gentlemen who had shied away from her were otherwise well-bred, so she could not be certain.

When she did not reply, he looked placidly about and, noting that the dance had begun, stepped to her side, away from the crowded floor. "I fear we have lost the opportunity of joining the set, for which I am greatly disappointed. I shall not lose hope, however, and in that spirit, wonder if I may impose upon your good nature a little longer by remaining with you."

She blinked, realizing that she was still staring rather rudely, and dropped her gaze with a blush.

After another space of silence, he spoke again in a lower but perfectly amiable tone. "You will pardon my presumption when I ask if it would distress you to know your mama has come out from the card room and is looking this way?"

Iris started, turning more fully toward him, her back to the card room door. "How does she look? Calm—or angry?"

"Quite calm," he said, glancing briefly toward Mrs. Slougham. "Even pleased, I should say."

"Oh, dear," said Iris, not daring to look. "Now I must not frighten you away, or I shall be in danger of marrying a toad."

He darted a curious look at her. "A toad? Dear me, how disagreeable. Please believe that I would do anything in my power to prevent such an eventuality, Miss Slougham—even endure whatever terrors you might inflict upon me. But were you considering trying to frighten me away?"

"Oh, no, sir, I need never consider it! It just happens!" Her hands wringing together again, she rushed on, "Say something—anything! Only do not cease talking to me!"

"I should be pleased to, ma'am," he said with admirable aplomb. "That is just what I wish, you know; therefore, I am even more at your service."

She nodded her perfunctory thanks and stood shifting from foot to foot, her attention absorbed by the turbaned lady watching them, at whom she did not quite dare to look.

Enjoying himself far more than he had anticipated, Mr. Blysdale said conversationally, "If I may, Miss Slougham, I wish to thank you for your excellent advice the other day."

"Certainly, sir," she said, only half listening in her anxiety. Then she blinked and looked at him. "What—what advice?"

"At our last meeting," he said, smiling. "In the Green Park, if you recollect. You were so obliging as to walk with me for a time, and were so acute as to conjecture my true purpose in coming there. You were entirely correct, you know, though it did not seem so at the time, nor soon thereafter."

She changed color at the memory. "I did not think you had under-stood me, sir. No one ever does, you know, beyond my very intimate friends."

"I am relieved to hear it, for I did *not* understand you at the time," replied Mr. Blysdale amiably. "Indeed, I found your words terribly cryptic, but I am a literal-minded fellow, and often cannot see beyond the nose on my face. Miss Marshall's assurance that you are not at all stupid resolved me, however, that there was nothing for it but to apply myself to working the matter out."

Staring unabashedly at him now, Iris said bluntly, "It would surprise me very much if you could," but then closed her eyes in embarrassment. Taking a deep breath, she tried again. "That is, I cannot see how you could have done so, sir, for I did not make any sense."

But he merely laughed and said, "It was a challenge, indeed, but you may have observed that I am a persistent sort of person, and came about quite well. Indeed, I may tell you that I have been successful, and have you to thank for my present acquaintance with Lord and Lady Gidgeborough, and with Lady Athena." He bowed.

Iris, regarding him with dawning satisfaction, said, "I am glad of it! I only hope it may do you good."

Before he could respond, the music ended and those who had been dancing came off the floor. Iris, recollecting that gentlemen generally did not stay very long by her side, anticipated at any moment that Mr. Blysdale would take his leave. But he did not, instead address-ing civil comments to her until Lenora returned, and then only requesting that he be introduced to her friend. Iris thought she saw then what his design had been and performed this office, preparing to fade into the background.

He continued the perfect gentleman, however, talking of this and that with both of them until the next dance struck up, and Iris fully expected that he should lead Lenora into the dance. She was utterly unprepared, therefore, for the renewal of his offer to herself, and she hesitated out of sheer amazement. Lenora's hushed encouragement to her to accept brought her out of her bemusement at last, however, and she joined him in the set.

Their two dances were as pleasant as they could be, for they were country dances that left little opportunity for talk. But even had they been a waltz, Iris flattered herself that she could very possibly have acquitted herself well, for she was far better able to manage her tongue when she was not terrified, and Mr. Blysdale had managed to put her very much at ease.

At the end of the set, Mr. Blysdale did turn his civility upon Lenora, securing her for the next two dances, and then took advantage of the interval to procure refreshment for both ladies. As they stood conversing, Mr. Tenby came up and joined them, and Iris, basking in the delight of being her natural self without disapprobation, was so contented that she forgot to hide.

Mr. Tenby bowed to Lenora and said, "Miss Breckinridge, may I have this next dance?"

"I am sorry, sir," said Lenora, smiling graciously, "but I am promised to Mr. Blysdale." With an almost imperceptible gesture, she indicated her friend and cast Mr. Tenby a significant glance, which was not lost on Iris.

His smile became a trifle fixed and he turned to look upon Iris, who imagined he was recalling their last meeting, and her champagne-induced observation of his straw-colored hair. For a moment, she knew a craven impulse to run away and save him the pain of partnering her, but this was forestalled by a stronger impulse to prove herself to him, and bolstered by the realization that she very much wished to stand up with him.

"I will dance with you, sir," she said, stepping forward just as he was in the act of bowing. They avoided a collision by a hair's breadth, and Iris colored, her mortification in once again having overstepped the bounds of propriety shaking her slim resolve.

Then he smiled, performing his bow at a safer distance. "I should be honored, Miss Slougham."

And as he stayed by chatting agreeably until the sets formed, she could almost believe that he spoke the truth. Their dance was a quadrille, however, and they were both tried a little by the long pauses occasioned by the movement of the dance.

Mr. Tenby spoke first. "You must pardon my having first asked your friend to dance, Miss Slougham. I was under a misapprehension. I had remarked you speaking very particularly with Mr. Blysdale, and so supposed him to be your partner."

"If you had continued to watch me, sir, you would have seen that I danced the previous two dances with him," Iris said.

He looked a little uncertainly at her. "I would not have you imagine that I am in the habit of watching you, ma'am."

Closing her eyes as heat rose up her neck, she stammered, "No—no, of course not, sir. Forgive me—that would—that is not what I meant."

"Indeed, you could not. Forgive me," he said, equally flustered, and faced the dance again. After another pause, he said, "Do you know Mr. Blysdale well?"

"Not yet," she said quickly. "He seems eager to know me better, however."

Mr. Tenby glanced at her askance, his lips pursing slightly as his brow furrowed—as though trying to make out what she meant. It was a look Iris knew well, and which generally signaled the end of a gentleman's attentions, but this time she was determined to make him understand her.

"He admires Athena—Lady Athena Dibbington, my friend," she hastened to explain. "I am much mistaken if he does not hope to improve his acquaintance with her through me."

Mr. Tenby's brow rose, but his lips remained tight. "I hope it is not so, for your sake, ma'am. I would not like to think him so ungentlemanly."

"No! He is everything that is gentlemanly—"

The dance required their attention at that moment, and they performed their steps in silence, he with a grave look and she in frustration. It seemed imperative to her that Mr. Tenby not mistake the matter between her and Mr. Blysdale.

As soon as they were again in their corners, she said, "He is prodigiously kind, and pleasant to talk to."

Mr. Tenby's countenance remained grave. "I beg pardon for tearing you away from him, ma'am."

"Pray, do not be stupid, sir!" she said, then pressed a gloved hand to her mouth. After a moment in which she collected herself, she said in a stifled tone, "Forgive me, Mr. Tenby. I ought not to have—oh, dear." And she relapsed into mortified silence.

After they had performed the next figure—she having shrunk more and more into herself throughout—Mr. Tenby cleared his throat and said, "I fear I am quite stupid, ma'am, for having been so presuming. I have injured your feelings and I beg you will forgive me."

Iris managed a nod and a choked, "It is forgotten, sir."

"Let us talk of something else," he suggested in a heartening tone. "What think you of books?"

Iris cast him a scared look, loath to own that her tastes ran to the Gothic, while his most likely kept to Latin or Greek classics, or to those horrid improving tales.

He smiled encouragingly. "Have you read *Pamela*? It is one of my mother's favorite novels, and she encouraged my youngest sister to read it."

"It is the only way a young lady of sense could be prevailed upon to finish that book," Iris blurted, then instantly looked away, her cheeks burning.

The proceeding pause was terrible to her feelings, and she did not dare look to see how thoroughly she had disgusted him. But when she could stand it no longer and did peep at him, she saw he was heroically keeping back a smile.

"You do not like *Pamela*?" she asked, incredulous but hopeful.

He gave her a look so full of empathy that her heart lightened perceptibly. He said, "I have never read it, but Marintha did not care for it at all. To own the truth, I only inquired of you because it was the only book I could think of that I knew young ladies read. But from what Minnie told me, I must say it is a relief that you also did not like it, for I should not have known what to say about it if you had."

She blinked, a smile tugging at her lips. "Your sister sounds a most sensible young lady, sir. I should like to know her."

He paused, eying her a trifle warily. "She is not out for another two or three years."

Iris's heart sank again in the belief that she had seemed forward. It appeared that she could never remain in any gentleman's good graces for long, no matter how hard she tried. They performed the final figure in strained amity, and when the dance ended, he delivered her to her mama, who had come to tell her it was time to depart. Lenora rode with them in the chaise, and after they had set her down in Curzon Street, Mrs. Slougham turned to Iris.

"A fine evening for you, my dear," she said. "Two gentlemen paid you very particular attentions, and you did not chase either one away. I own I had not thought it possible."

Iris swallowed, reflecting that Mr. Blysdale, if she was not much mistaken, was in no way interested in securing her affections and that Mr. Tenby was unlikely ever to approach her again. "Thank you, Mama," she said drearily.

Mrs. Slougham nodded, gazing out the window at the passing streetlights. "I had begun to believe that Mr. Slougham and I had wasted our efforts at putting by so considerable a portion as twenty thousand pounds for you, for it was no small thing, I assure you, to scrimp and save all your life. But we knew it to be essential if we ever were to have you off our hands, for even I am not so sanguine as to hope that a gentleman would take you without some inducement."

Iris sighed. "No, Mama."

"A very good night's work," said Mrs. Slougham, bending forward to pat Iris's hand with a warm smile. "You did very well, my dear. I begin to imagine that we shall see you happy at last."

Her mama sat back in the carriage, turning her gaze outside again with a satisfied smile, and Iris exhaled, overcome by relief and gratitude. Her mother's words—the sting of which she had long ago learned to ignore—were mere breadcrumbs of approbation, but they were balm to Iris's soul. Mrs. Slougham's hopes may yet be dashed, for

Iris could not be confident that tonight's success would be repeated in any way during the remainder of the Season, but she thought that the exchange of contentment—no matter the duration—for the perpetually harassed expression on her mother's countenance was worth the possibility of a future disappointment.

Chapter 7

DESPITE IRIS'S PREDICTIONS to the contrary, both her would-be suitors called on her at the correct hour for morning visits, to inquire as to her well-being and to forward their acquaintance. Mr. Blysdale arrived first in as agreeable a temper as ever, and charmed Mrs. Slougham with his good breeding.

Bowing over her hand, he said, "Forgive me for not begging an introduction to you before, madam, for I was made known to your amiable daughter and her friends, Lady Athena Dibbington and Miss Marshall, some three weeks ago. But I hope now to remedy that omission, if Miss Slougham would be so kind."

Shaken from her customary reticence, Iris instantly came forward and performed the introduction, after which Mrs. Slougham replied, "I can see that you are a true gentleman by your kind attentions to Iris, sir. She was almost overpowered by them last evening, as you may have perceived, for she is not quite so easy in society as one could wish."

He shared a glance with Iris, who had looked conscious at her mother's words. "On the contrary, Mrs. Slougham, I find Miss Slougham's conversation delightfully refreshing. One does not often come across a young lady newly out who is brave enough to be so honest and forthright. It says much of the excellence of her upbringing that she was able to be so without seeming forward or impertinent in any way."

Though perhaps not her daughter's most eloquent champion, Mrs. Slougham was not proof against such earnest flattery, and she almost simpered. "So fine a gentleman as yourself, sir, ought to be a judge, to be sure. I am only pleased that my poor efforts have not been wasted."

"Certainly not, madam," was the direct reply, and Iris was sensible of a growing respect for Mr. Blysdale's talents. That he was aware of her feelings she suspected, and it was only her own disregard for their importance—or her mother's habitual suppression of them—that prevented her from ascribing disinterested goodness to his motives. It seemed most probable that he defended her to her mother from the expectation that her gratitude would further his claims on her good offices with Athena. But far from disliking him for this, Iris welcomed the opportunity to assist him, for she could not be insensible of the immediate and continuing benefits of his good opinion.

Mr. Blysdale smiled at his hostess and inquired, "Miss Slougham seems often in Lady Athena's company. Is it possible that your families are related?"

"Not by blood, sir, but you are not too far off. Iris, Diana, and Athena might well be sisters, you know."

"I believe they are known as the Goddesses, Mrs. Slougham," said Blysdale smoothly, with a deferential smile to Iris. "One supposes that their names brought them together."

"Oh, no, sir, quite the contrary," said Mrs. Slougham, beguiled into excellent spirits by what she chose to assume was his extreme interest in Iris's suitability as a wife. "It was all their fathers' idea, for they were fast friends at Eton and then at Cambridge, and nothing would do for them but to ensure their offspring shared the same bond of friendship. It was fortunate for them that they all were to become fathers at approximately the same time, or such a design may have been for naught."

"Then they chose the names as the bond, I presume?"

Mrs. Slougham chuckled, in fine fettle. "Dear me, no, for they could not agree on the method before the children were born. It fell to their wives to fix on the solution, sir."

As it transpired, Lady Gidgeborough—true to her commanding disposition—took matters into her own hands, presenting her lord with the first child of the friends, and pronouncing her name to be Athena. Lord Gidgeborough, rather apologetically passing this news on to his friends, suggested they follow with other names from the Greek Pantheon, to which Mr. Marshall and Mr. Slougham agreed with alacrity, neglecting to consult their wives or even a list of Greek gods and goddesses—which Iris secretly believed may well have awoken them to the peril of their situation.

As luck would have it, Mrs. Slougham continued, she herself was delivered of a daughter only three weeks later, and Mr. Marshall and Lord Gidgeborough received the happy tidings that the goddess Iris had joined their little pantheon. Things seemed to be in excellent train until Mr. Marshall, succumbing to the anxiety of an arduous and perilous confinement for his beloved wife—from which she emerged exhausted but triumphant with a healthy daughter—suffered a lapse and announced his daughter's name to be Diana—a distinctly Roman appellation.

Two hastily composed and urgent letters were sent to arrest the ill-fated christening, but due to Mr. Marshall's general insensibility to the outer world, engendered by his utter relief and joy at having both avoided disaster and become a father, neither letter was opened until the event had taken place. The friendship inevitably stood upon a knife's point for a fortnight, but Mrs. Marshall, reviving more quickly than even her optimistic doctor had prophesied, wrote a lengthy letter of congratulation to the other two new mothers with the suggestion that they all combine to mark the occasion with a celebration of their three little goddesses, for were not they all divine? To this Lady Gidgeborough and Mrs. Slougham readily agreed, and their husbands, much struck by the simplicity of this solution, instantly forgot their grievance and endorsed the plan with energy.

"It is just like a gentleman to behave so insensibly," remarked Mrs. Slougham on the close of this history, "though I must beg your pardon for saying it, Mr. Blysdale."

His indulgence was not required however, for at that moment the butler announced Mrs. Tenby and her son, Mr. Tenby. Mrs. Slougham, delighted that her daughter had now two beaux to entertain, led Mrs. Tenby off to a chair by the fire and engaged her in chit-chat interesting only to older women.

Finding herself suddenly in the role of hostess, Iris did her best to rise to the occasion.

"You know one another, I daresay," she said, indicating each gentleman. When Mr. Tenby owned to never having been introduced to Mr. Blysdale, Iris performed this office, saying, "But you must have heard of him. You said as much last night."

Mr. Tenby stiffened, but Mr. Blysdale said smoothly, "I hope it is good hearsay, sir."

Clearing his throat, Mr. Tenby answered, "I doubt anyone has not heard of Mr. Blysdale. He is excessively well-known in certain circles."

"But not in yours," said Iris in an anxious attempt to erase her incivility. "To be sure, it is because you are not rich, while he is very much so."

She instantly retreated into a shell of mortification at her gaffe, but Mr. Blysdale, with admirable composure, said amiably, "More likely it is because we have very different histories. Mr. Tenby is a gentleman, you see."

Mr. Tenby, who had been resembling a particularly irritated waxwork, regarded his companion in surprise. He *had* heard of Mr. Blysdale, and some of what he had heard had not been at all complimentary. Blysdale was believed to have been born a commoner, with nothing approaching respectability in his ancestry, and to wish to bury this fact under the combined weight of an excellent education, high connections, and extreme wealth. He was presumed to be ambitious and headstrong in this purpose and mercenary in the means he used to achieve it. Mr. Tenby could not, from these rumors, have anticipated so self-effacing and gentlemanly a response to Miss Slougham's blunt statement of his circumstances, and he was not unmoved.

Unbending, therefore, he said gruffly, "It is not as though you are not a gentleman, sir. Anyone who is near you must believe it."

"You are very kind, Mr. Tenby," said Blysdale with a rueful little smile. "'It takes all sorts to make a world,' as Cervantes put it. It is simply a matter of finding a way to rub along together. We all have our little embarrassments, I am persuaded, do not we, Miss Slougham?"

Iris, who was quite as gratified as Mr. Tenby by Mr. Blysdale's smoothing away her blunder, managed a weak smile, but could not be brought to contribute more of her own brand of embarrassment to the conversation. The gentlemen got along well enough without her for another five minutes, at which time Blysdale rose to take his leave. Before he had completed this ceremony, however, the butler announced Lady Athena Dibbington and Miss Breckinridge.

Lady Athena's pause on perceiving Mr. Blysdale in the room was so infinitesimal as to be unnoticed by all but himself and Iris, who, wishing to recompense him for his great kindness to her, made a desperate resolution. As Athena greeted Mr. Tenby and made to pass by Mr. Blysdale with the merest nod, Iris moved to intercept her.

"You are acquainted with Mr. Blysdale, Athena?" she inquired boldly, her voice wobbling only slightly in her underlying fear—nay, certain knowledge—of remonstrance. "He is your father's friend, I understand."

Athena's gaze, sparking with otherwise unexpressed indignation, bored for a moment into her friend's before coming to rest on Mr. Blysdale. "He *is* my father's friend, Iris. How kind in you to remind me of my obligation. How do you do, Mr. Blysdale?"

He took her languidly proffered hand and bowed over it, releasing it at exactly the correct moment. "A pleasure to see you again, Lady Athena. Your father is well, I hope?"

"Tolerably, I believe," she replied in her cool tone and stepped past him to pay her respects to Mrs. Slougham.

Mr. Blysdale watched her go, a secret smile on his lips, and Iris said, "You were about to tell me more of your Oxford days, Mr. Blysdale. Lenora would be pleased to hear you, certainly."

"Oh, yes," said Lenora gamely, though in the dark as to why Iris should imagine her pleased to hear about Oxford. "Please, go on." And she seated herself beside Iris, both looking expectantly up at him.

With an appreciative look for Miss Slougham, Mr. Blysdale sat down again, launching into a humorous story of the bagwig who insisted upon rating the pranks of his students in such a way as to reward those who were more circumspect or clever and less uncaring of the consequences to others. He had nearly done when Mrs. Tenby came to collect her son, expressing her delight in the visit.

"But perhaps you are not ready to go, Nicolas?" she said, her gaze flicking between him and the young ladies, of whose handsome fortunes she was well aware. "You may stay behind, for I have the carriage, you know, and will do very well with Timothy Coachman. It is scarce two minutes home, I daresay."

Mr. Tenby rose, coloring at the intimation that there was more between him and either young lady than was evident to himself. "No need, Mama. I am at your service. Good day, Miss Slougham, Miss Breckinridge. Good day, Mr. Blysdale."

Lenora bade him a warm farewell, but Iris, too caught up in her hopes of keeping Mr. Blysdale with her until Athena was forced to acknowledge him, was rather more vague, a circumstance which did nothing to improve Mr. Tenby's notions of his importance in her eyes. He and his mother went away, and Iris wrung another ten minutes of Oxford stories from Mr. Blysdale before Athena at last came to them.

Her ladyship said, "I simply must tear you away, Lenora, and I fear we must forgo our walk, for Mama will be expecting me no later than four o'clock and we have already stayed here so long as to become almost irksome."

This was said without the slightest glance toward Mr. Blysdale—who had come before them and yet stayed—but if he did not feel the meaning of it, Iris felt it for him.

She jumped up. "Nonsense. It is not gone two o'clock. We may still have our walk."

"I would not presume to take you away from your guest, Iris," Athena replied, adjusting her gloves and hat. "It would not be civil, for Mr. Blysdale apparently has nowhere else to go. We may take our walk another day."

"Oh, no we will not!" cried Iris with energy. "Do not let her go away without me, Lenora. I must only fetch my things." She turned to Mr. Blysdale. "As you were just leaving, sir, I know you would be so good as to accompany us to the Green Park. Don't dare any of you go away."

All three of her callers gazed after her in varying degrees of astonishment as she flew from the room, and they had scarcely begun to recover themselves when she was with them again, her breath short and her hat askew.

"There!" she said, pulling her gloves on with satisfaction. "I have not kept you waiting, and we may all be on our way."

"Certainly," said Lenora, laughing as she adjusted Iris's hat. "But not until you look more the thing, my dear! We cannot have you disgracing us. What will Mr. Blysdale think?"

"He would be the only one unused to the circumstance," murmured Athena, "though I fancy he does not know enough to tell the difference."

If Mr. Blysdale heard her, he gave no indication of it, merely standing patiently as Lenora fixed Iris's bonnet more securely on her head.

No sooner was the task accomplished than Iris took Lenora's arm and tugged her toward the door. "We shall go together, Lenora. Athena, you may take Mr. Blysdale's arm. Goodbye, Mama!"

She was gone on the words, and Athena, her eyes snapping, inhaled deeply before taking Mr. Blysdale's arm as instructed.

"You honor me, your ladyship," he said, without a trace of triumph in his voice.

She glanced sideways at him, her lips pinching slightly. "On the contrary, sir, I must be the obliged. This is, as you may guess, an unusual position for me."

As they made their stately way out the door and down the stairs, he said in a slightly lowered tone, "As it is for me; however, I would beg you to think nothing of me, madam, were I not certain you already do not." He paused to receive his hat and cane from the butler, then turned again to her. "I will own to a concern for Miss Slougham. I would not have her injured for the world. She is only trying to be kind, I am persuaded."

Athena gave a little gasp, but instantly composed herself and raised her chin. "Do not tease yourself over Iris. This is all too common an occurrence in our relationship, but I have yet to throw her off."

"You are very angry."

"Anger is a paltry emotion." He raised his brows and she bit her lips, looking away. "I cannot easily overlook Iris's presumption, sir, but our friendship will take no harm, I assure you. As you may imagine, it has survived worse."

He smiled somewhat reluctantly in acknowledgment as he allowed her to proceed him down the steps. Iris and Lenora awaited them at the bottom and the four set off down the flagway in the direction of the Green Park, Athena's footman trailing behind. With characteristic perspicacity, Mr. Blysdale did not seek to press his advantage by attempted conversation with Lady Athena, remaining comfortably quiet for the short walk to the park entrance. He then very properly took his leave, thanking all the ladies for their excellent company.

"You are very welcome, sir," said Iris, shaking his hand and stolidly ignoring Athena's marked silence. "We all should be glad of your company at any time."

He pressed her hand, and with a measuring look at Athena, he tipped his hat and walked away. Iris watched him go, forcing Lenora to tug at her arm to tear her eyes away from his back, for Athena had not stopped longer than to give him a civil nod.

As they hastened their steps to come up with her, Lenora whispered in Iris's ear, "What on earth was all that about? Are you fallen in love with him?"

"Heavens, no," said Iris, lowering her brows at Lenora. "Besides, it would do me no good if I was."

"Then why—" But as Iris turned her scowl upon Athena, who was walking on as though they were not even there, Lenora blinked and said, "Oh."

She was not so long-acquainted with Athena as Iris was, but she had come to know her ladyship well enough to recognize the signs of her lacerated pride, and to guess what imprudent notion Iris had taken into her head. She had also some idea of Iris's obstinacy in matters about which she felt strongly, and suddenly glimpsed shoals ahead. There was an altercation doubtless brewing, and though she felt she had no part in it, neither could she abandon Iris to Athena's certain retribution, and she resolved upon the brave course of attempting to preempt any outbreak of hostilities—at least until she was gone from the vicinity.

She was frustrated in this noble purpose, however, by Iris saying abruptly, "You must not continue in so uncivil a manner toward him, Athena."

"I do not know what you mean, Iris," was the icy reply. "I am always unswervingly civil, even to those beneath my notice, or had you not perceived it these many years?"

Iris either dismissed or ignored the insult. "Mr. Blysdale is the acknowledged acquaintance of Lord Gidgeborough, and therefore more than worthy of your notice. Besides, he has ten times the breeding of half the lords in England and twice the fortune, or more. If he had been born a gentleman, I daresay he would be your sole object."

"But he was not born a gentleman, Iris," said Athena coldly. "I wonder that you continue to overlook it, though I ought to expect nothing less from one who goes about half-distracted. Even you ought to comprehend that a gentleman in Mr. Blysdale's situation could never be my object. He certainly could be yours, however. You are not under the same obligation to your name and family as I am. Your fortunes come from the same source, after all."

Iris glared at her. "That is neither here nor there, Athena. He does not want me."

"If that is so, he is unaccountably concerned for your welfare."

"He admires you," persisted Iris doggedly, "though I cannot tell why, when you are so waspish."

"And I cannot tell why I must repeatedly spell it out to you, Iris," said Athena, stopping short and turning to face her companions. "Mr. Blysdale is nothing to me. He is plainly both a mushroom and a simpleton. He obviously wishes to improve his lot in Society, and thinks to make an alliance with my family to achieve it. If he had a grain of commonsense, he would have seen from the outset that his aim is grossly misjudged. I must marry a title with an impeccable bloodline, which utterly excludes him—even were I to find his fortune or his person at all attractive."

"Your pride misleads you, Athena, for you are utterly blinded by it! He is excessively attractive, besides being clever and kind."

"His features are not out of the common way, his intelligence is middling at best, and he is arrogant, impertinent, presumptuous, and insufferably rude."

Iris shook her head, closing her eyes as she exhaled. "You had better take care, Athena, or you will end up married to that odious Lord Foxham, and it will only be what you deserve."

And so saying, Iris abruptly turned, towing Lenora with her, and marched quickly back down the path toward her home.

Chapter 8

M R. BLYSDALE COULD not but fear that the triumph of the afternoon—of having finally succeeded in gaining Lady Athena's public acknowledgment—had been dearly bought. Though the rumors that Mr. Tenby had heard were not far from the truth, they were hardly representative of the whole of Blysdale's character, for they neglected to admit his innate sense of right and a natural kindness, especially to those who were less comfortably circumstanced than himself. While Miss Slougham was in many ways his social superior, she was very much his inferior in address and connections, and he had been instantly struck at their first meeting by her unspoken but amply demonstrated desire to make herself understood, if not acceptable.

His subsequent attentions to her had therefore been precisely aimed to gratify that desire, and they had obviously impressed her deeply. Her prompt repayment of his kindness by sacrificing herself upon the altar of her long-standing friendship to Lady Athena could not be ignored; she must be protected. He had meant what he said to Lady Athena—he would not have Miss Slougham hurt for anything, and he would do all in his power to keep his word.

He was not so firm in his own esteem as to imagine he figured in Lady Athena's thoughts in general, but it was plain that his presence irritated her prodigiously. This fact gave him as much satisfaction as it gave him pause, for he flattered himself that it boded very well for his campaign, but so did it put Miss Slougham's sensibility in danger. Thus, he decided a retrenchment would be beneficial and withdrew his attentions to any of the Goddesses, secure in the belief that the strong friendship that had bound them for twenty years would serve to heal this latest wound.

He was far from beaten. Despite this setback, if he could not make the Lady Athena Dibbington his wife, he fancied he was not his father's son, for the late Mr. Ethan Blysdale had not risen from frame-knitter on a workshop floor to be the master of a textile empire for nothing. The Blysdale spirit was indomitable—and more than half responsible for the rumors that had shaken Mr. Tenby's opinion of him.

Sacking his plans for the following day—which had included driving out with Miss Slougham if she had been available—Blysdale sauntered down to his club. Here he discovered Lord Windon sitting in the parlor, gloomily perusing the social column of the Gazette. He settled in a chair beside him and after receiving no more than a grunted greeting, ordered coffee and regarded his friend.

"Now, what has you so down in the mouth, Windon? One of your flirts getting married?"

Windon cast him a look of annoyance and thrust the paper into his hands. "You could at least attempt to be conciliating, but it is all of a piece with you. Never trust a fellow to know his own mind, but I did, this time. Can't conceive of what she sees in that puffed-up gaby."

Blysdale glanced over the list of announcements and found Lady Serena's name among the newly engaged couples.

He tutted. "Told you she wasn't for you, my boy."

"Much you know about it!" replied Windon pugnaciously. "She was just the sort of girl for me, and I'd have made her very happy!"

The coffee was brought and Blysdale handed it to Windon. "For about a month, I think, at which time your interest would have gone wandering."

"Not this time! Not with her! She was the sweetest darling—I could never—"

"Precisely," said Blysdale calmly. "You could never contain your urges with so gentle a lady. What you need, my boy, is a strict hand to keep you in line. You must find yourself a governess to marry."

Windon spewed his mouthful of coffee onto the floor, to the detriment of the shoes of the gentleman who had just come up to them.

"Devil take it!" said Lord Alverton, regarding his shoes in dismay. "Why'd you do that, Windon? I only came to say 'How d'ye do' and to find out how your horses fared at Newmarket last week."

"Oh, beg pardon, Alverton," said Windon gruffly. "Nothing to do with you. This sapskull thinks I should marry a governess."

Alverton's brows shot up, but he turned a thoughtful eye on Blysdale. "Daresay that would do the trick. D'you think there's one that would have him, though? Prodigiously stiff-rumped, governesses. At least mine was, what I remember of her. No patience for shenanigans."

"Which is entirely the point," said Blysdale, waving him into a seat. "She won't stand for any of his havey-cavey business. She'd have to be enough of a beauty to catch his eye, but then she'd have the power to keep him in line with a look."

"Or one night of locking the door," mused Alverton. "I believe you're right, Blysdale. It's his only hope."

"I am right here, I'll thank you to remember," said Windon testily. "And I am fully capable of arranging my own future, which I can assure you will have no governess in it."

Ignoring this, Alverton said to Blysdale, "I hadn't taken you to be in the petticoat line. How come you to know so much about females? In the market for a wife yourself, are you?"

"As it happens, I am," said Blysdale. "Though it has no bearing on the present company. It is merely my knowledge of Windon, here, that gives me wisdom in this case."

"Ah, to be sure!" said Alverton, signaling a waiter for another coffee. "But you're avoiding the question, my boy. This is news, that you're finally ready to take the plunge, but I ought to have guessed it—my father hinted as much. And if I know anything of you, you've got a lady in your eye. Wouldn't happen to be that Slougham chit you stood up with at Lady Brixham's ball?"

Blysdale smiled ruefully but, though sorely tempted, did not attempt to mislead him. "No, sir. Though Miss Slougham is excessively interesting, she does not excite more than a friendly feeling in my breast."

"Glad to hear it," said Alverton, sipping his coffee. "I doubt even your reputation could survive marriage with that oddity."

"You wrong her, Alvie," said Blysdale, his intent gaze piercing his friend before dropping to the table. He continued in a conversational tone, "Miss Slougham's manner is out of the common way, to be sure, but one tires of commonality. Her converse is excessively refreshing, besides being to the point."

Alverton exchanged a look with Windon and said, "As you say, sir. But Miss Slougham is nothing to the point! You are trying to fob me off!"

Blysdale shook his head but Alverton was insistent. "Who's the lucky lady, Blysdale?"

"The only luck in the matter will be mine," said Blysdale, smiling dryly, "for I mean to have Lady Athena Dibbington."

Windon nearly choked again on his coffee. "Still at that?" he sputtered, shaking his head. "You're the devil of a gudgeon, Blysdale. Wise indeed! Lady Athena Dibbington? You're no better than a doormat to her mind. She'd sooner step on you than look at you."

Lord Alverton eyed Blysdale with a mixture of incredulity and respect. "Lady Athena, eh? No notion that was in the wind, though my father said you were after some big game. But Lady Athena—that's a mighty tall order. Not saying she ain't a fine woman—just above your touch, my boy. Hate to tell you, but so it is. I ought to know—she's above my touch, too."

"You see?" cried Windon, gesturing at Alverton for confirmation. "What did I tell you, weeks ago, when first you got her into your head? Above your touch, and so she is. Best leave off now and cut your losses."

"Fine advice from one so willing to follow it," said Blysdale wryly.

Windon's lips tightened into a line. "At least I know my limits."

Mr. Blysdale traced a pattern on the tabletop with his finger. "As do I, I assure you. They simply differ from those of other men, because I do not give up easily—nor do I begin a task where I do not feel sure of succeeding. You need not trouble yourselves to advise me in this case. I shall not fail, depend upon it."

Windon snorted. "It's not my consequence you're playing fast and loose with—by all means, destroy yourself."

"He's not far off," said Alverton reluctantly. "Really, Blysdale, you're in for it if you persist with Lady Athena. Take it from those in the know."

"Believe me, I have done," said Blysdale with a half-smile. "Just not those you might expect. And it has made all the difference. It may please you to know, gentlemen, that thanks to those truly in the know, I have gone from receiving the cut direct to counting both Lord Foxham and Lord Gidgeborough among my acquaintance, for which cause I may congratulate myself that only yesterday Lady Athena was induced to accept my arm for the length of not one, but three streets."

"No mean feat," said Alverton in awe.

"Heard it," said Windon, pursing his lips. "Didn't credit it, though. Are you sure you're not pitching it rum? She wasn't driven to it by twisting an ankle or having a fainting fit or some such thing?"

Blysdale chuckled. "When have I ever told an untruth? —and don't throw that rumpus with the Magdalen bagwig up in my teeth. That was an extenuating circumstance."

This allusion effectively assuaged Windon's desire for revenge as he instantly described the outrageous incident, in extravagant detail, to an excessively interested Lord Alverton, who had attended Cambridge and not met Blysdale until after his auspicious career at university had ended. The lively discussion that ensued so strengthened their camaraderie that Windon's mood made a reverse and both companions became consultative.

"Still can't recommend you continue pursuit of the Ice Maiden, my boy," said Windon, raising his cup in empathetic salute, "but if you're bent on it, better prepare for some frigid nights."

"Cold as the polar region, that one," nodded Alverton. "Even if you were to win her—which I don't yet admit as a possibility, mind you—should have to take a mistress to warm yourself up. Not saying it's right in general, but best thing to do, in these circumstances. No sense in getting frostbite, I say, when there are any number of cozier armfuls ready to have you at the snap of your fingers."

Blysdale glanced up. "Then I'd be as foolish as Windon. How can you speak of sense when you have none? I'll not win the finest woman in the country only to lose her esteem over a lightskirt."

Alverton shrugged, but Windon's eyes narrowed and he pointed an accusing finger around the cup still clutched in his hand. "Always was your weakness, Blysdale—pride. Must always have the best. I warn you, sir, your pride will carry you well into deep waters."

"Pride goeth before the fall," agreed Alverton sagely. "If it ain't your own that pulls you down, Lady Athena's is sure to drown you. "

"Regular 48-gun frigate, that one—her cool indifference drives all before it. As though you were a mere trawler."

Alverton nodded. "Either way, down you go, my boy."

Blysdale smiled. "If I may have the Lady Athena, I fancy it will be well worth it to set up my kingdom at the bottom of the sea. However, I fancy I am not so obliging as to allow anyone to drive me anywhere, even her ladyship."

"You're forgetting her mother, the Dragon," said Windon.

Blysdale considered this point, but only for a moment. "Unless I am much mistaken, Lady Athena is much like myself. She is properly respectful of her mama, but I should count myself shocked if she would allow anyone to dictate her future but herself."

Windon eyed him. "There is much in what you say—better take heed."

"I wouldn't want her unless I thought she could be brought to want me, Windon, I assure you."

"But that's just it!" cried Windon, sitting forward. "Lady Athena has too much of Lady Gidgeborough in her. Will never see past your birth—too starched up by half. Pity she couldn't take after her dear papa. Quite the cock robin, Lord Gidgeborough. Don't say I'd like to run with his set, precisely, but I'd take his society any day over his lady's."

Alverton hummed his approval. "Tolerable old cuff. Great friend of my father. Wonder how he ever got saddled with the Dragon."

"Depend upon it, he was as mad as Blysdale, here," said Windon, finishing his coffee. "Thought he had it all sorted out. Handsome woman, fine bloodline, excellent connections. How long into the honeymoon do you think his illusion lasted?"

Blysdale smiled peremptorily. "Perhaps I am banking on the likelihood of Lady Athena having more of a heart than anyone—least of all herself—realizes."

Alverton and Windon both regarded him narrowly, then shook their heads.

"Too much of a risk, I'd say," said Alverton. "Can't stake your whole life on such a flimsy hope, my boy! 'Til death do you part and all that! Mighty long time to be paying the piper, if you're wrong. Much better find a sweet young thing who worships you and won't freeze your gizzard every day—not to mention lock the door on you at night."

"Better be safe than sorry," agreed Windon.

Blysdale huffed a laugh, standing up. "Your notion of safety sounds tiresome in the extreme. A life of sweetness and light, with no friction or challenge? I thank you, but no. I thrive on friction, and must have a challenge. And I think I have found the very one for me. If I am wrong, I am willing to take the consequences. Thank you for your excellent—if unnecessary—advice, gentlemen, but upon due deliberation, I find I will continue my present course. No, no! Do not be dismayed. You may rest easy in having done your duty by me, and know that I shall not hold you accountable for what infelicity my decision may cause me. Good night."

He left them to murmur and shake their heads over his unwisdom and outright obstinacy, but he could not repent his decision or even feel uneasy. He possessed better information than either of his friends—they had not read Thomas's extensive report on Lady Athena's bosom friends. The other Goddesses and Miss Breckinridge were lively and sweet-tempered, and he had observed that her ladyship did not maintain her friendships without some fellow feeling. The traces of kindness he had seen were slight, but discernible nonetheless. It was enough to convince him that such gentle young ladies as Miss Marshall and Miss Breckinridge would not continue in Lady Athena's company if she were the absolute Ice Maiden that Windon and Alverton believed her to be.

And Miss Slougham's situation was even more significant. That the society of a young lady so awkward and even improper would not only be admitted by Lady Athena, but be welcomed and even sought by her was singular—if not entirely unheard-of. The circumstance suggested there must be something deeper behind their friendship beyond the mere encouragement of their fathers. Miss Slougham had had no compunction in taking Blysdale's part against Lady Athena yesterday—this alone was enough to suggest that she was sure of her old friend's forgiveness, even if it did take some time.

Still, he did not wish to stir the coals for Miss Slougham, and determined to try if he could not forward his suit without her help. The next morning, therefore, he paid a call in Curzon Street to Miss Breckinridge, an heiress with many admirers amongst whom his attentions would mean little. He did not worry for himself—Miss Breckinridge was known to be intensely interested in a newly minted Lord Helden—but he wished to keep her safe from Lady Athena's scrutiny as well.

Having succeeded in enticing Miss Breckinridge out for a drive in his curricle, Blysdale bided his time in an exchange of commonplaces until she mentioned their meeting at the Slougham's two days previous.

"I had not known you to be acquainted with Athena, sir," she said, eying him askance.

He smiled pleasantly. "I have only recently had that pleasure. I must admit it to be a dubious one. Lady Athena is infinitely elegant and superior, and I often wonder if I ought better to stay away."

"Oh, do not say so, sir!" cried Miss Breckinridge, but then she chuckled. "Though I must say Athena can be terribly superior—as you well know from her manner on Tuesday. She nearly froze me on our first meeting, but Diana—that is Miss Marshall, you know—made her laugh and took away all her stiffness."

Mr. Blysdale regarded her. "You are serious? I do not believe I have ever seen Lady Athena laugh."

"She does know how, sir, depend upon it," said Miss Breckinridge with a mischievous smile. "However, she does not choose to do so often. Only when among her intimate friends, I fancy, for I do not think she has ever relaxed her manner anywhere else. But it is only to be expected—Diana and Iris have known her forever."

Mr. Blysdale agreed, slowing a moment to greet an acquaintance who had brought his horse up beside the curricle. When the gentleman had ridden on, he turned again to Miss Breckinridge.

"But you have not known her ladyship as long."

"No, we met only this Season. But I have the advantage of having met Diana a year ago, and by extension have an honorary *entrée* into their little circle. Athena does not yet entirely approve of me, I am persuaded, but she has been excessively kind—in her way."

If he had constructed the conversation himself, it could not have run upon lines more suitable to his purpose. Smiling, he inquired in what way Athena could be kind.

Miss Breckinridge considered. "It is hard to discern, sir. She has been brought up to be quite superior, you see, and can be terribly rude—particularly when her consequence is threatened. But I believe she feels when she is wrong, especially amongst her friends, and will fairly quickly make amends." She went obligingly on to describe instances of her ladyship's forbearance with Iris, self-deprecation for the comfort of a friend, and advice given in good faith.

"I wondered at first at her acceptance of Iris, sir," she said meditatively, "for you must know that Iris is very awkward in Society. But she is the greatest dear, once one is accustomed. You seem to have overcome that obstacle, sir, and it does you the greatest credit! If only other gentlemen could be so perceptive."

"It seems Lady Athena is so perceptive," prompted Mr. Blysdale helpfully.

Miss Breckinridge nodded. "Indeed. One would not guess it to see her ladyship on most days, but she is a most fearsome champion of those she holds dear. I believe that if Diana or Iris were to come in harm's way, Athena should throw herself into the close without a thought but for them. I have quite amazed you, but so it is."

He denied having been amazed, returning her smile, but as he drove the vehicle through the Stanhope Gate and to her home, he could not but feel pleasure at having been so thoroughly vindicated.

After seeing her to her door, he drove back to Hanover Square, pondering the unquestionable existence of a heart beneath Lady Athena's icy exterior, and considered how it boded well for his unconventional suit. As he did so, however, he could not help but feel a deep admiration for her which went beyond any consideration of himself—but he did not long dwell upon it, not being generally in the habit of analyzing his feelings.

Chapter 9

IRIS, THOUGH SHY of confrontation with strangers, felt no such compunction with her intimate friends. Athena's cold disapprobation affected her only so far as her own sense of wrong gave it justice, but where she knew she was in the right, Iris could stand firm. And stand she did for three days through Athena's icy silence and dismissive looks, knowing from long experience that her friend would not withhold her amity forever. Diana, returning during this time from Brighton and being put in full possession of the situation, lent her what support she could, but was unable fully to approve Iris's methods.

"Even were he an eligible gentleman, Iris," said Diana regarding the previous Tuesday, "it is not the thing to force Athena's hand so. And in company, too! She must have been mortified, and you know how she dislikes anything of the sort. How could you?"

Iris looked away but said, "She had it coming, Diana. If you had seen how she has treated poor Mr. Blysdale—who is entirely eligible, for he has the approval of Lord Gidgeborough, you know—I cannot believe you would think me ill-judging in the matter. She could not go on so odiously."

"But you know that she only does so because Lady Gidgeborough is so high in her notions. It has always been thus—poor Lord Gidgeborough has not the sensibility to appreciate his lady's principles."

"Nor does anyone, I think!" cried Iris. "They are horridly misplaced!"

Diana bit her lip. "Of course, I agree with you, but there are those who would not, and one ought to take their reasons into account."

"Anyone whose reasons are so unreasonable ought not to be given such indulgence," retorted Iris.

"Come now, Iris," said Diana soothingly. "It behooves us to try for a little patience, especially with Athena. You know her situation—her mama so exacting and cool. Athena must do as she is expected to do."

"But her mama is wrong," said Iris doggedly.

"That may be so, but so are you for going so far on Tuesday. Forcing Athena to notice a person with whom her mama wishes her to have nothing to do? Think what would have been your sensations, had one of us done so to you?"

Iris blinked. "I should have been utterly shocked, for my mama wishes that I should have to do with any and every gentleman that ever breathed. You shake your head, but you know it is so! She would have married me off to Sir Isaac Hornaby, who not only looks like a toad but acts like one too. You have not seen him, Diana! He licks his lips when he sees me, as though he should like to gobble me up, and my mama sees nothing wrong in it! If a tinker had paid me attentions, not to mention a fine figure of a man such as Mr. Blysdale, she should have thrown me into his arms, I daresay. There is no gentleman, or any man moreover, against whom my mama would advise me."

Diana, who had been struggling against a desire to giggle at this outburst, was sobered to a degree by the mention of Mr. Blysdale's attractions. She regarded her friend thoughtfully.

"Do you like Mr. Blysdale, Iris? Is that why you are so eager to help him along?"

Iris gaped at her. "Don't be a ninnyhammer, Diana. A handsome, rich, well-bred gentleman such as he would be a sore trial to a middling girl like me. Imagine my waking every day to his perfections and having them constantly compared to my own lack of them. It could not be borne."

"Then why do you do it? For you do not, in general, design to risk Athena's displeasure."

Iris blinked. "He is formed for Athena, you must see that. They are both perfect in every way—except perhaps in pride, which both could bear a little less of. But I believe he would make her happy—far more than that stuffy, creaking Lord Foxham. For all her faults, Athena deserves to be happy, but she is too proud and too blind to accept that Mr. Blysdale will make her so."

"I see."

And Diana did see, for she, like Iris, had known Athena from infancy and, knowing all her ways, held the same conviction that she deserved happiness. She also knew Iris, and far from being offended by her blunt speaking, believed that she spoke the truth.

With a sigh, therefore, she took Iris's arm and pressed it, saying, "You are right, and I will help you to assist Mr. Blysdale to the best of my ability. However, you must promise never to place Athena in so disagreeable a situation again, my dear. She has not the humor to deal with it as she ought, and will not thank you—as you would not thank any of us to deal similarly with you."

Iris gave her promise, sanguine in the belief that none of her friends would serve her so, for they all did their best to guard her from the distressing effects of her wayward tongue. Her sensations the next week at the Tenby's ball, where Lenora Breckinridge entirely failed her, were therefore those of extreme ill-usage.

Lenora's fortune of thirty thousand pounds had made her the darling of Society, but it had also made her the target of not a few fortune hunters. An ill-judged walk into the shrubbery with one of these brought another hotfoot after them, to defend what he claimed was his right to Lenora's fortune and person—in that order. Iris came after him in time to see the issue—blows, a challenge, and Lenora so furious at their presumption that she might have come to blows with them herself had she not retained enough of her reason to suppress the desire. Leaving the gentlemen to have it out by themselves, therefore, she swept Iris back with her into the house.

"I hope they kill each other," said Lenora fervently, once they had gained the ballroom.

Iris, quite shocked at the gentlemen's odious behavior, said, "It would simplify matters, certainly."

But before they could share more hopes for the disposal of the two miscreants, Mr. Tenby came up all innocently to claim Lenora for the next two dances. Iris, knowing her friend was in no mood to share proximity with any member of the male sex in the foreseeable future, could only stare at both his insensibility and his apparent disregard for his own safety.

She was understandably unprepared, therefore, at being pulled forward by Lenora and recommended as a more desirable partner to Mr. Tenby. The existence of a dangerous glitter in his erstwhile partner's eyes must have penetrated his brain at this juncture, for he took Iris's hand with graceful civility, and she went away with him, too overwhelmed by events to formulate a demur.

By the time the set had begun, however, Iris had had time to resent Lenora's using her so ill, in thrusting her into just the situation that she dreaded. It was one thing to be angry, but another entirely to allow one's feelings to utterly overpower one's duty to one's awkward and defenseless friends. This was to be her first dance of the evening, and she had been given no opportunity to steel herself to it. She would certainly make a clodpole of herself, and drive away Mr. Tenby as she had all the rest, just when she had begun to hope that her mama had forgotten Sir Isaac Hornaby.

She cast a glance at Mr. Tenby, who was manfully maintaining his civil manner while trying to avoid her eye. As they were at that moment performing one of the figures, this was not much to be wondered at, until he was forced to grope for her hand because he would not look at her. Iris need not seek for the cause of his unease, for she had only to recollect the circumstances of their last meeting, and their last parting. She groaned aloud at her own stupidity at having treated him so cavalierly in her anxiety for Blysdale.

"Did you speak?" inquired Mr. Tenby with punctilious solicitude, as he led her back to her place to watch the others perform the figure.

Without considering, she said, "I did not mean to ignore you when you came to call, sir, but I really could not spare a thought for you."

He blinked at her for a long moment—during which time Iris could conceive of twelve different reasons why he should walk away then and there—but with a look of studious curiosity he at last said, "And why is that, pray? Are you often negligent of your visitors? Is that a symptom of your 'oddity,' as it is called?"

"Yes, sir, it is!" she replied, passing over this unflattering reference in her eagerness to explain herself. "There is so much to consider that I cannot think about it all with any degree of clarity. Some things, or persons, must fall by the wayside, and as I was entirely caught up in the problem of Athena's ridiculous pride at the time of your visit, you must see that I could not think of you."

His looked softened. "If that was the way of things, ma'am, then I can hardly be affronted. You take great care for your friend—it does you credit."

"Only so far as she will allow me, sir," said Iris feelingly. "You can have no notion of how trying it is to see clearly the solution to another's faults and not be allowed to discuss it."

"To be sure," he said, his smile faltering.

Iris saw instantly how he could be disturbed by what she had said, and began to shrink into herself once more, but their turn in the dance came up and as he reached for her hand, he smiled not unkindly and looked her in the eye. She felt suddenly lighter and, forgetting her embarrassment, performed the figure with tolerable pleasure.

Mr. Tenby did not come near Iris again that evening, but as he was the son of the house and had many guests to please, she was at pains to excuse his absence without thought for her own part in it. She experienced some surprise, and not a little delight, therefore, at his appearance the next morning in her mother's drawing room, full of civil inquiries after her health and happiness.

She managed not to utter a single solecism for the whole of his visit—beyond remarking on the odd pattern of his waistcoat—and was so pleased with herself that she nearly missed his polite request for her company the following morning on a drive in Hyde Park. When he had repeated himself and she had stopped gaping at him and given an acceptance more hasty than civil, he simply smiled and took his leave without retracting his offer.

After the last caller had departed, Mrs. Slougham congratulated Iris, saying, "It really is amazing that the thing had not gone off, despite everything you did to discourage him. That remark on his waistcoat—dear me, I thought I should sink! Mr. Tenby is most truly the gentleman to have let such an insult pass, and so you must remember, my dear, and take better care! Do not forget that it is nothing short of a miracle that he pays you any attention at all—though he is as poor as a church mouse and must marry money. But there are any number of rich young ladies on the Town whom he could have at a word, and yet he comes here to call! It really is unaccountable. How he has not conceived a disgust of you, I do not know. We must be grateful."

Iris was so heartened by this motherly encomium that she spent the next half-hour gazing desolately at her vague and unremarkable features in her dressing room mirror. The effect of this rumination was an extraordinary exertion to steel herself to face her broad-minded and forbearing suitor the following day. Part of her program was to be ready a half-hour early so as to feed her anxiety by keeping watch at an upper window for his approach, and she was both rewarded and greatly calmed by his leaping all unconsciously from his curricle and walking without hesitation up the steps to the door.

The sound of the knocker nevertheless struck fear in her heart, but she determined to overcome it by facing the situation head-on. Thus, before the footman could be sent to call her, she flew down the stairs and across the hall, tying her bonnet as she went.

"Shall we go, sir?" she inquired breathlessly, then colored and bit her lip, trying to recall her practiced speech. "That is, good morning,

Mr. Tenby. Thank you for coming—it is very kind in you to take me driving. Oh—what beautiful horses!"

As the door was open and she happened to turn to see his horses—which she had paid no heed to when she watched him so anxiously from her bedroom window—the rest of her speech flew out of her head and she hastened down the steps to go to their heads. Iris, though awkward with people, was comfortable with horses, for they did not expect their companions to speak clearly and sensibly, nor did they say cutting things or bemoan their companions' oddities. She had quite an affinity for most animals, and was a fine horsewoman and a notable whip.

Mr. Tenby, unacquainted with these characteristics of the otherwise strange Miss Slougham, took back his hat and gloves from the butler and followed after her down the steps to introduce her to his groom and to his dapple-greys.

"They look like rain puddles!" cried Iris, stroking their necks delightedly. "They deserve apples for their forbearance."

Gazing at her non-plussed, Mr. Tenby at last said, "They do get apples quite frequently, Miss Slougham."

"That is good, sir," she said with an approving look. "*We* should never be so patient with always hauling people about, I am persuaded. We must convince them it is worthwhile, or they might understandably revolt!"

This elucidation eased his mind somewhat, and he handed her into the vehicle with tolerable equanimity, and a quelling—if sympathetic—look to his grinning groom. They set off down the road toward Hyde Park and Iris happily inquired as to the horses' breeding and temperaments.

The discussion of this was so sensible that Mr. Tenby got up the courage to ask, "What did you mean about rain puddles?"

Iris looked at him, blinking. "Oh! Because they are grey on grey, and spotted. Like a rain puddle with drops of rain falling into it, and making darker circles. You must take in the rein a moment earlier on a turn, sir, if you wish to make it smoother."

He glanced at her in consternation, for not only was she a bewildering conversationalist, but he had before been complimented on his handling of the ribbons by many a young lady, and did not quite like to be made to feel foolish. Their dialogue had been so comfortable until then, however, that he was able to do justice to her innocence and concluded that she must be a squeamish passenger.

"If you do not like to go so fast, ma'am, I will drive slower."

"Oh, no, sir. What is the point in driving at a snail's pace? One might as well walk. This is an excellent pace, only the vehicle tends to swing less on a turn if you slow a touch earlier. Mind the horses, sir! You must not look away so long, no matter what I say. What *did* I say? I declare, it does not signify, for I begin to wonder if you know what you are about."

Rather than justly incur her censure a second time for gazing bemusedly at her while driving, Mr. Tenby pulled up his team and turned to regard her. "Do you question my skill at the ribbons?"

She returned his look frankly. "No, sir. I believe I know precisely your skill at the ribbons. Otherwise, I should not trust myself to advise you."

"And may I inquire as to your authority for judging my performance, ma'am?"

"Certainly! It is my own experience, which must be far superior to your own, sir, if you do not know such simple things."

His brows raised, and he looked away over the horses' backs as his mouth worked. After some minutes, he turned back to her and said, "Should you like to drive my greys, Miss Slougham?"

"I should love to, Mr. Tenby!" cried Iris, clapping her hands. "Though it surprises me that you should entrust them to me, without first testing my skill. They are such beautiful creatures that I should think you would wish to keep them from any harm."

"Oh, I do, ma'am, which is why I shall sit close enough to take the ribbons at the first sign of ill-handling."

"Very right, sir. I commend your good judgment. Here, we must change places. It would be easiest if you got down and allowed me to slide over."

He very amiably complied with this suggestion—perhaps because it was very sensible—and joined her again on the other side, placing himself so close as to press his leg against hers. Neither took much notice of this intimacy, however, for each was concerned with more important things, such as ascertaining the spirits of the animals now in her charge and biting his tongue against a retraction of his rather rash offer.

But he soon lost all his anxiety, for Iris obviously knew what she was about. As she took them expertly round the park, he gradually relaxed back against the seat, remarking on how well she managed a tricky turning or on the ease with which she passed an oncoming carriage, and listening with interest as she explained that she never used the whip if she could spare it. The outing was, in fact, so enjoyable that he was astonished, when at last he thought to consult his watch, to find that an hour had passed.

"Dear me!" cried Iris, instinctively turning the vehicle back toward the gate. "I am going to be late for afternoon callers. My mama requires me to be in the drawing room with her, in case an eligible young man may call—" Her face flushed red and she clamped her mouth shut, intent on the gate.

Mr. Tenby put a hand on hers, causing her to slow the horses from their over-fast pace. "One mustn't gallop in Hyde Park, Miss Slougham. Even your mama must allow for that."

She darted a glance at him and the placid smile on his face gave her instant relief. With a deep breath, she sat up straighter and inquired whether he would like her to drive them to Hill Street or if he should rather drive. He refused to take the ribbons from so expert a handler, however, and when she had pulled up in front of the house, he took her hand, saying, "It would be my honor to be driven by you again, ma'am. May I call for you Friday?"

Only after a positive engagement to drive to Richmond was reached did he climb down to hand her out of the curricle, and when he had seen her to the top of the stairs, he took her hand again, bowing over it and wishing her good day.

Chapter 10

Iris practically danced into the house, loosening her bonnet strings and letting the hat hang down her back as though she were a child. As she rushed up the stairs, tugging off her gloves, she thought that she had never had such a lovely drive with a gentleman before—indeed, a gentleman had never been induced to invite her out for a drive before, and it was almost too wonderful that it was not to be her last. How strange that the very frankness which had been her downfall was responsible for her present good fortune, for if she had not noted Mr. Tenby's lack at the ribbons, he would never have found in her a desirable teacher, and might not have invited her driving again.

When she entered the drawing room, she was brought down from these transports by her mama calling her to order and insisting that she give an account of her outing. This she happily did, but the response quite killed her delight.

"You advised him on his driving?" cried her mother in scandalized tones. "What next will you do, child? You drive me to distraction. Now he will never come again! Gentlemen do not want wives who point out their deficiencies, no matter how just the lady's observations may be."

Iris hastened to put her mother's fears at rest. "But he listened to my advice, Mama, and has asked me to drive him again on Friday! He wants to learn to feather-edge a corner, and we mean to go to Richmond so that he may get more practice."

Mrs. Slougham humphed. "Well, you are lucky this time, but there is no counting on luck to hold, depend upon it! No matter what maggot has got into Mr. Tenby's head today, gentlemen do not like to be dictated to, especially by a chit of a girl! If you do not wish to give him a disgust of you, you will not continue in these hoydenish ways! It is more imperative than ever before that you heed me, Iris! You must conform to the model of womanhood by which I have reared you or, mark my words, you will lose Mr. Tenby just as surely as you lost Sir Isaac Hornaby."

"But I never wanted Sir Isaac Hornaby!" cried Iris, horrified.

"That is neither here nor there, my dear," said her mother, unmoved. "You have only this one chance, I am persuaded, and you must not disappoint your father and me by wasting the expense and exertions of this Season when victory is within your grasp!"

Thoroughly dejected by this complimentary speech, Iris assured her mother she would do her best and escaped the drawing room, taking the stairs to her room as quickly as her suddenly exhausted body could carry her. On the landing, however, she met with her father, who stopped her with a hand on her shoulder.

"Now what has occurred to vex you, my love? Another young man gone away?"

"No, Papa, it is the one who has stayed. Mama insists that he does not like me and will only run away if I continue to speak my mind."

Mr. Slougham looked serious, but when put in possession of the details of her morning, he became thoughtful. "Now, dear, you seem to have made a friend, at least, if not a conquest of the heart. If Mr. Tenby values your advice, then by all means give it. Gentlemen are not all puffed up in their own conceit; advice thoughtfully given will always be considered as it ought by rational persons. I do not say your mama is wrong to advise against it in general, however. You know very well you must always endeavor to command your tongue, but I am persuaded that if this gentleman has not run away yet, then he may just deserve you."

With a trembling smile, Iris thanked her papa and kissed him, hurrying with renewed vigor to her room to change her dress. When she again entered the drawing room, she was in tolerable spirits and comported herself with enough conformity to satisfy even her mama.

Their guests did not include any eligible gentlemen, for Mr. Tenby could not be expected to visit twice in one day and Mr. Blysdale— whom Mrs. Slougham considered in the light of a suitor despite Iris's protestations—still kept his distance. There were several lofty matrons from Mrs. Slougham's set who came to gossip over the occurrences at the Tenby's ball, and whose daughters came to look sly and to try to get Iris to say something shocking.

Iris resolutely defied them for the first half hour, but then one Miss Hichin came to say, "I declare, Lenora Breckinridge is the most brazen creature—she disappeared for a full quarter of an hour into the garden with Lord Ratherton, and when she returned, she looked positively blowsy! I know! I saw her go and come back. It does not take a fanciful imagination to guess what happened. But it is all of a piece with one who takes so great an interest in that pretender Lord Helden. Pitiful."

This was too much to be endured. Iris instantly said, "Be quiet, Penelope. I never heard such a lot of rubbish in my life." She colored and added more civilly, "It—it does you no credit to speak in such a way."

"But I saw her!" said Miss Hichin, nettled. "You cannot deny it."

"I can and I will," returned Iris. "I saw Lord Ratherton take her into the garden and I went after her with Mr. Dowbridge."

"Ha! There you have it—even her friends were concerned," said Miss Hichin, but her exultation was belied by the heightened, angry color of her cheeks. "What can you imagine there is to say in Miss Breckinridge's defense, I wonder?"

Iris bit her lips against the anger swelling in her bosom. "She received an offer of marriage from Lord Ratherton, but nothing more."

Miss Hichin gasped and said waspishly. "No doubt he was entrapped. Was that your design? Did he offer before or after you saw them together, I wonder?"

"You are a jealous cat and should be horsewhipped!" retorted Iris, unable longer to restrain herself.

As this outburst had drawn the attention of the matrons, it was well that the door opened and Lady Athena and Diana were announced. The general stir this created put the subject of Lenora's discretion or lack thereof out of most minds, but when the newcomers were settled amongst the younger set, Athena turned to Miss Hichin.

"How do you get on, Penelope? I hear your prospects are significantly improved since the Tenby's ball. Now that Lenora has refused Lord Ratherton, perhaps he shall return his attentions to you."

The other young lady's awe of Lady Athena was so great that she hardly dared reply but, driven by hurt pride, she managed, "I am sure I do not care what his lordship does."

"Perhaps that is all for the best." Athena began removing her gloves. "His sudden and decided preference for Lenora does suggest a weakness for money. A pity that your fortune is not larger, for if it had been, he may not have been tempted away at the outset. One presumes that money is your only lack in his eyes. However, as you are now indifferent to him, it is of no consequence."

As Lady Athena then turned to other subjects, the matter was dropped, and Miss Hichin scraped up what was left of her dignity and left with her mother soon afterward. Lady Athena was one of the last to go away, and when she stood, Iris touched her arm.

"Thank you, Athena. I know I do not deserve it after what I did to you, but thank you."

Athena regarded her coolly, but her tone was soft as she said, "You are my friend, Iris. While much is said and done in the name of friendship that cannot be called praiseworthy, it is undoubtedly all done for the best."

Iris pressed her hand and Athena gave one of her rare smiles, going away in better spirits than she had come.

The past week had been one of annoyance to Athena, for she had been confronted by a new sensation: that of questioning her upbringing. Having been reared in an environment of the strictest principles, she was used to believe herself above reproach and to have an indubitable sense of right and wrong. Added to this was the firm conviction that her position as daughter to an earl was a divine right of her birth, and as such it was, and must remain, unassailable.

These two facets of her reality had never been materially

challenged. Iris and Diana, not being of noble birth, had at times questioned Athena's views, but there had never been an instance of outright challenge until the past Tuesday week. If it had merely been one of Iris's nonsensical flights, Athena could have brushed it off, and she did endeavor to do so. But observation and experience had since forced her to acknowledge that low-born and common Mr. Blysdale was not a mere mushroom, and it had shaken her confidence.

There was much about Mr. Blysdale that Athena had been forced to observe these last weeks, though she had meant to do nothing of the sort. She could not ignore that, notwithstanding his impertinence in pursuing her at all, he had persisted in a most flattering way, and gone about gaining an introduction with the utmost propriety. When she had tried to communicate her disdain for his advances by avoiding his society at every turn, his patience and ingenuity in involving her dearest friends was maddeningly thoughtful. And his air when at last she had been forced to undeniably acknowledge him in public had been not the least exultant, but had shown his extreme good breeding. Not one nobleman in ten could have carried the thing off as he had done.

And yet, no nobleman would have been made to go to such lengths, for his birth would have superseded all obstacles. And Lady Athena, in all the consternation of flattery, curiosity, and attraction, could begin to comprehend how Iris was so incensed by the injustice of birth as a barrier to Mr. Blysdale's chances.

That Mr. Blysdale was attractive to Athena, she could no longer deny. His bearing and looks were those of the gentleman born, and his quiet dignity paired exceedingly well with his self-deprecating humor—always properly applied. He was never rude or unkind, he seemed unconscious of Iris's oddities, and thought as he ought on all important subjects. Add to these perfections the charms of his tall, handsome person and dress and he was a paragon.

Such were the mortifying musings of a lady who had been intent upon snubbing and forgetting a gentleman far beneath her. Try as she might, Athena could not but take notice of Mr. Blysdale, wherever she might glimpse or hear of him—which was everywhere—and though in her waking hours she could still convince herself of his inferiority, her dreams had become disturbingly recalcitrant.

This would have been enough to try her spirits, but she had also to wrestle with the suspicion that she had been brought up with a wrong way of thinking. Faced with the fact that low-born Mr. Blysdale's character could compare more than favorably with any of the titled gentlemen of Athena's acquaintance, she could not but admit the doubt that the privilege of birth and rank was divine. It seemed—at times when she was overtired or under strain or simply thinking again about Mr. Blysdale—that privileged birth had done very little for a great many members of the *ton*, and that it was entirely possible that too much reverence had been attached to it.

It was a simple matter to dismiss such sacrilegious thoughts from her brain, for her mama constantly reminded her of her duty, and habit was excessively strong. But they plagued her more and more, as when her thoughts strayed to Mr. Blysdale's kindness to Iris or when she had occasion to observe his perfect manner when attending the same entertainment, and she found herself drawn to know him better.

Such was her mental state at an al fresco picnic given by the Countess of Carmichael, when he met her at the banquet table. She was considering whether he looked more gentlemanly in breeches and top boots—as she had seen him wear at the park—or in pantaloons and slippers—as he now wore—and she had allowed him to approach her before she knew it.

"Can it be that the Lady Athena is indecisive?" he inquired pleasantly.

She blinked, wondering how he had divined her thoughts, and then glanced down at her empty plate and took his meaning. Composing herself instantly, she said, "It is never easy to find just what one wants at these events."

"Yes," he said, reaching to take up a lobster cake with some tongs and placing it on his plate. "There is something to the idea of 'too much of a good thing.' It leads either to excess or indecision. May I assist you, madam?"

Her habitual instinct was to refuse, but the contrariness of her late feelings made her curious enough to accept, and within two minutes he had chosen several unexceptionable items to place on her plate. Perversely pleased and annoyed, she waited for his offer to accompany her to her seat so that she could refuse it, but either he anticipated her or he simply did not feel it proper or necessary, and instead wished her a hearty appetite and went away.

She could not tell if the slight depression of spirits that followed was from disappointment or from the veal croquettes. But after luncheon she had occasion to test both theories when, as she left her friends to gaze out over the duckpond, he came up to her and offered his arm.

"The path goes all the way round, my lady," he said, smiling charmingly, "if you would care to take a turn."

"It was my intention, sir, but to go alone."

His smile tipped higher on one side, emphasizing a long dimple in that cheek. "Ah! Then it is a settled thing, for we both of us know you think nothing of me, and so it will be as though I am not here."

Determined that he should remain ignorant of the true state of things, she tacitly agreed to this assessment by allowing him to take her hand on his arm and lead her down the path. Their conversation was desultory but pleasant, for he made only sensible and interesting observations and listened thoughtfully to what she said in reply. He even mentioned Yorkshire, and while she owned to having spent little time there, his descriptions of its wild beauty intrigued her enough to elicit several responses less tepid than she had intended.

He took leave of her directly they finished the circuit, for she was met by her friends, and though she was not so lost to all reason as to watch him stride away, she was hard-put to dismiss him entirely from her thoughts. She was still considering that evening the picture he had conjured of the moor in bloom when Lady Gidgeborough came into the drawing room, dressed for dinner.

"I have heard the most disturbing report, Athena," she said, adjusting her shawl in the mirror. "Lady Torrington has informed me that you have been seen on multiple occasions on the arm of that upstart Mr. Blysdale. I told her she was mistaken. It must be false."

Athena looked into the fire. "Forgive me, Mama, but it is true. Twice I have been obliged to take his arm out of common civility. I took it for the length of a street or two last week, and again today around the duckpond at Lady Carmichael's picnic."

Lady Gidgeborough's lips pressed into a thin line. "It must be uncommon civility that makes you stoop to such an action, Athena. Despite your father's unfortunate propensity toward him, we have thus far been clear as to *our* opinion of him, and if you had but continued to give him a wide berth, he might have been made to understand us. But now he is, no doubt, encouraged, as every encroaching sort of mushroom is wont to be at the slightest notice."

"It is to be lamented that Lady Carmichael does not consider him to be encroaching," said Athena, her grey eyes returning to her mother, "and nor does Lord Foxham or Lord Hollingsford, for we shall consequently be obliged to look down upon them."

Her mother regarded her narrowly. "Could it be that you are suggesting, by these comparisons, that we should allow into our circle—one of the highest in the *ton*, I may remind you—a commoner and a tradesman?"

Athena did not blink. "In truth, Mama, I am simply fatigued at trying to avoid him when he is everywhere. He is at every *ton* party, at Almack's, and could even be found, I daresay, at Carlton House! What would you have me to do, Mama? Did not you teach me that it is the height of impropriety to be puffed up in one's own consequence? And yet that is what it looks like, to be forever trying to cut a man who to everyone else is an unexceptionable acquaintance. It is known that he has been approved by my father and is acknowledged as a visitor in his house, which makes it even worse. Even were I to try to merely avoid him, he is underfoot wherever I go. I have begun to be of the opinion that it does me no credit to dismiss him."

"Underfoot is quite right, my love!" said her mother, sitting beside her with a huff. "Would that he would stay there—but there is something to what you say. Others will begin to talk if you continually act as though you question their decision to include him. And your father's acceptance, though ill-judged, is rather undeniable. It is excessively vexing to be sure, but I suppose there is nothing to be done. Very well, you must do as you think right. But he deserves no extraordinary treatment, my love. Do not think that simply because your Papa has whole-heartedly accepted him that he is an eligible *parti*."

Athena returned her gaze to the fire. "There is no question of that, Mama."

"Good." Lady Gidgeborough sat silent for several minutes, then said, "It is a great evil to marry beneath oneself, Athena. Do not, for a moment, consider it, for I may tell you without reservation that you will be sorry all the rest of your life."

She said no more, as Lord Gidgeborough strode into the room at that moment in all his bluff insensibility, and announced that he was famished. Athena silently stood and prepared to follow him and her mama into the dining room.

Chapter 11

AFTER WHAT HAD seemed a promising encounter at Lady Charmichael's picnic, Mr. Blysdale perceived that Lady Athena had experienced a recrudescence in her coolness toward him, but he was not discouraged. Nor was he much surprised, for if Lady Gidgeborough, the Dragon, had had nothing to do with it, he was a gudgeon. That lady had been at pains from the outset to annihilate him with her air and looks, while Lady Athena had merely tried to freeze him—an entirely different experience. Frost could melt, but utter destruction was permanent, and Mr. Blysdale was no longer under any illusion that his dignity was meant to survive her ladyship's disapprobation. It was well, therefore, that he was of tough Yorkshire stock and could withstand far more than Lady Gidgeborough imagined.

He did not mean to aggravate Lady Gidgeborough, however; nor did he wish to press his advantage—slight though it was—with Lady

Athena. Instead, he held himself for some days to polite greetings when they met in society, and no more than the briefest of interactions afterward. From observations made at various parties, Blysdale had concluded that Lady Athena and Miss Slougham were no longer at outs and, trusting that he could do Iris no more harm in pursuing their friendship, he engaged her to go driving with him to Wimbledon.

He handed her up into his finely sprung curricle and she instantly desired to be told the names of his horses and asked if they were of Arabian blood. This he confirmed, inquiring if she knew much about horses, and was more than entertained by her launching into a discussion of broad chests versus long backs and high-steppers versus sweet goers.

"I really don't know much more than that," she said after a quarter-hour's knowledgeable discourse, "though growing up I spent as much time in the stables as I could spare from my deportment lessons. Mama scolded me for hobnobbing with grooms, and deplored what I learned, but I thought it all fascinating. I very much prefer horses to people, for they are such comfortable companions. Do not you think so, Mr. Blysdale?"

"Not in general," he said, gallantly keeping back a smile. "But I own there have been times when I should very much have preferred a roomful of horses to a ball at Almack's."

"That is not what you wish to talk to me about, however," she declared with a sympathetic look. "Athena continues to be difficult."

He cast an astonished glance at her, huffing a laugh. "You do like to have the truth with no bark on it. Very well, yes, her ladyship is yet to fully accept my existence in her circle. However, I do not despair."

"I should think you a simpleton if you did," said Iris, then bit her lips, blushing.

But he laughed. "And I should agree with you! I could not think of a more poor-spirited thing to do than to give up after only a few minor setbacks."

"That is why you are formed for Athena, sir," she said, her color receding. "No one else could consider a month of snubs and slights as 'minor setbacks.' And if they had got through them, nine gentlemen out of ten would not have the tenacity required for the remainder of the business. I speak from experience, sir—I love Athena dearly, but it is hard work."

Smiling, he said, "I believe my success is owing to the notion, instilled in me by my excellent father, that hard work is worth doing if the outcome is very desirable. And, as you wish to have no bark on it, I find the prospect of Lady Athena as my wife increasingly desirable."

Iris regarded him. "I cannot comprehend why, sir. For *I* know she is well worth loving, but you cannot know anything about her but that she is beautiful, elegant, and well-connected."

"But I do know her. It is strange, ma'am, but though I met her only a month or five weeks ago, and have had little opportunity for interaction, I feel as though I know her intimately."

"That is all very fine," she said, wrinkling her nose at his poetic sentiment, "but it is only what any besotted young man would think. Perhaps it is unjust of me, for I am fully convinced that you are formed for Athena, but I must find out if you truly could make her happy— and that you intend to do so."

He drew up his team and turned to her, his countenance sober. "If you wish me to say I am in love with Lady Athena, I cannot satisfy you. I do not subscribe to the notion of love in general—but that does not mean that I will never feel such emotion for her. I cannot say, for I have never been in love, but I also have never been so drawn to a woman in all my life. All I can say is that I find Lady Athena beautiful in a way that transcends common beauty. It even transcends her excellent birth and connections. Her elegance and grace arise from something deeper, something more enduring than mere physical charms. These will all fade—they must—but even when she is an old woman and bent with age and infirmity, she will still be the Lady Athena in all her perfection."

Iris, having observed him intently during this speech, continued to search his face. At last she said, "I am more satisfied than you might think, sir. But I do not know whether to hug you or to endeavor instantly to disabuse you of the notion of Athena's perfection. She is rather wonderful, but rather awful, too. Your vision of her sounds very much like a glass house about to be shattered."

He only chuckled, setting the horses to again down the road. "I have never encountered the disappointment that could shatter me, ma'am."

Iris turned forward again with a sigh. "It may come sooner than you think. Athena will not come around easily. She is perfect only on the outside. She was bred to be so, and she exhibits very well. But inside she is just as complex as anyone else. She is proud and cool and condescending, but she is like a sister to me."

"That is a circumstance that I must own intrigues me," he said, glancing at her askance. "Forgive me, but your relationship does not seem natural to one of her temperament."

She shook her head. "It is not. I am everything that she has been taught to abhor—awkward and common, with low connections and a fortune from trade. If I were not the daughter of her father's best friend, she should have plucked both her eyes out before accepting my acquaintance. But she has never refused to acknowledge me. She can say cutting things and is the most provoking creature in nature, yet she has been my truest friend and the sister I never had."

"You give me hope."

"But I cannot imagine you understand me, sir," replied Iris impatiently. "Sisters can be the worst brutes of all."

He glanced at her, a brow lifted. "I suppose I do not understand. I do not have a sister, nor a brother."

"One loves them because of blood," Iris said, "but one does not wish to be forever with them."

He furrowed his brow. "I trust you do not design to give me a disgust of Lady Athena, for it will not do. I know my own mind and will not be dissuaded."

"Oh no! That is, I hope you do—that you are not. I assure you, Athena is not so trying as to make one wish her constantly at Jericho—but I am failing to make you see." She paused, ruminating. "Friends are not tied to one by blood, and may be turned off if one decides one cannot stand to be bothered with them anymore. But Athena might as well be my sister, for she continually overlooks my gaffes and always will forgive me. Believe me, she is horrid and odious, like many sisters, but so am I, in my way."

"So are we all, to be sure, Miss Slougham."

She nodded seriously. "And we all must make allowances. I do for Athena, and she does for me. It is friendship of the highest order. But you see, sir, though I know her faults and would have you know them, I would not see her unhappy for the world. For all she can be awful and vexatious, she deserves to be happy."

"Undoubtedly," he said, his forehead still creased. "There is nothing I would not do to ensure her happiness, ma'am, should she become my wife, no matter her imperfections."

Iris considered him for a moment, then turned away. "I believe you will do your best."

Mr. Blysdale drove on in silence for a few minutes and then said, "All you have told me merely proves my conviction that Lady Athena is more than she seems. It makes it all the more mysterious, however, that she chooses to assume a mask of indifference."

"It is not a mask, sir," said Iris with a significant look. "It is more a—a birthmark—or rather, a scab from a wound that she picks at—oh dear, that is not a very pretty picture." She hesitated, but his interested gaze spurred her to continue. "It is a little of both, I fancy, sir—a birthmark and a scab."

He nodded. "It is not unreasonable. She was born to her high position and responsibility—"

"No, she was born to her mother!" corrected Iris. "Lady Gidgeborough is worse than Athena, for with her it goes much farther than skin-deep—where Athena is cold and exacting, her ladyship is jealous and disappointed—"

"Disappointed?" asked Mr. Blysdale, surprised.

"She wanted a marquess and only got an earl, you see," said Iris. "That failure has plagued her all her life, and she has plagued Athena because of it. Athena must be better than Lady Gidgeborough ever could be, or her failure shall be complete indeed. She inflicted the wound of expectation very early in Athena's life, and has poked at it until Athena began picking at it too. So it is like a scab that cannot heal."

Mr. Blysdale contemplated this. "Lady Athena's experience with filial obedience to expectation is not so very dissimilar to my own. I have been driven to achieve every facet of my father's expectations for me. However, I have done it for myself, while Lady Athena seems desirous of satisfying her mother."

"Indeed," said Iris, turning her frank gaze on him. "And she must not succeed, for then she will become just like her mother, and even you will not want her anymore."

"That would never happen, Miss Slougham."

"It must not—you must win her, Mr. Blysdale," said Iris. "Then she can let that odious scab alone and the wound will heal and she can stop behaving for all the world as though she had no heart!"

There was no sign of humor in his voice or countenance as he answered, "I intend to." He was ruminative for a moment, then said, "Your vote of confidence means more than I can say, Miss Slougham, and I wish I knew to what I owe it."

"We are alike, you and I," said Iris simply. "We both are on the fringes of what some persons consider good *ton*, but we both possess a connection with the Dibbingtons. My connection was made before Lady Gidgeborough or Athena knew to escape it, and so it is winked at."

"I should be shocked if Lady Athena merely winks at your— uniqueness, ma'am. You have only just made the case that she is like a sister to you."

"To be sure, she is, but I am a sad trial to her." She turned to face him fully again. "But that is where she is the reverse of her mama, sir. She still knows how to love, and she winks at my oddity because she loves me, while her mama winks at it because it is unavoidable."

"If you imagine I wish for Lady Athena to be brought to wink at my unfavorable antecedents," he said, "you will pardon my telling you that you are much mistaken."

"Certainly not," replied Iris promptly. "It will be much better if she were to embrace your birth along with all the rest of you."

He could not resist a chuckle at the deep red that spread into her face and, seeking to dispel her embarrassment, said cordially, "I very much agree, ma'am."

After a few moments of composing herself, Iris said, "I do not pretend to have won all of Athena's favor just by virtue of being her lifelong friend—there is still the influence of Lady Gidgeborough to prevent that. But my relationship to Athena is proof that once her heart is touched, it remains open. It does not, perhaps, seem so. She is proud and headstrong and not warm-hearted, but she can be thoughtful and loyal and kind in her own way. If friendship can have so wonderful an effect upon such a person, then I am persuaded that romantic love will prove even more efficacious."

"Your view is an interesting one, ma'am," he said, "but I have told you that I do not pretend to be in love, nor do I anticipate Lady Athena will fall in love with me. I do not believe it necessary to her happiness, however."

"I suppose that is wise, sir, though I must hope you will find out otherwise. But I am romantic and Athena, assuredly, is not. There are very few people who Athena really loves, because her consequence requires that she sacrifice her pride in order to love. She seems only to love those who have a claim on her goodness. It is not a pitiable situation, sir—you must not think so, for it is my own, and I do not pity myself. But because Athena does not naturally or easily love, it is difficult for her to make the sacrifice at all."

"Then it is all the better," said Mr. Blysdale, "for I will not be disappointed—nor will I be in a position to be shattered in my glass house."

Iris pursed her lips at this sally, not quite satisfied, but merely turned forward again to gaze over the horses' heads. After some minutes, she observed, "You are a very fine whip, sir. Better than Mr. Tenby. But he will soon improve, for he has let me drive him."

"You are a whip, ma'am?" asked Mr. Blysdale with interest. "I should have guessed it. I am persuaded that Mr. Tenby cannot be in better hands."

She exhaled. "My mama is persuaded I ought not to have offered to teach him. She is of the opinion that all men are conceited and must be allowed to remain so. But I do not think they ought to be coddled so or they should all become spoilt—" She stopped short, closing her eyes upon the recollection that she was, in fact, speaking to a man.

Mr. Blysdale said merely, "Just so, ma'am, and I trust you would never allow any of the gentlemen of your acquaintance to run on in conceit when a just word would put them to rights. What a horrid world it would be to have men going about believing they were the pinnacle of perfection simply because females were taught always to conciliate them. It would be a most unsatisfactory turn of events, indeed."

"Precisely, sir!" cried Iris, grateful. "There is enough of that going on without it plaguing the entire human race! There is something to be said for respect and forbearance, but never to offer a kind word of advice would be terribly wrong, I believe."

"Indeed," he said amiably. "Do you wish to advise me on my driving?"

She paused long enough to watch him take a turning in very good style and said, "I do not think so, sir. But I should have to drive longer with you to be certain."

"I hope you will tell me if you do," was the grave reply.

She sighed. "Thank you, sir. You make me so easy in your company! Not like the generality of men. But it is all the fault of

Society, I am persuaded. I do not know how our customs have become so complex and restrictive, for it does not seem at all helpful. One is always walking on eggshells, wondering when next one will say something objectionable."

He murmured agreeably and she went on, "And when one is attracted to a gentleman, one cannot simply say so for fear of seeming forward. But how, pray, are we to promote our attachments without ever knowing the mind of the other? If we cannot begin by saying, 'I like you, sir,' and perhaps progress to, 'I admire you, sir,' then how do we know when we are at the point of 'I love you'?"

"I see what you mean," said Mr. Blysdale, admirably keeping his countenance. "We have built up a rather cold-blooded approach to love, have not we? That is, perhaps, one reason I do not subscribe to it. I imagine a great many broken engagements would never happen if one was allowed to discuss admiration more openly before an actual declaration was made."

"And think of all the unhappy marriages resulting from miscommunicated feelings! But Society is set in its ways, and one cannot depart from them, or one is a great embarrassment to one's relations. It is all very distressing."

With an empathetic look for his companion, Mr. Blysdale said, "But admiration is not so very difficult to discern, Miss Slougham, if I may. A gentleman who takes advice of a lady, for example, is at least respectful of her intelligence. And a gentleman who allows a lady to drive him is showing himself cognizant of her worth."

She glanced quickly at him as her cheeks pinked, and she did not answer.

He smiled and said, "A lady such as yourself is at a disadvantage, to be sure, for the quickness of your mind and the honesty of your nature compels you to speak your thoughts more freely than others are wont to do—or rather, are trained to do. But allow me to assure you, ma'am, that one tires of the conventions, and any time one is faced with a change, be it shocking or otherwise, it cannot be but welcome. I speak from experience."

The pink of her cheeks deepened, but she smiled shyly and said, "Thank you, sir." After a few companionable moments of silence, she said, "You loop a rein very well, sir."

He laughed and thanked her, and the remainder of the drive was spent between quiet enjoyment of the spring verdure about them and remarks on the equipages and teams they met along the way home. His curricle swept up to the steps of her house just as Mr. Tenby was coming up to it, and the two gentlemen exchanged greetings as Iris was handed down.

"Did you come to see me, Mr. Tenby?" inquired Iris, a little breathlessly, and then she blushed and looked away. "Or perhaps you are merely in your way somewhere."

Mr. Tenby bowed to her. "I was coming to call on you and your mama, Miss Slougham, but if you are otherwise engaged—"

"Oh, no, sir," she said quickly, turning to Mr. Blysdale. "Thank you for the drive, sir—it was lovely. Good day! Come up, Mr. Tenby. I won't be a minute changing my gown, but I daresay my mama shall be vastly pleased to entertain you."

Mr. Tenby, blinking at this whirlwind of welcome, nevertheless followed after her, taking a moment to say goodbye to Mr. Blysdale. That gentleman merely cast a knowing grin at Mr. Tenby's back, and told his groom to let the horses go.

Chapter 12

M R. TENBY HAD undergone a transformation of sorts in the previous weeks, having come to London in quite a necessarily mercenary frame of mind. His family, though ancient and respected, was at its last prayers of gentility, for too few of its members had bothered themselves with good stewardship, and the coffers had bled nearly dry. Nicolas Tenby had grown up in the discomfort of desperate expectations—the honor of the family depended solely upon his success on the Marriage Mart. But with only passable good looks and a decent style of living with which to entice a rich wife, the prospect was bleak at best.

It was with a sense of deep foreboding that Mr. Tenby had set out to find a bride that Season—a sense that was quickly justified by the excessive number of gentlemen on the town in a similar situation to his own. It was unseemly how many families had run through their fortunes and needed heiresses to rescue them, but so it was. There were only two consolations to be found: first, that Mr. Tenby himself could not be blamed for the state of his family's finances, as he was perhaps the first Tenby in a century to possess any sort of regard for the notion of frugality; and second, that there seemed to be an inordinate number of heiresses on the market.

Mr. Tenby had very fortunately come upon four of them at once, and had blessed whatever saint had caused the collection of these rich young ladies in want of husbands into a tidy group wishing always to be together. He was soon made to understand they were referred to as the Goddesses, which Tenby thought strange, for he could not for the life of him recall a goddess in any pantheon named Lenora. But their grouping made the process of perusal and selection much less time-consuming, and within a few meetings he had ordered them as to wealth, attractions, and compatibility.

Unfortunately, he was obliged to rule out one at the outset. It was not many days before it became plain to him that Lady Athena Dibbington was beyond his reach. It was rumored that she was sending out lures to the Marquess of Foxham who, though he was a pompous bore, was excessively plump in the pocket, and subsequently Lady Athena hardly spared poor Tenby a second glance.

Another, Miss Diana Marshall, was bright, lively, and pretty, but she was gone to Brighton a fortnight out of every month, and Tenby couldn't get on with her at all. She had been ranked last of the young ladies, however, for her fortune was a mere ten thousand pounds, and could scarcely pay off the mortgage on Tenby Place in Hampshire, much less the Tenby's numerous other debts.

That left Miss Lenora Breckinridge and Miss Iris Slougham. Miss Breckinridge's fortune of thirty thousand pounds was her chief attraction, but though she was as tall as Mr. Tenby and tended toward romantical ideas, she was pleasant and easy-going as well. Miss Slougham, however, was exceedingly shy and awkward, and it seemed an impossibility that she should ever be made to speak to him. Thus, he made Miss Breckinridge his object.

He did not prosper. Miss Breckinridge's thirty thousand pounds was also infinitely attractive to the numberless other gentlemen in want of money, and she was therefore exceedingly popular. This made getting within ten feet of her difficult, and procuring a dance with her nearly impossible. Add to this the watchfulness of her brother, Mr. Tom Breckinridge, who was rumored both to hate fortune hunters and to be mighty handy with his fives, and Miss Breckinridge's fortune quickly became less alluring.

Miss Slougham's twenty thousand pounds, however, were only a trifle more interesting, for the lady herself presented another set of problems. Skittish and only vaguely pretty, she was forever blurting out solecisms or incomprehensible observations, and then coloring like a chastened schoolroom miss. With the obstacles surrounding his other choices, however, Tenby concluded that he could not do worse than to have a go.

Great was his astonishment when he had steeled himself to get to know her better, and had found it not nearly so intimidating as he had imagined. Indeed, once he had got more used to her odd sayings and ways, he had found them quite refreshing, and the idea of seeing her again brought a smile to his features. He had begun to feel the weight of his duty to his family less, and to enjoy the business of romance more, and to think of Miss Slougham not as a mere prospect but as a potential companion for life.

Even her criticism of his driving, though it was a setback to be sure, could not long annoy him, for the lady knew horses, by Jupiter, and she could drive to an inch! She was undoubtedly out of the common way, and while this had been seen as a demerit before, it somehow became desirable in comparison with other young ladies. She never simpered or tittered or acted coy, and though she was a few years older than the usual new come-outs, to be sure, her maturity now seemed immeasurably attractive to him.

Such were his thoughts when he called upon her in Hill Street, only to witness her being handed down from a smart curricle by Mr. Jonathan Blysdale. That gentleman was nominally known to Mr. Tenby, as they were both members of Boodle's Club and their circles quite often overlapped. But Tenby had heard enough of Blysdale to be concerned that his newfound marriage prospect was in grave danger. If Blysdale was half so ambitious and cold-blooded as he was reputed to be, and if Miss Slougham was his object, then Tenby might as well be at Jericho. He was a Charlie's shelter to Blysdale's Carlton House, and no odds.

Before he could slink away, however, Miss Slougham spied him and smiled, sending a little thrill of joy through his chest. He managed a civil bow to Mr. Blysdale, who returned his greeting with a smug look that Tenby instantly took in dislike. But Miss Slougham was speaking, asking if he was in his way somewhere, and at his admission of having come to call on her, she blushed so charmingly that he felt the color rise in his cheeks, too. And when she invited him in, dismissing Mr. Blysdale out of hand, as it were, his sensations were so pleasant as to give him a positive charity for the poor gentleman as he drove away.

She took him to the drawing room, where he was induced to sit and trade commonplaces with Mrs. Slougham while Miss Slougham changed her dress, and to have his sangfroid tried.

"I declare I am taken by surprise, sir," said his hostess with a flat smile. "Iris was out driving with Mr. Blysdale, and it was he I took to be coming in for a visit."

Mr. Tenby bowed. "I beg your pardon, ma'am, but I trust you are not too disappointed."

"Oh, no, sir," she said, with a creditable attempt at a titter. "Any young gentleman is quite acceptable to us. That is, any gentleman of quality, which you undoubtedly are."

Endeavoring to ignore the note of condescension in this remark, he said, "Thank you, ma'am. It is a pleasure to be here."

There was a slight pause before Mrs. Slougham said, "Iris has so enjoyed her drives with you, sir. But I must apologize for her high-handed ways—she has been, I'm afraid, very rude. I tell you, I was mortified to discover she was so ill-judging as to comment unfavorably on your driving. I must beg you to forgive her."

"Indeed, no, ma'am," he said quickly. "That is, there is nothing to forgive. She was perfectly right, and has since rectified my lack with her excellent tutoring. She is a fine whip, ma'am, if I may be allowed to say so."

Mrs. Slougham looked as though torn between delight and uncertainty at the compliment, but said, "Certainly, sir. You are most gentlemanly to overlook this fault in her."

As Miss Slougham appeared just then, cheeks flushed and hair flying, Tenby was saved from further assurances.

"Good gracious, Iris," hissed her mother, almost leaping to intercept her daughter at the door. "What do you mean by coming in looking like a hoyden? Go back to Patty at once and let her do your hair properly. Go! Go!"

Miss Slougham disappeared but was back almost directly,

explaining hurriedly, "Patty was on the landing, and helped me pin up the rest of my hair in no time at all. Hello, Mr. Tenby. You are so kind to wait for me."

He had stood on each of her entrances and now, certain that she would stay, bowed before resuming his seat. "Mrs. Slougham has been entertaining me just as you said she would. That is, very ably, ma'am," he added with a quick glance to his hostess.

Her look of long-suffering made him uneasy for Miss Slougham's sake, but the young lady simply said, "Indeed, Mama, I knew you should be vastly happy to see him, for you have been quite pleased with his attentions to me of late."

Mr. Tenby did not know whether to be amused or discomfited as the two ladies' eyes simultaneously fluttered closed in mortification. Miss Slougham sighed, her cheeks ablaze, and her mother summoned up the travesty of a smile.

"And so I have, sir," she said, "for Iris is not used to such kind treatment as she has met with in Town. The gentlemen in our neighborhood are only too well acquainted with her—let us say they do not trouble themselves to be patient. But here in Town, it is just as I could have wished, and what I told Iris it would be! Only think, she has been out driving nearly every day this week, and with such unexceptionable gentlemen—beside yourself, you must know, there is Mr. Blysdale, whose attentions have been most acceptable. And there is Mr. Breckinridge, who is quite a good friend to Iris—indeed, there are such a number of kind gentlemen who are so very amiable and obliging."

Mr. Tenby said what was proper and then, in an attempt to draw the still mortified Miss Slougham out, said, "I have come to request the honor of your company, Miss Slougham, to see the spectacle at

Sadler's Wells on Friday. If you will permit, ma'am," he said, with a deferential nod to Mrs. Slougham.

"Certainly, certainly, sir," said his hostess, her smile still a trifle frozen. "That is, if Iris has not entered into any other engagements for that day. What say you, Iris? Was Mr. Blysdale so obliging as to invite you to drive with him again? Or to go anywhere, or do anything?"

This proof of Mr. Blysdale's superior attractions to the Sloughams quite dampened Mr. Tenby's spirits, and he nearly repented the idea of Sadler's Wells.

But Miss Slougham emerged from her silence to refute any thought of another engagement with Mr. Blysdale, saying, "He was in too much of a hurry to invite me anywhere, Mama, and would go. Indeed, I had nothing more to say to him."

"Iris," said Mrs. Slougham, a warning note in her voice. "Mr. Tenby will get a wrong idea of your gratitude."

Miss Slougham colored but replied, "I do not know how he can have any more of a wrong idea of me than he has already." As her mother looked as though she was ready to faint, Miss Slougham hurried on, "Mr. Blysdale and I have reached a most particular understanding, and if he wishes to see me again, he will call and say so. However, as yet I am unengaged for Friday, and may accept Mr. Tenby's invitation."

Having experienced a range of emotions during this speech, Mr. Tenby knew not how to look, and hesitated before committing himself to something that he was entirely uncertain was acceptable to the young lady before him. The expression of her eyes, however, led him to guess the progression of her own sensations, from determination to uncertainty to entreaty. This last convinced him that, whatever the meaning of the "particular understanding" between herself and

Blysdale, she did at least wish to accompany Tenby to Sadler's Wells, and he took enough courage at the thought to smile and be pleased. The visit soon closed and he went away with the wish of having made better progress.

By Friday, his doubts had become significant, for he had seen Miss Slougham speaking most earnestly to Mr. Blysdale at a rout on Thursday. But as no cancellation of their driving engagement was sent from Hill Street, he arrived punctually at one o'clock to take her up.

As was her custom, she did not keep him waiting above a minute, and must have been ready for him, for her hair was done and her hat affixed properly. He handed her into the curricle and climbed in himself, and once the groom had let the horses go, he set off toward Spa Fields.

The drive through the city was spent in her offering various hints as to improvements in his driving, and in his silently resolving to ascertain the exact nature of her relationship to Mr. Blysdale. Nothing much could be attempted until Holborn was reached, by which time Miss Slougham had become aware enough of his silence to cease her instructions.

She looked uneasily at him. "Are you quite well, sir? Have I overstepped myself in pointing out your many flaws? That is, they are not quite so many as Lenora Breckinridge's, but no one is as bad a whip as she is. You are much better, though not as accomplished as Mr. Blysdale, to be sure."

His gaze widened in dismay, and he wondered how he had been such a cod's head as to think she might prefer him over Blysdale. But when he dared to glance her way, he saw that she was biting her lips and looked so miserable that his heart went out to her.

"Your instruction is very good, Miss Slougham," he said with tolerable cheerfulness. "And very well-timed, I daresay. It would not do to have us overturned in the middle of High Holborn. What then would your mama say?"

Miss Slougham achieved a pitiful little chuckle. "She would not let you drive me again. But do not imagine that she would bar you from my company, for she is so desperate to get me off her hands that she would rather I marry a cow-handed driver than turn you away—oh dear!"

Her hands instantly went up to cover her face, and Mr. Tenby, caught between mortification and disbelief, began to laugh. He laughed weakly at first, but when she peeked at him from behind her fingers with a look of astonishment, he laughed more boldly, and then a dam burst within him and he laughed so hard he thought his belly would break. Her hands dropped and she stared openly at him, as though convinced of his madness. But when he nearly ran them onto the flagway from the blindness of his tears, she snatched the ribbons and righted the curricle before the groom could climb over the seat and take over.

"Really, sir!" she cried, her gaze flicking from the road to his reddened face and back again. "Really! I did not think you could be so nonsensical as to try the truth of my words. But I daresay I am so tiresome a creature that you would do anything to be rid of me—though why you would continue to seek me out is beyond my comprehension. I cannot fault you for trying to free yourself of my company, sir, but it will not answer, I tell you! If you try to kill me my mama will only consider it just cause to force you to marry me."

He had begun to regain his composure, but at this he went into whoops again and she was obliged to drive on up Saint John's Street, shaking her head and smiling at his insensibility. At last, he gave a final chuckle and sighed, reaching into his coat pocket for his handkerchief and wiping his face.

"I am obliged to you for stating the case so simply, ma'am," he said with as much solemnity as he could muster. "I own I had not before considered myself to be cow-handed, precisely."

"Oh, dear, no, sir!" she cried. "I did not mean it—not precisely! You are only cow-handed for a gentleman—that is, you are not nearly so bad as—"

"As Miss Breckinridge, yes, I thank you." He put up a staying hand as she began again to expostulate. "No, no, I fully comprehend your meaning. And if I had not been privileged to witness Miss Breckinridge's sad attempts at maneuvering during the hour of the promenade at Hyde Park, I should be less sensible of the compliment, I assure you."

"But you really are much better than that, sir," she said desperately.

He tipped his head to the side and gazed ruefully at her. "But not so good as Mr. Blysdale."

"Well, no, sir. For he has been driving since he was a small child, and has had every opportunity money can bring him. While everybody knows you have not two pennies to rub to—"

She stopped, clamping her lips shut and staring rigidly ahead.

He sighed and after a hesitation said, "I have not, to be sure, ma'am. It is the greatest trial to me, for it obliges me to marry for—that is, to act in such a way as to class myself among the fortune hunters of London."

She looked quickly at him. "But you are not, sir. You cannot be like them—like Lord Ratherton and Major Prewhurst and their ilk—for you did not lose your fortune, and you do not intend to repair it merely to game it away again. It is not your fault you must marry money."

"Pray, how do you know I will not game it away, ma'am?"

She lifted a shoulder. "You are not like that, forever in some gaming hell or lounging with 'knowing ones.' And you needn't look at me like that—everybody hears about it when a gentleman begins to hang about in gaming hells. And you do not do so."

He gazed at her in some bemusement, struck that she had troubled herself to find this out. "Does it not at all worry you that I must marry for money?"

"No, sir," she said, "for if it was not the case, you should not bother fixing my interest."

Her face flushed red and she clapped her hand over her mouth, thrusting the ribbons into his hands and looking anywhere but at him. His complexion fared no better and he stared ahead with unusual attention to his horses.

It would be an exaggeration to say her statement had shocked him—indeed, it had surprised him more than anything, but not in the way he had expected, nor indeed how she had guessed. All his breeding told him that she was an improper person to speak in so forward a manner about something so delicate as his intentions. These were still very much unformed, and her referring to them at all was too much akin to presumption.

He could not, however, find out that she had disgusted him. On the contrary, he had experienced a thrill of delight at her words that he was at pains to interpret, for it seemed only too much like attraction. But the situation was so complex—with her odd outbursts and her pushing mother and her "particular understanding" with Blysdale—that he could not trust himself to speak more boldly as yet.

With an effort, therefore, he fixed a smile to his lips and said cheerfully, "No, ma'am, I should not, and it would have been the most unfortunate thing, for then I should not have had the pleasure of getting to know you better."

This remark had the felicitous effect of easing both their discomfiture, and of enabling Miss Slougham to look him in the eye once more. It was not until Sadler's Wells was reached that she could again converse easily with him, but by the time they had viewed the spectacle of *The Battle of Waterloo Re-Enacted,* and had shared some few criticisms of the use of horses in the show, she seemed restored to loquacity. The return journey was made safe by their engaging in a long and involved discussion of the merits of training full-blood cattle to perform tricks, and the possible uses thereof, and Mr. Tenby was spared any more shockingly thought-inducing speeches by his companion.

Chapter 13

AFTER HIS ENLIGHTENING conversation with Miss Slougham, Mr. Blysdale commenced with his customary dispatch upon discovering in just what way Lady Athena's heart could be touched. He watched her more carefully at social events, attending to what conversation he could without being rude, and even went so far as to wait almost a quarter of an hour to make his presence known when he came up behind her group walking along the path at the park. The faithful Thomas's services were not called upon to augment what his employer had observed, however, for the tenor of Blysdale's pursuit had changed just enough that he wished to include no one else in his discoveries.

Lady Athena, meanwhile, struggled to balance her victory over her mama's prejudice against Mr. Blysdale with the demands of her own exacting disposition. She knew that her continual dismissal of her father's acknowledged friend had been wrong, but when she had been given the freedom to accept him, she had been prevented by a reticence to give more notice than was reasonable. Had he been less attractive to her, she could have trusted herself better, for she had long mastered the art of depressing pretension in those beneath her.

But he was excessively attractive to her, and growing daily more so, and when in company with him she was at pains to recollect just why his suit was not to be thought of. This was difficult for two reasons: firstly, his origins in Yorkshire trade were not well-known—or at least they were not often canvassed in her circle, for he was vastly well-respected—and so he seldom received a rebuff from anyone for that cause. Secondly, his good breeding continually outshone those gentlemen-born around him and caused everyone to forget or to dismiss that his upbringing was tainted by that necessity of the common man, work.

When alone or in company with her mama, Athena was not hard-pressed to recall his origins, but a very few minutes of his society were enough to quash any barrier she had since built and revive her serenity in being admired by a well-bred man. The recurrence of this unfortunate effect awakened her to a sense of her danger, and she resolved that it behooved her to cut short future meetings. Out of the following five days she met him, at engagements or about Town, she spoke more than commonplaces to him only two.

But the following week, at a meeting of the board members of a charitable society of which she was a patron, she was astonished by the announcement of a large donation that would enable them to greatly increase the efficacy of a new program among the poor, and learned that Mr. Blysdale was suspected of being the donor.

"There is no name ascribed to the donation, sir," pointed out a member when a general movement was made to thank Mr. Blysdale.

"It would be impolitic to thank the gentleman only to find it was not he, after all, who gave the donation."

The chairman waved this away. "It was his secretary who made the donation—wrote out the draft before my very eyes. Unless that young man has suddenly come into a great deal of money, there is no doubt as to the identity of our donor."

"Be that as it may, sir, the donor must wish to remain anonymous, else why should he refuse to sign his name?" pursued the member. "It would be highly improper for us to give recognition where none is desired, or where it is not due."

The point was debated some few minutes—for with the great obstacle of funding being removed from their program of highest priority, they had little else to discuss for their meeting—the outcome being that the anonymity of the donor, whoever he may be, must be preserved. But Athena, as she was handed into her carriage at the close of the meeting, still debated in her mind whether she ought to be affronted by Mr. Blysdale's obvious insertion of himself into yet another facet of her life, or pleased by his thoughtful and careful support of her interests.

This debate was settled two days later, when she met him at a select soirée. She greeted him as coolly as ever when he came to pay his respects, but when he would have gone away again, she invited him with a look to stay.

"I wonder if you are interested in charitable work, Mr. Blysdale," she said.

"Indeed, I am, ma'am," he replied. "I feel, as others in my position of privilege, that it is my duty to be so."

"To be sure," she said, looking away. "I wonder if you have heard of the Society for the Amelioration of the Situation of Unmarried Mothers Among the Poor."

He raised a brow at the name. "I believe I have heard of it, ma'am, but I might be mistaken. These societies—excellent enterprises, every one—all too often have such similar titles, it is hard to tell them apart."

"Indeed," she said, with a quelling look. "I have the honor of standing patron to the aforementioned society, and was rather gratified this week to discover that our most pressing project has at last been funded, and by an anonymous donor."

He nodded his congratulations.

She regarded him steadily. "Your secretary was seen somewhere in the vicinity of our chairman's home on the day of the donation, sir. Do you find that a singular occurrence?"

"Not at all," he said, shrugging. "Thomas may find himself anywhere in the City in the discharge of his duty. He is an excellent secretary."

"How salutary for you," she said, her mouth ever so slightly pursing as she considered whether to press further. At last, she concluded that to do so would be improper, for what gentleman, having once made a donation anonymously, would admit to it—and would she think better of him if he did?

She left it at that, therefore, merely changing the subject and allowing him to enjoy the benefit of her curiosity through her continued conversation.

The next day, she met him in the Green Park while out with her maid, and was obliged by common civility to allow him to turn back and walk with her as he would. He inquired after her charity work and she was inclined to think him sly, but his questions were so open and sincere that she soon forgot her suspicions and became quite engaged in the exchange of opinions and ideas that ensued. Before she knew where she was, he was walking her up the steps of Gidgeborough House, and taking his leave of her at the door.

It had been her intention to fob him off a street or two before Grosvenor Square, and it was all she could do not to sigh in relief that Lady Gidgeborough was out of the house, for she knew not what she would have said had her mother been a witness to her arrival with such a companion. As she handed her umbrella to the footman, she thought that she really must get a better command of herself while in his company, or next she may find herself inviting him into the Crimson Saloon for refreshment. But she was able to console herself, as she went upstairs to put off her pelisse and hat, that as she really had no intention ever to walk anywhere with him again, it didn't signify.

This, of course, was not the case, for two days later she was on Bond Street, where she had stopped outside the hat shop that enjoyed her custom to watch a young flower girl selling bundles of lily of the valley. The contrariety of emotions that this sight brought to her mind—stirred up by memories long suppressed—stunned her into momentary immobility. Mr. Blysdale, emerging from the bootmakers next door, caught her thus, and after startling her from her reverie with his greeting, he asked if it was the flowers or the girl who drew her interest.

"The girl, to be sure," she said, turning away slightly so as not to give away her discomfiture. "It is pitiful that she cannot find more profitable employment."

"But she seems to enjoy selling flowers," he said, indicating the girl's smile as she found a customer, "which makes her the more successful. It is not profitable, precisely, but there are far less enjoyable occupations she could be forced to take. Selling flowers, at least, has its delights and its usefulness. There will always be those who wish to buy pretty flowers."

Athena was surprised at the mild blush that she felt cross her cheek in response to the thoughtfulness in his reply. "I suppose you are right. Flowers are a thing of beauty, and will always be in demand."

"Especially lily of the valley," he said, with a slight lift to his voice, as though inquiring her opinion of the flower.

She turned onto the flagway, unconsciously allowing him to accompany her as her footman trailed behind. "They remind me of my grandmother, the Dowager Lady Gidgeborough—small, elegant, and pretty. They grow near the Dower House at Kemmerton, my father's country seat." She stopped, taking a moment to compose herself. "The girl is fortunate to have found respectable employment."

"Most fortunate."

They walked on in silence, crossing Bond Street to make their way to Hookham's library. She was insensibly grateful that he did not press her to speak, though she told herself it was presumptuous of him to have followed her this far. But before she could stir this conviction into irritation, he bade her good day at the door of the library.

"Unless there is any service I may render you, my lady," he said with civil propriety.

She demurred, indicating her confidence in the footman to carry out any of her wishes, and sent him off, glad to have the quiet of the library to herself to sort out her emotions. It had been many, many years since she had felt such sensations—of longing for her elegant, kind little grandmother who had died not long after her twelfth birthday. The lilies that grew in the wood behind the Dower House every spring were so intrinsically connected with memories of her grandmother that the sight of them in the hands of the young flower girl—dark-haired and slight as Athena had been at that age—had instantly taken her back.

It was distressing to have been overtaken by such strong and tender emotions, so wholly as she had eschewed them in the intervening nine years. It had shaken her, finding that she, so disciplined and reserved and cool, was susceptible to weakness of this kind. She required some time—spent browsing the titles in the catalog and requesting this book and that to be brought for her inspection merely so she could pass another quiet ten minutes in composing herself—to come to the conclusion that she was not herself of late, and must blame the over-exertion of the Season.

She took a day to rest, therefore, the better to face an evening at Almack's the day following. As she sat at her toilette, a maid brought up a posy of lily of the valley, and with a constricting feeling in her chest, Athena read the brief note wishing her an enjoyable evening, signed Jonathan Blysdale. The presence of the maid saved her from something like faintness; in the event, she retained enough reason to refuse to carry the posy, but stopped short of throwing it onto the fire. In the end, she coolly requested the maid to fix a stem or two in her hair, for they exactly complimented her white spangled gauze gown.

She had given up hope on receipt of the flowers that Mr. Blysdale would not be at Almack's, and accepted with fortitude that she should be looking for him all the evening, whether he sought her out or not. To her doubtful relief, he did not seem to be early to the Rooms, and she was at liberty to be impatient for his arrival while calmly mingling with her various acquaintance who were there.

At ten o'clock, a general stir was felt at the announcement of the arrival of the Duke of York. Though married, his title and long estrangement from his wife made him an object of interest, and the ladies in the room were all atwitter to see to whom the Duke's eye would turn. Lady Athena, whose interest in royal dukes was probably less at that moment than her mother would have liked, was the third lucky woman toward whom His Royal Highness bent his steps.

The honor of having been singled out by a royal duke was not lost on Athena, but the quaver in her mother's voice as she introduced her offspring was singularly distasteful to her. When His Royal Highness raised Lady Athena from her deep curtsey and looked her over—his eyes sweeping up and down her tall, elegant form—the feeling of distaste grew, and she suddenly wished that she had not worn something so thin as silk and gauze. He bent over her gloved hand, and she felt the press of lips that ought to have hovered an inch or two above—but perhaps he had simply not given up the custom that prevailed in his youth.

"This is not your first Season, I think, ma'am," said the Duke, a lazy smile creasing his once handsome features.

"No, Your Royal Highness. I have been out three years."

"Then you are a young woman of considerable experience, I fancy," he said, the smile tilting to meet the sly glint in his eye.

There were some titters around them as ladies sought to hide their shocked delight behind their fans. Athena wondered at the license granted to royalty, and even more that its impropriety had never yet occurred to her.

"There is much that I understand now about the pitfalls awaiting young women in Society that I did not conceive of before, Sir," she said coolly, her eyes averted.

He chuckled. "Certainly. One must be on one's guard at all times. The elevation of one's mind must be the object! And in Town, there are innumerable ways in which one may receive an education."

She would not raise her eyes to see the meaning that she had no doubt she would find in his—would not satisfy his desire to witness her discomposure. She had just resolved upon braving her mama's censure by excusing herself when another voice, familiar and surprisingly soothing, entered the conversation.

"Pray forgive the interruption, Your Royal Highness, but I could not help but overhear you are intrigued by education. It is the most fortunate occurrence! I must beg to be allowed to introduce Mrs. Goldentree to you."

The speaker was Mr. Blysdale, and he brought forward a lady dressed just this side of propriety, whose glittering jewels could not compare with the glitter in her eye as she regarded the Duke. "Mrs. Goldentree, you may surmise, is the widow of the lately lamented Mr. Goldentree, the celebrated educationist and orator."

Whatever affront Mr. Blysdale may have offered by interrupting His Royal Highness was forgotten in his instant assimilation of Mrs. Goldentree's charms. The Duke's eyes roamed freely over her ripe figure and clinging gown, which was nearly as transparent as Athena had imagined her own to be only minutes ago, and under which there did not seem to be anything by way of underclothes. His Royal Highness's attention, inevitably and thankfully, turned to the new arrival.

"A pleasure, ma'am," he said, kissing Mrs. Goldentree's hand as he had kissed Athena's. "I was privileged to know your husband, but cannot claim to have shared his interests."

"That makes two of us, Your Royal Highness," she said, then in a voice too low for most to hear added, "But perhaps we are not yet too old to gain an appreciation for education."

Athena, stepping away to allow more room for the couple, heard an appreciative chuckle from the Duke before their voices were blocked out by the murmurings of the crowd, and she looked up to see Mr. Blysdale before her.

"Good evening, ma'am," he said, bowing. "The crowd has made the room just here quite stuffy. Would you care to step away? Perhaps a glass of lemonade?"

The simplicity of his gallantry was infinitely welcome, and she took his arm, allowing him to lead her to the refreshment table. They stood in silence as she drank, and when she had placed her empty glass on a tray, he solicited her hand for the next two dances. It seemed only natural for Athena to accept, and she went without hesitation with him into the quadrille that was forming.

As they took their places and awaited their turn in the figures, she said, "I did not know you had been introduced to the Duke before. You are a man of wide connections."

He smiled. "Yes, I was so fortunate as to be invited to Carlton House last February, and made His Royal Highness's acquaintance there."

"But you did not meet Mrs. Goldentree at Carlton House," she said coolly.

"Oh, no. Mr. Goldentree and I worked together on some matters of education reform for the lower classes."

"A worthy cause. I must own I would not have imagined Mrs. Goldentree to share in such interests."

"She did not, and that is why I have not seen or met with her for some years."

Athena digested this. "It was a felicitous chance, then, that brought her to Almack's."

"Yes. As a friend of Lady Jersey, she has been admitted to Almack's for years, but she is only recently out of mourning. She was delighted to see me. When I mentioned I had the power of introducing her to the Duke, she was even more delighted."

"She seems very much to his taste," observed Athena.

"Yes," was his only reply, but his tone spoke everything she wished to know.

They performed their figures and talked of dancing, of common acquaintance, and of recent entertainments they had attended, but the subject of the Duke and Mrs. Goldentree was not revisited. Mr. Blysdale's gaze was on her through much of the dance, while they moved and while they waited, but never did she suffer discomfort, nor did she wish to get away. At the end of the set, he led her back to where Lady Gidgeborough sat speaking loftily to another matron.

"Thank you for the dances, ma'am," he said, bowing over her hand very properly. Then, glancing at the flowers in her hair, he said boldly, "The style of your hair is uncommonly pretty. One ventures to suggest that lily of the valley becomes you." And so saying, he smiled and walked away.

When her mama turned to scold at her having relinquished a royal duke for a commoner and a tradesman, she endured it patiently, agreeing so readily and so mildly that at last the lady imagined she was as annoyed as herself and let her alone.

Chapter 14

EXCUSING HERSELF FROM the next set by pleading fatigue, Athena left her mama and found a seat in an alcove out of the way. But it was fatigue of her senses more than of her body, for she was almost overcome by the stark dissimilarity between Mr. Blysdale, a commoner and tradesman as her mama pleased to call him, and a royal duke.

His Royal Highness, in displaying such condescension in his notice of her, had made her feel besmirched, his eyes sliding this way and that over her person as though she were a mere object for his delectation. The more he had looked at her, the less human she had felt, and the more strongly she had desired to get away. His tactless attentions had implied her obligation to him as her superior, and he had seemed to regard her admiration as his due. His opening salute upon her gloved hand, meant as an honor, had been taken by her as the basest insult—she intended to have the gloves destroyed as soon as she was safely home.

But Mr. Blysdale, in diverting the Duke's attention from her, had acted in a most chivalrous manner without expecting any obligation from her. His attentions, entirely free from calculation or self-gratification, had been as a burst of clean water flowing over her, washing away the cloying, clinging, distasteful impression of the Duke. When Mr. Blysdale had looked at her, he had *seen* her—a lady of quality and honor, desirable while also respectable. His looks had been admiring, appreciative, and indescribably more welcome than had those of the nobly-born Duke, whose divine rights held him far above.

The two were so widely different that they could not bear comparison. She thought that were she to receive an offer of marriage from both of them today, and be obliged to accept one of them, she should not hesitate but to accept Mr. Blysdale over the Duke. Even regardless of birth, Mr. Blysdale was His Grace's superior in looks, fortune, and breeding, and though it must be impossible for her to love him, she was confident that she—in person and in reputation—should be secure of his respect and care.

But as she considered accepting this imaginary offer from Mr. Blysdale, and all that entailed, she was struck by the suspicion that she could come to love him, for she was conscious even now of an interest in him that went beyond gratitude or esteem. She thought suddenly that if Mr. Blysdale were to become her husband, he would be permitted in all propriety, under certain circumstances, to undress her with his eyes, and she knew without a doubt that it would be not only a much more pleasant experience than what she had undergone from the Duke, but a very welcome one.

She was obliged to take her fan from her reticule and ply it vigorously for some minutes while purging these disturbing thoughts from her brain. What was she coming to? To entertain such thoughts—indeed, to have such hot-blooded and improper thoughts at all! It all came from mixing with persons beneath her—

But when she stole a glance at Mr. Blysdale, who was so elegantly dancing with his customary amiable propriety, she knew this was both incorrect and unjust. The thoughts had come because Mr. Blysdale had proven himself to be more worthy than a member of royalty—the highest and supposedly noblest specimens of manhood in the king-dom—who had shown how poorly he understood his divine right and how contemptuously he regarded moral principles. Try as she might, she could no longer utterly dismiss the notion that Mr. Blysdale was indeed a gentleman—nor could she suppress the regret that it made no difference in his eligibility as a suitor.

The following morning, Mr. Blysdale presented himself at Gidge-borough House, fully prepared to be turned away. It was only to be expected, after what he had done last night, but still, propriety dictated he call on the ladies with whom he had danced, and he would not be behindhand in any observance—it was what his reputation had been built on. The risk he had taken last night, of offending either the Duke or Lady Gidgeborough—or more likely, both—had been a calculated one, and he had gauged correctly on both counts. The Duke he had seen in sly discussion with Mrs. Goldentree just before he had taken leave of the Rooms, and the lady had followed soon after. Lady Gidgeborough—whose countenance upon perceiving Mrs. Goldentree's glittering person had been a sight to behold—had been stiff with anger, and had not so much as glanced his way the rest of the evening.

Great was his surprise, therefore, upon being ushered into the drawing room on the first floor and greeted quite pleasantly by Lady

Athena and almost civilly by her mother. He could only surmise that Lady Gidgeborough had had time to consider that His Royal Highness had not taken Mr. Blysdale's interruption amiss, which suggested a prior acquaintance between them—a fact that Athena might have confirmed, and that must not be carelessly overlooked. Nor had her daughter been slighted by the transaction in the least—Athena had been presented to a royal duke and been admired, and if the interview had been cut short, considering His Royal Highness's propensities, she must, as a woman of principle, consider that perhaps it was not a bad thing.

Athena, on the other hand, was laboring under mixed emotions. The shock of Mr. Blysdale's superiority to a royal duke had swirled into some very painful meditations upon her own principles, and she had gone to bed with a headache. Sleep had claimed her quickly, however, and her dreams had dwelt principally on her rescuer, and had deepened her sense of gratitude to him into something quite resembling esteem.

All this Mr. Blysdale might conjecture, for he had not come so far in Society without a keen judgment of human character, but what he guessed, he kept to himself. It was sufficient that he had entered the house a second time, and that both ladies were on the thaw. Being the only visitor at the moment, he was invited to take a seat beside Lady Athena on the sofa and the visit commenced.

"You may guess my astonishment last night, Mr. Blysdale," said Lady Gidgeborough, "upon finding that you were acquainted with the Duke of York. I believe you met at Carlton House?"

"Yes, madam. He was kind enough to recollect our meeting."

"Hmm." She regarded him blandly. "An invitation to Carlton House must have come as something of a surprise to one in your situation."

"On the contrary, madam, my father had been honored by an invitation some years ago. He had been considered for a knighthood, but died before the thing could be settled."

"Do you intend to apply in his place, sir?" she inquired, her tone mildly interested.

He smiled. "As it was my father's attainments that merited the knighthood, I can hardly presume to take his place. Perhaps I shall find myself in the way of such an application in the future, however."

She smiled thinly and looked away, but Lady Athena observed civilly, "Your father must have done something of significance, sir, to merit such an honor."

Lady Gidgeborough said, "I daresay it was nothing more than having been elected mayor, as is too often the case."

"In actuality, madam, he was instrumental in preventing an uprising of workers in the north. His intervention saved hundreds of livelihoods and thousands of pounds-worth of machinery and property."

"Luddites!" her ladyship declared in disgust.

"No, madam, for it did not involve the framework knitters but the factory workers."

"A mere squabble, then," sniffed Lady Gidgeborough. "It is odd that such low concerns merit the notice of the King, and that he should consider them worthy of reward! But His Majesty was not himself at that time, I daresay."

Mr. Blysdale smiled wryly. "As I have had occasion to observe, madam, Yorkshire is a large county, and the disagreement comprehended most of the manufactories in the county. In short, the danger was of a magnitude that if left unchecked, the issue would have disrupted textile supplies to all counties in the south, including London."

"Surely muslins and cambrics are not of such importance to the Crown," said Lady Gidgeborough.

"Clothing fabrics were not all that would have been affected, madam," he said, without a trace of triumph. "Some of the manufactories produced the sail-cloth for His Majesty's navy, which at that time was sorely needed in our struggle against France. A shortage would have harmed the war effort terribly. It scarcely wants explanation that the representatives of the Crown were exceedingly grateful to my father and the other masters involved in preventing such a calamity."

"Indeed," said her ladyship with a reluctant nod.

At all times sensible of appearing to advantage, Mr. Blysdale chose this moment to take his leave. He bowed deferentially over Lady Gidgeborough's hand and received a wary but civil smile in return. This was encouragement enough to prompt him, when he turned to Lady Athena, to beg the honor of her company the following afternoon on a drive. After a brief glance toward her mother, she responded in the affirmative, and with no more celebration than a grateful smile and a nod he took his leave, perfectly satisfied with the visit.

The next day was cloudy, and there was some talk of rain, but as the skies were not dark, Mr. Blysdale did not despair. He called for Lady Athena promptly at four o'clock and they set out for Hyde Park. Unlike Miss Slougham, Lady Athena did not comment on his horses other than to admire their neatness, but Blysdale was in a better mood than to cavil. He had attained the next goal, reached the next step in his plan, and if his companion did nothing but gaze stonily at the scenery for the entirety of the drive, he could be satisfied that she would do it by his side.

But Lady Athena had no intention of remaining silent. The conversation the previous day had reached that part of her heart that was opened only to those less fortunate, and she was moved to discover more of what had been Mr. Blysdale, Senior's, motives in the affair.

"I wish you will satisfy a point of curiosity for me, Mr. Blysdale, regarding the uprising you spoke of yesterday." She glanced up to find his brows raised, whether in surprise or in anticipation she could not tell. "Was your father's intervention prompted by a pricked conscience?"

Mr. Blysdale's brows rose higher, and he gazed at her perhaps a moment longer than was wise, considering he held the ribbons of a high-spirited pair. The next moment he slowed the horses to a walk, saying "It is no secret that many masters of manufactories abuse their power, to the detriment of those to whom they owe both their support and their gratitude. My father was not one of them. His—background gave him an intimate knowledge of the deprivations caused by unfair wages, and he resolved, upon becoming a master, never to stoop below his duty, no matter the effect to his pecuniary success."

With a nod, Athena said, "It is the duty of all in power, whether through birth or through—other means, to be diligent in the care of those in their stewardships. The rights of wealth do not extend to the neglect of duty."

"Indeed," he said, flicking a glance at her. "If everyone with means did his or her duty, there would be much less want in the world."

"Perhaps," she mused, nodding to an acquaintance walking beside the carriageway. "But where there is human weakness, there will always be want, regardless of the neglect of those in power."

"I suppose you refer to the vicious propensities often attributed to persons of the lower classes, ma'am. Allow me to argue that these propensities are attached not to class, but to disposition—selfish people are to be found everywhere."

"Certainly, there are those in any class who wish for more than they can get," she said, looking at him askance.

Ignoring this riposte, he said, "However, there will be much less occasion for dissatisfaction among those who truly want wherever they meet with the generosity of those who rejoice in prosperity."

Seeing that he meant to keep to the moral high ground, and really agreeing with him, she did not press further. Looking out over the park instead, she said, "I trust it was not imprudent for your father to put himself in harm's way."

"He took proper precautions, I assure you, but he was never in any real danger. He was too much respected. He knew his people would listen to him."

"And what of the other masters?"

He did not pause, but she saw that his jaw tightened infinitesimally. "They were soon brought to reason, as were their workers."

She regarded him with interest. "By the same means?"

"In general terms, yes. Both parties were mad with hunger—they were simply different sorts of hunger, appeased in differing ways."

She looked away again. "It seems a tiresome business. It is lucky for them that your father was not of the mind to have them all transported, or hanged."

"It would have done nothing but destroy families and perpetuate the problem if he had," he said, "not to mention ruin his business. My father was a pragmatist. He knew that hungry workers are inefficient and unprofitable. Once he had convinced the other masters of this, they joined him in alleviating the most pressing needs of their workers and when the workers had cause enough to listen, a compromise was reached."

Athena thought that she might have liked to have met the late Mr. Blysdale, but she did not long allow herself to entertain the thought. Instead, she said, "And you carry on in your father's footsteps, sir?"

He glanced at her. "In whatever ways I am able, ma'am. I was not raised to the business, so I have little to do with the day-to-day running of the mills, other than ensuring the comfort of my workers. I am merely the owner, and leave the work to the overseers I have hired."

"And yet, the work and the business are inextricably connected to you, are they not?"

"They are what has made me what I am." He paused, then said matter-of-factly, "I do not apologize for my background, ma'am. My family goes back in England as far as any nobleman's, and there are as many great names in my tree as any gentleman's. I do not find it shameful that I am descended from a surfeit of younger sons, for they have produced men as excellent as any of their elder brothers' progeny. And that my ancestors worked for their bread is a matter of pride to me, for it is their hard work that laid the foundation for my father's success, and for my present situation."

She was silent for some moments, not looking at him. When she did speak, it was to change the subject. "Your principal residence is in Yorkshire?" She turned to gaze steadily at him. "How near is it to your mills?"

He smiled wryly, as though reading into her words. "The nearest is fifty miles off, ma'am. I can neither see nor hear my machines or workers from any point on my property. Blyssmore is surrounded by hills and trees, with a park ten miles around. I am assured of privacy and quiet whenever I am at home."

"It is a recent purchase, I collect?"

"Of course, ma'am. As I am the first gentleman in my family for several centuries at least, it fell upon me to purchase. It was a daunting prospect, to be sure, for I knew that whatever property I settled upon would remain in my family for centuries to come, and I alone would be held responsible for any future dissatisfaction. However, I believe I may rest easy in my choice."

"I hope for your sake you are right, sir," said Athena with a slight, wry smile. "But I wonder that you did not choose a place on the moors. All your talk of the beauty of heather in bloom convinced me it would be so."

"Ah," he said, smiling. "I beg a thousand apologies for giving you a mistaken idea, my lady. The heather is lovely, indeed, but the moors are too wild for my taste—that is, my everyday taste. It would be too much to expect a gentleman with the power to choose his habitation to settle on so windswept and otherwise barren a location."

"One must use more caution when making so compelling a recommendation," said Athena disapprovingly, "if one wishes to retain one's character."

He glanced at her, then again, the smile growing to include his eyes. "I did specifically recommend a summer visit to the moors, ma'am—and only a visit."

Pursing her lips against a smile, she said, "You did. And yet, you have chosen the same county for your principal residence. I do not understand what you would be at."

"I am bound to my country, I suppose," he said, more seriously. "It did not occur to me to settle anywhere else than where I grew up." He turned to her. "And it is lovely, I assure you."

She lifted her chin. "Though the winters are exceptionally harsh, and not for the faint of heart?"

He chuckled. "It does not signify, for of course one comes to London for the winter."

A huff of laugh escaped her. "Very well, then I shall be obliged to take you at your word."

"I trust that someday, you will not have to, ma'am," he said very boldly.

This was too much for her. She stiffened and looked away. "I cannot imagine I should be so ill-advised as to travel to Yorkshire at any season, sir. It is much too long a journey to contemplate, when there is no one there I should have even the remotest desire to visit. You know very well, sir, that my mother should never wish to go there, and I should have no occasion to go if she does not."

It was his part to agree, which he did with so perfect a manner as to greatly annoy her, as did the secret smile that almost continually graced his lips as they made their way back.

Chapter 15

THE FOLLOWING EVENING at Brooks's Club, Mr. Blysdale met with Alverton, Hollingsford, and Windon over a convivial game of whist, accompanied by multiple bottles of a very tolerable burgundy. The spirit was one of celebration, for though Blysdale was too much the gentleman to boast of his conquests, he was so entirely pleased with his progress with Lady Athena that his manner belied him.

"You may as well cut line, Blysdale," said Alverton as the cards were cut and dealt. "It's as plain as day that you're proud as a peacock over something."

He cocked an innocent eyebrow. "But am I not always proud, sir? I seem to recall your saying that pride was my besetting sin."

"As it is," retorted Windon. "Who else would be proud of his pride?"

"There are few who could do so with such good cause," said Hollingsford, the voice of wisdom and age. "Would that my son had as much charm and sense."

"With all due respect, sir," said Alverton, nodding to his sire, "I am only as sensible and as charming as blood has made me."

The others called out in mock dismay, but Hollingsford merely passed the wine, saying, "You may hope that I have more sense than to re-make my will after tonight, my boy. Not all the property is entailed, you know."

This brought on another round of amusement hushed only by the commencement of play. As the tricks were taken, Windon mused, "You are far too pleased with yourself, Blysdale. You did not even attempt to be modest at winning that one. If you had cheated me cleanly you could not be more smug. Come now, what has given you so high an opinion of yourself?"

"Only my excellent choice of companions," Blysdale said, smiling. "See how well you play into my hands? I could not have chosen a more obliging set of friends."

"It is my belief," said Windon darkly, "that you are a Dead Setter. We should shake him upside down and see what he hides in that expensive coat of his."

"More likely he has scored a point with Lady Athena," said Hollingsford, calmly taking the next trick.

"By Jupiter, you're right, sir!" cried Alverton. "I saw him driving her in the park yesterday. Almost took me out of my skin—thought I was going mad!"

Windon gaped at them both. "He never did! What's this, Blysdale? Lady Athena wouldn't give you more than the time of day last I knew of it!"

"Well, sir," said Blysdale, laying down a card to take another trick, "it should teach you not to go off to Newmarket for days at a time. How fared your horses, by the by?"

"Worse than you, it seems," muttered Windon, casting down his cards in disgust. "How does a man get so lucky?"

"Not lucky," said Hollingsford, gathering up the cards as Blysdale jotted down the points. "Clever. And persistent," he added with an eagle glance at his son.

Alverton put up his hands. "I don't want Lady Athena, sir—never did! Don't know what put that maggot into your head—wouldn't have me if I tried!"

His father chuckled, dealing the new rubber as the wine went around again. "I know it too well, my boy. Not to worry—Blysdale is so far beyond you that I wouldn't presume."

"Lady Athena's still beyond *him*, I tell you," declared Windon, taking up his cards and tapping them smartly on the table. "No matter how far he wheedles his way into her good graces, he'll not make it into her heart. Hasn't got one!"

"Thought she hadn't any graces, either," said Alverton. "Leastways, not good ones. Got plenty of grace, can't deny that. And elegance, and beauty. Too bad she's so cold. Handsome woman!"

"Now don't get to sighing, Alvie," warned Windon, "or we'll turn you out. If Blysdale doesn't call you out, that is. Come to think on it, that's not such a wrong idea!"

Alverton cried, "What, getting my chest shot through? I thank you, no! Besides, already said I ain't interested in Lady Athena, no matter how handsome she is!"

"I've no reason to call you out, Alvie," said Blysdale soothingly, laying down his card. "Do not trouble yourself."

"What's got into you to promote a duel between friends, Windon?" inquired Hollingsford, his brow furrowing. "Foxed already?"

"No, sir! Scarcely a little wet! Besides, didn't mean anything of the sort. I meant Blysdale's got to have competition or he'll never come to his senses."

"He has got competition," said Hollingsford, taking the trick. "Lord Foxham, if I'm not mistaken."

"Yes, but I mean serious competition," said Windon, eying the cards with disfavor. "Fellow creaks. Lady Athena wouldn't consider a fellow who creaks. Couldn't abide the notoriety."

"Her consideration ain't needed. If he has not shown his preference to your satisfaction, her dear mama has very palpably approved him."

Windon threw down his hand. "I go out of Town for a few days and all the world goes to the devil! Did Lady Athena get engaged to Foxham while I was at Newmarket?"

"Why would she drive out with Blysdale if she had?" inquired Alverton, looking a trifle owlishly at his cards.

"Why does the Lady Athena do anything?" retorted Windon. "Because she can!"

"She has not got engaged," said Hollingsford pacifically, passing the bottle again. "But to hear Gidgeborough talk, his lady has set her cap at Lord Foxham. It would be tit for tat, to be sure."

"What's that, sir?" said Alverton, weighing the merits of the two cards in his hand rather too critically.

"If Lady Athena succeeds in marrying a marquess, it would at last remove the stain of her mother's failure to do so."

"To have a creaking son-in-law?" exclaimed Windon distastefully.

Hollingsford took the last trick, gathering the cards into his hand. "A creaking marquess is still a marquess, Windon. Ambition is blind to whatever it need not regard."

Alverton chuckled foolishly. "Better get yourself a corset, Blysdale. Only way to compete with the marquess."

"There will be no need, I thank you," said Blysdale, reckoning the points.

Windon shook his head, eying his friend narrowly. "Too dashed sure of yourself, Blysdale! Someone's got to drill some sense into you!"

"Can't be done," observed Alverton carefully. "He's too obstinate—like granite!"

"It could if he failed in this ridiculous pursuit of Lady Athena! And he will—I'll lay odds!"

Alverton blinked, "What odds?"

"Now, now, Windon, no need to ride grub," said Hollingsford. "Better quit the burgundy, sir! Always does turn you rusty."

Windon stood, on his dignity. "I am not drunk, my lord. And I wager that Blysdale will not succeed with Lady Athena—rather, Lord Foxham shall."

"But what odds?" inquired Alverton insistently.

"Three to one!"

Blysdale rose, handing the point tally to Hollingsford. "That's five and eight you owe me, sir, and Windon owes you two pounds ten. You may decide whether to take your other winnings out of Alverton's allowance. I must leave you, gentlemen, to my utmost regret. Your company, as your discourse, is ever grateful to me. Where else could I find such support in all my doings? Good evening, my lord," he said, nodding pleasantly to Hollingsford.

"Three to one, Blysdale," called Alverton after him, but he did not turn back.

Hollingsford stood, clapping Windon on the back. "Come home with us. Got a capital gun I'd like to show you."

"Thank you, no, sir. Tomorrow. I shall stay and play another game. Piquet, Alvie?"

Alverton nodded amiably and bid his father good night, making no objection to his taking the bottles away with him. Windon, however, squinted irritably at his lordship's back but, out of respect, waited until he was off the premises before ordering a new bottle of port from the waiter.

The two younger gentlemen played two rubbers of piquet—with widely varying outcomes, due chiefly to liberal doses of port—and losing all interest in cards and points, started in again on the bet they had agitated earlier. It seemed utter foolishness to both of them that Blysdale should pass up such an opportunity to bolster his claim, and seeing that it was in his best interests to bypass his permission, determined to write the bet in the book. This they dutifully did, therefore, signing their own names and then, after a meditative pause, signing his as well. Vastly relieved to have done so well by their friend, they left the club arm in arm, and sang ditties together until they were obliged to separate to stagger to their different lodgings.

The previous week, Blysdale had reserved a box at the theater, and had sent out invitations to the Goddesses and Miss Breckinridge and several gentlemen, including Mr. Breckinridge, Mr. Tenby, and Lord Heldon, for this Wednesday evening. All had accepted—apart from Lady Athena and Mr. Tenby, who each had sent their regrets at having a previous engagement. Lady Athena's refusal had given Blysdale little anxiety as much of a positive nature had occurred between the time of the invitation and now; however, Mr. Tenby's negative raised some irritation. Blysdale had invited Tenby expressly for Miss Slougham's sake, and the possibility of the gentleman's being jealous of him was annoying. He would simply have to find a way to disabuse Tenby of his misapprehensions.

The party at the Covent Garden Theater was a merry one, for Miss Marshall had once more returned to Town and all were in spirits. The play featured Mr. Young and Miss O'Neill, two rising stars in tragedy, and if they could not excite the interest of all the young people in the box, they could provide ample occasion for gratitude at the fall of the curtain and the enjoyment of the interval before the farce.

As Iris's intended companion was absent, she would soon have found herself as good as alone in the box, for the other couples unconsciously fell to private conversation between themselves. But Blysdale, also without his preferred companion, stepped to her side, ready to fill the void.

"Are you heated, Miss Slougham?" he asked. "Would you like to walk in the corridor for a while, to escape this stuffy box?"

"Yes, or I declare I shall melt," she said, rather too hastily for decorum. But recognizing this, she added demurely, "If you please, sir. Thank you."

He smiled and bowed her out, offering his arm and taking her at a comfortable pace down the corridor. As there were others strolling about, he would have engaged her with pleasantries, but she felt no such compunction.

"It was rude of Athena not to accept," she said. "But perhaps she has repented of it now that she need not fear being seen with you. Everyone seems to have witnessed you driving her in Hyde Park."

"Is that so?" he asked, with a smile of satisfaction.

"At least everyone is talking of it."

"Little escapes the eye of Society," he said dryly. "Would that its memory was so powerful. But it shall all be forgot tomorrow, which does not suit me at all. I shall not soon forget our drive."

"Was it so pleasant?" inquired Iris doubtfully. "I should not have imagined Athena to have unbent so soon as to make herself pleasant, precisely."

He laughed. "It was pleasant enough, for you must know I like a challenge. Indeed, I enjoyed it very much, for she was quite insistent upon disparaging my connection with the mills, and yet I do believe I managed to convince her both of their usefulness and of my own merit in keeping them running."

"But are they useful, sir?" inquired Iris frankly. "I have heard they are the horridest places."

"Mine certainly are not horrid, I assure you, ma'am," he said somewhat primly. "I have taken great pains to ensure that they are not, nor that they should ever be so."

Blushing fiercely, Iris begged pardon. "I did not mean to suggest—I know you are too much the gentlemen—indeed, you are too kind to betray the trust of those in your care."

"Thank you, Miss Slougham," he said, his smile losing its tightness. "It may interest you to know that Lady Athena expressed similar sentiments. Oh, not of my kindness—she most definitely has not unbent enough to do that—but of the responsibility of privileged persons to care for those within their stewardship."

"Yes," said Iris, grateful to have recovered so easily from her gaffe. "Athena has always felt strongly on such subjects, which is only to be expected of the nobility, for they are brought up to believe in duty and all that. But she does seem to feel it more deeply, sir. She can be quite passionate about her charity work, while most ladies simply embroider doilies to make the prisons seem more homelike, or some such useless nonsense."

"I have had occasion to witness her passion on the subject, ma'am, and must agree that it goes beyond the ordinary."

"It is evidence that she has a heart to be touched, sir. You must not give up."

"I do not intend to, ma'am," he said, somewhat taken aback. "What could give you any notion of it, pray?"

She sighed. "Only that Athena is set upon marrying the Marquess of Foxham. Oh, I do not think she really means it—that is, I do not believe it is real to her, and she merely talks of it as a certainty out of habit. Indeed, I do not think she could bring herself to do it—he creaks, sir!"

He chuckled, shaking his head. "I must try to follow Lord Foxham about next time I see him, to see if he really does creak. So many people have said it is so, I am wild with curiosity to hear it for myself."

"It is undignified, to be sure," said Iris, grinning. "To think a marquess should inflict such notoriety upon himself—it goes against all his breeding!"

"I cannot imagine what Lady Gidgeborough sees in him."

Iris's grin faded. "Nothing beyond his title, depend upon it. Lady Gidgeborough is rather obsessed with titles in general, and marquesses in particular. I believe I mentioned it has to do with a disappointment in her youth—but those are usually reserved for heroes in novels, and are made out to be much more romantic than what hers has been. I do not doubt it is to blame for all her prickles and thorns. It is very sad."

Mr. Blysdale murmured something proper, patting her hand on his arm.

She looked up at him. "It is why Athena is so unhappy, sir, depend upon it."

"I had not considered that Lady Athena is unhappy," he said, turning this over in his brain. "But it must be very lowering to have a mother who is so very disagreeable."

"It is not that sir—that is, not precisely. Her mother's disappointment has made her doubly insistent upon Athena's perfection. Athena can never be who she wants to be—only what her mama wishes. And it has become so much of a habit with her that she no longer thinks to feel ill-used, or to wish otherwise." Iris looked down. "If it goes on much longer, I fear she will forget what it means to be happy altogether. She certainly will if she marries Lord Foxham."

Blysdale stopped, taking her hand and pressing it. "She shall not marry Lord Foxham, Miss Slougham—of that I am determined. If I have anything to say in the matter, she will soon be free, not only to remember what makes her happy, but to live it."

He bent to kiss her hand, and her smile widened, her eyes speaking her thanks and pleasure in the promise. But when again they resumed their walking, she beheld Mr. Tenby standing still and pale at the turning of the corridor, watching them with an unmistakable look of injury. Iris was too struck by his appearance to do anything but stare and wonder at the meaning of it, and by the time she had collected her wits he had turned on his heel and strode out of sight around the corner.

"That was Mr. Tenby, sir," she said breathlessly.

"Yes, I saw him," said Blysdale, looking after him. "It is strange that he is here—I thought he would not be."

Iris looked up at her companion, vague and puzzled. "Why?"

"Because I invited him to be of our party, and he declined. Said he had another engagement—perhaps it was canceled." He smiled encouragingly. "Or perhaps he came looking for us."

"Hardly, sir. Did you see his face? He looked positively ill." She let go his arm, turning away and wringing her hands. "Oh, dear. I think I have finally done it! I have finally chased him away!"

"And why should you think that, Miss Slougham?"

"Because we went for a drive only a few days ago, and I said the most shocking things!"

"But you always say shocking things, ma'am. He can hardly have expected otherwise."

She huffed, almost a sob. "You don't understand. I as good as told him I should like him to marry me."

He hesitated, considering how to temper this. "Then you have tried the virtue of plain speech between romantically interested parties."

"And it has proved fatal!" she cried. "I have given him such a disgust of me that he will never speak to me again, and I will go home in disgrace!"

"Surely not, ma'am," said Blysdale, his glance flicking to the small groups scattered in the corridor who had begun to cast looks in their direction. "Do not make such wild assumptions. You do not know the truth."

"I do know the truth, sir! It is always the same—I cannot hold my tongue, and it ruins everything! You know my mother—she will wash her hands of me, and I shall have to marry Sir Isaac Hornaby!"

She ended on a soaring note of hysteria and he caught hold of her hands, turning her to look at him. "Come, Miss Slougham," he said in a low tone, fixing her with his steel blue gaze. "We are attracting unwelcome attention. You must compose yourself. Breathe deeply and walk with me. We shall go to the saloon and procure you some lemonade, and then we shall return to the box."

Iris swallowed, going pale at the thought of so many eyes upon her. "Yes—yes. Oh, forgive me, Blysdale. I am so terribly sorry to have made a scene."

"Do not distress yourself. All will be well. Do you have a fan with you? Give it to me."

Plying the fan before her face, he led her gently but firmly back down the corridor to the staircase, and down to the refreshment table in the saloon, murmuring loudly about the heat and her feeling of faintness. He procured the lemonade and, after superintending her disposal of it, he saw with relief that she had recovered much of her countenance and they returned to the box.

Upon seeing her friends, however, Iris's distress returned, and Miss Marshall and Miss Breckinridge gathered her to them, pulling her to a seat and instantly begging her to tell them what was the matter. Grateful that his charge was now in better hands, Mr. Blysdale turned with his usual pleasant manner to the gentlemen, smilingly engaging them in conversation—all the while mentally cursing Mr. Tenby's obtuseness, and his own stupidity.

Chapter 16

AT THE HANDS of her friends, Miss Slougham's condition immensely improved, and Mr. Blysdale saw her home in tolerable spirits. He called on her the next day, and from her pale but pleasant looks and Mrs. Slougham's unconscious manner, he concluded that the worst had passed and she would recover. He was still sensible of his guilt in the matter, however, and intending to set about immediately to repair the wrong, he went round to. Tenby House.

Mr. Tenby was not at home, however; nor was he at home the next day, or the next. He was out, and was not expected back at any specific hour. With some consternation, Blysdale asked for paper and pen and scribbled a note that he hoped would convey enough of the truth to be enlightening, without betraying Miss Slougham's confidences to him. He left the note with the butler, and went away, not quite content but obliged to be satisfied.

Upon entering his house in Hanover Square, he received from the hand of Stomes an invitation on gilt-edged lilac paper to the Marchioness of Foxham's ball the following Monday. He took it with the other post into the study and shut the door, considering if it behooved him to stay away from Foxham or to do as he had suggested to Miss Slougham and get as close to his lordship as possible. There was more than the creaking corset to consider, of course, for Lady Gidgeborough's ambition was very real, as was Lady Athena's inclination to obey her mother. In staying away, Blysdale would give Foxham a sporting chance to prove his right as Lady Gidgeborough's choice for her daughter. But in going, Blysdale would pay Miss Slougham the compliment of acknowledging her superior understanding of her friend, and allow Lady Athena an opportunity of direct comparison.

He sent his acceptance, therefore, and requested Hindley to see about the new coat he had ordered from Weston, and to collect his new evening slippers from the bootmakers. Hindley instantly produced the coat and slippers from his master's dressing room, having anticipated their necessity and taken steps to expedite their delivery. Mr. Blysdale smiled and thanked him, expressing the belief that he would be lost without him, which was all the commendation the faithful valet required.

On the night of the ball, the street outside the Marchioness of Foxham's residence was thronged with carriages and even some chairs, with gentlemen and ladies converging on the house from every direction. It was a feast, of sorts, for the senses, what with all the dazzling finery of both sexes, the sounds of link boys and carriage drivers arguing and hallooing, and the various smells associated with many bodies both equine and human.

Mr. Blysdale, percipiently choosing to walk around from Hanover Square, avoided the general chaos in the street and made his way through the crowds to the front door. Surrendering his hat and coat to the footman, he went up the stairs and was greeted by Lord Foxham, who stood dutifully at his mother's side to receive her guests.

"Blysdale, good of you to come," his lordship said, ponderously shaking hands. "You see my mother has filled her rooms—it is to be a squeeze, they tell me."

An unmistakable creaking sounded as Foxham moved, and Blysdale suppressed a thrill of triumph. "But it is not only your mother who has brought all these people," he said cordially. "The success of your bill is sure to have had some effect."

Lord Foxham smiled benignly. "Yes, well, it is to be expected. Not that I take credit—no, no, it was my father's bill, sir, and it is to his honor that I dedicate my success. Pleasure to see you, sir."

Having primed his host, Blysdale entered the drawing room, the doors of which had been thrown open to the enormous ballroom that took up the remainder of the first floor. The room was quite full already—as Foxham had pointed out—and Blysdale was obliged to edge his way here and there, greeting acquaintances and being introduced as he went. He did not expect to see the Marshalls or the Sloughams here, for they were not of the dowager's set, but there, across the room, stood Lady Athena with her father and mother on either side, like ill-matched bookends. Lord Gidgeborough, tall, large, and smiling, was infinitely the more approachable of the two. Lady Gidgeborough wore her usual stiff and sour expression, which only tightened when she became aware of Blysdale's approach. She turned to murmur something behind her fan to her daughter, which brought Lady Athena's eyes calmly to his.

She looked magnificent tonight, in deep blue satin trimmed in silver, with an underdress of silver-spangled white crepe. Her glorious dark hair was twisted up in bands about her head, woven through with silver ribbon, and with a spray of feathers at the side. The silver set off her eyes to perfection, and the creamy white of her throat was accented by a diamond necklet above the low-cut darkness of her bodice. Blysdale fancied he could stand all night and admire her, if he was in the habit of making a fool of himself. Instead, he walked steadily up to the group, addressing himself first to Lady Gidgeborough.

"My lady," he said, bowing with perfect grace. He turned to Lord Gidgeborough and said, "Sir, delightful to see you again. How did your horse at Newmarket?"

"Very well, sir, very well, thanks to your tip!" his lordship said, firmly shaking Blysdale's hand. "The jockey was just the thing! Excellent man. Hired him on the spot."

"I am pleased to have been of service, sir," Blysdale said, turning at last to Lady Athena. She seemed to have been measuring his person, for her eyes came up just as his turned to her.

"Lady Athena," he said, taking her extended hand. "I hope to be honored by your hand in the course of the evening. Perhaps a cotillion?"

"Certainly, sir. However, I fear I must keep you waiting until after supper, for I am quite taken up until then. The supper dance, of course, is promised to Lord Foxham."

This was said without the faintest intimation of her feelings on the matter, and if she wished to make him believe that she thought her choice superior, she had failed. Blysdale chose merely to believe her coolness due to the fact that his lordship inspired no feeling in her whatsoever. He smiled, therefore, and thanked her, and went away to ensure his evening would be well-spent, dancing as busily and as unexceptionably as Lady Athena.

It was a simple matter to make himself agreeable to young ladies of rank, for they were all that had been invited, and very few were as unattainable as Lady Athena. Mr. Blysdale, therefore, was seen to be dancing with several girls socially equal to Lady Athena, and chatting amiably with their noble fathers or mothers between sets. The circumstance did much to irritate Lady Gidgeborough and, indeed, her daughter, for it made their holding him at arms' length all the more nonsensical. This suited Mr. Blysdale very well, for his keen eye perceived their irritation and encouraged him to be all the more agreeable to his companions.

During an interval, Blysdale found himself beside Lord Foxham, who watched the proceedings with all the self-important satisfaction of a man who has the world in his grasp.

"Lady Foxham is to be congratulated, sir," said Blysdale, indicating the rooms full to bursting. "A squeeze indeed."

"An excellent party," replied his lordship complacently. "My mother has outdone herself. But it is only to be expected of the Marchioness of Foxham. We must live up to our privilege, you know. It would not do to be seen as lacking in any respect, be it in our duty to Society or in those to the kingdom."

"To be sure," said Blysdale. "Privilege is a responsibility that weighs heavily upon us all. It is well that one cannot wear it too easily, for then one may forget just how heavy it is, and then where would the rest of the kingdom be?"

His lordship eyed Blysdale warily, but did not reply. Blysdale only smiled and said, "Your wife will have great expectations placed upon her."

"She will be equal to it, depend upon it," said Foxham comfortably. "Lady Athena has received an excellent education in all the feminine arts, and Lady Gidgeborough's guidance has been unimpeachable. She will make an excellent marchioness."

This forthright statement took Blysdale somewhat aback, for though he knew of Foxham's intentions, he had not expected such outright presumption. "Am I to wish you joy, sir?"

Foxham glanced at him from under his stately drooping lids. "If you wish, though there will be no announcement until there has been an offer. But I have no doubt of a favorable answer once I have made the declaration."

Blysdale gazed out over the crowd, spying Lady Athena's dark head with its silver ribbons sparkling. "But what do you wait for, sir? If you are so certain of success, there does not seem to be cause to wait."

"It would not do to be hasty, sir. I will not go after my future wife in a scrambling way. No, we must be seen to be in company several more times before it will be prudent for my intentions to be made public."

"And the lady is aware of your intentions, sir?"

"Oh, yes. It has been an understood thing for months now." His lordship's chest expanded on a satisfied breath. "When first I met Lady Athena this Season I was struck by her suitability as a marchioness, and intimated that day my interest to her honored mother. My overture was received most favorably, and I have been making steady progress since."

"And Lady Athena herself has been apprised?"

"Certainly. I can only assume that her mother would have given her notice of the honor that awaits her."

Blysdale smiled his congratulations. "Lady Athena is eminently suited for a high position, I fancy. She is clever and capable and has been about enough in the world to be at ease in any situation."

"She has the air of a Great Lady, which she is," replied Foxham. "She will grace my arm and my home with all the elegance and refinement I require."

Blysdale's smile did not waver for an instant, and his manner in no way betrayed the disgust he felt at this woefully inadequate—indeed, terribly inapt—praise of Lady Athena. After another few commonplaces, he took his leave, going into an antechamber where a window had been opened to let in the cool night air. Here he stood, allowing the heat in his veins to subside and the hate he felt for all pompous, self-interested, conceited men to dissipate into the darkness of the night. It was an exercise he had often been obliged to undertake, through all the years of his ascent through the ranks of the privileged, and it had always served him well. Anger was, as Lady Athena had once said, a paltry emotion, and useless to his cause.

The supper dance came, and Blysdale had the honor of partnering a rather beautiful young lady—the daughter of a viscount—who danced delightfully, and who seemed as little interested in him as he was in her. Their position in the set gave him an excellent view of Lady Athena and Foxham, and he had the felicity to witness her incomparable elegance and her absolute indifference toward his lordship. This carried him through an annoying half hour of nothing-sayings with his partner, who seemed terribly keen on catching the eye of every other gentleman in the room.

He was obliged to lead the girl into supper, but as she insisted they sit beside her friends, he was soon able to leave her to their care and make his way over to Lord Windon, who had found himself a taking little thing with large blue eyes and a fetching smile. Blysdale noted with a wry look that she seemed quite happy in his lordship's company, as well. Nevertheless, Windon availed himself of the first opportunity to take Blysdale aside and hiss a warning in his ear.

"Didn't mean it, my boy, assure you! All a hum!"

Blysdale's brow furrowed, and he glanced at the half-filled glass of champagne in his friend's hand. "Are you foxed, Windon? Not the thing—not at a ball! What will your charming companion think of you? Best have done, sir." And he made to take the glass away.

But Windon gripped his arm and said, "What do you take me for? It's my first glass! No, I mean the bet, at the club. Th'other night? Don't know how it happened, but your name was signed to it, my boy!"

"What do you mean, Windon?" said Blysdale slowly, gazing fixedly at him.

"We entered the bet in the books, Blysdale. Alvie and I—signed it! And somehow, don't know how—likely the port, dash it—your name was signed to it as well. Devil to pay if Gidgeborough saw it!"

"Of all the—did you strike it out?" inquired Blysdale, his voice furiously low.

"Directly I saw it!" whispered Windon, the picture of regret. "But there's no telling who saw it before I did. Didn't recollect it until this afternoon!"

Blysdale's eyes dropped closed, his nostrils flaring as he breathed deeply.

Windon gazed miserably at him. "Blysdale—I'm terribly sorry. Will do everything in my power to smooth it over—Alvie too—but— well there it is."

Alive to the precariousness of his situation, Blysdale nevertheless retained control of his emotions, merely thanking his friend and moving away through the crowded drawing room and into the ballroom. He did not have time to fully consider how he might avoid the inevitable repercussions of his friends' drunken mistake, for his dance with Lady Athena was about to begin. With the slightest tightening of his lips to betray his consternation, he made his way toward her, watching for any signs that the rumor might even now be circulating.

None met his discerning eye, and he relaxed, bowing with ineffable grace before her and leading her into the set, but his brain continued to revolve possibilities for retaining his footing come what may.

"You have been busy tonight, sir," she said.

"If you mean that I have been doing my duty by my hostess, in ensuring that her female guests are well-entertained, then I must agree with you, ma'am."

Her brow rose. "If you see dancing as merely the fulfillment of a duty, sir, I do not know how to be honored by your standing up with me."

"Ah, but the honor is all mine, ma'am, so you need not concern yourself about it."

"That is very much in the way of a set-down, sir. I begin to repent obliging you with a dance. Your manners are worse and worse."

"Forgive me, ma'am. It was my very bad idea of a joke. I assumed you must know that dancing with you could never be seen as a duty, but a privilege."

She lifted her chin, gazing forward. "Very well, that will do."

They were separated by a figure of the dance and when they came together again, he said, "The dowager is something wonderful by way of a hostess. One does not wonder that you are considered fit to fill her shoes."

She looked quickly up at him. "I should hope that my upbringing has fitted me for any feminine duties, in any house." Then she looked away. "But as the daughter of the Earl of Gidgeborough, I am certainly better fitted for a marchioness than anything else."

"Then you expect a declaration."

"It is ill-bred to expect any such thing."

"True. But the masses may expect it—indeed, there are rumors to the effect. I do not wish to distress your ladyship, only to warn you."

She gave a short little huff. "Rumors are two a penny in Town, sir. I wonder that you do not understand that. Thank you for your kind warning, but it was unnecessary. I never heed rumors."

"You are wise, ma'am. Rumors are beneath us all."

Again, the dance claimed their attention. Blysdale admired his partner's grace, and more than once was gratified by a lift of her eyes to his, and a slight smile or blush as she did so. She was warming to him at last, but it was perhaps too late, if fate did not smile upon him a little longer.

"Your friend Windon seems to have made a conquest," she said when they were again together. "Miss Stowe is a very good sort of girl, and quite pretty."

"He seemed quite taken with her. I believe she is only just out and very green. But a sweet girl."

He did not think he imagined the look of satisfaction that came into her countenance upon hearing this tepid praise of Windon's lovely companion, but he did not depend upon its weighing very much with her. He must take care to obviate any other obstacles to ensure a smooth path in his courtship from here until its favorable issue.

His only hope, as he could see it, was that his signature was not noticed by anyone intimately acquainted with Gidgeborough's set, so that when the existence of the bet became known, it would take longer to get around to him, and thence to his daughter. If he was very lucky, he would be accosted by the earl himself and given the opportunity to clear his own name before his lordship made the matter known to his family.

But now he must enjoy Lady Athena's gentle smiles and light converse and graceful company as he may. The dance ended too soon and his partner was claimed by another gentleman, and Blysdale stayed to dance another set. But when Lord Foxham led Lady Athena out a second time, Blysdale was obliged to quell his instinct to follow suit in the next set, and took leave of his hostess, for it was not the thing to try to outdo a gentleman at his own ball.

The walk home was helpful in clearing his head, and in light of the urgency of fixing Lady Athena's interest, he saw the folly in awaiting Gidgeborough's seeking for the truth about the rumor of that misbegotten bet. Blysdale must head off the rumor himself if he hoped to retain any footing in Gidgeborough's circle, for if Gidgeborough heard of it first from another party, his pride could very likely override any friendly feelings he cherished for Blysdale, thus complicating matters in convincing him of the truth. Even more to the point, if Lord Gidgeborough reported the rumor to his wife and daughter, their hard-won good opinion of him—such as it was—would be lost, no doubt, forever.

Chapter 17

ATHENA WAS BLISSFULLY unaware of the thundercloud hovering on her horizon. She had enjoyed her dance with Mr. Blysdale, so much so that she had experienced a moment of impatience when Lord Foxham had petitioned her for a second dance. But one look from her mama had brought her to reason; she had danced with his lordship, and if she had thought him ponderous and ordinary, none could know of it from her graceful unconcern.

The following morning, she and Lady Gidgeborough received both Lord Foxham and Mr. Blysdale among their callers, and an onlooker might have smiled to see how the two ladies' manners were exchanged with each visit. When Lord Foxham came to give his lofty review of the delights of the evening, Lady Gidgeborough was all smiles and agreement, while Lady Athena was her usual coolly civil self. Lord Foxham ended his visit in the satisfaction of having obtained Lady Athena's hand for the first two dances of Mrs.

Pattershaw's upcoming ball, the honor of which was canvassed a full fifteen minutes by her mother to the matron who came next to call.

But when Mr. Blysdale came some time later, he was escorted and left at the drawing room door by Lord Gidgeborough, a circumstance which put up Lady Gidgeborough's back. Upon Lady Athena's perceiving him, however, her pale cheeks held an attractive blush and her eyes, if not her lips, smiled upon her visitor, while Lady Gidgeborough could scarcely recall how to smile and vigorously cherished within her breast the promise of a marquess over this upstart for her daughter. So full was she of this ambition, and so annoyed at Mr. Blysdale's continued existence within her daughter's sphere, that when the gentleman rose to take his leave, she dismissed him promptly, going to the door to see him safely off the premises.

But her daughter's admirer was undaunted, and as he took Athena's hand to say goodbye, he asked if they might have another drive together in the park. Vain were the urgent looks of warning and disapprobation Lady Gidgeborough directed at her daughter, who was suddenly deaf and blind to her presence.

"I should be delighted, sir," was Athena's reply, in a tone which her mother considered far too complacent for her own comfort.

The door was hardly shut upon the gentleman when Lady Gidgeborough gave vent to her feelings. "What do you mean by encouraging him in this way, Athena? I declare, you blushed like a schoolgirl on his arrival! One could almost imagine you to be falling in love with him—but it cannot be so, while you retain the use of your reason."

"I behaved no differently to Mr. Blysdale than to any of our other visitors, Mama," said Athena, raising a conscious hand to her cheek. "I daresay the day is too warm for a fire. I became heated, that is all."

Her mama regarded her narrowly. "Perhaps. But you needn't have accepted Mr. Blysdale's invitation so readily. It was exceedingly presuming of him, and yet you declared yourself delighted! What must he be thinking? If Lord Foxham received half so much encouragement, he should send a notice to the papers tomorrow!"

"I beg your pardon, Mama, but you grossly exaggerate the case. It is unlike you to take a thing up so. Lord Foxham should never do anything so improper, nor would you wish him to."

"Certainly not," said Lady Gidgeborough. "But who is to say that upstart Mr. Blysdale will not do the very thing? He has not the marquess's exquisite sensibility."

This struck Athena as humorous, and she actually bit back a smile in her mother's presence. So shocked was she at this uncharacteristic response to an admonition from her mother that she was obliged to avert her face and hastily compose herself before replying.

"Mr. Blysdale's sensibility is not exquisite, precisely, but it is excessively well-bred—one might almost forget he is a tradesman's son. Indeed, many of our acquaintance do."

"Next you will say he is as acceptable as Lord Foxham!" said her mother with asperity.

"No, Mama, for he has no title and his birth is inferior, but for all that Mr. Blysdale is surprisingly good *ton*. That is why I accepted his invitation to drive out. It does me great credit to be seen in his company, for though he is what one could term a new creation, you must own his breeding is as impeccable as that of the finest gentlemen of our acquaintance. And I make bold to say that it far exceeds some."

This statement quite robbed Lady Gidgeborough of speech, and Athena, sensing that she may have overstepped an invisible and long-honored boundary, took the opportunity to excuse herself to dress for walking out, and quit the room.

She had engaged to accompany Iris on her errands, and walked with a footman to Hill Street, where Iris awaited her.

They had not gone twenty feet before Iris accosted her with, "You are looking positively pregnant, Athena."

Athena's long-suffering sigh caused Iris to blush fierily and to glance behind at the wooden-faced footman—whose eyes seemed far too twinkling for unconsciousness. She lowered her voice.

"I do not know how it is that my thoughts forever come out wrongly! Pardon me, Athena—you seem preoccupied. Will you tell me what it is about?"

"I do not know what you can mean, Iris."

"Good gracious, Athena! Cut line!" Iris made a frustrated noise and tried again. "That is, you might as well confide in me."

"If I had anything to confide, you may be assured that I should think twice before sharing it with you, Iris. There is not a person in the world with less circumspection."

"Now that is unjust," cried Iris. "I may think and speak improperly ninety times out of a hundred, but I am never guilty of betraying a confidence."

Athena shook her head, a tiny smile on her lips. "No, but you may be depended upon to say something horrid, even if it is mortifyingly acute."

Caught off-guard by this compliment, Iris paused before saying, "Well, if you have not become inured to my ways by now, then you must suffer through them. You need not beat about the bush any longer, Athena, for I know now just what is weighing upon your mind—or rather, who."

"Pray, do not speak so loud," hissed Athena, casting a subtle glance about them. They had reached Bond Street, and though the footman was a respectful distance away, the flagway was crowded with members of the *ton* who would pounce upon any overheard gossip in a flash.

Iris, following Athena's example, said, "You are right. I will speak lower. What do you have to say of Mr. Blysdale?"

Athena sighed again but only partly in annoyance, with the greater part being resignation. "As you must insist upon knowing my mind, Iris, I will admit him to be a gentleman. You were right, in that respect, Iris, and I was wrong. I allowed myself to be blinded by his ungenteel birth, and must beg your pardon."

"Well, I own I had not expected your coming so soon to a right way of thinking," said Iris frankly, "but I did not despair of it, for you are, in general, just. But you would do better to beg *his* pardon, Athena."

"I will not do so, however," said Athena, resuming her cool manner. "He cannot expect it. Indeed, I do not imagine that he has at all felt any pain—he is too impudent for that."

Iris cast her an impatient glance. "If he has not, then it is all to his credit and none to yours, Athena. Not all of us are as insensible as you."

Athena pressed her lips together and looked away. They came to the modiste's shop where Iris was to have some alterations made to some of her gowns, and Athena rather grandly advised her on the number and style of her furbelows. Iris was not deceived by her manner, nor was she affronted, merely allowing her friend the license her bruised pride wanted.

When they had done at the modiste's shop, they went on to the other shops, not touching on the subject of Mr. Blysdale until they turned their steps back toward Hill Street.

"When do you expect to see Mr. Blysdale again?" inquired Iris abruptly.

"We are to go driving in Hyde Park tomorrow."

Iris regarded Athena with satisfaction. "He has a fine pair, does not he? And he is a very tolerable whip."

"If I was uncertain before of how you had come to converse so easily with Mr. Blysdale," Athena said dryly, "I can no longer be in any doubt. He does have a fine pair and is a tolerable whip, but that is not why I allow him to drive me."

"I never imagined it was, nor could anyone who knows you."

Pursing her lips, Athena said succinctly, "He is very good *ton*."

"He always was, you know," remarked Iris. After a pause, she added, "I hope you will be civil to him, Athena."

"I am always civil, Iris."

"Then I hope you will be truthful."

Athena turned her calm gaze upon her friend. "You are in rare form today, Iris. First you accuse me of incivility, and then of deceit. What next will you find me guilty of, I wonder?"

"Obstinacy," said Iris simply. "I cannot conjecture what you hope to gain by this continued display of indifference."

"You are impossible," said Athena, hastening her steps in her perturbation.

But Iris kept pace with her. "You said you were blind, Athena. You know it is a weakness, and you must resist it. You must give him a chance, for that is your only hope, I am persuaded."

"My only hope for what, pray?"

"Your only hope for happiness."

Athena looked in astonished indignation at Iris, but her friend's steady, guileless gaze smote her to the heart and she dropped her gaze.

"I cannot pretend to be ignorant of your meaning, and while I am grateful to you for the real solicitude which produced these expectations, they are simply ridiculous—pardon me, Iris. I must speak plainly, to check your imaginings before they run away with you."

Iris gazed in marked disappointment at her friend, at last shaking her head and turning away. "I am no more in danger of being run away with than you are, Athena—more's the pity."

Without saying more, she continued up the street with Athena, not unclosing her lips again until she bade farewell to her friend at the steps to her house.

As she went on her way, Athena told herself that Iris had always been unreasonable and ill-judging, but she could not dispel her own distress at her friend's disapprobation. There was nothing for it, however, for even if Athena could feel something like attachment to so ineligible a man, she had pressed her mama as far as that lady could be pressed in the matter of Mr. Blysdale, and Lady Gidgeborough would never sanction a match between them.

Athena's manner on the morrow, therefore, was a mixture of reserve and condescension, and Mr. Blysdale instantly understood that he had lost ground. It was a disappointment that he bore with fortitude, however, for he reasoned that he could not have hoped for his steady progression of victories to continue indefinitely. It would be foolish to imagine that Lady Gidgeborough's influence, having lasted a lifetime and been responsible for the formation of her daughter's character, could be vanquished after only a few propitious meetings. She was a redoubtable woman, and as proud and unassailable as her daughter. Indeed, he could expect her disapprobation only to grow stronger as the lady fought furiously against what she perceived as an insidious threat to her daughter's triumphant future.

His manner, therefore, was punctiliously civil and supremely unconscious as he handed Lady Athena into the curricle. His converse was composed entirely of unexceptionable commonplaces as they set off toward the park, and he was assiduous in his courtesies to the acquaintance which they happened to meet.

After a time, he perceived her manner had softened somewhat, and he ventured to suggest they get down and walk. "It is such a warm day, ma'am, that I imagine you would be glad to get out of this sun. There has been so little rain of late that we may be certain your footwear will receive no hurt."

This practical civility had the desired effect; Lady Athena assented, and they were soon walking along one of the shaded paths that criss-crossed the park.

"It is a welcome relief in Town to escape to the verdure of the parks," he said. "While the Season offers countless delights, the constant bustle and noise can be wearing. But in the tranquility of nature, one may find refreshment."

"The parks are certainly of value to one's health, sir," said his companion coolly. "Though they are nothing to the country."

He glanced at her. "Do you prefer the country to Town, then, ma'am?"

"Oh, no," she said, but then somewhat hesitantly amended, "That is, they really cannot be compared—they are too dissimilar. One must come to Town to find the cream of Society and the best entertainments, but the country is undeniably desirable during the summer months."

"It is certainly cooler," remarked Blysdale, casting a significant glance at the hot sun. "But this is unseasonably hot weather, I think."

"Yes, undoubtedly."

"This is one of my favorite walks whatever the weather, however," he said.

She rather quickly said, "And mine." Upon meeting his eye, she colored slightly, averting her face and saying in a more moderate tone, "It reminds me of the Dower House at Kemmerton."

He regarded what he could see of her face—the pale cheek now tinged with color, the elegant sweep of the neck, the dusky curls escaping from beneath her fashionable bonnet. "You mentioned your partiality for the Dower House before, I think—in connection with lily of the valley."

He thought he heard her inhale sharply, and it was a long moment before she answered him. "Yes. There is a walk near the Dower House that is lined with lily of the valley in the spring. I have not seen it for some time."

"You also mentioned your grandmother."

Her look when she glanced at him was startled but warm. "Yes, my grandmother used to take me on walks all round her house—she lived at the Dower House until her death nine years ago."

"I suppose she imparted her love of lily of the valley to her granddaughter."

She huffed, a tiny sound, but pleased nonetheless. "She did."

He looked ahead to help mask the satisfaction that doubtless showed in his features. "I own I am curious to know more of your grandmother, but I dare not hope you will indulge me."

"I do not mind, sir, if you mean it."

"I assure you, I do. She sounds a most remarkable woman."

"She was," said Athena, then bit her lip against the emotion that welled up. Resuming her air of reserve, she said, "She was my father's mother, and an excellent woman. She was my model of the ideal—though not everyone regarded her as such. Her devotion to duty was sometimes misconstrued as either vanity or indulgence."

"Those are widely different traits to ascribe to the same actions."

She cast him a wry glance. "But they were assigned by widely different parties, I assure you, sir—one motivated by awe and the other by jealousy."

"Then the matter becomes clear," he said, reveling in her openness. "The world is unfortunately full of fools, from all walks of life. You, however, Lady Athena, are possessed of a more discerning mind."

"Indeed not, sir," she said, and a becoming pink suffused her cheek. "I was merely privileged to receive her most tender attentions and thus understood her completely. But I was one of a very few, it seems. Even my mother did not get on well with Grandmama. They were a constant source of vexation to each other, and by the time of my birth had come to a truce of sorts wherein they each agreed not to darken the other's door. That is how I came to associate my grandmother only with the Dower House."

"Were her other grandchildren so fortunate?"

"I was her only grandchild at Kemmerton—I have two male cousins, but they came only once per year to visit. They were not invited more."

"Being boys, they were unable to secure your grandmother's complete affection, I am persuaded," he said with a knowing smile.

"Grandmama was never overly fond of them, to be sure, but in her defense, they were quite horrid. Indeed, they still are."

His brows raised and he said, "Then I may justly hope never to meet them—or do I know them already?"

She shook her head. "I do not imagine you can have met either of them. If my cousin Paul, Lord Northam, has been in Yorkshire, I have never heard of it, and he despises London for its dirt and noise. And my cousin Robert does not venture from his hunting box in Leicestershire if he can help it."

"Then I am saved a most uncomfortable acquaintance, for I am inclined to trust in your excellent grandmama's judgment and could never treat them with civility, I fear."

"As well you may trust her," she said with a significant look. "As I said, she had just cause to dislike them. They called her an old crone whenever she was obliged to refuse them anything, which was often, for they imagined all the world to be theirs for the taking. They tormented her cat and pulled my hair, and invariably picked the lilies and plucked off all the bells, scattering them about, the horrid creatures. Grandmama was incensed by that especially, and began refusing their visits excepting only at Christmas."

"Well done, Grandmama," he said. "You can have had no occasion to repine in being her favorite grandchild."

"No, indeed. We had the most lovely times together, Grandmama and I."

She smiled fully then, laughing for a glorious moment, and he was transfixed by the wonderful change that came over her countenance. The graceful planes of her face were softened, the color in her cheeks pronounced, the deliciousness of her lips enhanced, and the depths of her lovely eyes glowed. With an effort, he ceased his staring and applied himself to hearing and discerning her words.

"We made flower bouquets and took long walks and had tea and cakes in the middle of the afternoon," she said, her gaze far away. "She dressed me up as though I were a doll, and had her maid do my hair like a woman's, and trusted me with the most beautiful jewelry to wear. To be sure, I have her to thank for my impeccable taste."

He chuckled but did not speak further, allowing her to savor the delight in the memories that had been stimulated by this favorite walk. She spoke more of her grandmother as they retraced their steps to the curricle, and Mr. Blysdale was inclined to believe his notion of taking that particular walk had been pure inspiration. The magic of it followed them home from the park, and he credited it with the particular warmth with which she parted from him, even pressing his hand as he bowed over hers.

He went away full of satisfaction in the outing. It had been unexpected, how well smiles and softness became Lady Athena, for he had imagined that her elegance and grace depended upon her coolness and majesty. How utterly mistaken he had been! She was even more perfect in joy, and her laughter, brief though it had been, was nectar to his soul. He resolved by the time he arrived at his own door that if—when—he won her, it would be the business of his life to make her smile and laugh and look at him with those glowing eyes as often as possible.

Chapter 18

ATHENA WALKED THROUGH the following morning as though in a dream. She could not recall having been so happy before, except perhaps when she was with her grandmother at the Dower House at Kemmerton. She reasoned that it was the memory of those days, and the joy of sharing it with an appreciative audience, that had produced her present pleasure, but she knew that it was only half true. The audience, she could not deny, had much to do with it.

Her walk with Mr. Blysdale had been more delightful than it had had any right to be, for he could not be anything to her—could not hold a place in her future higher than a mere acquaintance, and certainly could not hold a place in her heart. Her future lay with the Marquess of Foxham, and once that bond was made, whatever she felt for Mr. Blysdale must give way, or be buried in oblivion.

But what was it she felt for Mr. Blysdale, precisely? Gratitude, certainly, for having prompted her to revive her happiest memories—to call them up from the place they had been consigned to years ago at her mama's insistence. She had never comprehended the loss those memories had been to her until now, and she must be grateful to the man who had restored them to her.

Gratitude, however, was too tame an appellation for what now stirred so powerfully in her breast. It was warmth and comfort and giddy delight, esteem and respect and hopeful longing—all emotions with which she had too little experience to order them reasonably. She had a strong suspicion that romantic persons, like her newly-betrothed friend Lenora, would call this jumble of sensations "love," but she hoped she would not so far demean herself as to believe that. Love was a commonplace emotion, fit only for the silly or the vulgar. The daughter of an earl would not stoop to feeling so improperly.

This conviction did not prevent her from spending the morning in unusually buoyant spirits, every moment in expectation of the arrival of Mr. Blysdale and his delightful society. Though this meant only that she exuded a gentle aura of contentment as she went about her usual tasks, more than once did Lady Gidgeborough comment on her lighthearted manner. Any attempts to depress her spirits, however, either by her ladyship or by Athena herself, were in vain. She was as unassailable in joy as she had hitherto been in indifference.

When her mama, exasperated by what she deemed unseemly cheerfulness, sent her from the Crimson Saloon to inquire something of the housekeeper, Athena went willingly, for she was as eager to remove from her mama's damping presence as her mama was eager to be rid of her. As she passed the servant's hall, however, she was stopped short, for she heard voices, and Mr. Blysdale's name caught her attention.

"It were a bet, alright, set down in the book, and he signed it, 'Jonathan Blysdale,' for all the world to see!" said John, the footman's, voice.

"I never! And he seemed so much the gentleman," said a voice that Athena thought belonged to Sarah, the upstairs maid. "I was happy to tell him little things about her, for I only thought he was sweet on her. Just goes to show you, you can't trust them nobs—they'll sweet-talk you right out of your shoes!"

"He give me a shilling every time he come!" agreed the man. "And that secretary of his give me a guinea to tell him where she went each day for a week. Thought nothing of it, until the bet, then I thinks plenty! Then I thinks, he's a cheat and a scoundrel, leading her on just to win a bet."

Athena could stand no more. She came round the corner and into the servants' hall, turning her most regal stare upon John and Sarah, now quaking in their shoes before her.

"Of what are you speaking?"

Sarah, eyes wide, edged behind John, whose impressive height and livery gave him fewer options of escape. Stammering, he said, "B-begging your pardon, my lady, w-we wasn't—that is, it's only gossip, my lady."

Her basilisk stare brooked no excuse, however, and he was forced to collect himself and answer her. "It were Mr. Blysdale, my lady, entered a bet in the book at Brooks's with two other gentlemen, that weren't very honorable, my lady."

"The bet, or the gentlemen?" inquired Athena tightly.

"The bet, my lady, to be sure! Though no gentleman ought to have—leastwise not one who was wishful of making himself agreeable—" He swallowed, shifting on his feet. "It were—the bet, that is—not quite complimentary to—to a lady."

A horrible, cold sensation had settled in Athena's chest. "What lady, John?"

His face went white and he swallowed again. "You, my lady."

"And what was the bet, exactly?"

"That he—that Mr. Blysdale—would beat Lord Foxham in winning your hand, my lady," he whispered.

Athena's throat constricted. "Where had you this information, John?" she asked quietly, the feeling of cold threatening to sweep over her.

"His lordship's valet had it from the bootmaker, who had it from Lord Galveston's valet, my lady."

Even the vulgarity of the chain of gossip could not prevent the premonition of disaster from coming to fruition, and she was plunged into a benumbed state that entirely destroyed her former good spirits. Only her years of self-command held her together enough to recollect the other distressing but important intelligence they had let fall.

"What is this about bribery, John? Did Mr. Blysdale purchase information about me from you?"

The footman looked about to faint. "I'm terrible sorry, my lady! I thought it was harmless! I thought he fancied you, truly, and wanted to know where you were so he could meet you. I'd never have done it if I'd known he was such a scoundrel!"

"The damage is done, John." She turned in icy dignity to the maid. "And you, Sarah? What did he want from you?"

Sarah wrung her hands, tears streaming down her face. "Oh, my lady, it was such little things—what flowers you liked and what color gown you was to wear, even if you liked animals and children—I thought he only wished to please you!" She ended on a sob, covering her face with her hands.

Athena was silent, the void in her chest gaping and frigid. These revelations ought to have prostrated her but she was Lady Athena Dibbington, and would not succumb to the vapors. She did, however, suddenly understand Iris's frequent longing to become invisible and to sink into the floor, which seemed an eminently suitable course to her feelings at present. Indeed, she felt blank to the point of numbness.

"What you have done is grounds for dismissal," she heard herself say. "You will pack your bags and be gone by dinner time. But as you were deceived by a gentleman—a very plausible gentleman—and your conduct hitherto has been unimpeachable, I shall not send you away without a character. I shall instruct Mrs. Beamish to write you both good recommendations."

Their thanks were as heartfelt as their misery could allow, and they scurried from the servants' hall, leaving their mistress standing motionless and silent, her breath shallow and her face pale. After many minutes, she turned and quit the room, her errand to the housekeeper forgotten. Ascending the stairs in her usual dignified manner, she went to her bedchamber, there to sit at her dressing table in morbid contemplation of this horribly unforeseen turn of events.

It was some time before her mind could conjure anything beyond the vision of Mr. Blysdale wearing the smile and the look that struck such joy into her heart, and a sense of disbelief that it all had been an act. The more she pondered it, however, the more his smile took on a sinister aspect, as did his actions. He had been too composed, too serene in his responses to Lady Gidgeborough's snubs, and to Athena's slights, which now spoke not excellent breeding but cold calculation. His determined pursuit now seemed motivated not by fierce admiration but by a mercenary spirit, with a view to conse-quence and self-gratulation.

She wondered that she had been so blind—that her blindness had not been that of improper pride, as she had convinced herself, but that of girlish romance—that in striving to right the one she had only fallen victim to the other. But this was the consequence of falling in love—for now that the circumstances had been revealed, she could append such a vulgar term to what she had felt for Mr. Blysdale. Love was only blindness, and led only to degradation, mortification, and pain.

It was only a step from pain to anger, and she allowed the white heat of it to purge her soul of any remaining tenderness for Mr. Blysdale before subsiding into a simmering tightness in her belly. It left her feeling exhausted and hopeless, but she only was to blame. Her father had introduced Mr. Blysdale into their circle, but Athena had chosen to accept his society and had at last opened her heart to him. Her mother had warned her a thousand times against entertaining Mr. Blysdale's ilk, but she had not listened, and had followed him down the path to her present state of pitiful weakness.

Providence alone had saved her from her ruinous course, for she could not but believe she might have gone so far as to consider him an eligible suitor after all. Athena was of half a mind to call back Sarah and John and reinstate them in gratitude for their having removed the scales from her eyes. But she concluded that this would be folly, and only indulging in the kind of weakness that had caused her present embarrassment. They must live with the consequences of their actions, just as she must. And the sooner she gave Mr. Blysdale his *congé*, the better.

She had not long to wait, for within the hour a footman—not John—came with the tidings that Mr. Blysdale awaited her in the drawing room. She thanked him and turned to the mirror, requiring only a moment to compose herself and to assume the film of civil hauteur that had inspired the sobriquet Ice Maiden.

When she appeared in the drawing room, he came to her from his station at the mantelpiece, smiling and bowing in his usual manner.

"Good day, Lady Athena. Allow me to say how well you look. I trust you were not fatigued by our drive yesterday."

"Oh, no, sir," she said coolly, not extending her hand to him. "I was not fatigued by our drive."

She made no move to sit, and he regarded her, turning the signet ring on his finger. "Is something the matter, ma'am? You seem a little pale. Will you sit? I might get you some wine."

"No, thank you, sir. I am perfectly well, but you seem to be all wrong. First, you say how well I look, and then you say I am pale. Perhaps you are not quite right yourself."

His brow furrowed as he tried another smile. "Perhaps I am not, ma'am. I do seem to be a trifle slow this morning." When she did not respond to this sally, he said with real concern, "Have I done something to vex you?"

"Nothing you do could vex me, sir, for such emotion is beneath me," she said with supreme indifference. "It seems, however, sir, that nothing is beneath you."

"Pray, what do you mean? What have you heard?" he asked, fully alert.

"If there is anything for me to hear, then you must know it already, having been the instigator. Your own conscience must tell you what it is that I mean."

"Is it the bet? Lady Athena, did your father not speak to you?"

"I have not seen my father today, but I do not know what he has to say to anything."

He bit his lips, an expression of extreme annoyance crossing his features. "I explained the matter to him, and to his complete satisfaction, three days ago. He assured me that he understood the supreme importance of—He has not mentioned it to you? Then I do not—I beg your pardon—Lady Athena, please bear with my anxiety—where did you hear of it?"

"Through the regular channels: the valet to the bootmaker to the valet to the footman to the maid. It is the only proper way to hear vulgar gossip, after all."

He swore under his breath, again begging her pardon and running an agitated hand through his hair. "I meant to prevent any such unpleasantness by bringing the matter directly to your father. Lord Gidgeborough said he would see to it that it was not spread about, and that you and your mother knew nothing of it, or that if you did hear, he would disabuse you of any wrong notions."

"Perhaps he did not see anything wrong in the notions that could arise from the news of a horrid bet made by a gentleman aspiring to the hand of a lady far above his station, that he would triumph against the odds—very favorable ones, too, I do not doubt—over a nobleman of far greater worth and character." Her voice had risen, and she was irritated to have lost some of her self-command.

In a calm but urgent tone, he said, "It is not what it seems, Lady Athena, I assure you. I beg your indulgence in hearing what I have to say."

"I cannot imagine what good it would do, sir," she said stiffly.

"Nevertheless, Lady Athena," he insisted, "I beg you will do me the goodness to hear me out."

"Very well, sir, but do not be all day." She sat rigidly on the edge of a chair and regarded him coldly.

He seated himself on the nearest chair, as far forward as he could without falling, and bent closer still, as though needing to be near her for this confession. She felt a tug of pity in her heart at the anxiety in his eyes, but she sternly repressed it, sitting farther back in her chair.

"It was all a—an ill-judged prank by my friends—Alverton and Windon. We were at cards at Brooks's and they became—they became too jovial and twitted me on my pursuit of you. Pray, do not think too ill of them, for they were—not themselves."

Athena turned her penetrating gaze upon him. "Pray cease this ridiculous skirting about the truth. They were drunk. Simply call it what it was."

He sighed. "Very well. They were drunk, and in this regrettable state took it into their heads to propose a bet regarding my chances with you against Lord Foxham. I refused to take the bet, nor even to listen to them, and the party broke up soon thereafter. However, Windon and Alverton stayed on, apparently becoming—even more drunk, and crowned their shameful conduct by entering in the book the very bet they had earlier discussed, and signing my name to it for good measure. I knew nothing of it until the night of Lady Foxham's ball, where Windon confessed and told me he had stricken out my name as soon as he recollected the business. But it had been several hours, during which time any number of gentlemen could have viewed the terms of the bet and noised them about."

She had remained stonily silent during this rehearsal, and he had watched her intently during the whole. When still she did not speak, he said, "I would not have had you hear of it for the world, Lady Athena. Gentlemen—men of any class—can be boors, and are not fit to grace the company of women."

"It is very true," she said at last, very quietly and very angrily.

It all sounded infinitely plausible, and she thought that she could perhaps be brought to believe him—she had her father and Windon or Alverton to turn to for corroboration, to be sure. Still, she paused a long while, her mind racing between flutterings of hope and indignation at the affront that, though not precisely from him after all, had still been offered and could still give her pain for days or weeks to come. The ignominy of having her name bandied about in the clubs was odious, and such notoriety was what she had lived to avoid all her adult life.

There was still the matter of the bribery, also, which she did not imagine could be so easily justified. It was one thing to have been merely associated with shameful conduct, but the servants had received the bribes from his and his secretary's hands—this could not be a drunken mistake.

Giving herself a mental shake, therefore, she said, still coldly, "I do not say that I am fully satisfied regarding this matter, but we will let it pass. There is something else of moment that I wish to discuss with you. It has come to my attention that you bribed my servants to give you information about my private concerns. What do you have to say in your defense?"

He sat up, his mouth open in a silent gasp, and regarded her in grieved astonishment. "That was weeks ago. I had forgotten—Lady Athena, I did not—"

"Did you bribe my servants?" she cut in, gazing frostily at him.

He averted his eyes, staring horrified into the middle distance. "I did," he said quietly. "At first, when you refused to acknowledge me, I did not know what else to do—so I bribed your servants to find a way to make myself acceptable to you." He looked up again, his gaze resolute. "It was wrong, and I am mortified at my own insensibility, my own shamefulness."

Her eyes pricked as she inquired flatly, "Is that how you knew about the lily of the valley? And that walk in Hyde Park?"

"No! No, I swear on my honor, it is not!" He started off his chair in his agitation, coming to kneel before her. "I had ceased that long before—You, Lady Athena, you told me about those things."

It was too much for her to bear—the crushing disappointment, the insistent hope, the degradation, the yearning, the betrayal. She stood abruptly, walking to the door.

"Get up, sir, and cease these protestations. They demean us both, and I will hear them no longer. I wish you good day, and request you never to call here again."

With that, she swept out of the room, ascending to her bedchamber without glancing back, while her ears strained to hear the sound of the door closing on his departure.

Chapter 19

Athena prepared with detached precision for Mrs. Patter-shaw's ball that evening, sternly suppressing the desire to curl up on her bed and feel sorry for herself the rest of her life. She managed to present a lovely appearance in her pale green satin gown with a white lace overskirt, despite the slight redness about her eyes from unshed tears and the furrow between them brought on by a persistent headache. Lady Gidgeborough remarked on the furrow, recommending she take steps to remove it, but Athena only gazed out the carriage window, not trusting herself to speak.

No looks or whispers greeted her entrance into the ballroom, so she could only assume her father had succeeded in stifling the rumors, but there was a hardness in her eyes and a biting edge to her comments which made her companions blink. Nonetheless, her usual admirers clustered about her, and she could almost forget the one who was conspicuously absent—whose easy elegance and fine figure compared so favorably to that of every other man in the room. With each flattering interchange, she could scarcely recall how the missing gentleman's eyes danced when he made her smile, or the resolution in his countenance when he spoke of his father, or the safety she had felt when he had rescued her from the Duke.

When Lord Foxham came to claim her for the first set, she received the first blow to her fragile sangfroid, for never before had he appeared so inferior to her idea of masculine perfection. The portliness of his frame, held in by the ubiquitous corset, struck her now as the obvious result of a life of indolence, and the assurance with which he led her onto the floor was an affront to her worth as an individual. A glance from Lady Gidgeborough luckily saved her from being overpowered once more by useless emotion, and she mercilessly repressed any comparison of her companion to an unnamable gentleman, who now more than ever had no business being in her thoughts.

The set was a trial to her, his lordship's unusual enthusiasm contributing to both the wilting of his shirtpoints and the irritation of Athena's nerves. When he brought her again to her mother and went away, she breathed a sigh of relief at the retreat of the creaking corset that had seemed to scratch away at her composure for the duration of the two dances. Her mother turned an inquiring gaze upon her, but Athena merely took out her fan and waved it before herself.

"It is insufferably hot, is not it, Mama?"

"It will only become more so, my love, as the ball goes on. You must take care to spare yourself now, for Lord Foxham may wish to stand up with you again, and you will not wish to disappoint him."

"No, Mama," she said, her tone impassive.

Athena was never without a partner for the rest of the evening, her rather more than usually intimidating air not decreasing her allure. There were plenty of ambitious persons present, whose sons had long wished to ally themselves with a family as powerful as that of the house of Dibbington, and they were not of the sort to allow a little superiority to put them off. Much to her satisfaction—and Lord Foxham's disappointment—Athena was promised for the supper dance to young Mr. Pattershaw, the scion of the house whose future inheritance included a large estate in Ireland and several smaller ones scattered about Scotland and northern England. He was a fine young man with long limbs and laughing eyes, whose interesting responses to her questions regarding his Yorkshire estate put them both at ease and whiled away the supper hour quite pleasantly.

After supper, however, Lord Foxham renewed his application for her hand, and with Lady Gidgeborough's eagle eye upon her, Athena accepted with as good a grace as she could muster. But by the end of the first dance, she had become so irritated by his creaking, his dancing, his consequence, and his smug look that she pleaded fatigue and begged to sit the second dance out. He instantly led her to a seat, going to procure her a glass of lemonade, which he brought back in very good time to catch her gazing out at the dancers with an almost bleak expression.

"Are you quite well, Lady Athena?" he inquired. "You look peaked. There is nothing catching, I trust."

She turned, taking the lemonade from him and returning her gaze to the crowded dance floor. "I am very well, I thank you, sir. It is only that I have never before participated in so energetic a reel."

"I am celebrated for my performance in the reel, ma'am," he said proudly, "and am sensible of the grace with which you followed me in every figure. You are, if I may say it, a credit to my own excellent style."

"The reel does generally require a level of energy above the usual country dance," she said with dangerous calm, "but I am of the opinion that it is possible to achieve an energy which renders the dance positively vulgar."

He hesitated in astonishment at her tone, then said a trifle stiffly, "I beg a thousand pardons, ma'am. As it is my wish to recommend myself to you by any means possible, I could never desire to offend your sensibilities, in this or in any other matter."

Biting back a rather too pointed retort regarding commendable but unattainable goals—which even in her present irritation of spirits she knew to be utterly injudicious—she merely thanked his lordship and did not look at him.

His discomfiture was palpable. "Are you quite certain you are not ill? Perhaps I should find Lady Gidgeborough, and she will decide if you are quite well."

"I assure you sir," said Athena tartly, "I am perfectly able to discern the state of my own health. I am quite well, and simply do not wish to dance so energetically. It is not enjoyable to exert oneself beyond one's wishes, and to be forced to view the excessive exertions of one's partner as well. I do not know how long I shall require to recover."

"I believe I comprehend you perfectly, madam," he said more stiffly. "You are not in spirits and wish to be left alone. I shall remove my irksome presence from you without delay. Good evening, Lady Athena."

When Lady Gidgeborough appeared five minutes later, she found her daughter in such a state of nerves as to be alarming, and her suggestion that they take their leave of Mrs. Pattershaw was met with an instant—if slightly tremulous—acquiescence. Having seen Lord Foxham himself leave not three minutes earlier, Lady Gidgeborough experienced a distressing premonition of doom and followed her daughter from the house with an expression of deep discontent.

The following morning, Athena's numerous callers did not include the Marquess of Foxham, and Lady Gidgeborough's impatience mounted through the seemingly interminable two hours until they saw the last caller out.

Instantly turning to her daughter, she inquired acidly, "And to what do you attribute this unpropitious occurrence, Athena? Ten gentlemen callers and not one of them Lord Foxham. I declare! What could have possessed you to anger him last night—for I know that is what has happened."

"His lordship's proprietary air was not to my taste, madam."

Her mother stared at her in horrified disbelief. "His proprietary— do you mean that he has declared himself, Athena? Can it be that you have refused him?"

The tone of alarm with which this inquiry was uttered caused Athena to wince, but she said, "No, Mama. He has not spoken, nor would he without your knowledge. It is merely that his attentions were too pointed—that he treated me with—" She pressed a hand to her head. "Forgive me, Mama. Perhaps I have behaved wrongly, or have been unjust. I have been suffering from the headache since last evening and it may have affected my judgment."

"Undoubtedly, it might!" cried her mother, leaping up from the sofa and taking a furious turn about the room. "That a mere headache might have ruined your chances at a marquess! It is not to be believed! It is not to be borne!"

She continued her feverish pacing but with lips tightly shut and her eyes insistently averted from her vexatious child. After several minutes, she had calmed enough to regain her customary composure and she sat down again, sternly regarding Athena, who sat rigidly, eyes closed.

"Well you might close your eyes upon the day, Athena. How you have damaged your reputation, your expectations—and how you have disappointed mine! This is what comes of lowering yourself— this is what comes of welcoming the society of persons beneath you! How strenuously I discouraged your acknowledging Mr. Blysdale, but you would not listen. You would demean yourself—blind, obstinate, provoking girl! This is how I am repaid for my tireless instruction and unswerving example! You have spurned the unexceptionable match that I have so carefully planned and worked and sacrificed for these ten years! A marquess! Oh! I can hardly bear to look at you."

Lady Gidgeborough hid her eyes behind a trembling hand and Athena, licking her dry lips, said in a deceptively steady tone, "My dear Mama, it is not so bad as that, I am persuaded. I have indeed demeaned myself, as you warned me I would, in accepting the society of Mr. Blysdale, but that is at an end. My eyes have at last been opened to his vulgarity, his perfidy, and his utter ineligibility as a companion. I shall never again refer to him even as a gentleman. But as none of my acquaintance has been in the least affronted by my association with him, I cannot agree that my reputation has been damaged in that respect.

"As to Lord Foxham, there has been a breach, but it is not irreparable. I was in low spirits and may have said something to offend him, but he behaved very gentlemanly and left me to myself. I owe him an apology, which I will make at the earliest opportunity, and if you will be so good as to write to invite him to call, it will be done directly. Once assured of my regret, I do not believe he will stoop to bearing me ill will, but shall forget it all and very soon return to paying me his usual attentions. Do not despair, Mama, I beg you."

This speech did much to soothe Lady Gidgeborough's lacerated feelings, and it was not many minutes longer before she was able to take a more optimistic view of the situation.

"Indeed, my dear, I believe you are right, and we can hope for a happier issue than I at first feared. It greatly relieves my mind that Mr. Blysdale is no longer admitted to your acquaintance—that he has proved unprincipled and dishonorable is only to be expected of one of his class. Bad blood will out, and it certainly has in his case. But his lordship must not be neglected longer. I shall write to him directly, and I trust we may expect his visit presently."

After she had gone, Athena stayed a few minutes more to compose herself and to adjust to the new course to which she had committed herself. That she must regain her footing with Lord Foxham was unquestionable; that she would find what followed to be distasteful was indubitable. She still was plagued by visions of Mr. Blysdale's various charms, but a mental review of his faults helped to cast him in a less favorable light, and she was soon in a fair way to steeling herself against him entirely.

A change of scene was necessary, however, as was a confederate in whom she could confide her disappointment, and going upstairs to change into walking dress, she summoned a footman to follow her and bent her steps toward Hill Street and the Slougham residence.

Iris, meanwhile, had been in something of a taking, wondering what had become of Mr. Tenby and why he stayed away. She had been on the point of adopting a desperate measure involving spying and creeping about and perhaps even fainting into his arms—all of which she knew her mother would strongly disapprove—but she had been forestalled by his sudden appearance in her drawing room.

After a long moment staring at him in mingled disbelief and delight, Iris jumped up and went to him, crying, "I declare, Mr. Tenby, I thought you had washed your hands of me! How glad I am to see you!"

This welcome could only strike him with its artlessness, and he took her outstretched hands in his. "And I you, Miss Slougham. Pray, forgive my long absence. I have been busy of late," he finished rather lamely.

"Tell me what you have been doing, sir," she said, pulling him with her to the sofa.

Here, her mother, who had been visiting with a friend nearer the fire, interposed. "Iris, you must not pull our visitor about and make demands. Pardon her, sir, I beg. She is in high spirits, merely."

Iris colored, but Mr. Tenby nodded to Mrs. Slougham and said, "I do not mind it, ma'am. A warm welcome must always be agreeable to me."

Mrs. Slougham seemed satisfied, and with a significant look to Iris, returned to her conversation.

Iris lowered her voice and said, "Thank you, sir. You are unerringly kind to me. But I shouldn't pull you about, for I don't know but that you had rather stay ten feet away from me!"

"I can assure you I do not wish for that, Miss Slougham," he said, pressing her hand which was still clasping his own.

She blushed again, but with pleasure, and released his hands, tucking hers in her lap. "Now, what shall we talk about, sir? Have you been anywhere nice? To Newmarket? Or the theater?"

Instantly, she regretted her eagerness, and wished that she could cut out her own tongue. His demeanor shifted from pleasure to supreme discomfort, and his gaze darted toward the door.

Seizing her courage, she said in a rush, "We saw you there—Mr. Blysdale and I—but you did not stay long enough for us to speak to you. Were you unwell? Blysdale said he had invited you to be of our party, but that you had a prior engagement."

He shook his head, not looking at her. "I thought I had—that is, I did not want—"

He trailed off and she said quickly, "You were greatly missed. Athena did not come either, and Mr. Blysdale and I were obliged to make what shifts we could, for the others were quite paired off. It was so disagreeable that we left them to themselves and took the air in the corridor. Lovers are, of all things, the most nauseating of companions—when one is not of their number."

"I cannot agree more," he said, at last raising his eyes to hers. "Miss Slougham, I—"

At that moment, the butler announced Mr. Blysdale, who came in with less than his usual ease. He greeted Mrs. Slougham first, then went to Mr. Tenby, saying, "Good morning, sir. I trust that you had my note?"

Mr. Tenby looked strangely at him. "No, sir."

"Then you would do well to inquire of the footman—tall dark-haired fellow with brown eyes?" Blysdale smiled, but it was rather weak. "You may find the note instructive."

"Thank you, sir," said Tenby, somewhat dubiously.

Blysdale sat down and Iris instantly bent toward him to whisper, "You look horrid! What has happened?"

"I fear I am *de trop*, ma'am, and must take my leave presently," he replied quietly.

"No!" said Iris, then with a glance at Tenby, she added in a low tone, "When he has gone you may speak freely. You will not go away until I am satisfied, sir."

Mr. Tenby stirred. "Miss Slougham, I came to take my leave of you. I am removing to my estate tomorrow. The Season is all but finished, and there is much to be done there."

"Oh, that is too bad," Iris said in consternation. "It cannot wait?"

But the stiffness of his countenance convinced her that she had lost what little ground she had recovered, and she lowered her eyes. "If you have business at home, then of course you must go. There is nothing to keep you here once the Season has done, I suppose."

His lips tightened. "No, there is not. I wish you well, ma'am, and trust that you will be most pleasantly occupied in the coming months."

Hurt that she did not warrant even a regretful look, she could think of nothing more to do than to shake his hand, saying, "Yes, well, I hope that you will too. I could hope as well that you would think of me, but I do not suppose that to be reasonable."

"Iris!" hissed her mother from across the room.

Iris flicked a glance to her mother and then at Mr. Tenby, then down at the floor. "Goodbye, sir."

He seemed about to say something, but with a look at Mr. Blysdale, he merely said goodbye, quitting the room in a rush. Iris, blinking, sat dazedly upon the sofa.

Mr. Blysdale looked after Mr. Tenby, his face a study in frustration. "Miss Slougham," he said, "I have made a botch of things, and I do not know how to tell you how sorry I am. I can only pray that Tenby's fool of a footman has not misplaced my note to him."

"What note?" inquired Iris. "What footman? What are you saying, Blysdale? Is this why you look so terrible?"

He closed his eyes and shook his head. "No, ma'am. That is another matter entirely, but it is just as much of a muddle as the other." He sank onto the sofa as he spoke. "I own I am quite at a loss."

"Good heaven," Iris said, her eyes searching his face. Perceiving the matter to be serious, she suddenly announced, "Mama, I am walking out with Mr. Blysdale. I won't be an hour."

She took Blysdale's arm and pulled him onto his feet and out the door. "I have never seen you at a loss, sir. You had better tell me the whole."

He shook his head. "I have been a fool, Miss Slougham, that is the long and short of it."

Appropriating the downstairs maid to accompany them, they came out onto the front steps and descended together, turning toward the Green Park.

"It is only what my friends warned me would happen," he continued. "My abominable pride has landed me in a pit of my own digging, and I can as yet see no way out." He stopped abruptly, his brow furrowed and his eyes pained. "My glass house is taking a beating, Miss Slougham, and I do not know if it will stand."

This pronouncement was as much enlightenment as he was to give her, for she just then perceived Athena coming toward them, her own face shadowed in consternation. Athena did not look up from the ground until she came up with them, and then her eyes widened first with shock, then with hurt, then with anger.

Iris watched the shift of emotions in her friend's eyes with fascinated horror. "Good heaven, Athena! You look dreadful!"

Athena's gaze snapped to Iris. "Thank you, Iris. You, on the other hand, look excessively comfortable. How strange that we should meet in this way, when I was looking for a friend."

Iris blinked. "Well, you have found two. And where else would you find me—this is where I live. Will not you walk with us?"

"No," said Athena, avoiding Mr. Blysdale's strained gaze. "No, Iris, I am going to—somewhere. I will not keep you. Good day."

But Mr. Blysdale stepped in her way. "Though I do not like to contradict you, Lady Athena, I am certain you wish to speak to Miss Slougham and I am in the way. Pray, do not mind me—you never have, you know—I shall take myself off." With a last searching look, he tipped his hat. "I am, as always, your servant, Lady Athena. Good day, Miss Slougham."

Iris stared after his retreating figure in open amazement, then turned to Athena, who bristled with irritation.

"Good heaven," Iris said for the third time, "what have you done now, Athena?"

Chapter 20

WHEN ATHENA ONLY glared after Mr. Blysdale's back with eyes suspiciously bright, Iris thought it wise to usher her into the house and take her up to her bedchamber. After shooing out the maid, she drew Athena to the bed and sat her down, taking her hand.

"Now what has happened, Athena? I know that is why you have come—to pour out your troubles."

"I have no troubles," said Athena, her voice rasping. She cleared her throat and lifted her chin. "That is, I have estranged myself from Lord Foxham, but that is of no consequence—"

"Indeed not!" cried Iris. "I only regret that your mama will be furious to relinquish her aspirations."

"Iris, do not be vulgar," said Athena in a restrained tone. "Lord Foxham's estrangement was a mistake—a lapse—that will soon be rectified."

"That is all well and good for Lady Gidgeborough's feelings, but what of yours, Athena?"

Athena glanced away. "I have the highest regard for Lord Foxham, and wish greatly for a reconciliation."

"I do not care about your regard for Foxham, Athena," said Iris impatiently, "and nor do you. What of your regard for Blysdale?"

Athena stood and walked in some agitation to the dressing table, picking up a hand mirror there and putting it down again. "What regard? Mr. Blysdale is nothing to me, and never was."

"Nonsense!" declared Iris, glaring at her. "You cannot hope to tip me the double, Athena, and so you shall learn. If you were not in love with him, then I am a spotted ape. What has happened?"

Athena shook her head, walking to the window. "You have built up in your mind a romantic illusion, merely, Iris. Mr. Blysdale imposed upon me, and I naturally would not stand for it. He is no longer welcome in my circle."

Iris threw up her hands. "If ever there was a ninnyhammer, it is you, Athena. Inside that fortress of impenetrable calm, you are a wreck of a woman—I know it! I have not known you for two decades and more for nothing. Now tell me in plain words what has happened between you and Mr. Blysdale to break your heart."

At the window, Athena gave a huff that sounded rather like a sob. "Since when have I a heart to break, Iris? I, the Ice Maiden, the Goddess of Wisdom, the Unassailable Citadel. I have never required a heart to realize my mama's wishes. Birth and breeding and attainments, grace and elegance and beauty are all that are required to make a brilliant match, and to succeed to the heights that she, herself, failed to reach." Her tone became more and more bitter as she continued, "I went on very well without a heart, Iris, until Mr. Blysdale precipitated himself into my sphere and overthrew all that I knew of the world. He has ruined me, and I will never forgive him for it!"

At this, she began to shake, and it was a moment before Iris perceived that she—that the Lady Athena Dibbington—was weeping. Overcoming her utter shock, Iris jumped up and went to her, wrapping her arms around her and holding her until her stiffness dissolved and she subsided onto her shoulder. Iris rubbed her back and murmured to her as Athena wept long and bitterly, until at last the sobs dwindled into sniffs, and then all was quiet.

She remained limply in Iris's embrace for a few more minutes before taking a deep breath and lifting her head, pushing herself away. "Well, I shall never do that again."

"I do not know why not," said Iris. "I find that a good cry is always very refreshing, and helps one to think more clearly."

"It is a sign of weakness in a female," said Athena.

"Pooh! That is a horrid fiction proliferated by prejudiced persons who have never indulged in a bout of tears," said Iris stoutly. "Only dare to tell me you do not feel ten times the better for it!"

Athena eyed her in annoyance, but then said, "Very well, I do. But I stand by it that I will never do it again."

"If we can get Blysdale back, then I can guarantee you will never want to do it again."

"No, Iris," said Athena, marching back to the bed and sitting hard upon it. "I was not overstating the matter when I said that I shall never forgive Blysdale."

Iris followed to sit beside her. "But you must forgive him. You love him."

"I do not—that is, perhaps I did, but he deceived me—used me—and I will not allow him ever to do so again."

"Athena, once and for all, what has happened? What did Blysdale do?"

The whole history of the bet and the bribery came out then, delivered in Athena's usual collected manner, and Iris was silent in contemplation for several minutes afterward.

"It is all very bad," she said at last, gazing at nothing with brow furrowed. "But he was not at fault for the bet—you must give him that. He would never have claimed to have informed your father if it were not true. Besides, Windon or Alverton could be applied to. It would be too easy a lie to expose."

Athena merely shook her head, her mouth a hard line.

Iris sighed. "But the bribery—I would not have thought it of him. It is really quite odiously indecent! And beyond the bounds of propriety—to have your private interests traded about by servants—it does not bear thinking of!"

"No," said Athena, her quiet calm almost menacing. "It does not bear thinking of, and that is why I shall not think of it, nor of him. I will reconcile with Lord Foxham and he will offer for me and I will become a marchioness, and my mama will be happy."

Iris tucked a hand into Athena's. "But you will not be at all happy."

Athena did not look at her, biting her lips and only briefly returning the pressure of her friend's hand.

"It is a hard thing, to be the daughter of a great family," said Iris, leaning her head on Athena's shoulder.

She did not see Athena's eyes close on a single tear that slid down her cheek.

Though Lady Gidgeborough's note to the marquess was elegant and polite in the extreme, it was returned unopened, for his lordship had been called away on sudden business. It was unknown when he would be returning, and Lady Gidgeborough, feeling acutely the danger of the situation, commanded that the letter be taken directly to Lord Foxham wherever he may be. It was with a grave countenance that she returned to the drawing room and summoned her daughter to attend her.

When Athena came, she wore the cool demeanor that her mother had ingrained in her, through years of instruction and example. Lady Gidgeborough had come to view it with pride, confident in the knowledge that it proved the excellence of her daughter's breeding, and her own considerable talents. But today she viewed her daughter's collected aspect warily, for she had begun to suspect that it hid a rebellious spirit that somehow had survived the strenuous tutelage of more than a decade.

"Sit down, Athena," she said, and watched her daughter dutifully obey. "Lord Foxham has gone away, ostensibly on business, but we both can guess his real motive for leaving Town with such precipitance."

"The Season has ended, Mama," said Athena. "Nearly everyone has retired to the country, or will do presently."

"That is nothing to the point, Athena," said her mother sharply. "Your ungracious conduct has driven him away, and I dare not think what might be the issue if we are unable to convince him of your contrition and regard. I wonder if it might not be permissible in this instance for you to write a note to him yourself."

"Certainly not, Mama," said Athena, looking quickly up. "Lord Foxham would take it as another affront, and think me very forward and encroaching. And the dowager would most assuredly take exception to such an improper action. Your letter must do the business, Mama, I am persuaded."

Her mother ruminated over the matter for a moment before saying, "Yes, I believe you are right. His attentions were most marked, and he did state his intentions months ago. I do not think one slight could drive him entirely away. Well, we must contrive a little. Mrs. Marshall intends to throw a house party in a week or two, and I shall request her to invite Lord Foxham. Two weeks in his company should provide ample time for you to mend the breach and convince him that he has found his marchioness. I shall write to her directly."

She stood and walked to the desk in the corner, sitting and arranging paper, ink, and sand before her. "You will do and say everything that is proper when next you see his lordship, I trust, Athena. There will not be another opportunity to fix his interest. We cannot afford another lapse."

"Yes, Mama," said Athena without expression.

In Hill Street, a similar conversation was going forward, as Mrs. Slougham had become uncomfortably aware of the prolonged absence of Iris's two suitors.

"It is only what I expected, however," she said with asperity. "You will insist upon stating your mind, and that is what no gentleman wants in a wife. If I have told you once, I have told you fifty times, Iris, that gentlemen want a quiet, well-spoken wife who does not question or challenge them."

"That is not what Papa wanted," said Iris. "At least, that is not what he got."

Her mother glared at her, pinching her lips together. "Enough of your impertinence, child! It was doubtless your design to thwart me this Season, for you never wished to come, and have been bent on punishing my generosity and patience all the while. How I have sacrificed and contrived and hoped for you—but it was all in vain.

You would chase dear Mr. Tenby and Mr. Blysdale, both, away. Oh, the hopes I had for you! Either one would have been famous, a capital husband, and I should never have mentioned Mr. Blysdale's low birth after you were wed. But it is not to be. Oh!"

"Mama, Mr. Blysdale never admired me, as I have told you often and often," said Iris, her patience strained. "He has only ever admired Athena and wanted me to help him with her, for she is the most provoking creature imaginable. But he has gone now and will very probably never come back again."

"Well, but Mr. Tenby has gone also, and you say nothing of that—"

"I wonder if he had a better motive for the bribery," mused Iris, oblivious to Mrs. Slougham's words. "I cannot believe that he did not love her, at least by the end. It must have been something that he did only out of desperation."

"Iris!" cried her mama, gazing at her in irritation. "Do not you care about Mr. Tenby?"

"Perhaps I might speak to his secretary, and discover whether he has changed."

"Good heaven, child, do not you hear me?"

"Unless they have both left Town, as everyone seems to have done."

It was perhaps fortunate that a footman arrived at that moment with a letter from Mrs. Marshall, inviting Iris and her parents to a house party at Findon Place in Sussex the following week. Mrs. Slougham read the invitation with impatience, then interest, then misgiving.

"I do not know. There will be eligible gentlemen there, to be sure, but what if Mr. Tenby should return to Town, and you are not here?"

"Then I have only a few days to reach him, and he cannot answer if he is in Yorkshire."

"Who is in Yorkshire?" cried Iris's afflicted parent, throwing down her arms. "If you have been going on about Mr. Blysdale all this while, then I do not comprehend why he is not to be considered your beau!"

Iris at last regarded her parent, blinking. "Oh, it is not on my account I am thinking of Mr. Blysdale, ma'am, but Athena's. I should have windmills in my head to imagine anything else."

Mrs. Slougham shook her head, pressing her lips into a tight line. "It is my belief you do have windmills in your head, regardless of Mr. Blysdale's inclinations. Indeed, he should have windmills in his head to wish to have you!"

"But I do not want him, Mama!"

With a visible effort of will, Mrs. Slougham refrained from screaming. "Well, Iris, if you do not give a fig for your beaux, then off with you to Sussex! I wash my hands of you! Your father may accompany you, for I dare swear I am in desperate need of a little quiet and solitude. It is not as though this is any sort of punishment, mind you, for you go to Diana, and if Athena is not also invited then I am a zany. But I can no longer stand by and witness your utter disregard for your future! Perhaps between the three of you there will be something of an awakening! I declare if I know what else to do with you."

Thus Athena and Iris posted together to Findon Place the following week, sharing the chaise with Mr. Slougham, whose air of resignation strongly suggested his being in possession of all the facts pertaining to their respective cases. Conversation, therefore, did not flourish on the drive into Sussex, though—due to Mr. Slougham's anxiety for a comfortable bottle of burgundy with his life-long friend to wash away the worrying effects of the past few days—this was accomplished in one day.

Diana, who had been rather alarmed at the silence of her dearest friends during the week preceding the party, took the first opportunity afforded her of gathering Iris and Athena into her bedchamber and demanding to be told what was in the wind. All their troubles of the past several days being soon revealed, Diana gazed at them in astonished concern.

"Dear me, it is not wonderful that you arrived with all the air of prisoners going to execution!"

Athena pursed her lips at this. "Pray do not exaggerate, Diana. We were fatigued by the journey, merely."

"Anyone would be cast into the mopes from riding in a chaise with my father a full day," said Iris.

"But he has good reason to be disappointed, Iris, for he is not generally so severe," said Diana.

Iris sighed. "It is very lowering, Diana. I have been used to continually disappointing my family, but of late Mama had such hopes. I would that I had not cast my prospects to the wind."

"You may have done so, Iris," said Athena haughtily, "but I am in no way despairing of regaining Lord Foxham's regard. He has been invited to the party, has he not, Diana?"

"Unfortunately, Mama received his regrets this morning."

Athena's composure slipped briefly, revealing her sensations on this announcement, but it was unclear whether her predominant emotion was relief or disappointment, for the glimpse was gone in an instant. "No matter," she said. "There will be time enough to contrive something."

"Yes, in the nature of a permanent separation!" said Iris in disgust. "Diana, we must convince her not to have that odious marquess over Mr. Blysdale!"

"But Mr. Blysdale is not quite the thing, Iris," said Diana reasonably, patting her hand. "He has resorted to underhanded dealing, after all."

"Even underhanded dealers have hearts, I am persuaded," Iris huffed, glancing at Athena, who gazed off in apparent unconcern. "It is as likely as Ice Maidens having them, after all."

"Iris!" cried Diana, glancing in alarm at Athena's pinked cheeks.

But Iris gestured impatiently. "I do not think he is underhanded, not really. I have been thinking, and what he did is no worse than what many gentlemen do to win favor with servants. My father is continually greasing someone's palm."

"How typical of your reasoning, Iris," retorted Athena, turning a distasteful gaze upon her. "But it is all of a piece, for you were ever in favor with Mr. Blysdale. It strikes one that, as you are so faithful a proponent of that gentleman's interests, you ought to entertain his suit yourself."

"He is in love with you, Athena!"

"He has an odd way of showing it. Never have I heard a gentleman prove his love by bribing his fair one's servants and placing odious bets on his chances with her."

Iris threw up her hands. "He did not place the bet!"

"But he did bribe my servants, which proves that his motives were mercenary."

Diana, wishing to ease Athena's consternation, hastily turned the subject. "But Iris, what do you think has happened to Tenby? You were going along so well when last I was in Town."

Iris dropped her gaze to her lap. "My mama believes I gave him a disgust of me by presuming to advise him on his driving, but I do not understand how that could be. He requested that I drive him, to show him how to improve, and when I had done so, he asked me to drive him again. If that is taking offense, I have truly learned nothing of gentlemen."

"To be sure, that seems very like approbation, Iris," said Diana soothingly. "But then his sentiments must have undergone a change."

"I suppose so. I first perceived it when I saw him at the theater and he would not come up to us. I was with Blysdale, you see, and Tenby went instantly away."

"You have been often in Blysdale's company," remarked Athena curtly.

Iris cast her an irritated look. "He was much in want of advice and comfort concerning the lady he loves, Athena."

"But that is it, Iris," cried Diana, bouncing a bit on the bed. "Tenby is jealous!"

Iris's brow furrowed and she gazed at Diana in disbelief. "It cannot be so! He must know Blysdale does not think of me. I have told him as much."

"Then I am persuaded he does not believe it, Iris. And even if he did, he might have been deceived into believing you to be partial to Blysdale, for the gentleman need not think of *you* for you to admire *him*. Do you see? I am resolved that Tenby deserted you out of mortification—he is in love with you and is jealous!"

Athena exhaled scornfully. "You both will allow your fancy to run away with you. It is unsound, and impolitic, too, Diana, for you to encourage Iris in this wholly unsubstantial belief when you know very well that she is prone to say utterly shocking things on the slightest provocation. If you go on in this way, what is to prevent her from declaring her conviction of Tenby's love for her, to himself or to anyone she meets, regardless of his true feelings? If you are wrong—and even if you are not—such an action could very well ruin her reputation."

Diana and Iris exchanged silent glances and Athena nodded coolly. "It is perhaps best that we leave off this subject altogether. Who knows but what Mr. Blysdale will decide that since he cannot have me, he may as well take Iris."

"Athena!" cried Diana, her brows drawing downward.

But Iris said simply, "I would take him if he loved me, Athena, for he is an excellent man. But he does not love me."

"As he does not love me," said Athena. She raised a hand against Iris's exclamation. "He was only in love with my consequence, Iris. Else, why should he resort to bribery to gain my favor?"

Iris clamped her lips shut and looked away, and Diana, looking helplessly between her friends, at last reached to take their hands and pressed them. "What a horrid burden you each have had to bear, and at the same moment! I wish I had been there to support you."

Iris looked her gratitude while Athena merely turned away—but she did not remove her hand from Diana's comforting clasp.

Chapter 21

WHILE ATHENA CARRIED herself with supreme unconcern through the following week, Iris could not be so dismissive of the gentlemen who had made up such a large part of her thoughts for the previous two months, simply because they both had disappointed her. How she was to deal with the problems at hand, however, was more than she knew, and she put many of the guests at the house party off with her vague manner as she puzzled it out.

Though Tenby—his whereabouts, his sentiments, and his hair that looked like straw—was in the back of her mind constantly, her active thoughts were chiefly occupied by the problem of Athena's disenchantment with Blysdale and how to effect a reconciliation. Convinced as Iris was of Athena's having fallen in love at last, it had become of dire importance to ascertain Blysdale's motives for pursuing Athena, and if they were as pure as Iris believed, to convince Athena of it.

In this cause, Iris had set upon a course while still in London that would have scandalized Mrs. Slougham, had she been privy to it. But Iris, though rather ramshackle, had a lively sense of self-preservation, and had taken good care that her mother should never suspect a thing. Her bribe of a sovereign to her maid seemed it would be wasted, however, for no letter arrived under cover to Rowley before they were obliged to depart for the house party.

She came into Sussex, therefore, with great anxiety which, despite Diana's kind ministrations, enjoyed no alleviation in the first several days. On the morning of the fifth day, however, she received a letter from Suffolk which, upon her perceiving the frank, caused her to blush and hasten away with disjointed apologies. Once in her room, she locked the door and plumped down into a chair to read it.

> *Suffolk, 14 June, 1818*
>
> *My dear Miss Slougham,*
>
> *You will excuse the extreme astonishment with which I received your letter, which found me at last at Newmarket, and which might have occasioned much remark among various gentlemen present had I not with great presence of mind spilled wine on Alverton's breeches and thus created a diversion while I spirited away your letter into my pocket. Your reputation, dear lady, is thus intact, as is my own.*
>
> *In answer to your pressing and—I do not scruple to say—rather distressing inquiries, I shall endeavor to both satisfy your desire for justice and secure a measure of your mercy to myself—Alverton I will leave to shift for himself. Our part in the bumblebath you understand*

well, and I can only affirm, on my honor as a gentleman, that Blysdale had no part in it whatsoever, and behaved respectably throughout.

What I must say in my defense is this: I should never have got the notion for such a bet into my head—for you were nothing less than right, ma'am, though I am ashamed to own it, in describing my state that night as "odiously foxed"—had I not in the numerous sober moments leading up to it been convinced of Blysdale's wanting a heavy set-down. He is the best of good fellows, but his obstinate pursuit of Lady Athena could only make him ridiculous, for the match is unequal in the extreme.

I will here insert that I have never seen him so fascinated by a lady, and without reason, for he has little need of her connections or fortune, having plenty of each in his own right. She is, without doubt, a handsome woman, and possessed of innumerable excellent qualities, but no man in his right mind would present himself to a Dibbington without a title.

Blysdale has never heeded my arguments against his suit, however, and in my deplorable state that night at cards, it seemed to me that the only way he could be made to see reason was to announce my support of a competitor who could not be beaten. The bet was entered into the books and the signatures set to it, but without Blysdale's knowledge.

There you have the whole history, ma'am, and if it has not softened your heart toward me, it has gone some way toward clearing my conscience in this affair. I promised

Blysdale—an excellent, Christian fellow—that I should do all within my power to smooth it over and make things right, and I trust that your being in possession of these facts will assist me.

I only add my civil desire that this letter not be seen by any other eyes than your own, and trust to your principles that it will be burnt as soon as may be, for we neither of us would wish to be compromised in any manner, though I hold you in the highest esteem, etc.,

Peter Holydale, Viscount Windon

This letter furnished Iris with much food for thought, particularly regarding how best to turn the information to good account. Windon's answer had been highly satisfactory—though Iris did not believe she could forgive him so easily as he had wished. She rather thought he knew how horridly he had destroyed Blysdale's prospects, and it would take much more than a hastily written explanation to bring matters to a satisfactory conclusion and thus earn himself a pardon from her.

However, the written testimony of a man of the world that Blysdale was innocent, excellent, and fascinated by Lady Athena despite her connections was very much to Iris's taste and, it was to be hoped, to Athena's. Yet, it was not quite enough to make the case she had built up, and the success of her schemes hung upon a felicitous response to the second part of her correspondence.

After receiving a scold from Diana for having her head in the clouds, Iris endeavored to put the matter from her mind, but it was uphill work. She knew there was nothing more to be done until another letter arrived with additional evidence, but so eager was she to give Athena cause to soften her frosty air that she could not help conjecturing upon the contents of the letter to come, counting and recounting the days that had elapsed since she had written to inquire, and haunting the hall at the times of the post. Her oddity caused some to whisper behind their hands, but it was only as much as she had experienced since coming into Society. Her reputation did not have long to suffer, however, for not two days later, another letter arrived and was carried hastily upstairs to be devoured in the privacy of her apartment.

London, 17 June, 1818

Dear Madam,

I beg your pardon for the tardy reply to your letter dated ten days ago. Mr. Blysdale was obliged to leave town that very day, and carried me away with him. We are only today come back to Town and catching up our correspondence.

I need not state that your inquiry caused me an hour's quandary, for it is highly improper for a subordinate to impart information that could very well be used to blacken his employer's character. But as Mr. Blysdale has spoken often of you as a friend, and you have assured me that your intentions are entirely benevolent, I have resolved to render you what assistance is in my power.

I have another motive in answering you which I do not scruple to disclose: Mr. Blysdale is not himself, and has not been since the day we left Town so suddenly. He has not changed openly—in public he is very much what he always was—but in private, madam, he is gravely altered. I do not exaggerate when I say that I am excessively concerned for his welfare. As his close friend, madam, you may apprehend my urgency in wishing to alleviate his distress, and the contents of your letter have given me hope that in clearing up this misunderstanding we may join in doing just that.

In regard to the claims of bribery to which you refer, and to which Mr. Blysdale has already admitted guilt, I cannot excuse either his or my own involvement. I may only attempt to explain why it was done, and in what spirit, and trust his fate to your justice and, indeed, mercy.

I have often used bribery to obtain what information Mr. Blysdale has required of me, and it has never before occasioned me a moment's guilt. I have never been encouraged to resort to extortion to succeed in my aims, and the classes among whom I have dealt are generally glad to be paid for such innocuous bits of intelligence as my employer desires. A lady such as yourself may not be aware of the infinite number of bribes freely given and happily taken every day in London—indeed, one may argue that vails are nothing but an acceptable and expected bribe.

But this seems as though I am endeavoring to justify improper conduct—I am not. I only wish to help you see how entirely innocent Mr. Blysdale is of intentional wrongdoing. His reasons for wishing his information were never harmful, and he has never used it for such underhanded activities as blackmail or coercion. The information is generally such as will allow him to assist or get to know someone with whom he wishes to have a connection.

This case, though similar in nature, was quite different in its effect—and here I venture into avenues that are both private and theoretical. If it were not for my employer's present pitiable state, I should never presume—but I feel it imperative that I do, and I pray it will do him good.

Mr. Blysdale's interest in the Lady Athena Dibbington was personal, and he was more determined upon success than I had ever seen him. I believe the challenge of overcoming her scruples in acknowledging him served only to increase his fascination, for he told me once that she was well worth the trouble. I do not believe I have seen him happier than when he at last was honored by her company for a short walk. He was a trifle smug, to be sure, but you will pardon the liberty when I assert that it was the satisfaction of a man falling in love.

He ceased to request my services after successful contact was made with Lady Athena, and afterward only referred to his success in the most oblique manner—he did not boast or gossip to me or to anyone else that I know of. He also did not inform me of the cause of his extreme dejection the day before we left Town, but he did burn several papers I believe to have contained my initial reports on Lady Athena, and during the brief conversation we had touching his mood, he told me only that he was a fool. He has since expressed a resolution to dispense entirely with those of my services which involve the gathering of information.

Though it is only founded upon observation and long experience of him, I hold to my opinion that he is a man truly, deeply, and now quite hopelessly in love. That is all

> *that I can tell you, madam, in relation to the matter, with-*
> *out reiterating my concern and my desire that through*
> *your timely intervention all may come to a happy issue.*
> *God bless you,*
> *Thomas Shaw*
> *Secretary to Mr. Jonathan Blysdale*

This was so exactly what she had hoped to receive that she jumped up from the bed directly and ran to find Athena. She was out in the garden watching some of the others play at battledore and shuttlecock, and it was no difficult matter to get her to come back into the house. Indeed, as Iris seized her hand and dragged her up the stairs and into her own room, there was not much her ladyship could do but protest against such treatment.

Locking the door once more, Iris turned to her startled guest and thrust the letter into her hands.

"Read that!" she commanded, her tone triumphant.

Athena looked at the letter in annoyed puzzlement, but had hardly read the direction when Iris plucked it from her hands again.

"No, stupid! Not that one—" Iris ran to the dressing table and rummaged in the drawer, pulling out another letter and returning to thrust it at Athena. "This one! Read it!"

Athena raised her brows and sighed. "If I did not know better, I should say you are mad. You cannot mean that I am stupid."

"No, I mean myself! That is, you are quite, but only recently, I assure you."

"You are all kindness," was the bland reply as Athena began to peruse the letter. After a moment, she looked up, brow furrowed. "What on earth is this about, Iris?"

"Just be quiet and read!"

With another, more irritated sigh, Athena did as she was directed and read the letter through, her jaw tightening the more she read. When she was finished, she tossed the letter aside with a moue of distaste.

"I do not know what you were thinking, Iris—or rather, I am not surprised that you did not think. What did you hope to accomplish, other than wreaking havoc on your reputation? It is quite a shambles as it is, but at least you are not entangled with any gentleman—as yet. You are fortunate that Windon—though he is a rattle and a reprobate—is principled enough to think to protect you."

"He was only afraid of being obliged to offer for me should the word get out that we were in correspondence, Athena. But he is a gentleman, and you cannot doubt his word!"

Athena huffed. "Certainly I can. Indeed, why should I heed anything he says when in the same breath he freely admits to drunkenness, impertinence, and fraud? 'Conscience,' indeed. He is a disgrace to the name of gentleman."

Grimacing in frustration, Iris flourished the other letter in front of Athena. "Very well, then read this one. It is from a very different quarter but I hope it will convince you."

"Convince me of what?" said Athena dryly, taking the letter. "That Blysdale is 'the best of good fellows,' despite his trickery?"

"Oh, just read, Athena!"

She did, with much the same effect. "It is a parcel of falsehoods and excuses. Did you think that I would be swayed by this moving appeal to your friendship? You are far too trusting, Iris."

"And you are far too obstinate!" cried Iris, stamping her foot. "Do you not see, Athena? Two friends of Blysdale state, separately and without cooperation, that he is in love with you—with *you* Athena! Not your station, nor your family name, nor your connections. Blysdale has only ever wanted you. Would you like to hear what it was that drew him to you? He said that your elegance came from something deeper than birth, and that even when you are old you will still be the Lady Athena in all your perfection."

Athena averted her gaze in apparent distaste, but not before Iris perceived a flash of longing in her eyes. Iris sat down next to Athena and took her hand in both of hers.

"Dearest Athena, do consider—everything he did was to please you. You may term it bribery or deceit or what-have-you, but none of it was mercenary. It is no different than your having paid Madame Fleurie an extra ten guineas to have your dress a week earlier than promised. It benefited both of you and harmed no one."

"It harmed me—my sensibility," said Athena in a suspiciously choked tone.

Iris pursed her lips. "You have no sensibility, Athena. And if you had, it would never have been hurt had not you eavesdropped on the servants."

Athena stood, wrenching her hand from Iris's grip. "Very well, I have no sensibility. My pride was hurt, but that, to me, is more important than any sentiment. If I do not have my pride, what do I have? Merely a hollow existence leading to a meaningless union of insensibility. At least my pride will make my actions worth something."

She crossed her arms and gazed out the window, pointedly turning her back.

Iris stood as well, shaking her head. "You and your horrid pride. It is a fearsome thing, just as Blysdale discovered. I only hope you may realize just how lonely you are, when all you have is your pride for company."

With that, Iris quitted the room, closing the door forcefully behind her. Athena stayed staring out the window for some minutes, then turned to gaze thoughtfully at the door, her countenance no longer cold, but wistful. After a few moments, her eyes drifted to the letters on the bed and soon her feet followed, and she was unable to resist picking them up again. She reread Windon's letter, sitting absently down as her gaze dwelt on a particular passage regarding fascination, her lower lip caught between her teeth. Then she turned to the second letter and reread it, holding at the phrase "man in love."

Dropping her hands with the letters into her lap, she closed her eyes and let her mind recall Blysdale's delight as she had spoken of her grandmama. She saw again his offering of the lily of the valley, and his comment of how lovely they had looked in her hair. She relived the moment of exquisite relief when he had rescued her from the Duke, and the happiness of their two dances together.

With a sigh, she lay down on her side on the bed, her arms clutching the letters to her chest. She could not forgive him. What he had done was unforgivable—and yet, she was almost certain that she no longer cared. The hurt seemed to have gone, or to have dimmed so far as to be insignificant. She tried to revive it with recollections of her feelings upon hearing John, the footman's, testimony, but she could only think of his protestations that he had only done it because he thought Mr. Blysdale was sweet on her. It had been that insolent bet that had turned John and Sarah from their good opinions, and that had been nothing of Blysdale's doing.

Perhaps she had been hasty in dismissing them. Accepting bribes to divulge personal information about their employers was a serious charge, but they had imparted such harmless information, after all. The color of her gowns, the errands she was to run, the parties she was to attend. There was really nothing in it to shame her. It was all so that he could see her, be with her, and know her better. All because he was falling in love with her.

A little thrill passed through her, from her chest to her toes, which curled in her slippers. She thought of what it would be like to feel that—or something akin to it—every day as a married woman. Could she hope to feel that with Lord Foxham? She thought not. Even if he did not wear a corset, he did not inspire anything like the thrill she had just felt. Indeed, she was greatly mistaken if she inspired that sort of a thrill in him. Had he not demonstrated at the Pattershaw's ball that he thought of her only as an ornament to his position? Indeed, his views were as mercenary as she had thought Blysdale's to be, and quite as mercenary as Lady Gidgeborough's.

She shook her head, trying to clear it of the disturbing conclusions that then crowded in. Owning to Blysdale's innocence changed nothing except to reinstate the possibility of friendship. Indeed, as soon as she returned to London, she would take the first opportunity of making amends to him—he deserved that as a gentleman, surely. It certainly did not mean that she wished for more, for that was, and always would be, impossible.

She stood, feeling lighter than she had in a fortnight. But before rejoining the company, she resolved to do one thing more when she returned to Town—to seek out John and Sarah and beg them to return to Gidgeborough House.

Chapter 22

For the remainder of the house party, Athena endeavored to retain her superior air, but somehow Iris saw through her. Perhaps it was the disappearance of the two letters Iris had received that gave her the hint, but she could not but smile at Athena's supreme indifference to any reference to Mr. Blysdale or returning to Town. Athena's frank recommendation to Diana to fix her interest with the gentleman of her choice without delay strengthened Iris's suspicions, and when the mention of Lord Foxham only deepened Athena's reserve, Iris was satisfied that her friend Blysdale would soon have occasion to smile and hope again.

The day before the house party broke up, Mrs. Marshall received a letter informing her that Mrs. Slougham had determined upon staying in London for the summer to wait out repairs on their house in Berkshire. She was pleased to add that Lady Gidgeborough had resolved to bear her company, and so Lord Gidgeborough would remain as well. Thus, Mr. Slougham would be returning to London rather than go into the country, and both Iris and Athena would stay with their parents in Town.

Iris accepted this scheme without demur, for it would only improve Blysdale's chances with Athena. For Iris's part, it mattered not whether she was in Town or in Berkshire or in Bombay, for none afforded her the prospect of seeing Tenby, at least until the winter. It was tempting to repine her fate as a woman, dependent upon her relations to approve her accommodation—how easy it was for a man to move about the country with complete freedom. If she were a man, she could follow Mr. Tenby into Hampshire and—but here her reasoning broke down, for she did not know what she could do in the situation, for she was yet unconvinced that his desertion was merely the effect of jealousy.

The news that she was to pass the summer in London was rather surprising to Athena, for she had quitted Town in the belief that Lord Foxham had retired to the country, and she had fully expected that her mama would contrive a way for them to follow him wherever he had gone. That Lady Gidgeborough had willingly stayed in Town suggested one of two things: either Lord Foxham had not answered her letter and she had not yet decided upon a prudent course, or his lordship had returned to London. Neither possibility excited an emotion warmer than impatience in Athena's breast, a circumstance that she was at pains not to analyze.

The Goddesses bid each other farewell in their various manners—Diana sentimental, Iris resigned, and Athena calm and cool. Mr. Slougham, refreshed from two weeks without the nagging of his wife, was a far better companion on the return journey, and the drive from Sussex to London seemed half as long as that from London to Sussex.

Their arrival in Town was greeted by widely different emotions in Grosvenor Square than in Hill Street. Mrs. Slougham accepted her husband's kiss with equanimity, then gazed at their offspring with a heartfelt sigh.

"Well, you are back again, Iris," she said, turning to lead the way up to the saloon. "There does not seem to be much point in your staying, except that Mr. Slougham will wish to keep Gidgeborough company and we cannot spare a servant to travel with you into Berkshire."

"Yes, mama," said Iris, pulling out a parcel that Mrs. Marshall had given into her keeping. "I will do my best to be a comfort to you while we are here, and Mrs. Marshall has sent you some cuttings from her roses to root in the garden."

"At least someone takes a thought for my comfort." Mrs. Slougham took the parcel, handing it immediately to a maid and instructing her to take it to the housekeeper's room. "It is good that I shall have something relaxing to do, for I do not anticipate much enjoyment from remaining in Town in this heat and dust."

"Come, my dear," said Mr. Slougham, "we may just as well go home, if you do not like it here."

"I did not say that, my love," replied Mrs. Slougham. "We came to marry off our daughter, and we shall remain until we have exhausted every possibility. Besides, I daresay there is more dust at Stowe Hill than here, even for all the heat."

Sighing, Iris excused herself, going to her room to remove her pelisse and hat and stretching out on top of the bed. If Tenby had returned, her mama would have apprised her of it, so Iris also could not anticipate much enjoyment from staying in Town. If only she could be certain of his sentiments, then she could make some sort of plan. As it was, the reasonable thing to do was to put Tenby from her mind and to focus her energies on assisting in a reconciliation between Athena and Blysdale.

In Grosvenor Square, Lady Gidgeborough greeted her daughter with the intelligence that Lord Foxham had returned to Town and had spoken with her.

"He was excessively civil, my love, and quite ready to forgive your hasty temper. My note vastly relieved his mind, and brought him back to Town post-haste. Indeed, he owned to having been out of sorts himself at the ball, and that he took himself off to his estate to recover his spirits. He is now awaiting an opportunity to see you, that you may make good your apologies."

Athena regarded her coolly. "How good of him. I wonder if I ought to go to Foxham House on the instant, and beg his pardon on his doorstep."

"Do not be vulgar, Athena," said Lady Gidgeborough crossly. "You know very well that you are in the wrong, and though he may have expressed himself somewhat ungraciously, he has owned to it and you will forgive him. It is much more important that he receive an apology from you, especially now that it is expected."

"Certainly, Mama," said Athena. "I must not forget what is due my betters."

Lady Gidgeborough eyed her offspring narrowly. "Your mood does not seem to have improved during your sojourn in Sussex, Athena. I am disappointed. I have been lately possessed of the suspicion that you are growing wayward, and I will not have it! You are the daughter of Lord Gidgeborough, of the House of Dibbington, and must never disregard what is owed to your name."

"I assure you, ma'am, that I am constantly aware of what is owed to my name."

"As you should be! Your birth and privilege require it, and it is only what you have been bred up to do. Therefore, you will make your apology to Lord Foxham at the first suitable opportunity and then you will make yourself agreeable to him. With any luck, you shall be engaged by August, and we may retire to his estate for the remainder of the summer. I have never seen London so insufferably hot."

Athena thought it wiser to accede to this demand than to continue to push against her mama, but the notion of going meekly into wedded shackles with Lord Foxham only served to irritate her. A sennight earlier it had seemed desirable, and she had forced herself to overcome her distaste for the marquess's sterile sentiments. Now, though she held to her duty to comply with her mother's wishes, she somewhat hazily trusted that something would prevent the marquess from wishing to offer for her, while her whole determination was to find and reconcile with Mr. Blysdale.

Iris was more than happy to assist her in this, and they walked out every day, hoping to see him out and about. Even his secretary or a servant would do, for such could be prevailed upon to apprise his master of their interest in meeting him. But no such fortune smiled upon them, and though they walked down all the principal streets and lingered outside his favored shops, he never appeared. Athena began to be anxious that he had quit Town after all, but when they recklessly strolled past his house in Hanover Square, the sight of the knocker still up suggested otherwise.

As the Season had ended, London was extremely thin of company, and the usual round of parties, balls, routs, and picnics had diminished into one or two entertainments per week. There was still the theater and public concerts where one could meet one's friends, but even in all this, Mr. Blysdale did not appear.

It was with real disappointment that Athena encountered Lord Foxham at a musical soirée and was obliged to reconcile with him before even she had seen Mr. Blysdale. Lord Foxham's condescension was infinitely more disagreeable to her than ever Blysdale's impudence had been, but upon reflection, she was made to own that Blysdale's pursuit of her had not been disagreeable in the least. Indeed, she rather missed the satisfaction of being chased by a desirable rather than a merely eligible suitor.

The thought of Lord Foxham chasing her actually caused her to chuckle, which was unfortunate, as that gentleman had just made a comment on the delight occasioned by music well-performed. She was obliged again to soothe his feelings, an effort which gave her to think on the tiresome quality of their conversations, and the insupportability of those conversations if they were to be multiplied over a lifetime as his wife.

He, however, was so well-pleased by her ministrations that he invited her and her honored parents to the theater the following evening, and as Lady Gidgeborough was close enough to hear the invitation, Athena was obliged to pay penance by accepting with a good grace. All the way home in the carriage she was thus subjected to the transports of her mother, who extolled the virtues of my Lord of Foxham, counted the days until an offer could be expected, and congratulated herself that Athena had overcome her perverse mood—while Lord Gidgeborough dozed in the opposite corner.

The next morning, Athena met Iris for their usual walk and was so intent upon going first to Hanover Square that Iris commented upon it.

"If I did not know better, I should imagine you to be anxious. Has something happened?"

Athena denied it. "It is only that I am not in a dawdling mood. Come along, Iris! You are very slow this morning."

"I am not so slow as to believe you," retorted Iris, picking up her steps. "Has Lord Foxham approached you? I have seen him about town. Your mama must have been in fits to bring you together."

Athena blew out a breath in a manner most unlike herself. "I have seen his lordship. He could not be within the same county and my mama not effect a meeting."

"Then he has forgiven you? How dispiriting." Iris watched her keenly. "Has your mama ordered your wedding clothes?"

"Pray do not be odious, Iris. I am in no mood for levity."

"No, how could you be? I, however, should be wondering whether to run away to join the gypsies or to throw myself in the river."

"You would choose the latter, of course," said Athena, pursing her lips. "You are fond of threatening to throw yourself in the river."

"It is no threat, I assure you, Athena. Only someone is always on hand to prevent me." She paused, considering. "For which I am necessarily grateful. One is not at one's best when one is in despair."

Athena sighed. "No, I suppose not."

They had reached Hanover Square and yet again caught no glimpse of Mr. Blysdale. It was with gritted teeth that Athena turned toward home, after a quarter hour of fruitless wandering up and down the street, but as they came up to his steps one last time, the door opened. Both girls stilled, staring in eager anticipation, one all relief, the other half hope, half fear, as a man emerged. Both let out their breath in a huff upon perceiving that it was Mr. Shaw, the secretary.

He looked up as he started down the steps, his pace slowing as he recognized Athena. His mouth opened in silent shock and he came to a stop before them, his gaze flicking between their two alert countenances.

"Good day, your ladyship," he said at last, fumbling with his hat and his bow.

Athena nodded, her lips between her teeth until Iris nudged her with an elbow and she said, "You are Mr. Blysdale's secretary, I presume."

"Yes, ma'am. May I be of assistance?"

"Yes—that is, no. I do not wish—that is—"

Again she bit her lips and Iris was obliged to come to the rescue. "Sir, I am Miss Slougham, Mr. Blysdale's friend. You were so good as to correspond with me."

"Iris!" hissed Athena, earning an anxious glance from Mr. Shaw.

But Iris was unmoved. "We are on the verge of success, sir," she said meaningfully, tipping her head toward Athena. "We must see Mr. Blysdale."

"Oh!" he said, looking wide-eyed at Athena. He blinked, then said with more animation, "Oh! By Jupiter—pardon me, ma'am—would do anything to oblige—but Mr. Blysdale is not at home."

Both Athena and Iris wilted a trifle, but Mr. Shaw said quickly, "He is only gone into the City on business. He will be at home later— however, I do not perceive how—it is not proper for you—"

"Precisely," said Athena, resuming her air of cool superiority as she fished in her reticule for a shilling piece. She held it out to him. "Perhaps you know where he may be met with this evening, sir."

His mouth dropped open again as he stiffened and stared at the coin in her hand, but after a moment he relaxed, a rueful smile playing about his lips. "Yes, ma'am, but I would not dream of taking a bribe from your ladyship. You, of all people, are welcome to the intelligence that my employer is attending a concert with a party of friends tonight."

Athena blinked. "Oh. How unfortunate." Slowly, she pulled back her hand and replaced the shilling in her reticule.

"She is engaged to go to the theater tonight," explained Iris, shaking her head. "The most infamous luck. However, you may tell us where he shall be tomorrow, I daresay."

He could and he did, outlining his employer's engagements in enough detail to earn a sovereign—if he had been taking bribes. The two ladies were grateful, Iris excessively so and Athena with proper reserve. When they turned to go their separate ways, Iris took his hand and pressed it.

"Thank you, sir. We have done good work today."

Mr. Shaw smiled, tipping his hat and walking away with a jaunty step.

With a head full of tomorrow, Athena prepared for the theater, so engrossed in her thoughts of Mr. Blysdale that she nearly started back when Lord Foxham appeared in the drawing room. Recovering instantly, she came forward, saying all that was proper, and endeavored to attend to his ponderous greeting while wishing that his predilection for entertainment had carried that day to concerts. But it was not to be, and she resigned herself that it was likely better that she not be in the same place with both Mr. Blysdale and Lord Foxham until a reconciliation with the former had taken place and she could discover upon what footing she stood.

For Athena still did not know her own heart. So long had she prepared to make an advantageous marriage that even when faced with disagreeable feelings for him, she could not utterly dismiss the Marquess of Foxham. Her whole identity was caught up in her mother's designs, and as there had never been room therein for anything so demeaning as love or romance, it was entirely unnatural for Athena to embrace such things. But she could feel them, and having felt them, she could appreciate them to a degree that her usual patterns of thinking were disturbed, and it became much less difficult for her to envision herself marrying for love rather than solely to oblige her family.

The play was a tragedy, with Mr. Kean in the lead role of Hamlet, and though he played his part with all the energy of emotion for which he was famed, Athena could not but opine that his age was beginning to show to disadvantage. Indeed, between Lord Foxham's instructive attentions before the play, and his self-important communications during the interval, Athena believed that the theater no longer held any charms for her.

When at last they adjourned to the foyer to await their carriage, Athena applied herself to the civilities she owed to Lord Foxham as her host, and was listening with fading patience to his laborious review of Kean's abilities when a tall, dark-haired figure caught her eye. She started, stepping away from her companions so as to get a better look, and perceived Mr. Blysdale in a small group of people near the door.

He saw her at the same moment and stilled, his eyes widening in a face gone slightly pale. When she did not turn away from him, he bowed to her, and when she returned his bow with a blush and a tremulous smile, he excused himself from his friends and came to her.

"Lady Athena," he said, bowing again over her outstretched hand. He nodded to Lady Gidgeborough, who regarded him with lifted brows, but who forbore to dismiss him when Lord Foxham extended a hand. "My lord," said Blysdale. "Did you enjoy the play?"

His lordship smiled condescendingly. "Certainly, sir. But how else may one describe the sensation of witnessing a master of the art of dramatics? I was just telling Lord and Lady Gidgeborough and Lady Athena my opinion of tonight's performance. Splendid, quite splendid. Mr. Kean cannot fail to delight."

Mr. Blysdale nodded pleasantly, but his eyes held that spark of humor that Athena had missed so terribly. They were obliged to listen politely to Lord Foxham's discourse for only a few more minutes, however, for another couple came up, quite fortuitously, to draw Lord and Lady Gidgeborough into conversation. The marquess inserted himself at the mention of fine dramatists, and when Lady Athena held herself back, Blysdale turned to her again.

"I had heard you were returned to Town," he said with cautious civility. "Do you remain much longer?"

She nodded, somewhat shocked at the feeling of wholeness his presence gave to her. "We remain for the summer, sir. And you? I had heard that you had gone out of Town for a time."

"Yes, but only to Newmarket. Windon convinced me to accompany him there, to support him in his horses losing every one of their races."

She laughed, a light huff filled with relief and unexpected plea-sure. "You are an excellent friend."

His gaze became pensive, searching her face. "I try to be, ma'am, but do not always succeed. It is a weakness of which I have not before been aware, but which now—"

"Mr. Blysdale," she interposed, "pray do not take all the fault to yourself. Friendship is a treaty of sorts between imperfect beings, and therefore is prone to mistreatment or neglect from either party." She paused, dropping her gaze. "Where both make mistakes, one must only hope that neither is irredeemable."

He took her hand and brought it briefly to his lips. Releasing her just as quickly, he raised his eyes to hers and said, "You are an exceptional woman, Lady Athena."

She swallowed, her hand trembling at her side. "And you are without doubt a gentleman, Mr. Blysdale."

He held her gaze for a moment longer, then stepped back with a deferential nod, before the interchange attracted the undue notice of her companions. The Gidgeborough carriage was then announced and there was a general stir among them, forcing Athena to part with Blysdale in civil propriety. He withdrew and returned to his party and Athena, blinking against a sudden pricking in her eyes, followed sedately after her mother and father and the man she suddenly hoped would never have the opportunity to prevail upon her to marry him.

Chapter 23

DESPITE THE SIGNIFICANT lift to his spirits from the meeting with Lady Athena, it was not to be expected that Mr. Blysdale would instantly revive from his strong self-disapprobation. The weeks she had been away had been filled for him by hours of sometimes painful, often mortifying reflection. For a man who prided himself on an honest rise to success, it had been a blow to have flaws in his character so unequivocally pointed out. He had almost immediately accepted that Lady Athena's disgust in him was entirely justifiable, and for the first time in their acquaintance he had questioned his worthiness for her.

Even now, her extension of an olive branch by no means assuaged his conviction of her disappointment in him. It did teach him to hope, however, and the intense introspection of his private hours was replaced by a restless energy that drove his butler to remonstrate with him.

"Pardon the liberty, sir," said old Stomes diffidently, coming into the library to replenish his master's wine decanters and finding him pacing about the room, "but I suspect the carpets might not hold up much longer under such treatment."

Blysdale looked up at him, startled out of his reverie, and smiled. "Am I a great trial to you, Stomes? I beg your pardon."

He came over to partake of the new supply of brandy, offering a glass to the retainer. This was politely refused.

"I'll not take that liberty, sir, not soon nor ever. Indeed, it has me in a puzzle how you expect I should take such condescension, sir, seeing as how you know it is not the thing to drink with one's butler—not the thing at all."

Blysdale chuckled as he regarded Stomes with tender respect. "I beg your pardon once again, Stomes. It seems I have lost my head, and must be retaught how to behave. It is a lowering thing, but I trust that I may be brought to a right way of thinking, with the right handling. May I count on you for that?"

The butler shook his head but bowed. "If you will allow me, sir, it seems that the tender handling you require won't come from the likes of me. If I may be so bold, that is the province of a lady—and not just any lady, sir."

"That is perilously close to a liberty, Stomes," retorted Blysdale, one brow lifting in challenge.

"As you say, sir," said Stomes, unperturbed. "Some liberties are more necessary than others, sir, and I'll take the liberty to say you'd best walk outside on the pavement and save your carpets. I suspect those thoughts of yours need an airing just as surely as your legs, sir."

He bowed again and turned away, leaving his master to smile rather ruefully into his glass. Placing the glass down again beside the decanter, he gazed ruminatively at the door, the smile disappearing from his lips, until at last he went out of the library and up to his bedchamber, calling for his valet. Hindley came forth from the dressing room to place himself at his master's service.

"Going out sir? Shall I retrieve the blue coat?"

"No, Hindley," said Blysdale, pulling on his gloves. "The brown will do. I'm going merely for a visit to a friend."

Hindley bowed, disappearing for a moment into the dressing room and returning with the coat. As he held it for his master, he inquired in a tone of supreme indifference, "A lady friend, sir?"

Blysdale eyed him askance. "Yes, Hindley, though I do not know how that should interest you."

"Oh, no interest, sir," said Hindley, expressionlessly smoothing the coat across his shoulders and handing him a Malacca cane. "No interest whatsoever. Merely delighted to have you going out and about again. Shall I expect you back before dinner, sir?"

"I believe so, Hindley," said Blysdale, moved despite himself. "Thank you."

The valet bowed and went away into the dressing room to continue pressing his master's coats, and Blysdale, shaking his head with a tiny smile, went out into the corridor. As he descended again to the entry hall, Stomes entered, his countenance wooden.

"Going out, sir?"

"I am, Stomes, on the excellent advice of a friend."

The butler nodded and handed him his hat and gloves, the twinkle in his eyes the only hint betraying his smug delight. "Very good, sir." He opened the front door and bowed his master out. "Enjoy your walk, sir."

Blysdale assured him he would and set off down the steps and onto the flagway in the direction of Hill Street. At the Slougham's townhouse, he took the steps two at a time and plied the knocker with vigor. He was ushered into the house and up to the drawing room, there to await Miss Slougham, who entered not two minutes later, her eager gaze searching his face.

"How do you do, sir? You look much better than I had been led to believe. How are you so happy—oh, I do hope you are not driven mad by this business, for I tell you there is no need in the world to be so!"

He came forward and took her hand, bowing over it. "No, Miss Slougham, I am not mad, though I might well be if I do not speak to you, and at length. I wonder, may I prevail upon you to walk out with me to the Green Park? Are you at leisure?"

Her searching gaze intensified, but she answered, "Certainly I am, sir. I must get my bonnet and spencer, but I shall be with you directly. Do sit down."

"Thank you, I would rather stand," he replied, bowing and fidgeting with the hat in his hands.

"Very well," she said and, eying him rather warily, left him to pace about the room.

She was back quickly, tying her bonnet as she re-entered, and they descended to the front hall, where she informed the butler that she was going out with Mr. Blysdale.

"But do not tell Mrs. Slougham unless she particularly asks my whereabouts, Brentridge, for she will believe all sorts of wild things and I shall never hear the end of it."

On this injunction—which the butler, long inured to his young mistress's vagaries, merely acceded to with a nod—she left the house, Mr. Blysdale following behind her. Their dialogue as they walked up the street was comprised of no more than commonplaces, but once in the relative quiet of the park, Iris demanded to know what had brought him to her door.

"I met Lady Athena at the theater last night," he said, watching her response.

She was patently surprised. "But Mr. Shaw told us you were to go to a concert."

It was his turn to show surprise. "When had Mr. Shaw occasion to tell you that?"

"We met him on the street outside your house yesterday," admitted Iris, coloring.

"Ah," he said, still eying her closely. "You and Lady Athena? I wonder what can have brought you to Hanover Square."

She shook her head impatiently. "If you cannot tell that, sir, you are more a cod's head than I give you credit for. What took you to the theater? And what happened there?"

"I was invited by an old friend to be of his party, and having no great inclination for my own company, I gave up my ticket to the concert. Afterward, I saw Lady Athena and she—she spoke to me. She welcomed me, Miss Slougham. I had not imagined she would do so, so soon after what had occurred between us."

"Oh, excellent!" cried Iris triumphantly. "She was as good as her word. Now, if only Lord Foxham were not in the picture."

His countenance became pensive. "Does she still consider him?"

"She would have Society believe he is her object, but that is her mama speaking, depend upon it. Who could seriously consider marriage with a man who is so full of himself he creaks?"

He was silent a moment, walking on. "Her mama is very insistent. To be sure, in the eyes of Society, his title makes him an excellent match for her."

"Pooh! The Duke of York is a royal and yet you cannot tell me he would make an eligible *parti* for any young lady."

He agreed to this but yet was quiet. "It is not so simple as I once imagined."

Iris looked quickly at him. "Simple? You cannot ever have expected that with Athena, sir."

"No, never," he said with a huff. "I should have said it is not so straightforward as I had imagined. Before, I only knew I wanted to win her, but now... I am not certain what it is I want."

"Good heaven!" cried Iris, rolling her eyes. "What am I to do with the pair of you? You do not know what you want, Athena will not decide—it is a wonder anyone is ever married at all! I begin to understand why so many marriages are arranged, else the parties should wander about forever, continually bumping into one another like an eternal game of Blind Man's Buff, and never coming to an understanding!"

She turned on him, pointing a finger into his chest. "You are in love with her, Blysdale, that is the long and short of it. And don't give me any more blather about not subscribing to the notion of love, for it is neither here nor there. You are in the middle of it, whether you subscribe to it or no."

He blinked, letting out a long breath. "I suppose you are right. It is more difficult an emotion to handle than I had imagined, for now I only care for her happiness, whether or not I figure in her future—though I very dearly hope to do so, for I should not like to contemplate the alternative."

"Would that I could foretell her future," said Iris with a sigh, turning again to walk on. "But I cannot. I suspect she could not herself, even should she give anything away. I told you she is the most provoking creature imaginable! But I have good cause to believe she is quite as much in love with you as you are with her. She has only to discover it."

"But if she does, will it be enough to overcome her filial scruples?" he inquired. "This is why my suit is no longer straightforward. I should never wish to occasion her distress in going against the wishes of her family."

Iris gave a groan, shaking her head. "For my part, I take exception to the justice of being bound by the wishes of a most unreasonable parent."

"In all other cases, I should agree with you, Miss Slougham, but my position is no longer so strong as I once thought it to be. I have shown myself to be scarcely better than a deceiver and a mercenary."

"Not a mercenary, Blysdale," said Iris staunchly, a hand on his arm. "Your pursuit of her was never influenced by mercenary motives, as she is well aware."

"How dissimilar were my motives to those of any fortune hunter?" he inquired pointedly.

Iris lifted her brows. "The fortune they are after is pecuniary. The fortune you are after is Athena herself."

He looked down, contemplating this, and Iris took his arm, leading him down the path.

"Your motives at the outset might have differed from more recently, but they were just what any gentleman's are when embarking upon courtship. He wishes to forward his own interests in some way, be it through connections or wealth—or love." She gave him a significant look. "But that does not signify. The breach between you was precipitated by your bribery of her servants, which was very bad, you know."

"Certainly, I know it," he said, casting her an annoyed glance.

She patted his arm. "But Athena has forgiven that—which, I will tell you I sometimes despaired of, for she is a high stickler, to be sure. But, if I am not much mistaken, you shall no longer resort to such means, so all is well."

"At present we are on good terms, but it is not certain I can hope for more."

Iris looked quickly up. "But you must! Blysdale, do you love Athena or not?"

"I love her enough to respect her wishes, ma'am," he said testily. "If she does not love me, then I will not force myself upon her."

"And I suppose you will stand by and allow her to marry Foxham?"

"If it comes to that, I can have nothing to say in the matter."

"Great merciful heaven!" cried Iris, dropping her hand from his arm. "You are become so poor-spirited, I cannot look at you!"

And she strode away up the path, fuming under her breath about men who were infants and women who were too proud to realize they were in love. She had gone on in this way a full two minutes when a gentleman stepped into view around a bend and she stopped still. It was Mr. Tenby.

He stilled as well, gazing at her in astonishment before coming slowly forward and removing his hat to bow. "Miss Slougham."

"Mr. Tenby," Iris managed in almost a gasp.

They gazed at one another in mounting embarrassment until he inquired, "You are well?"

"I—yes—tolerably, sir, I thank you. And—and you?"

"I am well—very well, I thank you." He shifted on his feet and looked down.

She blinked several times and then said, "You left and you are back—in Town, that is."

"Yes, I returned." He swallowed, licking dry lips. "I had not thought to return. There is always much to be done on the estate."

"Then how come you to be in London?"

He opened his mouth, shut it again, and then said, "I was given reason to believe—that is, I heard you had gone away as well."

Iris paled. "You came because you thought I was gone away?"

"No!" he said, stepping closer in his anxiety to correct her. "No, I came back and then heard you had gone away. Was I mistaken?"

She had regained her color. "No, sir. I was gone away. Merely a house party. Our home is undergoing repairs. It was in Sussex. A dear friend. Mama wished to stay."

"In Sussex?" he inquired, valiantly trying to follow.

"No—no. In Town. Mama wished to stay in case Mr. Blysdale came back, but—"

"Miss Slougham!" called Mr. Blysdale, coming up behind her on the path. "You mustn't go so far ahead alone!"

He stopped upon seeing Mr. Tenby, who had stiffened and replaced his hat.

"Mr. Blysdale," he said tightly.

"Tenby, you're back." Blysdale looked from him to Iris, who seemed bewildered, and back again. "I seem to have interrupted—"

"No, sir, you have not. Good day. Good day, Miss Slougham," said Tenby, and he stalked off.

Blysdale called after him, but Iris, blinking at Tenby's fast receding figure, was too overset to think clearly. She turned her bewildered gaze on Blysdale, who swore under his breath as he put out a hand to steady her.

"Are you well, Miss Slougham?"

She laughed, an edge of hysteria to her tone. "He asked me that, too. And I told him I was tolerably well. But I am not! I am not! Why must he do so? Why must he speak so kindly to me and then—and then go away?"

Mr. Blysdale put a brotherly arm about her shoulders, holding her up and murmuring soothingly, "Because he is a cawker, ma'am. Perhaps we should turn back."

Iris shook her head, slowly at first, and then more vigorously, as though clearing cobwebs from her brain. She looked up at Blysdale, her brow furrowed.

"Mr. Blysdale, you are a man."

"Yes, ma'am, I hope I am."

"Then you may tell me, is Mr. Tenby jealous?"

Mr. Blysdale's brows went up and he glanced down the path where Tenby had disappeared. "I should say decidedly, yes."

Iris closed her eyes, her hands clenching into fists. "But why?" she wailed. "Why must you always be about to make him jealous? Why are you so handsome and rich? And why are you my friend, and in need of so much guidance? For that is the only cause for our being so often in company! But he cannot see that! No, he sees only that you are forever by my side, and that we are intimate and—" She broke suddenly from his hold, leveling an accusing glare at him. "Do not comfort me, sir! He is sure to come back for some stupid reason and see you with your arm about me and—and he will—he will come to some ridiculous conclusion again!"

"I should be extremely surprised if he turned back, ma'am."

She started after Tenby. "I must catch him and make him see what a foolish mistake he has made—he cannot go on like this, Blysdale! I cannot bear it!"

But when she had gone several yards down the path and he was yet nowhere in sight, she stopped, turning indecisively to peer down a branching path. After a few moments, she looked back to Blysdale, who stood some feet away, watching her solicitously.

"He is gone, Blysdale."

"Yes, ma'am, I imagine he is nearly to Tenby House by now."

Iris tried to speak, failed, and stood trembling on the path, half-way between misery and fury. At last, fury won out and she turned and stormed down the path, ranting as she went.

"Oh! I hate men! They are horrid, provoking, odious creatures who cannot be rational and reasonable! And they imagine *women* to be weak-minded! Oh, they should look more closely in the mirror! Why must I care so much for him? He has only brought me sorrow and suffering. Perhaps I am mad!"

"Miss Slougham, stay!" called Mr. Blysdale, catching her by the elbow and forcing her to take his arm. He slowed her furious pace, bending close to whisper, "Pray speak lower, ma'am, or soon you may have all the world agreeing with you and they will clap you in irons and shut you away."

She colored and glanced about, but then pressed her lips grimly together. "Perhaps it would be best, sir. All I am good for is to marry, but men are stupid creatures and I want none of them."

Soberly he said, "We certainly are stupid creatures, ma'am, but you must take pity on us, for we all are in desperate need of female guidance and forbearance."

"But how can I take pity when all he does is come to nonsensical conclusions and walk away?" she inquired, exasperated.

"It is a quandary, ma'am," said Blysdale pacifically. "But I feel sure you will come upon the solution in time—when your head is cooler, and I have had time to knock some sense into Tenby's."

She eyed him askance. "Would you really do so?"

"If you wish me to, ma'am," said Blysdale. "However, I believe I should even if you did not wish it, for his pig-headedness is beginning to annoy me."

"Well, I give you leave to box his ears, sir, or whatever it is you do. Serve him a wisty caster, or plant him a facer, or—or whatever you like. *I* should certainly like to do so, but it is one of the injustices of this world that a woman never can."

"Oh, there are female pugilists, ma'am, who exhibit very well," said Blysdale reassuringly. "Perhaps that is your calling, if you are not to marry."

They had reached her house steps and she let go his arm, lifting her chin. "Perhaps it is, sir. And it would serve him right!"

With that, she stomped up the steps, leaving Blysdale to regard her with a grim smile as he settled his hat more firmly on his head and set off in the direction of Tenby House.

Chapter 24

THE SLAMMING OF the front door woke Mrs. Slougham from the doze she had fallen into on the sofa in the saloon, and she went to the head of the stair to remonstrate with whatever servant had been so remiss. But as the footman who stood by the door merely stared in undisguised wonder as Iris whirled up the steps like a virago, she quickly comprehended what had happened and intercepted her daughter, guiding her into the saloon.

"Whatever is the matter, child?" she inquired, shutting the door against the curious gazes of the servants.

"Nothing, mama," said Iris in a shaking voice. "Only that I wish I could throw myself in the river!"

Mrs. Slougham, inured to such statements by her daughter, sat down upon the sofa and fixed Iris with a grave eye. "What now have you done? Let me know at once, so that I may steel myself to the consequences."

A look of injury flashed through Iris's fury. "I have done nothing—that is, I do not think I have. No, it is all Tenby—that horrid, odious, ridiculously stupid man. Do you know, Mama, he has been jealous all this time? I could not comprehend why he should act so strangely toward me—friendly one day and wishing to avoid me the next. Indeed, I would not wonder at his avoidance if he had not been so kind to me, for it is all of a piece with the generality of gentlemen I have met. But he acted as though he liked me, Mama, and he did! Letting me drive him and dancing with me and being so kind as to overlook my oddities. Only Blysdale has been so kind as that, and he is my friend."

"I have often pondered the incomprehensibility of my having so foolish a child," said Mrs. Slougham with asperity. "You speak of Tenby, but it is Blysdale who is continually in your mind! How you can even compare the two gentlemen is nonsensical, Iris. Tenby is not half the gentleman Blysdale is, and has not a fraction of the fortune. You had better put Tenby out of your mind and set your cap at Mr. Blysdale."

Iris turned a look of horror upon her mother. "I could never set my cap at Blysdale, Mama!"

"You can and you will," said Mrs. Slougham, dismissing what she assumed to be Iris's scruples out of hand. "It is too late in the day to be straining at trifles—Society may dictate that a damsel be demure and biddable and await the attentions of a gentleman, but Society never had a daughter like you. Mr. Blysdale is your man, and is merely waiting for encouragement."

"But Athena—"

"Oh, hang Athena!" said Mrs. Slougham forcefully. "She may have any number of gentlemen, of rank and title, too, and if she does not mean to have the Marquess of Foxham, I am a gaby. But you must take what you are given, Iris, and be thankful. But this is nonsense—Mr. Blysdale is far and away the best catch. His birth is nothing—he is handsome and gentlemanly, besides being rich, and he is not disgusted by your disgraceful manners. He is everything that is charming, and far more than we have ever dared hope for you, my dear. You must fix his interest, and quickly, before he changes his mind."

Iris set her jaw. "So I am to entrap him before he can think better of it, Mama? For no man in his right mind would marry me willingly. No, it must be a mad flight of fancy, or a careless mistake! I am so out of reason strange that no one would want me, least of all my own family!"

"Do not enact me a tragedy, Iris! Of course we want you," said her mother. "It simply would suit us best—"

"And if Mr. Blysdale is not so obliging as to take me, you are so anxious to be rid of me that you would fob me off on Sir Isaac Hornaby—a man who could be my father, who looks like a toad and likely thinks like one, too."

"You exaggerate, Iris," said Mrs. Slougham, blinking. "Sir Isaac does not—well, he might, a little—"

"It makes no odds if he might or not, Mama," said Iris with a sharp shake of her head. "I will not marry him, or any man who does not love me. I would not enter into a lifetime of slights and snubs simply so that you may be more comfortable. No, I would rather be a—a governess, or a cookmaid!"

"This is just another of your ridiculous starts," replied her mother with a doubtful little laugh.

But as she watched, a look of mulish intent came over Iris's angry countenance. "I assure you it is not, Mama! I was never more serious in my life! Why, pray, should I stay to be married off to whatever gentleman will have me, to consign myself to a lifetime of ill-usage, when I may enter a similar relationship which it is at least possible to leave? It is a simple thing to register at the employment office, I have heard, and I might be off your hands within a fortnight, on a stage-coach to my new charges in Northumberland or—or Cornwall."

"Iris, my dear," said Mrs. Slougham, becoming alarmed. "Do not talk so! We do not wish you gone simply so that we may be comfortable. We wish for you to be happy, and a woman is never so happy as when she is the mistress of her own home."

"Only when her husband loves her," returned Iris, "or at the very least esteems her."

"Well, I suppose that is true, my dear, but many marriages begin with very little more than an equality of character."

Iris huffed. "Then you believe that I am equal in character to Sir Isaac?"

Her mother, stunned, could not speak.

Crossing her arms over her chest, Iris moved to the fire, her back to her mother. "At any rate, I must do what I can for Blysdale before I settle what must be done for myself—and do not take him up again with me, Mama! I will not think of Blysdale, simply because he does not think of me. He wants Athena, and I could never press a gentleman to take me over my best friend, for it would be infamous, besides being destined for failure. For who would take me over Athena?"

"But Athena will not have him," said her mother quietly.

"Oh, she will if I can bring her to her senses. She is as in love with him as he is with her, if only she will own it."

Mrs. Slougham was silent for some minutes, ruminating over the faults that had been so suddenly and forcefully brought to her attention. She had never set out to hurt her child—indeed, she cared deeply for Iris and wished only her happiness. But she could not deny that she had become rather cynical of late, and had allowed the mortifications of Iris's unbridled tongue to sour her mood and put her in a perpetual state of irritation. The previous two weeks without her daughter had been rejuvenating and restful, but she had not used them to renew her maternal forbearance, nor had she thought much beyond the disappointment of having had two eligible suitors for her daughter's hand disappear into thin air. Throughout the whole, she had never considered what could be Iris's feelings on the matter, and had simply resumed hostilities, as it were, upon her return, without attempting any sort of truce or understanding.

Now, humbled and chastened, she intended to do so, inquiring quietly, "Do you care very much for Mr. Tenby?"

Iris sighed heavily. "I do, Mama, though I do not know what that has to say to anything. He is a gudgeon if ever there was one, and will not stay to hear reason."

"You say he is jealous? What cause do you have to think so?"

"He is continually coming upon me when I am counseling Blysdale regarding his troubles with Athena, and jumping to the most ridiculous conclusions—" She turned to face her mama. "He imagines me to be in love with Blysdale! Blysdale! Who is head over ears in love with Athena—and is practically perfection himself. The two of them belong in the pantheon, I dare swear! What a clodpole Tenby must think me to imagine Blysdale would consider me!"

"Do not say so, Iris. You are very pretty, and—once one has got to know you—your manners are quite—taking! Tenby, at least, must think so, for if he did not, he could not imagine another gentleman to be in love with you."

Iris stared at her parent. "You have never described my manners as 'taking,' Mama."

Mrs. Slougham colored, averting her eyes. "I considered them so when you were a child, Iris. I had forgotten—or I had put it behind me. But I well remember smiling at your sudden bursts of candor, for they were often so well-deserved! I declare, I was glad of your little oddity then—at least, much of the time—for some of our neighbors wanted a set-down, and I could never bring myself to give it."

"I had not thought to hear you say so, Mama," Iris said, subsiding onto the sofa in bemusement at this view of herself.

"I am very sorry that you did not, Iris." She paused, gazing in contrition upon her daughter. But then she sat up straight, resuming her businesslike tone. "But we must decide what to do about poor Tenby. If it is true that he is jealous, then he must be in love with you, and we must give him encouragement. But you must be certain that it is jealousy that hinders him."

"That is Blysdale's opinion, as well as Diana's, for I told her all about it and that is what she concluded. I did not credit it, but today— well, it could not be any clearer."

"Then we must contrive to bring you together, my love," said Mrs. Slougham energetically. "I am fairly well acquainted with Mrs. Tenby, you know. I believe I shall pay her an afternoon call and try if I may drop a little hint into her ear."

The door opened and Mr. Slougham came in, looking with interest on the scene. "This is very snug, my loves. What is it that engrosses you—or is it a secret meant only for ladies?"

"Do not be nonsensical, my dear," said Mrs. Slougham, rising and kissing his cheek. "We have had a counsel of war and have decided where the next battle is to be fought. Pray, excuse me. I must go instantly to change my dress, for I am going out."

She swept out the door and Mr. Slougham, gazing after her, said, "I do not believe she has kissed me like that in two years." He turned back to Iris, his head cocked. "What sort of war is this?"

Iris went to him, still somewhat in a daze. "A very strange one, sir. I do not believe that I understand quite what has happened, but Mama is on the rampage and cannot be stopped. Indeed, I do not wish her to be, for my happiness depends upon her success."

"Is this anything to do with Mr. Tenby?" inquired Mr. Slougham, watching her closely.

She colored, the vague look on her countenance giving way to a bright-eyed smile. "Yes, sir, it does."

He chuckled, taking her hand and patting it. "Then I wish her godspeed, and you happy."

Iris thanked her papa and kissed his other cheek for good measure, earning herself another chuckle.

Meanwhile, Mrs. Slougham had ordered the carriage and then changed her morning dress to walking dress, descending the stairs in dignified urgency and sweeping out the door. Her coachman drove her quickly to Tenby House and deposited her at the door, where a footman was ready to hand her out and to usher her into the house.

Mrs. Tenby greeted her with civil coolness in a saloon decorated in muted shades of yellow and pink. "How do you do, Mrs. Slougham? What a pleasure it is to see you here. There are so few families left in London that I declare I have had only two other visitors today."

"It is frightfully dull, is it not, Mrs. Tenby?" answered Mrs. Slougham, glancing about at the furnishings, which were handsome though a trifle shabby. "But it is only to be expected with such hot weather. I daresay Brighton is quite lovely. We must certainly either be out of our senses or have something urgent to keep us here."

"There does seem to be much business to attend to in Town this summer," said Mrs. Tenby, eying her guest speculatively. "My son was quite adamant that he stay, though we always retire to Hampshire at the end of the Season."

"Indeed. I had heard that he retired into the country very recently, at least for a few weeks."

Mrs. Tenby straightened the folds of her shawl. "There was some pressing business at Tenby Place that called him away. I did not go with him, for I would have had to shut the house up early and I was not prepared to do so. Perhaps I ought to have gone, however, for then he would not have been obliged to return to Town in such inhospitable weather."

The bland smile that accompanied this intelligence was not lost on Mrs. Slougham. "I am sure his journey was not wasted, ma'am, for he will be a welcome addition to our restricted society."

Her hostess lifted a brow and said, "You, also, have had occasion to leave Town and come back again, I believe."

"Oh, I have remained throughout, but my daughter, Iris, and her father traveled down to Sussex to attend a house party. They returned, however, and Iris hopes to find something to engage her during our protracted stay."

Mrs. Tenby became involved in disentangling the fringe on her shawl. "She must have strange notions of entertainment, ma'am, for there is very little to interest a young lady here at present."

"She does enjoy one activity in particular, for she is such a good girl. She has recently been much caught up in assisting a gentleman friend of ours to navigate a very delicate matter, which I do not scruple to tell you has quite broken his heart." In a lowered tone, she said, "A lady is involved, who is one of Iris's lifelong friends. It is a sad business, but Iris is determined to forward his suit, though the lady is rather out of his reach."

Mrs. Tenby blinked, regarding her with interest. "It is very good of Miss Slougham, to be sure. One does wish for one's children to behave benevolently at all times. Nicolas is often hasty, and cannot always be trusted to see the best in certain situations."

"It is, unfortunately, an impediment of youth," said Mrs. Slougham philosophically. "He will soon, I trust, outgrow such faults of reasoning, and find much in others to recommend them to his heart."

"Certainly. Nicolas ever was a generous boy." Mrs. Tenby again fiddled with her shawl, saying casually, "He would be more generous had he been more fortunate in his inheritance. But he is an excellent steward, ma'am, and has made me quite proud at how he has managed with what little his father left him. If he were to be blessed with wealth, he should do much good with it, I am persuaded."

Mrs. Slougham smiled benignly. "Wealth is too often put into the wrong hands, I believe. It is my opinion that fortunes, such as those endowed on young ladies, ought to be handled so that the greatest good may be done with them."

"There is much good that can come of a marriage where fortune is well-spent," said Mrs. Tenby pleasantly. "Where there are excellent principles, there is sure to be respect, if not love."

"It is even better when love exists from the beginning of a union, do not you agree?"

Mrs. Tenby's eyes widened. "Certainly, though it is not always possible. Love matches are not so common as they were used to be, I fear."

"Perhaps they would be more common if love was given higher priority," said Mrs. Slougham meditatively. "Love is often swept aside as unnecessary, but I believe it is quite essential for the strength and longevity of a marriage. It most definitely contributes to the happiness of the couple."

Her hostess seemed to be heartened by this idea. "It is excessively desirable, to be sure. One does wish for such a union for one's child, does not one? How better to dispose of a beloved child in marriage than in a love-match?"

Mrs. Slougham gravely agreed. "When the parties concerned are in perfect accord, there is nothing more felicitous. But it is ofttimes the misfortune of one or the other to experience doubts in the matter, which may result in delay or even frustration of the issue."

"A sad, sad circumstance, certainly," said Mrs. Tenby, tutting. "One cannot but feel it could be avoided by a very little interference of an interested party."

"In my experience, successful matches are more likely to be achieved when the parties are often in company," said Mrs. Slougham thoughtfully. "One is put in mind of the many matches made between gentlemen and young ladies who have grown up together, and cannot but consider the certainty that admiration kindled from a short acquaintance may be stoked into a greater feeling by continued interaction."

"Yes," said Mrs. Tenby, thoughtful. "A few parties or outings in a matter of days might do the trick."

Mrs. Slougham nodded and gathered up her reticule. "Thank you for receiving me, Mrs. Tenby. Our dialogue has been most enjoyable, and I am pleased to have met with a lady of so sound an understanding. I trust we will meet again soon?"

"Certainly, Mrs. Slougham. I believe I shall throw together a party for a few days hence, if I may prevail upon you to attend?"

"We are not at all engaged this week, ma'am, and will be delighted to attend you. You may be sure to receive a similar invitation from me, perhaps Tuesday next? Very good."

Mrs. Slougham rose and took her leave, returning to Hill Street excessively pleased with both herself and her new comrade in arms.

Chapter 25

AFTER LEAVING MISS Slougham, Mr. Blysdale walked directly to Tenby House and inquired for Mr. Tenby, but was again told the master was not at home. Taking a sovereign from his pocket, he placed it into the palm of the butler.

"I must and I will speak to him. If you have any desire to see your master happy again, you will send round a note when next he is at home, and I will come directly."

This being agreed to by the butler, who regarded Mr. Blysdale with new respect and not a little curiosity, Blysdale turned toward Hanover Square and the quiet of his library. He had much to consider. Miss Slougham's words had not been perfectly relieving, for the unfortunate meeting with Tenby had suspended all relevant discussion between her and himself, but he had taken much comfort from them. He at least knew that Lady Athena had, in fact, forgiven him from her heart, and that Miss Slougham believed her to be in love with him or, at the very least, tempted by the notion.

This was enough to justify his determination to win her, but his recent humbling had not been without effect. He would go gently this time, and not press the issue. His object had not changed, but his purpose had; he loved her, and desiring her love in return, would do all in his power to earn it. He would watch and wait and allow her to come to him—should she wish to do so—and leave himself open to the possibility that she would not, after all, choose him. If this required letting her go, he knew he must do it. She was not a commodity to be bid on and taken by the winner, but a lady whose choice would be hers, and that choice—no matter how painful to himself—would be respected.

In this frame of mind, Blysdale went to the mantelpiece, upon which rested some invitations for the coming weeks, and selected from among them the most probable engagements at which he might meet her ladyship. Calling Thomas to him, he handed him the invitations and requested that they be added to the schedule.

"At once, sir," said the faithful secretary, glancing over the names on the cards. Having drawn his own conclusions, he added with extreme blandness, "Perhaps you should like me to narrow them down for you? I could set about some inquiries."

Mr. Blysdale cast him a sideways look, not without humor. "No, Thomas, for you know that I have sworn off that sort of thing. It is imperative to me to be on the square, if ever I wish to succeed."

"Very good, sir," said Thomas, turning toward the door.

"Do you miss it, Thomas?" inquired Blysdale over his shoulder.

Thomas turned again and regarded him, the ghost of a smile playing about his lips. "Sometimes, sir, I own I do. Gathering information has been a large part of my activities for as long as I can remember, and was exceedingly useful to my success in school. Indeed, without that particular talent, I may not have survived to become your secretary, sir. But it has been borne in upon me that one must be extremely careful with talents such as mine. I would not wish to find myself again in a position such as we—such as I have recently been in."

Mr. Blysdale lowered his eyes, considering. "Perhaps we may find a proper use for your particular skill in the future. It would be a shame to waste it."

"Yes, sir," said Thomas, his smile more pronounced.

He bowed and retired, leaving his master to meditate upon whether he could give up his secretary to the Home Office, or if he was too indispensable. Perhaps he might share him. The matter was not destined to occupy his thoughts long, however, for a note was shortly brought in by a footman who said the messenger awaited an answer. Unscrewing the note, Blysdale read that Mr. Tenby was now at home and could be prevailed upon to receive him.

"Thank you. Tell him I shall come round directly."

He followed on the footman's heels, taking the stairs two at a time to change his coat and to inform his valet he was going out, but would return in time to dress for a rout party that evening.

In a matter of minutes, he was again at Mr. Tenby's door, thanking the butler for his efficiency with a half-crown. Mr. Tenby was to be found in the study and, judging by the look on his face when Mr. Blysdale was announced and stepped into the room, he was not expecting his guest.

"Blysdale," he said with scarcely disguised loathing.

Blysdale gave him a friendly smile and removed his hat. "Hello, Tenby. I wish you would not be a cod's head and refuse to see me. I had to grease your butler in the fist in order to achieve this meeting, which you must own is quite uncomplimentary to my efforts on your behalf. Did you not read my note? I had congratulated myself that its contents had brought you back to Town."

"They had," said Tenby, putting down his pen and coming round the desk. "But it was all a waste of time, and you can go to the devil."

"More and more uncivil, sir. What stands in your way, I'd like to know?"

Tenby set his jaw. "I could call you out for your insufferable disregard for—do you not have a care for what you have done to her? She is an innocent, sweet girl who trusts in your honor as a gentleman, and you have led her on to believe you—"

"Are her friend? Yes, she believes me to be her good friend, and what's more, she knows—and has done from the outset—that I am in love with Lady Athena Dibbington."

Tenby looked taken aback at that, but gamely returned with, "Then it is all the more shameful how you have trifled with her. She is obviously in love with you, and yet you impose upon her good faith for your own ends."

Blysdale almost laughed, but commanded himself enough to say with tolerable calm, "They say love makes one blind, but I have never before seen the proof of it. I am now enlightened. You, sir, are a gudgeon, and I am beginning to question my desire to further your suit with Miss Slougham, for I would not wish a lady for whom I cherish the highest regard to saddle herself with a nitwit as her life's companion."

"Do you think that encouraging my suit will absolve you from guilt, sir?" cried Tenby, jabbing a finger at Blysdale's chest. "A lady of Miss Slougham's quality will not so easily change her affections, not when she has been so masterfully manipulated."

"I shall call you out if you continue with these ridiculous insinuations," said Blysdale in a forceful tone. "If Miss Slougham is in love with me, Tenby, I am the gudgeon, and will own it before all the world, but I will swear to you now, on my honor, that she is not. And if you would be so wise as to stand your ground when I am in her vicinity, you should see that I am right. She is like a sister to me—and more to the point, she treats me like a brother. Only today, just before you met us in the park, we had disagreed over the mode of my pursuit of her friend."

"Because she cannot wish for you continue!" said Tenby, as though unwilling to hope.

Blysdale lifted a brow, shaking his head. "No, you sapskull, because she wants me to succeed with Lady Athena so much that she became irate at my hesitance. She is my faithful champion, sir, but only with her friend, I assure you."

Tenby exhaled, the fight leaving him. He regarded his guest warily for some minutes longer, then dropped his gaze to the carpet. "Is that why she is forever with you?"

"It is the only reason. I have had an uphill battle, but she is determined I shall succeed." Blysdale smiled. "She is a redoubtable lady, sir, and one who deserves a man of strong character."

Tenby's brown-eyed gaze flicked to the steely blue one and away again. His jaw worked and he said, "I suppose I owe you an apology, Blysdale. If it is as you say, you have done me a good turn, and I am in your debt."

"Do not give up with Miss Slougham, sir, and we will call it even," Blysdale said, reaching out to shake hands.

Tenby saw him to the door and Blysdale, relieved of a great weight, returned home with a vigorous step, determined now to deal with his own concerns as efficiently as he had Miss Slougham's.

The following weeks saw Blysdale more active in Society than he had been for over a month, attending nearly every entertainment thought up by the few matrons unfortunate enough to have been obliged to remain in Town for the summer. That these included an al fresco picnic and a dinner by Mrs. Slougham and a rout party and soirée by Mrs. Tenby did not weigh with him in the least, for he was glad to observe that Mr. Tenby had an abundance of support from all quarters.

That Lady Athena attended the majority of these events was of primary importance to him, and each time he entered a house, glancing casually about to ascertain the identities of the guests and finding her to be one of them, he was obliged to suppress the excitement of his heart. This was a new experience for Mr. Blysdale—he had never before been motivated by an emotion other than determination. The thrill that overcame him on sight of Lady Athena—her graceful carriage; her elegant movements; her dignified air; and the slight, secret smile that came to her lips when she met his gaze—was entirely new and intoxicating.

It was not in the least disturbing to him, however, except in the quiet hours after leaving her entrancing presence and returning home to his empty house. Then, doubts invariably crowded in, and he wondered if all his machinations to attain his position in Society had been in vain. His goal had always been impeccable placement, which had not required more than respectful acknowledgment from high-born friends. That he possessed a number of these attested to the quality of his character and attainments, but he could not be certain that this was enough to earn him the love of the lady of his choice.

When he had first fixed on Lady Athena as his future wife, it was merely with the view of crowning his achievements. She was excellent in every way: face, form, air, address, and that certain something that bespoke her superiority to all other ladies in his eyes. Her connections were merely an additional incentive, for the many powerful connections he already possessed more than sufficed for his aims, and her fortune could only complement his own. He had not reckoned on falling in love with the lady—indeed, he had not considered love at all, in the beginning.

But now that he had recognized that he was, indeed, in love with Lady Athena, he was unable to avoid the vulnerability that came with that most tender of emotions. Even without the humbling effect of her recent reproaches—so well-earned—he was assailed by doubts of his worthiness for her affections whenever she was too long out of his company. As this was necessarily often, his torment was great. He was in alt one moment, in despair the next, and he often was obliged to take himself rigorously to task, holding long and strident sessions before the dressing table mirror.

Whenever he was in her company, however, he was instantly refreshed, his soul cradled in the persuasion of her esteem. He was easily able to convince himself that her eyes would not brighten so upon seeing him if she did not return his affections, and that the secret smile she continually wore in his presence was for him alone.

But he could not be certain, and so did not dare openly press his suit. Her rejection of a month ago still stung, and he was resolved not to be so confident in his success again. She must be persuaded of his loyalty and respect first, and she must give him an undeniable sign of her own esteem. That he watched for this at every meeting went without saying, but he had yet to see it when he arrived at a ball given by a matron whose husband had been obliged to remain in Town for his health.

He approached Lady Athena without haste, stopping to greet and converse with various acquaintance before coming to request her hand for the set that was forming. She was unengaged, and took his hand gladly, allowing him to lead her onto the floor with all the appearance of delight.

"You are in spirits tonight, Lady Athena," he remarked, watching the faint blush rise so satisfyingly into her beautiful countenance.

"There are so few balls at this season that I can hardly be expected not to be in spirits, sir," she said coolly, but with that secret smile he loved to see.

He returned the smile with one of his own and led her down the dance, she having taken the lead as the principal lady in the set.

When they were at leisure to speak again, he said, "I dare not hope that your stay in Town will last all the summer, ma'am."

She looked down, the becoming color still in her cheeks. "I believe it will, sir. My mother is desirous of remaining, and my father is fond of Town, when he cannot hunt."

"I am persuaded it is an unusual circumstance that keeps you here in this heat," he observed.

"Yes, but I do not regard it. Indeed, I have occasion to be pleased."

This was said with an almost shy glance, and he took it as an indication that he had something to do with her pleasure in staying. They went down the line again, which movements took up the remainder of the dance, and as she retained the position of lead for the whole set, their conversation during the second dance was again limited by these increased demands on their attention.

He was obliged, therefore, to leave her after the set without knowing precisely the nature of the business that kept Lord Gidgeborough in Town, and why she and her mama had chosen to remain with him. But as he could only be grateful for the circumstance that kept her near him, he did not think much of it.

He had danced with two other young ladies and was considering asking Lady Athena a second time when he found that Lady Gidgeborough had joined him and seemed intent upon engaging him in conversation. She addressed only commonplaces to him at first, until the dance had begun and he resigned himself to standing out. As his position afforded him an excellent view of Lady Athena as she danced with Lord Foxham, however, he did not repine, and answered Lady Gidgeborough with every evidence of civil pleasure.

"You stay often in Town for the summer, sir?" she inquired, gazing up at him with cool civility.

"Not often, madam, for Yorkshire is rather more pleasant than London in summer."

One of her brows raised and she replied, "Then one is given to wonder why you should do so now."

Ignoring the impertinence of her manner, he took Lady Athena's example, saying, "There is more business than usual keeping me here, madam. I suspect it is so with Lord Gidgeborough."

"It is, sir," she said, gazing out into the crowd. "We have long been expecting a desirable event, which has at last taken place. It is too early to crave your felicitations, sir, for the announcement has not yet been put in the papers, but I have no doubt you, as one of Athena's many friends, will be the first to congratulate her when it is known."

Immobilized by these words for some moments, he at last found strength to turn his head, following her satisfied gaze to where Athena turned in graceful ease to meet Lord Foxham's more ponderous steps in the dance. Athena's smile had vanished, but she gazed with such complacence about her, even looking graciously when her eye met his lordship's, that he was struck with a certainty that he had been utterly and disastrously mistaken.

"I have been aware for some time of Lord Foxham's interest in Lady Athena," he managed, though his tongue felt as heavy as his heart.

"It has been a settled thing for some time now, sir, but his lordship is so very punctilious a gentleman that he did not wish to appear hasty." She gave a little sigh of delight. "Such an excellent match. I own I have long dreamed of it, and am so excessively pleased that it has at last been achieved!"

"I trust that Lady Athena is also pleased."

She looked archly at him. "You may have noticed her tender looks of late, sir. There is something so charming in having gained the affections of a gentleman of the marquess's stature. One cannot wonder at her happiness."

"No, madam." Blysdale forced a congratulatory smile and nodded to her. "Nor can one wonder at your own."

She gave him as close to a simper as one of her superior air could stoop to and thanked him, leaving him to wonder—from the blank void that had taken up residence in his chest—if any of his heart had survived her revelation. He stood at the edge of the floor, automatically greeting those acquaintance who passed him and allowing all vestiges of hope to slip away. It was apparent, both from her mother's words and from Lady Athena's present expression, that this course had been her choice, and he was forced to acknowledge that she never had shown himself a decided preference. Indeed, she had always been either less than impressed by his advances or merely tolerant of them, and her kindness to him of late had been nothing to do with him.

It was something of a wrench to accept that her present happiness was owed to so unromantic a figure as Lord Foxham, but he forced himself to do so. He was assisted in this by recalling Miss Slougham's warning that his lordship was a grave obstacle to his own success, and it was with some sorrow that he wished he had not trusted in her conviction of Lady Athena's regard. But he only could be blamed for his mistaking Lady Athena's affections, though he did think he was justified in misunderstanding the source of her recent tenderness, for it had seemed—oh, how unquestionably had it seemed! —directed toward him.

After being held spellbound by these meditations several minutes, he realized that he was in danger of making himself disagreeable and resolved to take leave of his hostess. As he did so, he formed the determination that London was too small for both him and Lord Foxham at this present, and that it would do the world good for the unsuccessful of the two to retire from the field.

Chapter 26

WHILE BLYSDALE HAD been enjoying the thrill of believing his affections to be in a fair way to being returned, Iris had been entertaining a similar sensation, for Mr. Tenby had not, as she had feared, given up and run away to Hampshire for good. In fact, he appeared with astonishing regularity at the parties and picnics that suddenly cropped up, and Iris could not help but credit her mother's interference for it. She knew from experience that a mother's influence was powerful, but not being intimate with Mrs. Tenby, Iris had no way of gauging that lady's strength or determination, and so had not put much faith in Mrs. Slougham's scheme of enlisting her aid.

It seemed, however, that she had wronged Mrs. Tenby, for that lady, whom Iris had scarcely seen before—despite the superfluity of engagements during the regular Season which both Iris and Mrs. Tenby had attended—became a most energetic supporter of young people's activity and could be depended upon to make up a party on the spur of the moment to fill an idle afternoon. Mr. Tenby, too, exceeded Iris's expectations, for not only was he willing to seek her out and to speak to her, he also appeared to have overcome his former habit of running away whenever Mr. Blysdale was in the vicinity. As Tenby did not seem the worse for his alteration, she suspected that Blysdale had not been obliged to literally knock sense into him, for which she was at first regretful, having cherished for some days a desire to plant him a facer herself.

But all memory of this desire faded before the steady increase of his attentions, and the multiplying enjoyment of his society. He asked her to drive out with him again, this time to watch and correct his driving and perhaps to teach him some new tricks, like the way she had of catching the thong of her whip. This she was pleased to do, very honestly complimenting him on his improvement since last they had driven out together.

"I drove all the way home to Hampshire in my curricle," he said, a little conscious. "It was a long way, and I—I had a particular wish to be active. You were—that is, your instructions continually came to my mind, so I fancied I had better put them into practice."

"It was well done, sir," said Iris approvingly. "An excellent use of the time. Your driving is no longer an embarrassment—" She stopped and colored, looking away. "That is, I am quite proud to be seen driving with you now."

He gave a dry laugh and she turned back to see him smiling. Taking courage, she said, "I wish you will not mind me, sir, for I speak nothing to the purpose. Your equipage and animals are unexceptionable, to be sure. No one can deny you are an excellent judge of horseflesh. I have seldom seen a finer pair than your dapple greys."

His smile broadened and he thanked her, inquiring whether

she should like to drive them, and she very gratefully accepted. This drive seemed to have restored them to their former friendship, and afterward they met without a trace of embarrassment. He did not take exception to Iris's candid opinions and she, therefore, became less conscious and was able better to think through her words before they were spoken.

When she had occasion to meet and converse with both Tenby and Blysdale together, Iris was finally convinced that all jealousy on Mr. Tenby's part was at an end. Whatever had passed between the two gentlemen had scotched Tenby's misapprehensions, she was persuaded, and she was excessively pleased. It seemed that everything was in train toward a happy conclusion, and she awaited with fond expectation a hint from Athena or Blysdale that they also had reached an understanding.

She was therefore quite stunned when she received a flying visit from Blysdale, dressed for traveling and in a state of high agitation.

"I will not stay longer than to say goodbye, for I am removing to Yorkshire at once."

She blinked at him. "What? Are you mad? What of Athena?"

An expression of infinite pain flashed in his eyes, but he looked away with a forced smile. "It has been borne in upon me that I have made a terrible mistake in presuming to care for her. Indeed, I might well have heeded my friends' warnings from the outset, but I was ever obstinate. She will not have me."

"Good heaven! She refused you?" exclaimed Iris, gripping his hand. "I do not believe it!"

He shook his head, his lips turned up in a wry smile but his eyes desolate. "No, I imagine not, for you have always been on my side, ma'am. But it is not quite so simple as that, for I did not make an offer, as it was luckily made clear to me only last night that she never meant to accept me."

Iris gasped, but Blysdale brushed away her concern. "I beg you will not keep me here in vain explanation. No doubt you will hear the happy tidings from Lady Athena herself at any moment. You must understand how I should like to get away. You have done everything possible to forward my suit, Miss Slougham, for which I will be eternally grateful, but it was not enough. *I* am not enough."

With faltering composure, he again said goodbye and Iris, perceiving he did not wish to make a scene by falling to pieces before her, let him go. As he reached the door, however, she called out, "I will get to the bottom of this, Blysdale. Do not despair."

"My glass house has shattered, ma'am, as you feared it might," he said over his shoulder. "Until I can find the will to gather up the pieces, I can promise nothing." And he was gone.

Iris stared intently at the door for some minutes, her mind reeling and racing. When last she had seen Blysdale and Athena together, they had seemed perfectly content, amicable, and even tender. She had not seen Athena so happy in weeks, and imagined her to have entirely given up her mama's schemes for Lord Foxham. Blysdale was the gentleman for whom Athena smiled, blushed, and hoped. What, then, could have occurred to make her drive him away at last?

She plumped down onto the sofa and sighed. Lady Gidgeborough, of course. Either Athena had rebelled against her own change of mind and heart—which Iris could not bring herself to believe—or Lady Gidgeborough had somehow forced her to it. Iris knew her ladyship well enough not to doubt she had never admitted Blysdale as even remotely eligible for her daughter. And if she had observed Athena's altered demeanor toward Blysdale of late—which she should have to have been blind not to have done—she must have recognized the danger, and taken steps to warn Athena away from him.

Iris pushed herself up off the sofa with a most unladylike exclamation. "Devil take Lady Gidgeborough! If she is not the most selfish, heartless, calculating baggage there ever was!"

In a matter of minutes, she had dressed for the street and had flung out of the house, her maid nearly skipping to keep up as they hastened to Grosvenor Square. There she rapped on the knocker and scarcely waited for the door to be opened before she pushed her way in, inquiring for Lady Athena.

"Her ladyship is laid down upon her bed, miss," said the butler, but Iris was already halfway up the stairs by the time he had finished.

She knocked lightly on the door but did not wait for an answer before turning the handle and pushing it open. The room was dim, the shades being half-drawn, and Athena had just sat up from a recumbent position on the bed. She looked narrow-eyed at the intruder, but upon recognizing her friend, she sighed and looked away.

"If you are come to tell me Blysdale is gone, you may save your breath. He took leave of us not half an hour ago."

Iris came toward her, untying the ribbons on her bonnet and tossing it onto the bed. "Why did you not stop him, Athena? How could you simply let him go?"

Athena huffed. "He was determined, Iris. It is not the privilege of a woman to question a man—"

"Pooh! Lady Gidgeborough questions your papa innumerable times a day."

"She is his wife, Iris. There is a difference."

Iris sat beside Athena, regarding her intently. "You could have been Blysdale's wife, Athena."

Athena's head swung toward her, the grey eyes stormy. "Perhaps we were both mistaken in him, Iris. I collect that he visited you as well this morning? It occurs to me that perhaps Mr. Blysdale feels more for you than he ever felt for me."

"Nonsense," stated Iris unequivocally. "You do not believe that any more than I do. More likely, he did not receive the encouragement he wanted to proceed. How can you have so mismanaged his affections?"

"Do not ask me, Iris!" cried Athena, standing and crossing her arms over her chest. "Perhaps I was too much myself—I do not know! I am only who I have been trained to be, and that is not what he wants."

Iris tutted. "He never wanted anything *but* you, Athena. How can you be so stupid?" She sighed, looking away. "But in justice to you, I am as much at a loss—unless you think your mama had a hand in warning him away?"

"Does it signify?" Athena made an angry gesture. "He is gone. He must not have been half so in love with me as you would have me believe if a few discouraging words from Mama drove him off so easily."

"You are right," said Iris, pursing her lips. "He never was deterred before. But that was at first—after your falling out, his confidence was injured, Athena. It might not have taken much to convince him you did not care for him."

Athena shook her head impatiently, going to the window. "Then he is poor-spirited, and I do not know but that I am glad to be rid of him."

"Now you are simply being churlish."

"I have a right to be, Iris. Why did not he fight for me? If he loved me, he would not have run away. I cannot help but feel I was gravely mistaken in his character, or at the very least in his constancy. Perhaps it is better that he has gone for now I have no other recourse but to marry Lord Foxham."

"That is the most ridiculous lot of fustian I have ever heard," said Iris, glaring at her.

Athena swung round to face her. "It is what I must do, however. I feel certain he will offer for me and I cannot in good conscience turn down so eligible an offer when no other is forthcoming."

Iris eyed her distastefully, saying, "How you can so calmly acquiesce to such a thing is baffling to me."

"It is an excellent match."

Iris made a face. "Only if one closes one's ears to—"

"If you dare speak of his creaking corsets, I vow I shall scream," warned Athena, her chin high. "Lord Foxham is a gentleman, a nobleman, and a statesman. He is respected and admired, and his fortune is good. His person and intellect are—they are adequate. He is in every way my equal."

"Why do not you go after him?" inquired Iris angrily.

"I am going after him!"

"Not Foxham, you ninny—Blysdale! I am much mistaken if this is not all a hum occasioned by your honored mama's meddling, and that if you went after Blysdale he would not instantly take you in his arms and carry you off to church in Yorkshire. He might even get the Archbishop of York to marry you."

For an instant it seemed as though Iris had broken through Athena's reserve and touched her bruised heart, for an unmistakable longing shone in her eyes as she hesitated to answer. But long habit overthrew her indecision and a look of steel replaced whatever emotion had momentarily overcome her.

"Only you would suggest such a hoydenish thing, Iris," she said. "As though I should stoop to scrambling after a man who has plainly sought to toy with my affections, and who has signally failed, I will inform you! He duped me once but he will not again, as I told you in Sussex. I am glad to be rid of him, and will welcome with relief and satisfaction Lord Foxham's addresses when they are paid me."

With an exhale of frustration, Iris stood, facing her friend. "You may talk until Doomsday to convince yourself that you are happy, but it will yet be a lie. You can never be happy when you know that Jonathan Blysdale was the perfect man for you and you let him go. No title or fortune or bill in Parliament will compensate for the misery and loneliness of a loveless marriage."

"Love was never a consideration for me," said Athena, turning away.

"Perhaps it was not for Lady Gidgeborough," retorted Iris. "But though you deny it 'til your dying day, you considered it very well of late. I hope that consideration will not haunt you every time you are addressed as Lady Foxham."

Athena did not answer as Iris scooped up her bonnet from the bed and quitted the room, marching straight back home to vent her feelings in pounding out Mozart's concertos on the pianoforte.

Athena did not stay long at the window, but went to sit at her dressing table, toying with the gilt-handled brush and mirror that lay there until a glimpse of herself in the mirror made her get up and take a hasty turn about the room. She could not even bear to look at herself, so disgusted was she. Much as she should like to blame Blysdale, his defection was only her fault.

Iris had been right—Athena had not given him enough encouragement. She choked on a sobbing laugh at this, for it was only as much as she had warned Diana against at Findon. Diana had been entertaining two beaux at Findon—Tom Breckinridge and another young man—but plainly preferred one over the other; however, she was so universally charming that neither beau knew where he stood. Athena had been obliged to drop a rather sharp hint to her to beware losing the man she preferred from giving too little encouragement in the right quarter. Diana had taken the hint, and things had moved along in a more promising direction. But Athena had better have taken her own advice, it seemed.

It was too late to repine, however. Much as Iris detested her for it, Athena would never do so unmaidenly a thing as to chase after a man, whether or not he loved her. Not only was it not the thing, but she did not believe her heart—so newly tried and sorely tested—could survive a third disappointment, should he prove not to love her after all.

In a burst of rage, she seized a small figurine from the mantelpiece and threw it into the fire, reveling in the satisfactory crash and tinkle of the shattered pieces. Like her heart, she thought savagely. It were better that it had never been touched. But she had learned that hearts were of no more use than love to a girl in her position, and she would be careful in future to keep hers safely encased in ice.

As she was dressing for dinner, she was interrupted by a knock on the door followed by the precipitate entrance of Lady Gidgeborough into the room.

"Oh, my love, I am glad you are wearing the peach silk, for it becomes you so very well," said her mama, scrutinizing her person. "But you had better wear the gold fillet in your hair, and the pearl set, for they are perfectly suited to a demure young lady."

"Certainly, Mama," said Athena, betraying none of the curiosity she felt at this strange intrusion. "We have always trusted Wardley to assemble my toilettes, for she is quite capable."

"Yes, my dear, but tonight we are to entertain Lord Foxham—" she lowered her voice impressively, "who is at this moment in the study with your papa, and I do not doubt shall have something of a very satisfying nature to say to you after dinner."

Her bosom swelled with a sigh to match her smile and she gazed off into the reaches of her fancy. "Such an excellent match—a marquess! Oh, Athena, at last you are to make me happy. At last we are to have our due in so august a connection! It is everything that I could wish. Now do make haste, my love, and come down, for we would not wish to keep his lordship waiting. I am certain he is the sort of man to like his dinner and he must be assured that he will receive every attention in this house! Do not disregard me, my dear. Wardley, I depend upon you."

When her mother had swept from the room, Athena contemplated her striking reflection in the mirror without expression or pleasure. This was the moment she had awaited all her life—the moment of fulfilling her own destiny in realizing her mother's ambition. She had always imagined it would be infinitely satisfying, a thrill of triumph and a welcome relief.

That it was none of these things did not come as a surprise to her—not after the events of the past six months. She had been the Unassailable, but had been so unwise as to descend from her Olympian heights to taste the forbidden fruit, and now the heights held no fascination for her. She had been ruined for consequence by love for a tradesman's son and the prospect of an alliance with Lord Foxham no longer had power to excite her in any way.

She knew a moment of panic at the vision of another twenty years, and twenty more, and twenty more, of upholding the pretense of the Ice Maiden, of projecting perfection and superior reserve with no hope of a reprieve. Her life's companion would be a man for whom she could cherish little respect and no esteem and who thought her no more than an ornament to his ambition, a prize for the privilege of his birth. The bleakness of the picture startled her, and Wardley remarked upon the sudden paleness of her features, inquiring whether her ladyship should like some wine or her vinaigrette.

Athena shook herself and refused these ministrations, claiming only a slight giddiness at the news her mama had imparted, and with a deep breath banished all thoughts of weakness from her mind. She was the Lady Athena Dibbington, of the House of Dibbington, and she was Unassailable. Nothing would impede her progress through the highest ranks of Society, and nothing—not well-meaning friends nor tradesmen's sons nor unrequited love—would keep her from accepting the Marquess of Foxham's offer tonight.

Chapter 27

IRIS WAS UNABLE to bring herself to speak to Athena for some days, especially after Mr. Slougham pointed out the announcement of the engagement of the Lady Athena Dibbington to Lord Ambrose Tippleton, Marquess of Foxham two days after Mr. Blysdale's exit from the Metropolis. She was so incensed over this insanity that she pulled to pieces a hat that had been a gift from Athena during the previous Season, only to mourn its loss and grieve over the insensibility of the giver.

She was almost as angry at Blysdale, too, for she could not but agree with Athena's astonishment that he should so easily have given her up. He had gone through hell and high water for her before, and had shown himself exceedingly resilient—Iris could not imagine what Lady Gidgeborough could have said to so thoroughly put him off. For she was increasingly convinced that Lady Gidgeborough had been the real villain of this piece, and the more time passed, the more hard-pressed she was to form a charitable thought for the woman who had stood in the place of an aunt to her for the whole of her life.

These thoughts and more consumed her mind as she sat listlessly in the drawing room, plunking the keys of the pianoforte at random. Her papa found her there and came in, frowning and shaking his head as he greeted her with less than his usual placidity.

"It's the devil of a thing, my dear, but our friends seem marked for disappointment—ho there! What's this? You look hagged to death! Can it be that you have already heard?"

"Heard what, Papa?" asked Iris, patently ignoring his unflattering assessment of her looks. "I have heard nothing since Athena's horrid engagement."

"Then whatever is the matter?"

"It's Athena, Papa," she said in a melancholy voice. "And poor Blysdale. They *are* marked for disappointment, and I can never forgive them for it! Look how it has upset me! I cannot sleep for wondering if I could have done more to ease their way, but they are both such obstinate creatures that I doubt I could."

"No, no," he said, leading her solicitously to the sofa and going to pour her some wine and water from the decanters on the sideboard. "You've done your best, and they must shift for themselves. You are a good friend, but the best of friends cannot force a matter where it is not acceptable."

"But this was entirely acceptable—even desirable, Papa! I have never seen two people more suited, nor more in love. But they were too stupid and foolish to acknowledge it—at least at the same time, or long enough for it to lead to anything tangible." She gulped down her wine, handing the tumbler to him and saying dully, "It is such a lowering thing to watch the friend of your childhood, the sister of your youth, make such a wretched, wretched mistake. She will regret it for the rest of her life, Papa, mark my words. Who could not, when Foxham is continually spouting nonsense about his consequence and importance and suitability for advancement in Parliament. I tell you, if his ilk are running this country, I had rather emigrate."

Mr. Slougham chuckled, placing the glass on a side table. "I wish you will not, my dear, for what should I do without you? Your mama has made great strides of late, but I should still wish to be able to visit you without the Channel or, heaven forbid, an entire ocean between us. But enough of this! You must come out of your blue devils, for if what you say is true, all may not be lost with Lady Athena, even if her family is ruined."

Iris glanced sharply at him. "What do you mean, ruined?"

"It is the most shocking thing," he said, pacing in a haphazard circle with his hands behind his back. "I never could have imagined it of Edward, but it seems to be all too true. It has upset me terribly, but as I said, perhaps there will be a silver lining out of it for Athena—if Blysdale does not regard the shame as Foxham certainly has. Either way, Athena is in for some rough waters."

"Papa!" cried Iris, pounding the arm of the sofa in annoyance. "What has happened? Pray, do not be so mysterious and tell me!"

He went over to the sideboard and poured himself some wine, eschewing the water. After taking a judicious gulp, he turned to her. "I have just returned from the club, and everyone is talking of it. Apparently, Lord Gidgeborough was accused of cheating over cards late last night, and there's been the devil of a dust kicked up. Whole club was in an uproar, even so late as I went there this morning—couldn't even get coffee for the longest time—"

"I don't care for that, Papa," cut in Iris, bending toward him in her anxiety. "What does it have to do with Athena?"

"Well," he said resolutely, "the long and the short of it is, Lord Gidgeborough has been blackballed at the club, and he's out! That is bad enough in itself, for it is the worst scandal the town has seen this year, and I do not know how he shall ever live it down—not to mention Lady Gidgeborough! Dear me, but she shall be in fits. Poor Edward."

He refreshed himself at his glass and shook his head in silent meditation, causing Iris to say again, "Papa! How can this be good for Athena? It seems everything is horrible for her!"

He blinked at her and moved a chair to sit down. "You see, Lord Foxham apparently witnessed it and is in a taking over what it all means for his engagement. Can't bear the notion of the smudge on his reputation, having a father-in-law who was blackballed. Can't say I blame him. Poor Edward," he said again, and downed the rest of his drink.

Iris gripped her hands together, her eyes becoming unfocused. "He will desire an end to the engagement. Athena will be free."

"He most certainly will," agreed her father, shaking his head. "Foxham never could stand any sort of public notice. This will be nothing short of torture for him, while poor Edward is as good as done for in Society—at least for a time. He will bluster through eventually, I daresay, but Drusilla—" He shuddered eloquently and stood to refill his glass. "I must be grateful that your mama was never so fastidious a creature as Drusilla Dibbington."

Iris stood and began to pace the room. "Lord Foxham was there, you say? So he learned of it last night?"

"Yes, he saw it all. Was playing Macao at one of the other tables when the cry of cheating went up. Gidgeborough stands to it he's innocent, but three other players say he fudged the cards. It's pretty black for him."

"Yes, it is," mused Iris, her eyes lighting and her hands clenching together and unclenching before her bosom. "Oh, it could not be better! But Blysdale must know of this! He will not hear for days, and may not even see the newspapers at all! I must send for him."

"Yes, very well, my dear," said Mr. Slougham distractedly, putting down his glass and meandering toward the door. "Poor Edward."

As he left the room, the butler stepped in to announce Mr. Tenby, who followed on his heels.

"Have you heard, Miss Slougham? Lord Gidgeborough is ruined, and there's the devil to pay."

Iris glanced up from her ruminations and nodded mechanically. "Yes, I have, Tenby. Thank you for coming to tell me, but my papa has already done so. Now I must think what is to be done, for I want Blysdale as soon as he can be got. How does one send an express? Tenby, do you know?"

Tenby had stiffened at the name Blysdale and now stood regarding her with a pinched expression. "Why?"

"Why?" repeated Iris incredulously. "Because Blysdale must return to London without delay! I have so much to tell him—stay! You must go to bring him back, Tenby! That is it! I will write the note and you will take it to him in Yorkshire, and then I will be assured of its getting to him!"

She hastened to the writing desk and prepared to write while he stared fixedly at her back, silent.

She looked up. "What do you stand there for? You may sit while I write the note. Or at least take some wine. I daresay you will need your strength for the journey. It will be a long one, to be sure, but I have no doubt of your being equal to it."

She was rummaging around in the desk while she spoke and he cleared his throat to get her attention. "I shan't go."

"What?"

"I shan't go. I don't see what this has to do with me, at any rate. You may send whatever letter you must write to him express. Those riders know their business. It will reach him in plenty of time. You have no need of me."

She turned, her brow furrowed, and said, "Certainly you are right, and perhaps I will send it express. But it is most disobliging of you to refuse to go, Tenby. Blysdale must get the news as soon as possible. You may take the mail coach, if you dislike riding, but you could beat the newspapers if you were to ride night and day."

With that, he snatched his hat up off the table and crammed it on his head, gathering up his gloves and cane as well. "You must excuse me, ma'am, for I do not know how you could think me such a sapskull as to fly up to Yorkshire on a fool's errand. If you want Blysdale so much, I wish you had told him so, for he told me you treat him like a brother! Ha! I'd give a monkey to see the look on his face if I were to come dashing up in a post chaise and four, jumping out to declare that you want him!"

"If you give him my note, he should look very happy indeed!" she cried, coming toward him. "And why should I not want him in this case? You are being singularly stupid, Tenby."

"I wish I were, ma'am, but I am persuaded I am not," he said, turning his face away, his chin raised. "It gives me no pleasure to say this to you, but I would save you pain. Blysdale does not think of you, and if you believe that apprising him of Lady Athena's family's shame will change his feelings, you have entirely mistaken the matter. Indeed, he believes you do not care a rap for him, and is of the opinion that you care for—" He stopped, pulling at his coat cuffs and saying in a slightly choked voice. "At all events, whatever you feel for Blysdale, I do not know what it has to do with me. It is my belief that you have been driven distracted by all this meddling in his affairs and do not know what you are about. Well, I shall not stay to distract you further. Good day, ma'am."

But Iris had had enough and she stepped in front of him, her eyes ablaze. "You, sir, are a numskull, and have given me more grief these past months than I have experienced during the whole of my life, even considering my innumerable, self-inflicted mortifications. How dare you stand there and lecture me on mistaken feelings when you have no notion of the matter? I thought you had come to a right way of thinking—indeed, I ought to have known better, for everyone who should have come to a right way of thinking has sadly disappointed me and I am left to pick up the pieces of their stupid, idiotic, nonsensical decisions!"

She paused for breath but he was too astonished to speak, and she went on in the same angry tone. "I am sick to death of persons I love, persons who mean the world to me and whose haphazard choices pierce me to the soul, acting like the worst sort of gudgeons! Do any of you have eyes in your heads, or brains either? I do not believe so, for none of you act as though you see or think! For it is plain as the nose on my face that Blysdale loves Athena and that she loves him, but do they admit it? No! They run about like hens without heads, kicking up a dust and falling over useless at last. And when I have done my possible to put them to rights, engaging in most unladylike conduct to obtain information vital to their happiness, do they take it to heart and make good use of it? Of course they do not! They moon about for a week or a fortnight, smelling of April and May, and then all of a sudden throw up their hands and scurry off in the most unnatural directions! I declare, I have had my fill of insensible persons!"

She turned on him, a finger pointed at his nose. "And you, sir! You have been the worst of all, for what must you do but fling evidence to the wind and cherish this nonsensical notion of my admiration for Blysdale despite my best efforts to convince you otherwise! After Blysdale himself told you we are no more than brother and sister, you remain jealous! Provoking, vexing, impossible man! *You* will drive me distracted! It is too much for me to bear, and I beg your pardon if you must wait, for I cannot make such a stupid person my priority at present. Athena's happiness is paramount, and time is of the essence! You must go away. I am too angry to speak longer to you anyhow."

She marched to the door, wrenching it open, then, changing her mind, pushed it shut again and marched back to him as he gaped in awe and shock. In one motion, she grasped the lapels of his coat and yanked him forward until their lips met and she held him there a long moment.

When she pushed him away again, he gasped as though a drowning man coming up for air, his eyes a trifle wild.

"There!" she said, eying him defiantly. "If you cannot comprehend that, then I wash my hands of you."

She marched away again, but he stumbled forward to catch her hand, stopping her. "Stay, Miss Slougham—Iris. Pray, do not go. I see I have been a fool, but—I still do not quite understand. I wonder," he said, as she looked at him askance, "would you explain it to me again?"

Her lips pursed and she said, "I do not imagine it will do any good, for you are as thick as a brick, Mr. Tenby."

"I am very sorry, Iris," he said, gently tugging her toward him, "for I own I am a stupid fellow. But notwithstanding, I assure you that I learn quickly, and I am certain that if you show me just once more, I will comprehend you perfectly."

Grumbling, she obliged him, and his arms stole about her waist, holding her to him longer than the first kiss. She did not seem to mind it, even putting her arms up around his neck and encouraging him to kiss her more deeply.

When they did at last pause for breath, she said rather huskily, "I trust you comprehend me, sir?"

He smiled, pulling her back and saying against her lips, "I think just a little more explaining will do for me."

As he was so close and so insistent, she thought it no trouble to oblige him, for a teacher does wish her student to understand a lesson thoroughly, and he seemed an excessively eager learner. She was quite enjoying the lesson herself, and was in no hurry for it to end. The sudden opening of the door, however, brought the kiss to an abrupt halt, and both pairs of startled eyes turned to find a maid holding a coal scuttle standing in utter shock at the open door. No sooner did their eyes meet hers than she bobbed a quick curtsy and fled the room, pulling the door shut behind her.

Iris turned her gaze to her swain, her countenance intently grave. "Well, Mr. Tenby, if you do not now comprehend me, it is of no use, for I am thoroughly ruined. You will have to marry me, or my mama will plague your life out, besides Society holding you in derision for having compromised my reputation beyond repair."

"That is no reason to marry," he said with a look of distaste. "I am affronted that you believe me so easily worked upon. I should never stoop to marrying for so sordid a reason."

With an arch look, Iris pushed away, propping both forearms against his chest. "Well! Your principles are certainly singular, sir. And here you accused Mr. Blysdale of trifling with me! For shame!"

"But I am so enjoying myself," he said smugly, managing to evade her resistance long enough to stop her mouth with a kiss, and earning a gasp of delighted outrage.

Iris held him at arm's length, her chin raised. "I wonder how you shall enjoy yourself in court? For if you are to be difficult, I shall insist my father take an action against you, though we will join our friends the Dibbingtons in ignominy. Indeed, your character will be ripped to shreds alongside ours, for yours shall not wear any better in the courts than ours shall, I assure you, sir."

"Would you really take such trouble only to make me marry you, Iris?" he inquired, dazzled by her determination.

"Certainly, Nicolas," she said, her fingers wandering to toy with his neckcloth. "Recollect, I have already gone to vast amounts of trouble for you. After all that, if I cannot get you, I may as well assure myself that no one else shall."

He chuckled, pulling her to him again and nuzzling her neck. "I relent, ma'am. I would not, as a gentleman, dream of putting you to so much trouble. Indeed, I relinquish my principles, and am as putty in your hands. Shall we ring for the butler for another witness to your ruination, my love? For if I am to commit to an engagement, I should not wish to do it by halves, and leave you any avenue for escape."

In answer, Iris put her arms about his neck, twining her hands in his hair that looked like ripe straw, gazed into his deep brown eyes, and kissed him again, very, very thoroughly.

Chapter 28

AT THE SAME moment that Mr. Slougham made Lord Gidgeborough's shame known to Iris, Lord Foxham arrived to do the same for Lady Gidgeborough and Athena. Under such untenable circumstances, it was only through the strength of Lady Gidgeborough's iron will that she had avoided flying into a screaming fury or fainting dead away onto the floor.

This was no mean feat, for not only was Lady Gidgeborough called upon to bear the news of her husband's public humiliation, she must also encourage Athena to agree with grave equanimity to Lord Foxham's request that he be instantly released from his engagement to her. But Lady Gidgeborough was not a marquess's daughter for nothing, and throughout the ordeal she betrayed not a hint of her wild desire to make use of the elegant pair of dueling pistols reposing in their box in her husband's study upon either one or the other of the lords at present under her roof.

After Lord Foxham's hasty exit from the house, Lady Gidgeborough bore down upon Athena as she sat in humble silence on the sofa and cried, "This! This is to be the end of all my preparations! I trust you are satisfied, my dear, in having thwarted the desire of my heart, and all through your nonsensical fascination with the upstart son of a tradesman!"

"It was not I who brought this disgrace upon us, madam," said Athena quietly.

"It was you who wasted precious weeks in prevarication, however," insisted her mother, pacing furiously about the room. "If you had not been so long in fixing his lordship's interest, you would have been married by now, and there would have been nothing to be done about it."

"Yes, madam," Athena replied, "and I should have been allied for life to a man who held both myself and my family in abhorrence."

"That is nothing to the point," said Lady Gidgeborough testily. "It should have blown over, and you could have shown by your impeccable behavior that you do not bear the taint of your father's indiscretions. Oh, that horrid, horrid man! Would that I had not allowed him to prevail upon me to marry him! Had not the Marquess of Limhurst ceased his attentions so abruptly and gone after that Fairborne chit, I should have been less likely to have accepted a mere viscount out of pique, and we should not at present have been in this odious predicament!"

As Lord Limhurst had, not three years ago, been rumored to have spent the six months of his reputed business trip to the Continent in wild orgies with various classes of women, while his staid and faded wife resided quietly at home, this conviction did not carry much weight with Athena, and she merely replied that it was useless to repine over such timeworn considerations.

"I experienced a feeling of deep foreboding upon my engagement to your father that something of the kind should occur to throw all my comfort to the wind," declared Lady Gidgeborough, paying no heed at all to her daughter's advice. "And here it is borne out! Cheating! At dice, at his club, in full view of the highest members of Society! He certainly did the thing very thoroughly!"

Choosing not to answer this, Athena merely picked up the embroidery that had been abandoned upon Lord Foxham's entrance and resumed her work, which methodical action soothed her frayed nerves, and allowed her to endure her mama's continued ranting.

"I am now a laughingstock," Lady Gidgeborough said bitterly, "but I do not know why I should expect you to care a fig for that, Athena. You would have married that upstart, I have no doubt, if I had not exerted myself in depressing his pretensions. It seems I may not have occasion to congratulate myself on my success, however, for now that you have lost Lord Foxham, there is not another so eligible to take his place, and at least the tradesman's son had a fantastic fortune."

Athena, who had looked quickly up at mention of Mr. Blysdale, said urgently, "What do you mean, Mama? How, exactly, did you depress Mr. Blysdale's pretensions?"

"Oh, a mere implication that you had already received and accepted an offer from Lord Foxham, but it is of no consequence, for your horrid father ruined everything!" She passed a hand over her eyes, shaking her head. "Cheating! And he denied it—denied it though three of his cronies saw it with their own eyes! What can have possessed him, Athena? What have I done to deserve this wretchedness?"

But though she paused long enough to receive an answer, Athena was unable to oblige her, for she had succumbed to the shock of one who has just discovered a betrayal of the worst kind. As her mother subsided into a wing chair to sigh over her injuries, Athena sat as one frozen, considering that Iris had suggested that Lady Gidgeborough was capable of such perfidy, and Athena had dismissed the notion in favor of Blysdale's poor-spiritedness. This grievous misuse of her powers of reason smote her to the heart, for now it seemed entirely likely that, had she taken up Iris's second suggestion that she follow after Mr. Blysdale and express the violence of her feelings for him, he would have reciprocated.

It was utterly too late for that, however, as the positive news of her engagement to Foxham must have reached him with the London papers he no doubt received in Yorkshire. But the reality of it still stung, and Athena was only prevented from serious consideration of making the journey after all by the lowering thought that Mr. Blysdale may well view her family's disgrace as distastefully as had Lord Foxham.

Thus, she relinquished any such schemes in the shared humiliation of her house, and resigned herself to the necessity of a quiet acceptance of Society's rejection, followed by an even quieter removal to Kemmerton, there to live retired until such time as Lord and Lady Gidgeborough deemed it possible to show their faces in polite Society again.

For some days after Lady Gidgeborough's initial outburst—and a second to Lord Gidgeborough upon his waking, conducted behind closed doors but loud enough to be heard by the whole house and half the street—her ladyship preserved a frigid silence. The news of Diana Marshall's engagement served only to give her a sudden and violent dislike for a Sevres vase, which was found later in pieces by the housemaid.

From thence refusing to look at the mail, Lady Gidgeborough undertook her usual activities about the house, ordering the servants with curt demands and sitting punctiliously at her embroidery during visiting hours, but refusing to admit the few inquisitive acquaintances who were so vulgar as to dare to call. The disgraced earl and the upper and the lower servants walked about on tiptoe and uttered not a word above a whisper, as though there had been a death in the house, or they were afraid that any untoward comment would bring their fragile existence down about their ears.

Athena, however, moved about listlessly and quietly out of grief that, though the disaster of a distasteful and unhappy marriage had been miraculously averted, she was nonetheless powerless to effect any sort of alliance to alleviate her pain. Mr. Blysdale she was persuaded was lost to her, and no other gentleman could make her happy. Iris had prophesied rightly—Athena would die an old maid. These depressing truths served to remove all vestiges of pride from her demeanor, and she very soon felt that her impending removal to the country could not be more desirable, for she could then take up the life of a spinster without loss of time, and without a moment's regret.

On the afternoon of the fifth day, while in the midst of such sobering reflections as had subdued her mind of late, Athena was approached by the butler who, with many apologies, announced the arrival of a visitor and proffered a salver with a white visiting card. The name on the pasteboard rectangle had the effect of bringing her to her feet, then sinking her again into her chair with a halting request to be told how the gentleman looked.

This question did not seem to strike the butler as odd, for he replied in staid accents, "Quite agitated, my lady, if I may. I should not have allowed him in, but for his recent status in this house, and his absolute insistence that I bring your ladyship his card."

This intelligence did not allay the fears that had started through her brain at sight of his name, but it calmed enough of them that she was able, without a tremor, to say, "Thank you, Ormsby. I shall see him."

She then disposed herself more gracefully on the sofa and bent to her neglected embroidery, only to toss it away after a very few moments upon perceiving that the trembling of her hands would not allow even the pretense of occupation. The rapid pounding of feet on the stairs set her heart pounding equally quick, and she watched the turning of the knob in the door with sentiments too tangled to identify.

Then Mr. Blysdale stood in the doorway, his expression as unidentifiable as her own, his appearance lacking all the suavity and precision for which he was famed and his eyes darting instantly to hers. He paused on meeting her gaze, as if drinking in her every detail, and he stepped into the room only after he had taken several visible breaths.

The door safely closed behind him, he advanced slowly, his hat in his hands. "Pardon the intrusion, Lady Athena. I am only just returned to Town. I came as soon as I heard—" He hesitated, running a hand through his already tousled hair. "Pray, forgive my appearance. I hardly stopped to change out of my traveling clothes, so anxious was I—" He paused again, his eyes searching her face. "Is it true? Is your engagement to Foxham at an end?"

Athena's gaze dropped to her hands, which were clutched in her lap. "It is, these four days. Lord Foxham insisted—my father—"

"I know it all, ma'am," he said gently. "Tenby brought the news— Miss Slougham wrote to me."

"Iris?" She looked quickly up, but then dropped her gaze once more. "But why should I be surprised? She would of course do so improper a thing, though from the purest motives, I am persuaded."

He watched her for some moments, her eyes downcast and her hands still clasped before her, before saying quietly, "I am grieved for your situation, Lady Athena. This double blow is monstrous, and I would not have had it happen to you, or to your family, for the world."

Athena looked up, a slight furrow between her brows. "Do you mean the double blow of two defected suitors, sir?"

"No, not—" He looked horrified and came forward impetuously, his hand held out. "Surely you do not imagine that I—Lady Athena, I could not stay—I could not trust myself while you were engaged to Lord Foxham."

She blinked, inhaling unsteadily. "That is all at an end, Mr. Blysdale."

"Yes, forgive me," he said, withdrawing his hand. "I did not mean to give you pain."

"There is no pain, sir," she said quickly. "Indeed, I do not know that I could have gone through with it at last, even without my father's disgrace."

"No?"

The word held such tremulous hope that she was drawn to meet his eyes. "No, sir. I did not love him, nor he me."

His breath quickened and he gazed at her, as though searching for words. "Lady Athena, why, then, did you engage yourself to him? Did you not understand me?"

She gave a pathetic huff, shaking her head. "I thought I understood you, sir, but your hasty removal from my vicinity a sennight ago proved my mistake. What else could I understand but that you wished to retract every hint of pretension to my hand?"

"But you were engaged before I left, madam," he said, looking keenly at her.

She returned his gaze, saying, "No, sir, I was not."

His brows lowered. "Your mother—"

Her eyes closed upon the recollection of Lady Gidgeborough's perfidy. "I think I understood you too well, and my mama knew it."

He blinked, color coming into his cheeks. "She told me you had accepted Foxham—I would not have gone away had she not made me believe—"

"That I did not think of you?" supplied Athena, looking up at him, the misery of the past sennight full in her eyes.

"Athena," he said fervently, and came to one knee at her feet, taking her hands in his own.

But she pulled them away, averting her gaze as she said haltingly, "Forgive me, sir, I—I am no longer fit for—for you to consider. My father's disgrace—it is mine as well—"

He recaptured her hands, bending to force her to look into his face. "Darling Athena, how could I care for that? I rode night and day to reach you. As soon as I heard, I threw myself on a horse and did not stop until I could know how you were, so that I might comfort you."

A sob shuddered through her and her hands trembled in his. "I do not want your comfort, sir."

"No?" he inquired, uncertain.

"No, Jonathan." She looked into his eyes then, smiling through her tears. "I want you."

He took her into his arms then, nearly pulling her from the sofa, and reveled in the feeling of her, warm and yielding, no more the Ice Maiden but his own Lady Athena.

Pressing his face into her hair, he murmured, "And I only ever wanted you."

She turned her head, accepting his kiss as one starved, and it was many minutes before she came to her senses and admonished him to get up off the floor and sit beside her like a civilized gentleman.

He did so, putting his arms about her again, and she leaned her head on his shoulder, smiling.

"I am not the paragon you thought me, I fear, Jonathan."

"How is that, pray?"

"My blood seems to have a taint we none of us suspected."

He gave something much like a snort and said, "I never cared a button for your bloodline, my love. You are all I saw—your grace, your beauty, your kindness—"

"Kindness?" she repeated, incredulous. "I am not kind!"

"You are," he said, kissing her forehead, "though you endeavor to hide it. But anyone who has seen you with Miss Slougham, or who has caught you watching flower girls who sell lily of the valley, cannot imagine you are otherwise than kind."

She sighed. "Very well. But you ought not to noise it about, or everyone shall say that the house of Dibbington has gone utterly mad."

"That may be unavoidable, my love, for when the announcement of our engagement is put into the papers, following so quickly upon the heels of the breakup of your engagement to Lord Foxham, what else may the *ton* think?"

"They may think what they will," she said, snuggling closer. "I cannot find out that I care anymore. I am a daughter of the House of Dibbington, after all, and I know my worth."

He smiled, turning her chin so that she faced him again. "As do I." And he kissed her again, long and deeply.

It was at this moment that Lady Gidgeborough came into the room, her aspect an odd mixture of quelling hauteur and curiosity. When Ormsby had informed her that Mr. Blysdale had called, she was at first irate that he had the temerity once again to present himself in her house, and at this most delicate of moments. But a very few minutes of reflection had impressed upon her the felicity of the circumstance, for though his birth was execrable, his fortune was immense and his *ton* excellent. He was not a marquess, to be sure, but his notice could do much to improve the present fragile standing of her family.

Upon finding her daughter in so improper an attitude with the son of a tradesman, however, her reason was almost overset, and she knew a strong inclination to send him to the rightabout without a care for his fortune and standing. But the iron will that had stood her in such good stead during Lord Foxham's ultimatum did not desert her now, and after taking in several breaths and thinking fiercely on the benefit to her name an advantageous marriage could do, she at last was able to compose herself adequately to address the happy couple on the sofa.

"Well, Athena," she said, eying the pair with reluctant approbation, "it seems that your disappointment has not lasted long."

"No, mama," said Athena. "But that was to be expected."

Taking this rightly to indicate that Athena meant to have Mr. Blysdale, Lady Gidgeborough forced herself to address her future son-in-law, saying stiffly, "I congratulate you, Mr. Blysdale. You have had quite an excellent bit of fortune, I think."

"Yes, Lady Gidgeborough," he gravely answered.

She looked them over again and sniffed. "I suppose we must also be thankful. To be sure, you are a good sort of man, sir. I shall inform Gidgeborough that you should like a word with him."

"I would be very much obliged to you, my lady," he said, as she sailed majestically out of the room.

Exchanging a look with Athena, he said, "That went rather better than I had imagined."

"It did," Athena agreed, "but I daresay she will stipulate our instant removal from Town—even, perhaps, before the announcement can be printed."

"I am in full agreement; however, we cannot go before I may procure a special license, for I do not intend to have you more than five miles out of my reach again, my love. It nearly killed me to hie all the way to Yorkshire without you."

"I believe Yorkshire is just the thing, Jonathan," said Athena, sitting up. "If certain claims are to be believed, it is rather lovely this time of year. I imagine even my mama might be persuaded to take a journey that far northward, considering our circumstances."

"However," he said, regarding her coolly, "I should not like it in the least, and will strenuously discourage her from considering so rash a journey."

She lifted her brows at this. "Where has all your pride in Yorkshire gone, I should like to know, sir?"

"It is present as ever. Only, I intend to have my wife all to myself for the first few months at least. And then, the winter months will have set in, and we shall be obliged to endure them from the fastness of Blyssmore, for we should not wish to set foot in Town again until February at the earliest—more likely March or even April—so that the furor over our ill-assorted union can have died down."

"Oh!" Athena cast him a speculative look. "But my father will certainly wish to hunt in Yorkshire during the autumn, and as his son-in-law, you could not tell him nay."

"I most certainly could, ma'am," he said haughtily.

"Yes, I expect so." She settled her head on his shoulder again, running her hand up and down his coat lapel. "Thank you. It will be quite restful without them for a time. Do you think we may hope to be detained in Yorkshire by snow?"

"Oh, almost certainly. The roads are often impassable through the winter."

"Delightful. I congratulate you on your choice of county, sir. I feel sure I shall soon become as hardy and indomitable as our mill workers."

"*Our* mill workers?" he said, shifting to look at her face.

She straightened again, looking seriously at him. "Why, yes. I suppose I may think of them as our concern now, for there is no ignoring the fact that your fortune was made possible by them. I am excessively intrigued by the mills, Jonathan. Could you arrange a tour of one? I should like to know what the conditions are like, so that I may know how to help our people."

"I should be glad to arrange it, my love," he answered, a strange gleam in his eye. "And after you have satisfied yourself as to the comfort of our workers, we must plant lily of the valley in the Home Wood at Blyssmore."

She blinked, her eyes suddenly bright, but as he began to reach into his pocket for his handkerchief, she abruptly pulled his head down and kissed him soundly.

"I had far rather marry you than a marquess, Jonathan Blysdale."

"I am glad to hear it, my Lady Athena."

But he could not speak more, for she was kissing him again, and though the butler at last came in upon them, his was so stealthy a step that neither knew of it, and he instantly retreated and closed the door as silently as he had entered.

If you enjoyed this book, please consider leaving a review at the library or store site where you found it or on your favorite review site.

Reviews help others discover their next favorite read and are incredibly appreciated by authors.

Thank you!

Be sure to visit judithhaleeverett.com to find out more about The Branwell Chronicles series, and to get your free book!

Author's Note

ENGLAND'S HISTORY IS so rich and vast that it is daunting to try to discover everything that I might need to know in writing these books. I take it one bite at a time, however, and little by little I am coming to understand how it all combined to create the social and legal structure of the Regency. With every story, I am more fascinated by what made it all tick.

England is one of several countries that adopted a hierarchical class system early in its history. While many countries have given up this system for all intents and purposes, England's social structure continues to strongly affect individual identity, and it was only more so during the Regency. The belief in the divine right of leadership was so deeply rooted that most did not question their "place" in society. By the Regency era, the upper class lived by the notion that they were intrinsically better than the lower class, and looked upon any encroachment into their world by mere commoners as a breach of decency and divine decree. Thus, Lady Catherine de Bourgh in *Pride and Prejudice* liking "to have the distinction of rank preserved." The rise of the wealthy working class in society was not unheard of before the Regency, however, and the Industrial Revolution and the discontent of the poor accelerated a shift in class perceptions during that era.

The Luddites—named after a fictional figure named Ned Ludd, whose name was appended to several letters from the group to members of parliament—were violently opposed to the Industrial Revolution. This group took responsibility for several acts of vandalism committed in the name of preserving the cottage weaving industry. Their actions, no matter how eloquently defended by perpetrators and sympathizers alike, were heartily condemned by government, and the uprisings as quickly and cruelly suppressed. Thus, the growth of textile manufactories continued at an incredible pace, and by 1830, they dotted the north and blackened the skies and the towns where they were located. Most factories and masters lived up to the evil reputations they were given, but some did not; a lucky few workers were given fair wages and decent working conditions, including schools for their children.

The idea that gentlemen should not work stemmed from the idea that earning money was "common" or even vulgar. Thus, any connection to trade was looked down upon by the upper classes. However, more upper-class persons than we think were connected to trade. In *Pride and Prejudice*, Mr. Bingley's fortune came from trade, as did Sir William Lucas's, while Mr. Gardiner "lived in sight of his warehouses." The degree of acceptability of these persons did depend upon how far they had been able to remove themselves from the taint of labor. Mr. Bingley had never been actually involved in trade and therefore could forget his fortune derived from it; Sir William had only left his trade recently, but might have buried that fact if he had not been so proud of it; while Mr. Gardiner still oversaw his warehouses and so incurred the derision of Mr. Bingley's sisters. Since Jonathan Blysdale was only the son of a tradesman and had never actually worked himself, his success in penetrating the highest circles of the *ton* is not inconceivable.

The distinction of knighthood was another evidence of upward mobility during the Regency. All noble titles were originally conferred at one time or other by the king, as a reward for loyalty or extraordinary service, such as during wartime. The practice still obtained during the early 19th century, and King George III would have been the one to grant Mr. Blysdale, Senior, his knighthood, as he would have been the one whom Sir William Lucas in *Pride and Prejudice* addressed to receive his knighthood. It was common practice to have mayors knighted, especially if they impressed the king somehow, and Sir William must have made his case well. Mr. Blysdale, Senior, did not apply but was singled out for the honor out of gratitude by the king for averting the disaster of a canvas shortage during the Napoleonic Wars.

Sadler's Wells was a theater north of London that enjoyed varied success through the years. During the Regency it was a popular destination for those wishing to get out of the city and enjoy some fresh air. As non-musical drama was restricted by law to Drury Lane and Covent Garden, Sadler's Wells put on burlettas, pantomimes, aerial and aquatic shows, and farces. The famous Grimaldi, the clown, divided his performances between Drury Lane Theater and Sadler's Wells until 1820. The proximity of Sadler's Wells theater to the New River enabled the installation of a tank under the stage for aquatic re-enactments, such as the *Battle of Trafalgar*, and other nautical shows. Another specialty of the theater was battle re-enactments using live horses, such as the one Iris and Tenby went to see.

Travel from Yorkshire to London was long and difficult. The distance is over 200 miles to York, and would take a fast coach (traveling six mph with brief stops) thirty-two to thirty-six hours. If the weather was wet or cold, it would affect the state of the roads, and people rarely traveled during the night, so a journey to York from London could take four or five days. The fact that Mr. Blysdale rode night and day to return to London shortened his travel time to less than two days.

Sources:

Walter, Floyed. "British Class System: Explore the Social Strata." https://uniacco.com/blog/british-class-system

Sale, Kirkpatrick. *Rebels Against the Future: The Luddites and Their War on the Industrial Revolution.* Addison-Wesley Publishing Company. 1995

Hansen, Viveka. "Textile Manufacturing in Britain: A Case Study from 1700-1850." https://www.ikfoundation.org/itextilis/textile-manufacturing-in-britain.html

Jeffers, Regina. "What Does it Mean to Be Knighted?" https://reginajeffers.blog/2015/11/19/being-knighted/

Ackerman, Rudolph. *The Microcosm of London.* Ackerman's Repository of the Arts, London. 1808.

"Sadler's Wells Theater." Wikipedia.com. https://en.wikipedia.org/wiki/Sadler's_Wells_Theatre

Glover, Anne. *Early 19th Century Coaching Routes.* Regrom.com. 2022.

If you would like to learn more about these Regency history topics and many others, please join me on my blog at judithhaleeverett.com, or scan the QR code below.

Acknowledgments

I AM ALWAYS AMAZED at how monumental an effort it is to write and publish another book. This one has been in my head for a couple of years, ever since I introduced Athena and Iris in Book 2, *Romance of the Ruin*. Their characters were a challenge to write, as were their stories, but I had so much fun doing it that I'm thrilled to finally share them with my readers. But writing any story would not be possible, nor so rewarding, without all the people who help and support me.

First, to my readers, who are always so kind and generous with praise and support. Thank you!

To my beta readers, Laurie Harris-Wirz, Emily Menendez, Diane Paredes, Karen Pierotti, and Liz Prettyman, you are the best! Thanks for taking time out of your busy schedules to read my book and tell me so specifically and constructively how I can make it better. I owe a lot of my growth as a writer to your excellent abilities.

To Rae Allen, whose covers always make such a great impression on my readers. The cover of a book is often the first thing to draw a reader, so I owe much of my success to you!

To Paul Midcalf at Audio Sorcery and Clare Wille, my narrator, for bringing my books to life in amazing audio, I can never express how much I love your work!

To my friends and neighbors who talk up my books and offer encouragement and support along the way, I couldn't do it without you.

To my family, who totally believe in me and try to find ways to help me succeed, I love you!

And to my husband Joe, who is my number one fan, most vocal cheerleader, and who gives out more of my business cards than I do, I would much rather be married to you than to any marquess—or earl, or viscount, and most definitely not any duke!

Judith Hale Everett is one of seven sisters and grew up surrounded by romance novels. Georgette Heyer and Jane Austen were staples and formed the groundwork for her lifelong love affair with the Regency. Add to that her obsession with the English language and you've got one hopelessly literate romantic.

You can find JudithHaleEverett on Facebook and Instagram, or at judithhaleeverett.com.